FRIDAY NIGHT AT HUMBLE HOUSE

DANE ERBACH

Cover design and interior layout by: Dane Erbach
This book is typeset in Baskerville, Canela, and SF Pro

Published in Chicago, Illinois

ISBN 9798224994366 (paperback)
ISBN 9798224884452 (ebook)
LCCN 2024910693

*For Jack and Leda
and their family,
my family*

*And for Mitch,
who I never knew
but whose spirit lives on*

Becky McLaughlin
September 21st, 2011

"Sir?"

The voice tickled her ear like a blade of grass. Somewhere between slumber's dizzy narrative and the snap of consciousness, it swirled into words, a sentence that said, "Sir, you're not allowed to sleep in study hall."

"Oh my god, did he just call her *sir*?" someone else whispered, that last syllable striking like a hammer hitting steel, then fizzing into a snicker that seemed to fill the room.

Becky awoke but was unable to lift her chin off her bare, freckled wrist. It took two seconds to identify the blurry silhouette hovering above her as Mr. Hamilton, her study hall teacher. "Sorry," she said, unable to correct his mistake, uncertain how.

One snicker sparked another until laughter flared all around Becky, circled her until she swore she heard someone say, "Well, she *does* sort of look like a guy." The heat radiating from her face made the spectral hairs on her arm fizzle.

Outside her head, the spectacle was short-lived. But the laughter echoed in her mind, disrupting the small, unprotected piles of self-confidence she had been storing there. To distract herself, she fixed her gaze on the shallow trough on her desk where pencils are supposed to sit; some artist from the past had carved "FUK U" into the resin, saying what she couldn't.

Her phone purred silently in her pocket, but she ignored it since the school day would end within the hour; if Mr. Hamilton confiscated her phone, it would drain her of whatever self-worth remained. But then the phone shuddered a second time and, soon, a third. With a sly, subconscious motion, she crammed her hand into her pocket, tucked her phone in the nook of her palm, and dropped it onto her lap. After poking the screen, she read a triptych of texts from Frances:

omg someone wrote something in the c hall bathroom about u

people r stupid

r u there????????

She almost forgot to pocket her phone before she rose from her seat and stepped toward Hamilton's desk. "I have to go to the bathroom," Becky whispered, hoping he would look up from his phone and notice her feminine cheekbones, her fingernails painted in the color of dried blood, her petite but apparent breasts. He didn't. Instead, he pointed to a plywood hall pass on the corner of his desk.

During passing periods, the high school's hallways roared to life with the release of stifled conversation—girls who squawked "Oh my god" at boys who spread their peacock feathers and punched one another. Stairwells thundered with the echo of footsteps, and intersections clogged with kissing couples. Becky preferred this chaos to the implications of its emptiness. In it, she felt the presence of every student that walked these halls in the school's sixty-some year history—and, sometimes, saw them. On the first day of school, she had sworn she watched a boy in an outdated jean jacket stumble into the locked theatre.

The abandoned corridors always produced a caffeinated feeling in her muscles, as if they were being readied to fight or fly. Because of this feeling, Becky shut her eyes while she walked through the halls during class periods, listening for her steps as they echoed off of the aluminum lockers. Every sixth step, she peeked and readjusted her trajectory, hoping not to stumble into anyone alive or deceased.

When she heard the patter of footsteps, Becky froze and kept her eyes closed, unconvinced that the approaching body was breathing, or even there. As it shuffled away, her freckled cheeks flushed. As embarrassing as it seemed, she was more worried about what she'd see if she opened her eyes.

She cracked one eyelid as she approached the girl's bathroom, relieved to see Frances's reflection in the mirror.

"Oh my god, look," she said, clutching Becky's speckled arm and tugging her into the handicapped stall. Scrawled onto its periwinkle wall in jagged handwriting was a list of five "Ugly Freshmen."

Becky McLaughlin's name was number three on the list—and misspelled.

She landed on the shut toilet seat, rested her elbows onto her thighs, and gripped the plywood hall pass.

"Are you okay?" Frances asked.

"Yeah, it's just stupid. Does it come off?"

Frances spit into a fistful of toilet paper, her unnatural copper curls swinging in front of her face as she scoured the stall's wall. Mr. Hamilton would never mistake Frances for being a guy. She dressed in a manner that mixed modesty and display, which made Becky both envious and delighted to be seen walking beside her. "No," she reported. "I'm smearing some of it, but it's Sharpie or something."

Becky was used to teasing like this, or so she had convinced herself. Still, something about the list's permanence, visibility, and anonymity provoked a sense of powerlessness in Becky. Her name's incorrect spelling sparked a paranoia that convinced her of the author's cruel genius. "What do we do?"

"Well," Frances said, standing like a superhero, "I'm going to go to the office and tell one of the assistant principals right now. Come with me, okay?"

Becky hunched over on the toilet. "I'm just going to sit here for a second, I think."

"Okay," Frances said. "I'll come back with Ms. Broyles, though, and we'll make sure it gets cleaned off." She hugged Becky—more an impersonation of affection than an actual demonstration—before storming out of the stall and stomping out of the bathroom.

As soon as Frances left, Becky slipped from the toilet's ledge and shattered onto the floor. Hot tears tumbled down her face, leaving pink, puffy lines where they seared her cheeks. Her sad, quiet squeaks sounded more like hiccups than sobs. When she couldn't catch her breath, Becky squeezed her eyes shut so much that her muscles cramped. Her tears puddled on the hexagonal tiles, marring the grey grout between with their heat.

When she swore she heard someone say, "Are you alright?" Becky sucked in her tears and breath for a second, embarrassed about the way her extremities lay scattered across the stall. She sniffled. "Sorry, yeah. I'm fine, thanks." When she pulled open her eyes and peeked beneath the stall, though, no feet treaded on the tile anywhere in the bathroom.

Each hair on Becky's arm porcupined into sharp, silken needles, and a cold sensation climbed her spine. She sat up suddenly and backed against the clammy toilet. After some still and silent seconds, it occurred to her that someone outside the bathroom had heard her crying, that this person was merely speaking out of sight, that Becky was being silly. "Hello?" she asked, worried that no one—or someone—would respond. No one did.

Becky sat motionless, hushed and holding in hiccups and tears, hoping for Frances to return with Ms. Broyles when the bell rang, the school day over. The bathroom filled with visible, breathing adolescents who chattered as they checked their make-up and called their moms. Becky counted six sets of shoes before she allowed herself to breathe. Her courage crumbled again, however, when the bathroom emptied and she realized she still had Mr. Hamilton's plywood hall pass. She had hidden in the bathroom for forty-five minutes. Frances would probably not return, had probably headed home.

When her phone hummed in her pocket, her hunch was confirmed. She read Frances's text from the floor: r u at ur house???????

Becky pulled herself onto brittle legs and came

face-to-face with the list. The script was bold and harsh. The fact that Frances left her with this inelegant list intact infuriated her. But Becky withered further at the realization that the school's dependable adults probably shooed Frances away, assuring her that they'd handle it, but ultimately unwilling to help her recoup her identity, her dignity, even her goddamned name.

She pulled a silver gel pen from her backpack—hardly the best tool for the job, but it was all she could find. Then, in wild scribbles, she obscured the bastardization of her last name and rewrote "McLaughlin" correctly.

Charles Stonebreaker
May 25th, 1910

He sunk his hands into the wet cement, a dull-colored and dusty porridge. He didn't try to hold what flooded into his palms. Instead, he simply let his hands rest, let the cold cement soothe his blisters. He believed with an unspoken sincerity that stone, like all of nature's elements, could cleanse his spirit, absorb his stress.

"Charles, get your hands out of there!" Elizabeth scolded from the road, clutching her skirt as she stepped carefully between the tracks carved in the mud. Her hat, illuminated by the sun, cast a complex shadow onto her face. Strands of hair stuck to her unsettled smile. Even unkempt and irked, Elizabeth was more beautiful each time he saw her. "Goodness, you have been acting more childish and reckless since we moved here."

Rebecca galloped behind her mother. "Daddy!" she squealed, her blonde curls bouncing in time with the bottom of her white dress to the beat of each careless step.

"Becky, slow down," Elizabeth scolded with calm authority, spotting the speckled hem of her daughter's dress. "Oh, no. Becky, look what you've done. You've ruined your dress. And your shoes! They're full of mud!"

"Daddy!" she giggled, ignoring her mother's

concerns. "Why are your hands in there?"

"What do you mean?" Charles played.

"Your hands! They're in that muck!" Her voice sparkled like the puddles that adorned the muddy road.

"Charles, why *are* your hands in the cement?" Elizabeth asked, her smile melted into an unamused scowl.

"My hands?" Charles asked. He gasped sharply, shrieked with gay horror. "Goodness! Where are my hands? Becky, help me! I have lost my hands!"

Rebecca's cackle kindled a fire within Charles's chest—subtle, but very bright. With a snarl, he pulled his hands from the wet cement. His eyes widened and an erratic smirk stretched beneath his suddenly upturned and terrifying mustache. He twisted toward his daughter, cement sliding from his wrists and fingers onto the trampled grass like blood from an assassin's dagger. "I'm sorry, daughter," Charles growled. "It seems to have taken control of me-e-e-e!" His final syllable rose into a howl as he stepped toward Rebecca, revealing what seemed like sharpened teeth as his hands curled into hellish claws. Rebecca screamed in playful fear and fled as her crazed father chased her through the yard.

Elizabeth winced with each shriek. "Darling, don't yell," she said. "It's only eight o'clock in the morning." But Rebecca screeched into the road, splashing through puddles and slipping in the mud, pursued by her father. "Stop," Elizabeth instructed with palpable impatience. "Charles, please stop. You're acting mad."

Charles slid to a stop and grinned at his wife. "Oh, Lizzy," he said. "We're just playing."

"Wash off your hands, please, unless you want to treat your daughter to a new dress."

Charles kneeled next to a puddle in the road. "Sorry," he said with a resentful stare. "I don't get a lot of time to play with my daughter, so I'll take every moment I can." His knees sunk into the road as he splashed lukewarm water with one hand onto the other. A grey cloud bloomed in the rusty puddle.

"And whose fault is that?" Elizabeth snapped. She crossed her arms and shot a coarse stare at her husband. "You're the one who wanted to build a house instead of buy one. You're the one who wanted to take on a job in the city."

Charles stifled a snicker at the thought that Wisnago was a city. He had shivered in the brisk shadows of Chicago's skyscrapers once, experienced the weight of the World's Fair as a child. Wisnago was no city.

In his periphery, he watched Rebecca hop birdlike back onto the lot and wander toward the cement slabs. She inspected the concrete clods within the wheelbarrow first. In his mind, he tried to imagine what her eyes saw—the thick compound, grainy and grey, like the stony stuff dripping between the bricks in their bedroom, only still squishy. A smirk bent beneath his mustache when she plucked something out of the sludge and wiped it onto the wet grass.

Charles slid his hands on the back of his slacks as he stepped towards Elizabeth. "Sorry," he said, this time with sincerity. He wrapped his arms around her, careful to keep his wet hands away from her dress, and ducked his head beneath the brim of her hat. "I know this move has not been easy for you." He squeezed harder, nestled his chin in the nook of her neck, and tried to draw the tension from her like the cement had for him.

Finally, her hands landed on his waist. "I just don't know why—" she began but stopped herself. "It has just been a difficult three weeks."

"I understand," Charles soothed.

"And Becky has been such a handful," Elizabeth continued, tilting her head against his. "I think she's restless, but I just do not know what to do with her, especially when you wake us up at six on a Sunday morning."

"I know," he said.

Fifteen feet away, Rebecca rolled a stone between her thumb and forefingers as she studied the wide cement slabs—and their misshapen holes. Again, Charles wondered what she saw, if she knew what those grey rectangles would become, and if their stair shape gave them away. Her eyes bounced from tool to dented tool, bucket to wheelbarrow, then behind the worksite toward the big hole she was warned not to play near, finally landing on the big pile of rocks.

Charles pulled away from Elizabeth and stared into her ashen eyes. Her smirk returned, endlessly disapproving but playful and pleasant. It was one of the first features Charles fell in love with. "I just don't know why you needed to come out here so early," she said, combing the cement specks out of his mustache with her fingernails.

"The storm woke me up. I figured I'd get the steps finished before it grew too hot." He looked up at the hazy yellow sky and couldn't decide if it was cloudless or cloudy.

"Yes, the steps that lead to the house you haven't built yet."

Charles smiled. "It's symbolism," he said, proud of how intelligent his answer sounded. "They are the first part of the house a person will ever experience. Seemed like a fitting place to start."

"Becky!" Elizabeth barked suddenly at her daughter, who was creeping toward the cement clutching a trowel in her fist. "Get away from there! You'll ruin it!"

"Nonsense," Charles smiled, stepping toward his two slabs. "Do you want to help me fix that stair?" he asked his daughter. Her bangs bobbed in a brisk nod.

Charles guided Rebecca's troweled hand toward the wheelbarrow and, together, they stole a scoop of cement. "Careful," he commanded half-heartedly as they made their way toward the settling steps. Rebecca giggled as cement dribbled off the trowel and onto the grass. They dumped what remained of the dollop into one of Charles's hand-holes, then went back for another scoop.

Elizabeth's smirk settled into something warmer and rounder—a real smile—as she watched her husband guide Rebecca's hand across the step, smoothing it with the trowel's edge like they were decorating a birthday cake. Rebecca gazed up at her mother and grinned.

"There!" Charles exclaimed when the step looked level enough. "Look at that! When this cement dries, we'll have a perfect step."

"What do you have in your hand, darling?" Elizabeth asked, now close enough to notice her clenched fist.

Rebecca held out her open palm, revealing something almost unnaturally round. "Just a stone I found. See?" After her mother inspected it, Rebecca pushed it into the center of the second stair. "It's a decoration, now."

"Lovely," Elizabeth said with sincere but momentary amusement. When she noticed Rebecca's hand, which the drying cement had turned a decaying grey, she snatched it, spat into it, and scrubbed it with a handkerchief.

Charles watched his wife stare at the first two steps, as well as the foundation a few feet behind it. The basement's dirt floor was already level, and stonework was already installed on three walls; he would finish the fourth sometime that week. It was a massive basement, already more impressive than the modest farmhouse they had somehow shared with Elizabeth's parents and her brother's family. "How long will it take, again?" she asked, though she already knew the answer.

"A year," he said, "but we can move in as soon as we have heat and water, when we have a way to cook food and keep ourselves warm and use the toilet."

"And how long will that take?" she asked.

"Before winter, if I'm working by myself. As long as I do a little every day."

Elizabeth sighed and surveyed the unnamed dirt roads that intersected in front of what would become their first home. Mud and manure climbed out from the street, sullying what used to be a proud stretch of prairie. A handful of pathetic oaks rose beside hissing gas lamps. There were one or two houses on each block, some circled by drunken fences, their limp pickets leaning toward the street; others were guarded by knee-high brick walls and iron bars; only their stable doors provided access to the street. Where Charles saw potential and promise, he knew Elizabeth perceived a snobby "city" too busy to keep itself clean.

But when he looked at Rebecca, stabbing the soggy ground with the trowel, Charles tried to imagine what she saw: A place where she could play, a town she could explore, a house where she could hide. Bugs to catch and wildflowers to pick. Neighbors to bother, gardens to raid. Oaks to grow alongside—and later climb—and gas lamps to pinwheel around. Fences to rattle with sticks. New friends. A place on a map she could point to when someone asked, "Where are you from?"

For him, that was enough. Even if Elizabeth couldn't see it, he could. Despite these unpleasant appearances, they would make it beautiful somehow.

Barbara Farmer
July 5th, 1941

The way the fireworks splashed against the sky reminded Barbara of fruit hitting a wall. She grinned at the thought that those pops and crackles were nothing more than blackened apples, chucked by her brother Barney, splattering against the barn's roof. For an instant, it reminded her of home.

But it was only for an instant. As she and John, newlywed, wandered beneath the setting sun and casino signs that danced in self-serving desperation, another fruit hit the sky—an orange spraying citrus on the city around them. The casinos, the cars cruising noisily up and down the strip, the fireworks whistling in the distance—it made this city, this moment, more surreal than any other she had ever stepped into.

She wrapped both her arms around John's torso as they stepped together over cigarette butts and gummy black blotches on the sidewalk, mashed her cheek into his cotton khaki shirt, and smiled. Being clumped together made walking awkward, annoying the pedestrians they passed.

Barbara lifted her head to see John's shaven smirk, his eyes like smeared soot daubs looking down at her. As she squeezed her eyes shut, squeezed her stone of a man, she heard him say, "So now what?" They stumbled to a stop in the middle of the sidewalk beneath the hot breath of some massive marquee.

She pulled away from John so she could watch him while they talked. She wanted to study him, steal a snapshot of him on this day in this place. "Oh, I don't know," Barbara said simply. "What is there to do?"

John snorted, then snickered. "We're in Las Vegas," he said. "We can get away with whatever we want here."

"Well, what do people do in Las Vegas?" she teased. Her neck stretched six inches as she stuck a kiss on John's cleft chin.

A corner of John's mouth curled up as if lifted by an invisible string. "Well," he started, "I suppose there're casinos, and there're diners. The nightclubs are likely to start filling up soon so, if we wanted to do some dancing tonight, we'd want to get into those before long." He stopped, peered up and down Fremont Street, and his smirk hardened. "I'd suggest we go to one of those famous Las Vegas reviews but, Barbara, I'm a married man now."

A mousy laugh bubbled out of Barbara, but mostly at the reminder that they were married. She snuck a peek at her ring, a buttery gold band punctuated with a small stone—probably a diamond—that shimmered each time a firework sparkled overhead. They had bought it only an hour earlier for fifty dollars at some consignment shop near city hall. Since John slid it onto her finger at the courthouse, it felt uncomfortable, and she tried to decide whether it was a size too big or too small. In her other hand, Barbara clutched a compact white postcard with the words "Just Married at

Las Vegas!" printed in black letters beside a picture of two cartoon cowboys, one with wide chaps ringing what she assumed was a wedding bell; on the card they had written their names and the date in pencil.

"Say, I have an idea," John said. "Let me go get Glen and Anita and we'll catch a movie and go dancing afterward." Delight rounded the sharp corners of his eyes, and his rigid smirk bent into a full smile. "Go get a cup of coffee at that diner," he added, "and we'll meet you here in—oh, I don't know—fifteen minutes."

Barbara hung a half-hearted smile across her face like an "out to lunch" sign. It's not that she didn't like Glen and Anita; in the weeks they had lived together on the West Coast, the four had become fast friends. She just wanted to spend as much time with her husband as possible, and at least some of it without company. Plus, waiting in a coffee shop for her husband fifteen minutes after murmuring their vows was not how she envisioned their first moments of marriage. Barbara figured, though, that being a wife meant honoring her husband, trusting him even if it made her an afterthought. In the end, she said, "That sounds fine."

But he smiled, pulled her close, and kissed her with a delicate force she had never experienced before. "Let's have some fun tonight," he said, pulling away. "I love you."

He left her catching her breath beneath the marquee, jogging lightly against the current of distracted pedestrians. "I—" she started, stopping short of "love you" as he disappeared. Barbara felt suddenly like a stone, smooth and dense, at the bottom of a riverbed.

Another fruit splattered against the sky—something

white this time, a pear perhaps. Around her, the crowd howled and chuckled in the direction of whichever hotel was shooting off their leftover Fourth of July fireworks. "Golly," she heard one young man say to his gawking girlfriend. It took a couple of attempts before Barbara was able to budge from the riverbed; Las Vegas—its lights, its noise, its continuous activity— seemed suddenly a little scary without John at her side.

She crossed Fremont Street between two rows of traffic and approached the diner on the other side crammed between two bright, bus-sized signs; a more modest sign glowed "Dino's" in drunken script above its door. Inside, the atmosphere was calmer, brighter, and quieter. Silverware clinked on porcelain and the low susurration of old men hung in the air like cigarette smoke.

"Just you, hon?" a waitress asked as she approached, already peeling a menu from the stack. She looked like she couldn't have been much older than Barbara.

"Just me. And I'm fine at the counter with a cup of coffee."

By the time Barbara sat down, there was a warm cup of coffee waiting for her, steam rolling slowly from the top of the speckled mug. The counter was uninhabited, save some lump of flannel bound by suspenders at the far end whose still and enlightened posture implied that, during his daily dinners at Dino's, he had discovered the perfect position on that specific stool.

"You just get married?" the waitress asked.

"Oh, uh," Barbara stuttered. It took her a second to realize that she had the "Just Married" postcard still pinned between her fingers; she had smudged the pencil marks so their names floated within a cloud of lead. "Yes, no more than an hour ago at the courthouse."

"That's nice," the waitress said. "My husband and I married there just before he went overseas. He heard there'd be a draft, so he enlisted in the Navy, figuring it'd be better to join on his own will."

"That makes sense," Barbara nodded. She detected her server's sadness but had to take a sip of coffee to stifle her despair.

"I suppose," the waitress sighed, shuffling behind the counter. She wiped down its surface with a rag frayed and grey from use. "For the past few months, he's been on a warship in the Atlantic," she said. "I feel like I've married a ghost."

The restaurant felt like the inside of a conch shell; its white, clean walls and stainless steel accents conveyed a sort of pearlescence that made this counter seem safe. Barbara finally gathered the courage to say aloud what had been haunting her mind for weeks. "My husband is leaving next week for the Philippines," Barbara admitted, focusing her gaze on her coffee cup. "He's in the Air Force and just finished his training. That's why we married today."

"Oh, hon," she said, hovering over the counter's crumbs. "I'm so sorry. I don't wish my position on anyone."

"Well, I think it'll be just fine," Barbara stated. Inside, her muscles ached at the thought of John's departure, but her waitress's response seemed melodramatic, especially for someone padding around the restaurant in the same shoes. "Sometimes, I think some distance would even do us good."

"Then you're a stronger woman than I am," the waitress said. "It hasn't been easy for me at all, especially going home after my shift. There's no one to talk to, no one to play games with, no one to drink wine with or laugh with or listen to the radio with." The same distant, idle expression clung to her face as before, a burden that slumped her shoulders and slowed her down. She released a pressure cooker sigh. "But we all have to do what we all have to do, right?"

Barbara's muscles no longer ached; instead, she felt them smolder, felt the smoke fill the inside of her body. She had obsessed about John's voluntary deployment for months, visualized life without him over and over, re-enacted their final moments in her mind a million times. She convinced herself that she was ready, but it took talking to this waitress—witnessing her limp smile and heavy shoulders, hearing her hard, deflated voice lay out her feelings to a stranger—for Barbara to realize how lonely she would be without him.

A shadow loomed in her periphery and she felt soft, damp lips on her cheek. Behind her, Barbara heard Glen's unmistakable cackle. She turned around to see him standing in his khaki airman's uniform, one corner of his mouth turned up. Glen stood behind him in an identical outfit, a dizzy smile stretching across his face, and Anita hid behind him with a look that Barbara wouldn't have recognized before today. "Did I surprise you?" John asked.

"Sure did," Barbara answered, smelling the savory stench of her own smoke.

"Look who I found walking up and down Fremont

Street watching the fireworks," he smiled, tilting his head toward their friends, when he noticed the waitress behind the counter. "Say," he said, "who's this handsome young lady you've been talking to?"

"Oh," Barbara started, "this is my waitress…um…" but stammered to a stop; she didn't know her name.

"I'm Joy," the waitress answered suddenly. "Hey, do you three want menus? Or do you want a booth that'll fit all four of you?"

"No, we're actually on our way out," John said. "You ready, Barbara?"

Suddenly, Barbara wasn't so sure.

Lester Lancaster
March 20th, 1982

His shadow flickered on the ceiling above him. With his head curled over the top of an aluminum lawn chair, Lester watched the dark lumps dance, side-step an inch to the left and shimmy, sharpen, blur, and dim before hopping two steps back.

Of course, his shadow wasn't really moving and he knew it. Color flashed and swirled around the shape, fading like a bruise from red to violet to blackish blue, snapping to white and yellowing slowly, as if his silhouette was in the middle of an empty disco dance floor. He snickered at this thought: As if he would be caught dead dancing at a nightclub.

But, framed by the crown molding, his shadow seemed as alive as the images on the television whose light cast it. He knew the television's images weren't real, that they were merely images in a box. The shadow on the ceiling, however, was real. In a weird way, Lester was comforted by this thought. His shadow was there to keep him company.

A vaguely red splotch on the ceiling added a layer to these lights and dancing darks. The spot had been there since he moved in; it too felt comforting, like a burgundy galaxy watching over him.

It took all of Lester's strength to tug his neck over the back of the aluminum chair so he could see the band pantomiming on the TV—the drummer who hit cymbals where none splashed in the song; the bass player with the white-toothed smile who, uninhibited by any cumbersome cables, plucked his instrument playfully; the guitarist whose blonde Telecaster complimented his dusty hair suspiciously; the keyboard player whose fingers must have galloped across the keys during that mean solo, though the camera only managed to catch his tawny mane as it bounced to the beat.

Then, of course, there was that girl in the blood-red dress and tights. Cropped just beneath her chin, her midnight hair was styled in an unintended bedhead. She shuffled from foot to foot, bounced with the graceless innocence of a toddler, and flirted with each of her bandmates—or so the video's editing made it seem. Her bottom lip bulged as she gazed with wide gazelle eyes into the camera, at Lester in his living room; she seemed to be pouting throughout the song, especially when she sang, "Goodbye to you!"

Lester smirked in disbelief; she didn't really want to leave, did she?

He had seen this music video dozens of times. He loved the song, but he was mesmerized, literally in love, with Patti Smyth, that girl in the blood-red dress and tights. Despite her silly dancing and lip-synching, she howled in pain during the song's most climactic sections and whispered seductively during its most intimate. He thought a lot about this song and video's push and pull—Smyth's powerful, confident voice belting, "Goodbye to you!" beside the bouncing, the bedhead, the stary-eyed smirk, the flirting, the pouting and parody and underlying innocence that undermined her message made this video strangely sophisticated, adding a level of meaning that the song alone seemed to be missing—the uncertainty of her departure, or a playfulness in its declaration.

Lester's analysis was cut by a succession of furious cracks at the door. Lester didn't budge from his lawn chair. Instead, as "Goodbye to You" slowly faded out and transitioned into "I Know What Boys Like" (another video that he thought about often since Patty Donahue's apathetic voice seemed soaked in both hubris and sarcasm), he sunk into the seat's nylon webbing and turned down the television.

The cracks echoed a second time, sharper than the last. "Come on Lester," a voice said, "I know you're in there. Let me in." He recognized his little sister Angela's voice—slanted, wooden, serious.

She's bluffing, Lester decided, locking his eyes on the music video. *She'll go away after a while if I ignore her.*

When the front door opened, daylight flooded into the room like water on the *Titanic*, spilling onto the floor and splashing against the walls, stirring up empty Olympia cans and pizza boxes, which seemed to float before sinking silently back onto the ground.

"First of all," Angela said before taking any steps into the house, "if you aren't going to answer the door, you should at least lock—"

Angela's rant was suffocated by the smell—like body odor and spoiled food left to ferment so long that it smelled chemical, synthetic, like diesel exhaust.

The smell didn't prepare her for what she saw:

Lester in weathered red UW-Madison sweatpants, his bare, hairy belly ballooning over its stressed elastic waistband, gawking at MTV in an otherwise empty living room. Used paper plates and maranara'd napkins, half-crumpled cans of soda and beer, compromised and soiled pairs of sweat pants, and unopened mail spread around him. Unshaven, the tips of his shoulder-length hair curling in the house's man-made humidity, Lester squinted at Angela's silhouette from his seat. He looked like *something* in headlights, maybe mangy a bear, but definitely nothing as elegant as a deer.

"This…" is all Angela could say, though her jaw seemed to have rusted open.

"Angela, get out of my house," Lester demanded.

"This is…"

"For serious! Get out!" he said, making no effort to leave his lawn chair.

For a moment, only a derisive and condescending laugh staggered out of her. "This is why I come and check on you," she finally said in a Kindergarten teacher tone that startled Lester. "This is…" she started again, but let the sentence corrode in the stench.

"For serious, Angela! I'm going to call the cops if you don't get out of my house right now," Lester said, well aware that there wasn't a working phone on the property. "What do you even want?"

"Mom sent me here to pick up the rent you owe," she said. "She hasn't seen any money for two months." Angela pulled her attention away from Lester to eyeball the rest of the room—the paint peeling from the walls and flaking from the ceiling, the dull hardwood floors peeking through the trash, the mildewy towels duct-taped over each window. "Truthfully, though, I think she wanted me to make sure you weren't dead."

"Pssh, you wish."

Angela picked up the closest pieces of trash, starting with a pizza box torn in two, on which an order for Chinese food had been written in Lester's loopy handwriting. "Get out of that chair and find me the $400 you owe mom," she demanded. "And get a garbage bag or something. I'm going to help you clean up a little." She spotted the cherry-colored splotch on the ceiling. "Is that blood?" she asked. "How do you get blood on the ceiling? You know what? Never mind."

Lester didn't move. There was something about the thought of his little sister picking up his trash that amused him—the way her rosewood hair dislodged from behind her ear and fluttered in front of her face when she crouched down to pluck something off of the floor with her manicured nails. *Really*, he thought, *anyone in a $200 crimson trench coat with matching heels deserved to struggle with a juice box stuck to the hardwood floor.*

"I don't know why you only ever visit when you're collecting mom's money," Lester whined. "And, when you *do* visit, all you ever do is criticize." He watched his sister inspect a hardened rag that had been duct-taped into a ball for reasons both unknown and unsettling. "Don't touch that one," Lester warned.

Angela snarled, then stared at Lester with an expression that conveyed both disgust and disappointment. She had her brother's eyes—cold and bold and bright, more like gel toothpaste than ice. But Angela's face complemented these eyes; round and symmetrical, comforting and friendly, it looked younger than its twenty-five years. Lester's eyes looked foreign, like leftovers implanted into an imposter's face.

"I don't have any money, Angela," Lester confessed.

Her disappointment stretched into a look of disbelief. "Are you serious? You afford *this*?" she asked, gesturing at the television. Lester noticed that it was playing a Billy Idol song he had scrutinized a hundred times.

"You know that mom bought me a year of cable for my birthday," he answered. "That was like my *only* present."

"What about all of this takeout? How can you afford all of this beer? And what about the water bill or the electricity?"

"Oh, come on," Lester snorted. "Mom pays the utilities. That's been the deal since day one. And I will always find a way to acquire pizza and beer."

Angela carefully returned the trash to the ground, leaned against the living room wall, and restrung her hair behind her ears. "Okay," she sighed. Her exasperation felt suspicious to Lester. To him, every word she said, every gesture, it all seemed strategic, like this was some scheme she and their mom had hatched, perhaps even practiced. "Mom really needs the money and if I come back without it, she'll be devastated unless I have some plan."

"What do you mean?" Lester asked. "What kind of plan?"

"Tell me when you last worked and where."

He leaned back in his chair, the webbing and aluminum creaking uncomfortably, and stared at the silhouette-less ceiling in thought. "I worked as a cashier at Sullivan's until that bitch freaked out at me about coupons, but that was over a year ago."

"Do you think they would give you your old job back?" she asked. "I mean, even if you just worked a couple of shifts a week—"

"No way," Lester said. "That place was the *worst*. Plus, they wouldn't want me back there. I would probably sabotage the meat freezers or something. They know I'm a loose cannon."

Angela rolled her eyes. "Well you're getting a job somewhere, and by the end of the week."

"Listen," Lester said, still reclining. "There are some people who get up every day, complete a 'to-do-list' at their mundane job, and commute home. But some of us are meant to contribute to society in more subtle, but more important ways."

Angela's mouth curled into an incredulous smile, and an uncontrollable snicker bubbled out of it. "You are the laziest sack of shit," she said, "and I can't believe you are so willing to use your own mother like this."

But Lester lost interest when he noticed that MTV was playing Tom Tom Club's "Genius of Love," an animated video that had always fascinated him. He sensed Angela's anger rising, the tense timbre of her voice about to break, but lost himself in the spiraling artwork, which reminded him of something that a ten-year-old girl would draw with those "smelly" Mr. Sketch markers. Visually, he hated the video— the pseudo-psychedelic drawings giving way to a parade of abstract shapes—but the fleeting images helped bring to life the narrative, which was easy to lose in the song's hypnotic beat and dazed singing. Lester always soaked up the song's first few lines: "What you gonna do when you get out of jail?" a pair of girls ask a third, who replies, "I'm gonna have some fun." Here, she confesses that she's "in heaven with her boyfriend," who is "the genius of love" and "so deep," but does so in a frame that alters the entire narrative; this imprisoned protagonist's devotion to her boyfriend—and, with it, her character—seemed suddenly unreliable. Lester never loved the song or the video but, whenever it came on TV, he couldn't help but watch and wonder if the "fun, natural fun" she hopes to have equates snorting coke and dancing to Smokey Robinson; and if her laughing, unhappy boyfriend actually exists or not; and whether or not this love—

"Listen to me, goddammit!" Angela screamed.

Lester and his lawn chair squeaked in tandem. "I was listening, Angela!" he whined. "Jeez!"

Angela shut her eyes and kneaded the lines from her forehead. "Then what do you think about collecting unemployment for a while?"

"Unemployment?" he asked. "That's, like, getting money for nothin', right?"

Angela seemed to roll her eyes beneath her sealed lids and released a conceding sigh. "Yes, if you qualify and are looking for a job," she stated impatiently as if she had just said it moments ago. "Why, do you think you'd be willing to try that?"

Lester turned his attention back to the Tom Tom Club video and shrugged. "I don't know," he said. "Maybe."

But he beamed inside. Luckily for him, he thought, the daylight kept Angela from detecting the subtle glow beneath his skin.

Preston Assad
January 12th, 1996

The snow crunched under his bootstep, holding his weight for a split-second before collapsing beneath his weight. The cold dark swirled around him as he walked home. Some streets were well-lit— including Liliac and Sixth, whose sidewalks were shoveled and even salted. When he turned onto Coneflower, though, there were no more sidewalks and he was forced to contend with chunks of ice in the street. So long as he was out of the office, though, he couldn't complain.

A block from his house, a wave of anxiety swelled inside him about his appearance—his thick Buddy Holly glasses, whose smooth fames complimented his clean-shaven cheekbones; his black peacoat and his earth-toned scarf that matched his khakis; his Jansport camping backpack crammed full of files; his boots that helped him crunch through the snow but lent him no punk-rock credibility. He recognized his concern as an absurd remnant from his adolescence, but momentarily considered slipping on the dirty white Converse All-Stars stashed in his backpack so that he could be seen walking into the house wearing them but shook the shameful thought out of his head.

As he approached the house, thin silhouettes cast

shadows across his front porch. Glowing cigarette tips danced through the cold air between the porch's pillars like molten insects. When he stepped onto his property, he heard hushed voices. "Is that the guy?"

He spotted the rusty conversion van catching its breath in the driveway as he hopped up the cement steps. "Hi guys," he said with a natural, unsuspecting smile. "I'm Preston."

"Preston!" one of the silhouettes bellowed. It shuffled quickly from the shadows and revealed itself to be a muscular goblin of a man. "Dude!" he said in a bold, blaring voice as he wrapped his arms around Preston. "It is so good to finally meet you! I'm Alvin."

"It's good to meet you too," Preston replied, patting his back. Despite his stale odor, Alvin's affection felt neither uncomfortable nor forced; in fact, Preston had waited all week to receive this stranger's hug.

"This is the rest of the band," Alvin said, gesturing to five other young guys and introducing each by name; in response, each shivered beneath a ripped, stretched hooded sweatshirt and hunched over a cigarette like it provided some sort of warmth.

Preston smiled at them as he approached the front door, his keys clutched in his hand. "How is it," he asked, "that the band driving more than two thousand miles makes it before the bands driving forty-five minutes?" He turned the door's deadbolt, and the front door swung into the dark silence of the house. "Welcome to Humble House," he said with modest fanfare. "Make yourself at home."

Preston let the band file into the unlit living room

first; he followed, flipping on the lights, kicking off his boots, and hanging his backpack from a hook on the wall, all while reciting a set of directions in a rote, automatic manner as if he's said them hundreds of times. "One bathroom's upstairs," he pointed. "The other is behind that door. There's a phone in the kitchen. If you guys want to get into the basement, the door is around the corner. You can load in through the cellar; there's a gate leading from the backyard to the driveway that'll let you in." As the band split into six different directions, Preston walked from room to room, turning on lights, locking closets, tidying up.

"Hey Preston," a skeletal band member approached him. "I'm George, the drummer. A couple of us got really sick and I'm wondering if you have any, like, medicine lying around or something." As he spoke, Preston noticed not only his age—he couldn't have been older than nineteen—but also his skin's oatmeal hue.

"Sure, man," Preston replied. "Let's look in the kitchen."

The house seemed suddenly alive with sound: footsteps, closing doors, crackling floorboards, flushing toilets, the dull murmur of conversation wafting from the basement. It was chaotic, but this kind of commotion made Preston comfortable.

In the kitchen, Preston pawed through a small drawer, rattling bottles of vitamins and pain relievers. He pulled a half-full of bottle Nyquil, poured the red syrup into a shot glass conveniently drying on a nearby counter, and passed it to George, who, after sipping it, looked like he had swallowed whiskey and not decongestant. "Thanks, man," he said.

"No problem," Preston replied. "I'll keep pouring shots of this stuff to whoever needs it. Just pass them my way."

When George left, Preston turned the oven to 350 degrees and removed a casserole dish covered with aluminum foil from the fridge. He drew back its silver bed sheet to study its contents—chunks of pasta and peppers barely recognizable, coated with a muddy, rusty-colored sauce and adorned with black beans and bits of avocado— then stashed it in the unheated oven.

"Preston, when do doors open?" a voice yelled from the basement followed by the thud of flight cases cascading down the cellar stairs.

"7:30," he answered, "though I guarantee we'll start getting lurkers within the next hour or so." He loved the lurkers, those kids, usually teenagers, who lived four to five towns away and arrived early so they could scope out the scene before committing; they walked around the block in pairs, peeking into the backyard or the kitchen window, or stood uncertain on the sidewalk leading up to the porch— that is, until Preston noticed them and invited them into the house early. Lurkers became the ones who returned every weekend.

"How long is it until 7:30?" the voice yelled back. The whole house seemed to snicker in response. Preston heard a bandmate mutter in a low murmur, "Buy a watch, Jeremy. Jesus."

"It's 5:15 now, so about an hour and fifteen minutes," Preston replied. "You guys don't play until 9:00, though, so set up your amps along the back."

He stomped toward the basement, realizing that he could be helping the band load in, at least until the food finished baking. The narrow stairs buckled as he stepped down them, which always worried him. The basement at the bottom seemed immense, at least twice as long as the house above it, but he knew that when it filled with people, it shrunk considerably; every weekend, he found himself fretting about fire codes and maximum occupancies and other regulations that didn't apply to his private residence.

The basement was unfinished. Two walls had been slathered over in cement at some point, and the slab floor had been poured back before contractors cared about making them smooth or level; otherwise, the original foundation's stones remained. It was clean, though, and no longer possessed the "haunted house" aura it had when he moved in. Preston attributed this to the lighting system he installed, comprised of eight sockets and bulbs, connected by electrical conduit. He also stretched fabric across several two-foot by three-foot frames to create sound panels; they in no way made the basement soundproof, but it didn't echo much, and the music barely made it to the street.

On the opposite end of the space, cold air curled beneath the cellar door and wove between tottering stacks of drums and amps. Preston heard footsteps scuffing down the cellar stairs before the door flung open; Alvin and another, presumably Jeremy, shuffled into the basement with a speaker cabinet between them, wincing and grunting softly.

"Do you guys need help?" Preston said, scurrying toward them as they grounded the caster-less cabinet.

"No way," Alvin said, catching his breath and cracking his knuckles. "We're so used to this by now that other people just get in our way."

"I think we just have the bass cab and amp and a couple of guitars left," maybe Jeremy added, "so it's only another couple of trips, tops."

"Cool," Preston said. "Just let me know if you need help."

"Just want to say," Alvin said with a wild but sincere smile, "that your setup down here is pretty awesome."

Three microphone stands lined up like soldiers guarding a stained, scuffed Persian rug, centered along the back wall. Cables snaked up from each microphone into the rafters and followed the electrical conduit toward the back of the basement. They descended from the ceiling into a modest Mackie soundboard on a wooden workstation that Preston had made himself and positioned in front of the washer and dryer beneath the stairs. A pair of speakers flanked the mic stands, each hoisted on an aluminum tripod as close to the ceiling as possible.

"Thanks," Preston returned. "Sorry I don't have any monitors or anything, but you should be able to hear yourselves well enough. It's a small space"

"Hey, man," Jeremy answered as he breathed hot air onto his hands. "We've played with worse PAs on this tour at much bigger places. This is perfect."

As they turned to ascend the cellar steps, Preston heard the stairs groan. McCauley, almost too tall for the basement, ducked beneath the threshold as he dropped from the bottom step to the basement floor. He was still wearing his parka; wedges of bright blonde hair peeked from beneath his beanie. "Hey dude," he said, "Whatever you're cooking is sizzling pretty good in the oven. It might be done."

"I didn't even hear you come in," Preston replied, following him back into the kitchen. "Did you stop at the bank to pick up singles?"

"Yeah, I have a hundred," McCauley answered. "That should be enough, right?"

"Should be." Preston and McCauley had been best buddies in high school and through college. It was Preston's idea to book bands in his own basement, and he happily performed almost all of the legwork—connecting with bands, making flyers, purchasing sound equipment, offering his home to strangers, playing "stage manager" and "sound guy." But McCauley had become Preston's official Humble House partner and performed smaller critical duties, like handing out the flyers before and cleaning up after. Recently, Preston taught McCauley how to take money and monitor the door; while McCauley maintained the first floor, Preston could make sure the show was running smoothly in the basement.

"You'll never guess what else I picked up," McCauley said with a smirk. They turned into the kitchen and saw two teenagers, one terrified and one star-stuck. Neither wore coats—just black band t-shirts and jeans—and both shrugged like they were just starting to thaw. They were obviously lurkers.

"Hi guys. I'm Preston." He offered his open hand to the girl, then the boy, both of whom shook it weakly. "Are you two here for the show?"

"Yeah," the guy said, his eyes darting at every person who swooped past the kitchen door. The girl, meanwhile, said nothing, barely breathed; she stared at Preston and McCauley, enamored, unsure of who she might be staring at.

"Cool," Preston said as he moved toward the oven. "Well, if you're hungry, you should eat with us before people show up." He cracked open the oven and studied the sizzling casserole dish before using mitts to move it from the center rack to the stovetop.

"Watch this," McCauley grinned at the teenagers as he unplied a stack of paper plates. "Food's ready!" he screamed. The resulting rumble wasn't quite a stampede, but the house did stir noticeably. When all five band members entered in a cloud of conversation from every direction, the lurkers froze like amphibians trying to blend in with their surroundings.

Thirty minutes earlier, this band had been shivering in the silent shadows of the front porch, sucking down cigarettes, distracting themselves from the midwestern winter the best they could; in the kitchen, though, they scooped pasta and beans onto paper plates, cackled at each other, spoke in booming voices, came alive. "Hey guys," Preston shouted over the ruckus, "In case you didn't meet him earlier, this is McCauley, my counterpart. He's going to run the door. And two other friends showed up a little early. They are…" he stopped short, clearing space for the teenagers to introduce themselves.

"Jennifer," the boy said after a few uncertain seconds. "I mean—"

"I'm Jennifer," the girl interrupted. "He's Jake, my older brother."

The room responded with welcoming noise. It was difficult for Preston to pick out every question and answer, every joke or sarcastic comment, every short or tall tale, but it was apparent how suddenly the teenagers were sucked into the scene.

"Preston, what is this?" George asked, his voice cutting through the cacophony as he scraped his plate with a plastic fork.

"It's vegan enchilada casserole."

"Wait, this is *vegan*?" Alvin screeched.

"Cool," Jennifer said, suddenly brave enough to contribute to the conversation. "Are you vegan?"

"I'm not," Preston said, "but most bands that come through are. My goal is to make something vegan that non-vegans would like too. That way, everyone wins."

"Dude," maybe Jeremy added. "I might have to become a vegan."

"I'd *love* to see that," Alvin said.

"With food like this…" George added, spooning another dripping bite into his mouth.

Preston paused to notice the moment around him. Here were eight scruffy humans—strangers he had never met before this night—and his sole best friend, all splitting a space that comfortably fits five, slurping the casserole he had warmed moments before, sparring, sharing stories, tugging each other from one conversation to another. As he scooted himself onto the countertop, making more room in the cramped kitchen, he thought about how strange this would seem to an outsider, and then wondered why welcoming strangers into his house should seem strange at all.

Becky McLaughlin
September 30th, 2011

The leaves crunched under her shoesteps, having abandoned their branches in a splendid leap of faith. Above these trees, beyond the stuck-up noses of each haughty house, the sky stretched in an endless sapphire. Power lines separated the suburban scenery into long, rectangular frames so that, for a moment, Becky felt the fleeting sensation of walking through an art gallery.

She gripped her backpack's straps as she snaked through the streets, walking out of her way to step on the crunchiest leaves. It made her feel better about the day's bitter defeats—her failed Spanish test, that girl who called her a cunt, the continued graffiti scribbled in the C bathroom. These were difficult to forget, but the autumn sun warmed her and helped her put it all aside.

As she hopped up the steps toward her front porch, Becky heard her mother's muffled shrieking within the house and froze. "What the fuck is wrong with you, Tom?"

Becky knew better than to inch inside, especially after she heard her brother's response. "Mom, will you fuck off? I've been suspended a million times."

"I am so fucking sick of this!" Becky's mom screeched. "What the fuck are you going to do if you don't graduate this year? Because I can tell you now you're not living in this house."

"I don't care." Tom spoke in an articulate calm that Becky considered more intimidating than her mother's volume. "In fact, I'll do you a favor." Becky heard the floorboards thump inside as he walked toward the front of the house. "I'd rather be homeless than live in this shit hole with you." The front door reared back, the screen door flew forward, and Tom stormed from the house.

Stuck on the steps, Becky watched her brother barrel toward her, his tattooed arms swinging with each stride. "Tom," she said, "what's going on?"

"Fuck you," he murmured at her as he cascaded down the steps, pulling a cigarette from his back pocket and lighting it in his mouth in one graceful motion. Becky watched as he stepped down the street in a slant, his brown recluse haircut stuttering in the breeze to the beat of his rippling black t-shirt, until he carved around the corner.

With a sigh, Becky stepped onto the porch and through the screen door where she was slapped by the stench of stale tobacco. Amber-colored vinyl blinds fell over every window on the first floor, casting the disheveled living room in a hazy half-light. A pile of laundry sat next to an empty basket on the couch, and used ashtrays lay strewn across the floor, each placed with the strategy of a landmine.

Misty, Becky's mother, sat on the floor reclining against the couch wrapped in a dusty bathrobe. She smoked a cigarette and put one of the landmines to use. "What the fuck was his problem?" she croaked, exhaling silver spirals of smoke.

"I don't know," Becky answered from the doorway. "I don't see him during the day."

"Well, he's an asshole," Misty said. She dragged at her cigarette again and locked the smoke in her lungs before she continued. "You hear he lit some kid's shoe on fire?"

"What?" Becky hadn't heard, but couldn't care less. Her brother was always doing something stupid, and her mom was always doing nothing about it. None of it seemed new or interesting to Becky.

As Misty exhaled, smoke spilled and rose from her slack lips, uncoiling somewhere above her head. "Well, all I wonder is what those teachers are even doing over there if they don't notice their students lighting each other's shoelaces on fire, for fuck's sake."

"Teachers suck," Becky answered, focusing on the comforting purr in her pocket. She pulled her cell phone from her side pocket. **whats up**, the screen blinked before fading into an electronic coma.

"Listen, before you disappear for the night, do your laundry," Misty said, the cigarette wriggling between her lips as she picked up her own phone and started poking at its shattered screen.

"Why can't you do it?" Becky asked.

"What, am I your fucking maid or something?"

She decided not to insult her mother, not to murmur or sigh, not to stomp up the stairs in some pouty performance. Instead, by the time Misty finished pecking her message, Becky had simply disappeared, absorbed silently by the house.

In her room, Becky sat cross-legged on her bed in a

swirled nest of fleece blankets dotted with little bits of lint. The afternoon sunlight slid through her blinds and sliced her face into shadows and bright lines. She took two seconds to type, **ugg im doing laundry**, back to Frances before slipping the device into the front pocket of her faded jeans.

Outside her room, the floorboards creaked. Someone was coming upstairs—her mother, she assumed. *Maybe she's spying on me*, Becky thought, removing an iPod from beneath a pile of lifeless pillows. Music, she knew, was an effective method of scaring her mother away.

The touchscreen flickered on, obscured by pocks of dead pixels. Becky swiped at it mindlessly and stuck it into a cradle connected to a set of speakers. She didn't know the name of the song that started but recognized it as Pierce the Veil by the singer's taffy-like whine, which twisted around itself and everything else.

Becky let it wrap around her as she laid back on her bed, forgave herself for allowing her still-sneakered feet to burrow into the blankets. She subconsciously pulled her phone from her pocket. **tom lit some kids shoe on fire toady**, she typed, then dropped the device.

As the song rose, Becky closed her eyes, spiraling in the song's helpless free fall. She clung to the reins at the melody rose, a sunbound rocket, the singer's elastic vocal chords stretching with it into the sky, thrusted by lowing guitars, braying guitars, shrieking guitars shaking their matted manes, dragging this reeling chariot toward some calamitous finale. Suddenly, the track flamed out in the atmosphere, and Becky dropped back onto her bed.

The floorboards creaked outside her door again,

continuing as smoke from the song dissipated in the air. With a sigh, Becky bounced from her bed and stuck her head out the door, ready to complain.

"Becky!" a bullet shot from the living room beneath her. "Laundry! Let's go!"

She cocked her head, stood sideways in the doorframe studying the vacant hallway with a crumpled brow. When one of the floorboards sunk, cracked beneath the weight of nothing, she felt the hairs sharpen where her skull met her spine. The sensation crept down her shoulders. She shut the door quietly, whispering, "Holy shit," as she backed into her room's far, barren wall.

"Becky?" a hushed voice murmured in the hallway. It was a man's—murky and dismal. The crystal doorknob rattled.

"Tom?" Becky asked, her voice trembling. She knew it wasn't him.

"Becky?" it murmured again. It sounded sad, like his head was resting against the solid door.

"Holy shit, holy shit, holy shit," she repeated, breathless, her heart beating in time with each syllable. She slid down the wall, landed into her overflowing laundry basket.

"Becky, I know you're there. Please open the door," he pleaded.

A high-pitched squall rose from her throat—the sort that shook warped window panes and spooked the grackles hiding in nearby bushes. Her adolescent lungs deflated, Becky took a shallow, desperate breath and squealed a second time. The doorknob continued to rattle, shook from side to side.

"Becky, please."

Someone stomped up the stairs, tripped and trampled down the hall. The door drew open, and Misty stood wide-eyed in the doorway, her claw clutching the shimmering knob. "What?" she shrieked back, bands of sun striping her straight face, her bathrobe swinging. "What's going on? What's wrong?"

But Becky's scream collapsed into a bawl. Tears flushed her clenched eyes, cooled her pink face, dribbled down her freckles and onto her chest.

"Becky, what's wrong?" Misty cawed, her voice hardened with frustration. "Dammit, just tell me!"

Becky wiped her nose on her sleeve. "I heard—someone, a voice," she stuttered. "Someone said—was calling my name."

"That was me, you dumbass."

"No!" she spat, her voice sparking. "It was a man's! A ghost's!" she screeched.

Misty simply scowled. "Get your ass out of that laundry basket and grow the fuck up," she said and stormed out.

Unconsciously, or for comfort's sake, Becky slid her phone from her front pocket. To her surprise, Frances had returned her text. **omg thats scary**, it read, and the hairs on the back of her head crept like ivy toward her ears.

"For fuck's sake," Becky heard her mother mutter as she stumbled down the stairs. "Both my goddamn kids are crazy."

Lester Lancaster
March 26th, 1982

A *tiny bell jingled*, and Lester stepped once again between the marble buildings downtown. A thin brown sleeve swung from his left hand, a stained paper sack from his right. As he waddled from the comic book store, the glass door still swinging shut behind him, his Sylvester and Tweetie tie lifted in the wind and lapped his trimmed mustache. *This is why I hate ties*, he thought.

In the bakery's windows, he caught his reflection, spotting the black socks peeking beneath his khakis; they didn't match his slacks, but they complimented his black and silver cross-trainers just fine. Ovals of sweat seeped through his olive shirt beneath his arms; he tried his best to ignore them.

His ponytail drooped from the back of his head like a wet dog's tail. That morning, Lester worried about pulling his hair into a ponytail, which his sister instructed him to do. But, as he strutted past a line of banks, he saw why: *I fit in with all these bankers*, he noted. Slicked back with mousse, his hair was calmer and classier than usual. Lester smirked at his reflection as he walked—until he slammed into a pebble-studded ash urn.

Lester crossed into the square downtown, still faded

from the harsh winter, and found a wooden bench to sit on. The grey Civic Center, which sat across Fourth Street from him, seemed to watch in disapproval as he removed a fat sandwich from the sack; shards of lettuce and onion tumbled from the bun and vinegar left oily circles on his khakis.

Lester rested his breakfast on his knee and glared back at the building. An hour before, he had been intimidated by its sixteen cement steps, which led him between Ionian columns and beneath an enormous awning three floors above the front doors. When he entered, he found himself in a lobby whose floors and walls were made of whole slabs of granite, each flecked with what shimmered like copper in the morning sun. Facing an information desk, he had to calm his breathing to ask where the unemployment office was: up two flights of spotless marble steps, each lit by windows that stretched the height of the first and second stories, then down a hall with white quartz walls.

The meeting with Mrs. Beverly Thatcher was far less intimidating. It began with her invitation for Lester to sit down on a ratty office chair, which he obeyed dutifully. The meeting ended, however, with Mrs. Thatcher falling out of her chair, laughing until tears tumbled down the curves of her cheeks. Lester, wagging his tie in front of his face, had done his best impression of Sylvester's lisp—who'd have thought she'd find it so funny? She wiped her cheeks with one hand as she shook Lester's hand with the other, her eyeglasses dangling from a chain around her neck, then instructed him to visit a kiosk two levels below where he could pick up a check for $450—his monthly allotment during his first six months of unemployment. Lester wasn't sure if she was allowed to waive the week-long wait for benefits, but she had seemed pleased to do so.

Lester bit a corner off of his sandwich. As he chewed, a condescending snicker rattled in his chest, and he hoped the Civic Center—with its furrowed forehead and protruding bottom lip—could hear it. Lester's smile seemed to say, "You're not as scary as you thought you were, are you?" However, mid-smirk, he felt vinegar drip from his mouth down the smooth bulges of his chin. Lester wiped the oil onto Tweetie's face. Considering that he bought it at a garage sale on the way to the interview, it was no big loss.

As he placed his sandwich back onto his stained slacks, Lester removed *Amazing Spider-Man* 226 from its paper sleeve. Spider-Man was his favorite superhero, and Black Cat was easily his favorite female villain—anti-hero, really. It wasn't just her lush, platinum hair or her tight leotard— admittedly, he found her physically irresistible—but her undying adoration for Spidey that attracted him to her. He also found Felicia Hardy decidedly un-evil as far as villains go; she may be a bit immoral, but Lester didn't consider it a deal-breaker.

Tearing further into his Italian sub, Lester flipped open the cover, his fingerprints and staining the newsprint, smearing the ink. Felicia was on the second page, her platinum hair swaying as she walked through the psychiatric ward where Spider-Man had sent her after their last meeting. As he chewed, he read and re-read the copy floating in each bubble carefully studying every colorful dot printed on the page, especially the black curves that outlined Felicia's sullen face.

Around him, downtown was quietly alive. The sun smoldered through a thin blanket of clouds and between the still-bare branches of a tree lurking over Lester's left shoulder, which cast fidgety shadows across his book. A sudden breeze fanned the pages beneath Lester's fingers. "Dang it," he muttered, the sub nearly slipping from his grasp as he slapped his hand on the book to keep it from flying away. As he flipped back to his page, Lester noticed the traffic on Fourth Street farting back and forth—station wagons and pickup trucks, Grand Ams smiling in the sun, garbage trucks tipping their hats at the Civic Center as they passed. Six panels into *Amazing Spider-Man*, Lester was already regretting his attempt to enjoy the outdoors.

As Felicia told her distracted nurse about her encounters with Spider-Man, Lester heard footsteps pad past him. "You're looking great," a voice said in a humble whisper. "This weather does marvelous things for you."

Lester turned to see a man in khaki pajama pants and corduroy slippers wandering past, his steps tiny and seemingly aimless. His satin jacket rippled in the breeze, its silver snaps reflecting the haze. He walked slowly, unsteadily, clutching a cane, its dark-stained wood dented and scratched after years of use. Behind a set of saucer-sized plastic glasses, deep creases scored his forehead. His sparse, close-trimmed hair was white, almost transparent.

With a newspaper tucked beneath his armpit, he slid his slippers to the corner mumbling beneath his breath the entire way. "You look stronger now. Do you feel stronger?" Lester heard him say. "Well, isn't that something! You're getting stronger with age! It's a lovely thing, a lovely thing." It was endearing, Lester decided, but definitely a sign of insanity. *Maybe he's homeless*, Lester wondered, *yet another reason why eating lunch outside was a dumb idea.* He picked up his sandwich and, after biting off another corner, subconsciously clenched the sopping thing in his fist.

When the light at Lily turned green, the man took minuscule steps across Fourth, mere inches at a time. As Lester stared, a morsel of concern bubbled up from his stomach. He tried to return to the psychiatric ward with Felicia, her face overlaid in crimson and contorting into an evil—no, immoral—smile. Locking the nurse's arm behind her back, Felicia shoved the overweight woman violently into her former room, cackling, "It's so much easier to bide your time and escape from a hospital…than from a prison!" As he read this dialogue, Lester released a giggle into the air. He really loved a character how many steps in ahead of Spider-Man—and the reader—Black Cat was at any moment. He wanted to flip-forward to where Felicia would inevitably don her sleek, skintight costume and the simple mask that obscured just enough of her identity to display her devious beauty. But he held back, instead imagining her in his mind's eye, tracing the delicate curve of her calf; following it past the subtle, ticklish recess behind her knee to her thighs, long and lean; to her butt, firm but bouncing softly with each feline-like step, the satin spandex of her disguise stretching slightly between both cheeks; to the small of her back—

A honking car horn interrupted Lester's concentration. He glanced up to see the homeless man only halfway across Fourth, the "Do Not Walk" sign in a solid red, and a Pinto wagon snarling, swerving around him into the opposite lane. Other cars careened toward the crosswalk, their tires barking briefly as they slammed on the brakes. The pajama'd man inched toward the other side of the street, his cane trembling with each step; it was obvious that he was shuffling across as quickly as legs would take him.

"What's going on over there?" Lester heard his sister's voice behind him.

He turned to see Angela wearing her work attire: a suit coat, bolstered with shoulder pads that made her look more masculine, and a blouse unbuttoned just enough to emphasize her femininity. "What do *you* want?" he said, casting a squinting stare.

"You see that poor man over there being honked at?" Angela asked. "Do you think he's okay?" Cars swerved around the homeless man, his cane still quivering, only a few steps from the curb.

"Just some bum. He'll figure it out."

"Hey, you look spiffy," Angela said, pawing at his ponytail. Her smile sunk into a half-hearted smirk, though, when she noticed his athletic shoes, stained pants, streaked Sylvester and Tweetie tie, and the old cotton Boy Scout belt straining at his waist. "Well, you tried," she concluded, sitting down on the bench beside him.

"What are you even doing here?" Lester whined.

"My meeting ended early. I looked out the window and saw you sitting here, so I thought I'd come and say hi."

"You mean *interrogate* me," Lester sneered, ripping menacingly into the remaining nub of his sandwich.

"Where did you get that?" she asked. A corner of her mouth curled upward, the only hint of the snicker she was suppressing.

"See?"

"Seriously, though," she added. "It's nine in the morning. Who sells sandwiches that early?"

"I know a guy that'll make me sandwiches whenever I want one."

"I thought you didn't have any money," Angela said suspiciously.

"If I told you any more about my sandwich guy, I fear I'll lose him," he argued. "He's put everything he has on the line for me, and I'm not about to risk that."

Across the street, the man stood safely on the corner of Fourth and Lily, staring at the Civic Center, his head bent back and mouth cracked open. He seemed to bask in the building's cold, stern supremacy. Angela and Lester paused to observe this strange scene. Lester conceded that the building was the most impressive and intimidating structure on this downtown square, but the man's wonder only convinced him further that he was crazy.

"So," Angela said, "how much money are they giving you each month?"

"Are you serious? Is money all you care about?"

"Jeez, I'm just curious. Is it enough to pay back mom? She really needs it."

Lester sighed again, though subconsciously this time. He look again at the comic sprawled across his lap, into Felicia's lustful eyes and mischievous smile, at Spider-Man swinging though the city completely unaware of the Black Cat's escapades.

"They're giving me two hundred dollars a month,"

Lester said. "It's enough to pay rent, but, unfortunately, not enough to pay mom back what I owe her."

"Well," Angela responded, "I suppose it's something."

Lester glanced again at the man across the street, still staring at the Civic Center's pretentious facade. His jaw bounced in quiet conversation with himself, or maybe the building.

"Pitiful," Lester spat, shoving the butt of his sandwich into his slimy mouth.

Barbara Farmer
July 14th, 1941

A steady cadence clattered beneath Barbara as she walked the length of the train car. She felt it in her feet, but more in her lungs. Halfway to her seat, the beat tangled itself with her body's rhythms so much that she confused the two; her breathing stuttered, and she walked in unsteady strides, mistaking her the sound of her steps with the furious shuffle of the train bearing down the tracks.

When Barbara stopped, desperate to separate these rhythms from one another, the felt a sob inch its way up her throat. *Why is it so difficult to walk on a train all the sudden?* she wondered, collapsing into the nearest seat, tears dribbling between her fingers as she tried to hide her face. Though the car's bystanders noticed, no one budged from their business. Men in hats lowered their newspapers and peered through eyeglasses at Barbara before returning to the news from overseas; elderly women snuck quick peeks from the corners of their eyes before returning their attention to the naked Nevada landscape. One boy in a small necktie asked his mother, "Is that woman sad?" but his question went unanswered.

Barbara didn't want consolation anyway. She thought about John, his pudgy smile and subtle dimples, and where he was at that moment—probably on a train headed to San Francisco, fidgeting with the buttons on his uniform. In the darkness beneath her hands, Barbara returned at the train station, buried in John's arms. She remembered the way he smelled, the sweet bite of his cologne mixed with his savory skin, and the delicate scent of his cotton uniform. Buried within his embrace, she heard his parting words to her: "Oh, sweet lovely lady, be good."

In that moment, Barbara emerged from his arms, gazed past the tears shimmering in his eyes, and giggled while he wiped her cheeks with his thumbs. He knew it was her favorite song, one that they had danced to dozens of times. The lyrics, of course, carried a new meaning in that context; it was no longer a line sung by some slick-haired band leader with a saxophone swinging from his neck. Here, they seemed to plea for loyalty, for sanity, for peace while he was gone. "I will," she whispered.

While they kissed, the grey roar of pedestrians brightened, the rumble of footsteps and luggage softened, the murmur of restless trains faded. Surrounded in white silence, his lips slipped against hers, his hand clasped her shoulder, her fingertips raked through his hair. An hour after this kiss, she swore she could still feel him on her lips and fingertips and tongue.

Barbara felt the beat once again beneath her feet, but it felt different. It no longer competed with her heartbeat; her breathing seemed to cycle in time with the train's heavy clacking rhythm.

With a sigh, Barbara wiped her eyes with her forefingers and blinked out any tears that might have remained. Through still-cloudy vision, she noticed how eager the riders around her were to avert their attention, to ignore the woman drenched in her own tears. To Barbara, their indifference seemed insincere; their eyes suggested that they understood her tears, that they cared, but were unsure how to console her, a military wife, as war waxed more and more every evening.

She noticed something else—that the song "Oh! Lady Be Good" was swinging through her head, perhaps inspired by her husband's parting words. In her mind, she heard the splaying horns and woodwinds, the hi-hat's lazy shuffle, the bass's stubborn bump bouncing in time with the train. She pulled herself carefully from the seat. As the train bobbed and swayed, Barbara found herself able to stay on her feet. She stepped slowly in time with each measure's downbeats until she made it to the far side of the car.

The heavy doors seemed easy to heave, the canyon between cars bridgeable with the song skipping through her head. Though she clung to the leather seats she passed, Barbara became more confident as she moved, her stride aligned with first and third beat of each measure. She closed her eyes and let the song's swagger propel her through the train. A clarinet solo swirled wildly, then settled into something softer, stirred by that stuttering hi-hat and a polite piano, and a man in her head crooned, "I am so awfully misunderstood, so lady be good to me." When she had treaded the length of the car, barely aware that she was humming along with this man's warm warble, Barbara cracked open her eyes to see passengers staring at her strangely. *Now they notice*, she thought with a smirk, transferring cars before she could care any further.

On this next car, Barbara no longer took small, cautious steps. Instead, her eyelids sealed, she shimmied down the aisle, almost hopping from beat to beat. A saxophone wiggled in her head, and the train's whistle blasted beside the brass section. She still held the back of each seat she passed, but more lightly; they became the sweating hands of her dance partner, the train, which bounced beneath her footsteps, let her pivot and twist and lightly kick. As the solo subsided, she heard herself whisper along with the sly voice in her head. "Oh, please have some pity," she begged beneath her breath, "because I'm all alone in this big city. I'm just a lonesome babe in the wood, so lady be good to me."

On the outside, Barbara looked like a woman traveling gracefully but blindly through the train, touching each tawny seat and mumbling to herself, her toes occasionally flicking the air in front of her. On the inside, though, Barbara bounced on a dim and slick dance floor, the air hot and dense, her fingers knitted with John's, kicking her heels forward and her toes back, tilting and twisting to the bobbing beat, colliding tenderly with other couples; ten gentlemen in matching teal tuxedos swaying in time a room away, their fingers climbing up and down their saxophones, their cheeks puffing air into their trumpets and trombones, sweat loosening locks of hair that swung over their brows, over the body of a stand-up bass, a vibraphone, a snare and pair of tom toms; and the tickle of her dress fluttering around her knees, the darkness above, the steady and reckless palpitation of the room around them, and John's petroleum eyes dripping up and down her body, the commotion whirling around her, making her one with her husband and everyone around her.

Her rapture was interrupted by a familiar voice. "There's Barbara," it said. "Where have you been?"

Barbara opened her eyes to see Anita leaning out of her seat near the back of the car; Joy, facing the front of the train, twisted around to spot her friend, her concerned smirk curling quickly into a look of relief.

Breaking with the beat, Barbara dropped into her seat. "I'm back," she said breathlessly, her disheveled curls framing her pink face. Discolored rings circled her eyes like stains around a drain.

"Oh, hon," Joy said. "You've been crying, haven't you. Are you okay?"

"Yes," Barbara replied, sighing, resting her arms on the table between their seats. "But I'm better now."

"We were worried sick about you," Anita said. Her hair fell forward into a pile of coils and waves that she had pinned to the top of her head in a style that Barbara found particularly fashionable. She adored the color of Anita's hair—it looked like rich potting soil—and how well it matched her almond complexion.

"We thought you might have fallen in the loo," Joy smiled. In Las Vegas, Barbara and Anita had visited her at Dino's almost daily to ask her questions and keep her company. They sipped black coffee and forced themselves to laugh until the day before their departure when they half-joked that Joy should return to Wisconsin with them. But Joy loved the idea; she had no real reason to stay and argued that a new adventure might revitalize her. The effects were instant: Joy still strained beneath the weight of her heavy heart, but her sky blue eyes seemed cloudless, and her hay-colored hair (cropped a little too short for Barbara's taste) stuck out playfully. She seemed suddenly younger and a lot more fun.

"No," Barbara snickered, shaking her head. "About halfway to the bathroom, I realized it was the first time I had been alone—you know, really alone, without John or my parents or anyone." She fiddled with her wedding ring, twisting it around her finger. "And, on my way back, the thought just became too much."

Joy reached across the tabletop to lay her palm on Barbara's hands. "Well, you have us now, so you won't be alone," she said.

"While you were gone, we got to talking," Anita added, glancing at Joy's smile.

"We should get a place to share for as long as we need to," Joy jumped in. "Like an apartment, and we could split the rent."

"We could make supper together," Anita continued, "and go out on the town sometimes, and help each other with laundry and sewing, and share clothes—"

"But, most importantly," Joy concluded, making careful eye contact with Barbara, "be there for each other. Each of us is going to need support at some point."

"Where?" Barbara asked.

"We'll stay out of the big cities, like Milwaukee," Anita said, "so we're a little safer. But we need to find somewhere big enough so we can get jobs. That way, we can split the rent even-Stevens."

Barbara drew in a long breath. The thought of living

together thrilled her, but she had never permanently lived anywhere other than her parent's farm. The thought of living anywhere else scared her. Her mouth stiffened into a frown.

When she closed her eyes, she could smell John again, especially that clean cotton uniform. She thought about her husband in that uniform—nineteen years old, a teenager, playing soldier—but reminded herself that he went through basic training, that he was prepared for war.

Who could ever be prepared for war? she wondered.

She imagined him on a ship puttering across the ocean—smoking a cigarette, staring across the horizon, wondering what hell was waiting for him. Would he let himself feel fear?

She imagined him startled awake in his bunk, first at the sound of sirens, then at the sound of distant gunfire; his helmet crooked, his rifle loaded, his eyesight streaking, would he he follow a line of other soldiers into the night?

She imagined him cowering against a tree, the leafy canopy above him turning day into night as guns snapped all around him, bullets tearing through the darkness. In her mind, his sweat left clean lines on his filthy face, Barbara's tear stains on his uniform long-since dried, replaced by oil, mud, the blood of his new brothers.

Barbara stopped herself from imagining any more. In her heart, she knew John was scared too, despite the confidence he carried himself with. He was sleeping somewhere unfamiliar, unsafe, alone. And if he could, she could too.

"Okay," Barbara sighed and tried to smile. "Let's give it a go."

Preston Assad
January 30th, 1996

Most days, he could tune out the clicking. But, today, Preston struggled to conceal his frustration—and all because his mouse wasn't working. He double-clicked on icons that refused to respond; they sat blind and oblivious, unaware of their directives.

Near Preston, Fred reclined in his office chair and clicked his mouse recklessly. Preston couldn't see Fred's screen, but could see his face: eyes focused and blank, lower-lip hanging limp, jowl wobbling. Preston knew that he was playing that game again—the one with the spaceship that required Fred to click the mouse continuously in order to exterminate his enemies.

Windows wrapped around three sides of the interior office that Preston shared with Fred, sheets of mint-tinted glass that stretched to the ceiling, offering a view of the floor's many cubicles and occupants—men in sandy suits and maroon ties reading the daily paper at their desks, women with perms in pantsuits, movement and activity and a surprising lack of actual progress.

Preston returned to his mouse, clicked it, double-clicked it, triple-clicked it, scribbled it across the mousepad adorned with Wisnago's circular seal. He mimicked Fred's frantic technique, his fore- and middle-fingers popping the button with such violence that his glasses slipped from the bridge of his nose. "Hey Fred," he finally said. "Can you help me? My mouse isn't working."

"What's wrong?" Fred asked, his attention still stuck to his screen.

Preston slid his thick-rimmed spectacles back onto the bridge of his nose. "My mouse's button isn't working. The arrow's moving, but it won't let me click on anything."

"Unplug it," Fred instructed, "then plug it in." The words tumbled from his lips and plopped onto the floor in seven distinct syllabic lumps.

"I did that," Preston said, then sighed. "I have this thing due before noon, so I need it fixed."

"I dunno, man," Fred concluded. "Not sure what's wrong."

Preston spun his chair away from his useless computer and colleague, releasing steam as slowly and delicately as he could. On the back wall, four stout windows disrupted provided Preston a view of a icy city in perpetual twilight. Crown moulding, the color of settled caramel, hid the corners where the wall met the twelve-foot ceiling. All these details, including the dizzying carpet, made the building seem older—like an office from a movie set in the 1930s.

He heard four quiet cracks at the door and, coincidentally, Fred's clicking stopped. Preston knew it was Doria, his supervisor, before he turned from the snowscape outside simply by her needless knocks. "Hey Preston," he heard her trill, "We need that new letterhead done in the next few minutes. Is that possible?"

Preston spun his chair toward the door. "I thought you needed it by noon?"

"Well, Schooner wants to send a letter to our sister city in Belgium, so he needs to get it into the mail by the time it's picked up at nine."

"I can try," Preston replied, clicking his useless mouse. "It should be easy, but my computer's mouse isn't working right now, and I'm not sure why."

Doria smirked. "It's moments like this where I bet you're glad you share an office with the IT supervisor. When you're done, print it out on a few blank pieces of the nice linen paper and put the file on a disk for Tammi." Then she slid like a shadow out the door, closing it with no more noise than a considerate clunk.

Fred's clicking resumed, bouncing around the room, off the back office wall, the windows, the swirling rug, until he realized the mouse was no longer working. "The hell?" Fred mumbled. The clicka-clicka-clicka continued, but Preston's trained ear detected panic in the pattern. When the mouse scurried out of Fred's hand, he searched the room like a disoriented toddler; his gaze finally landed on Preston, who loomed over his computer holding his broken mouse by its tail like a dead rat he just discovered beneath the garbage disposal—and his colleague's mouse in his other hand.

"What the fuck, Preston?"

"I have work to do, so I'm going to use your mouse," Preston said. "You can use mine if you can fix it."

Fred sat up in his chair and held out a plump, blotchy paw. His concession was silent, but his raised brow, tightened lips, and tilted head hinted at his disapproval. Preston swung the defective rodent into Fred's hand and retreated to his desk.

After sending the new letterhead to the printer, Preston unplugged his new mouse, stuffed it in his back pocket, and headed out the door. He chose his gait carefully as he approached the printer near Doria's office. He wanted to seem swamped, too busy to stop and talk, so he leaned into each step. The mouse's cord swung behind him like a tail.

Preston picked up the piece of paper waiting for him in the printer and turned toward the copy room, pretending not to notice both Sarahs as they stirred instant coffee near the water cooler. He focused on his printout when Will limped by, then smirked at Schooner as he snuck past his office toward the copy room where found Maryanne photocopying some packets for a presentation. "It'll only be another minute," she said smiling.

As he waited, Preston looked out from the copy room's window at the rest of the first floor, noticed how many of his coworkers cackled with their colleagues between cubicles or hid at their desks, how many flipped through issues of *Harper's Bazaar* or *Sports Illustrated* in some perceived privacy or telephoned their friends, their fiancés, twisting the curly cord around their fingers.

"I don't think I saw you yesterday," Maryanne said. "How was your weekend?"

"Oh," Preston said, caught off guard. "Fine, I guess."

"That's good," she replied, almost shouting above

the copier's backbeat.

Preston noticed Maryanne's plum hair hanging to the center of her spine; she climbed onto tip-toes to turn the pages of her packet, place it on the platen, and closed the lid. As aqua-colored light squeezed out from the Konica's and outlined her pear-shaped silhouette, Preston realized he should have asked her about her weekend. He winced, wondering how he always seemed to miss this simple social protocol.

"Do you still put on concerts at your house," she asked.

"Uh, yeah, actually," he answered, surprised that anyone at work knew about what happened at Humble House on Friday nights, or that anyone cared. "Not last week, but we will this Friday."

"Cool," she said, her smile sparkling in the copier's glow. The corners of her mouth stuck into her round cheeks, creating rows of perky dimples, and it occurred to Preston that Maryanne was much younger than he thought—maybe younger than him. "What kind of music?"

Preston stopped himself, knowing that he could become too easily enrapt when discussing music; one time, after an intense debate about CBGBs in the 1970s, a friend compared him to a puppy that peed all over the linoleum every time his owner came home. Preston was aware that most people had never heard of his favorite bands and would hate them if they had. So he kept his answer simple. "Rock 'n' roll bands, mostly," he said.

Maryanne snickered as if she though he was being playful. "Okay, what *kind* of rock 'n' roll?"

"Punk-rock, I guess," he started, his tail starting to wag. "Mostly post-hardcore bands these days, but I think the house is developing a reputation as the house in the midwest to play if you're in a band that plays anything loud and/or fast."

The Konica's hypnotic murmur stuttered to a stop, and the aqua light drained back into the copier's mechanical depths. "That sounds cool," she said, stealing her packets from the lower tray and tapping the "reset" button at the top corner of the copier's toothy smile. Her hair swung during this gesture, and Preston swore he saw the outline of a star tattooed in blue ink behind her ear. "It's all yours," Maryanne said toward the office's florescent glare, once again a silhouette, as if she had been cut out from the scenery with scissors.

Preston's eyebrows tangled behind his glasses, more suspicious than surprised that these bands sounded "cool" to anyone who worked in Wisnago's government offices. "Do you like post-hardcore music?" he asked.

"Like Quicksand?" she replied. "Or Sunny Day Real Estate? Is that what you mean?"

"Yeah," he answered, flattening his document onto the copier and stabbing the machine's buttons. The Konica wheezed the shrill whistle of something about to detonate before rollicking to life; electric light brimmed beneath its lid as its belly hummed and rumbled.

"I have a couple of Sunny Day's tapes," she said. "Actually, I just got their new one a week ago. I really like it so far."

Preston swiped a page from the copier's tray and

handed it to Maryanne. "Here's a flyer for Friday's show," he said, his smile slanted. "If you like Sunny Day Real Estate, you'll like these bands."

"Cool," she said. "Do I get in for free?" Preston sensed a smile somewhere within the depths of her silhouette.

"Of course," Preston smirked.

"Cool," she repeated. "I'll consider it. Thanks." And she disappeared into the idle bustle behind her. Preston swallowed and realized his mouth had gone dry. He wasn't sure why.

He found McCauley spinning in Fred's empty chair when he returned to his office with half a ream of flyers overstuffing a manilla folder. The fur-lined hood of McCauley's sage parka made him seem hunchbacked, and its swollen size made his head seem tiny, but it didn't stop him from wearing it everywhere until April. "Where's Fred?" he asked.

"I think he's pissed at me because I made him do his job," Preston said, tossing the folder onto his desk. "Why are you here so early?"

"I didn't sleep last night," McCauley replied, still spinning, "and I have nothing to do until work at noon, so I figured I'd see if you had the flyers finished so I can start putting them up."

"I do," Preston said. "I just finished copying them, actually. Good timing."

McCauley stopped mid-spin and pulled himself to Preston's desk, his heels stabbing the carpet's paisley fronds. He drew the flyers from the folder and scrutinized them like an art dealer. "You do good work, Assad," he said. "I'm giving you a raise."

"Man, I hate working here," Preston said.

"I know."

"It's, like, rare to see anyone doing anything. But, somehow, all of my work needs to be done in a rush. It's annoying."

"And what have you actually done today, besides photocopying flyers?" McCauley said, staring at Preston with a crooked and knowing smirk.

"Oh, come on," Preston snarled. "I couldn't do anything because my mouse was broken. I would have been swamped with bullshit all morning if it hadn't been."

"Is it because you sat on it?" McCauley asked, pointing to the gray cord dangling from the back pocket of Preston's Dockers.

"Don't ask." Preston pulled the hardware from his pocket and tossed it onto Fred's desk.

"Forgive your coworkers," McCauley climbed from Fred's chair and slid the flyers and folder into his coat, where they fit perfectly into an enormous pocket. "They can't all be bad."

Outside his office—across a landscape of cubicles and abandoned, disarrayed desks—Preston glimpsed Maryanne organizing sheets of paper into mindless piles at her desk outside of Schooner's office, headphones hugging her ears. He couldn't quite see her head bobbing, couldn't hear her humming beneath each breath, but noticed her hair as it swayed from side to side. He wondered what she was listening to.

"You're right," Preston conceded quietly.

Charles Stonebreaker
June 3rd, 1910

Eight straining, cussing men hauled a burlap-wrapped bale of hops, shuffling their feet through the firm dirt between the train yard and storehouse where four other bales waited in refrigerated darkness. Dust swirled in the air, stuck to the sweat and saliva seeping from the team.

"Gentlemen, pick up your feet please," Charles said as he coughed. "We don't want that dust to dirty the hops." He fanned his paperwork in front of his face as he followed the bale.

"Go die, Stonebreaker," one of the men grumbled through clenched teeth, but Charles couldn't determine which. It didn't matter, though. He couldn't blame them for being irritable. The train with the week's last shipment was held up in Ames, Iowa for two hours, and he required his team to stay late and unload the six bales when they arrived. His demand, however, meant his men would remain two hours after work on a Friday—a payday—and lug six five-hundred-pound bricks through the summer sun. Of course, as the shipping and receiving manager, Charles didn't do any lifting, which likely made these hot laborers hotter.

As the men disappeared into the shadows of the storehouse, Charles considered laying in the dirt beneath the door and allowing the plumes of cool air to uncurl onto him. Instead, he wandered beneath the sun back toward the train, where the hissing steam needled his eardrums. Sweat slid down his face, stung his eyes with each blink.

One by one, each member of his team materialized from the shade and slogged with leaden steps toward the train car. Sullivan was the first to arrive. "You helping with this last one, eh Stonebreaker?" he teased, though the way his forearms stretched the seams of his rolled-up shirtsleeves made even high-spirited statements seem vaguely threatening.

"Yeah," Bowman yipped behind him, removing his hat to wipe the sweat from his forehead. "I'll hold onto the receipt and you can take my side."

"They don't pay me enough to do labor," he said, his bite tight behind his smile. "Anyway, we—you only have one more bale before we can pick up our wages and head home for the weekend."

Sullivan and Bowman smirked, leaning against the boxcar beside Charles. When the rest of the team arrived, they hauled the last bale to the storehouse, kicking up a cloud of dust and profanities. Drops of sweat fell with each scuffled step, leaving dark circles in the dust beneath their feet.

Meanwhile, Charles slow-walked along the tracks to tell the engineer they were done. He hated the engine's terrible hissing—hated it even more than dealing with his laborers. The sound pierced his skull, impaled whatever thoughts he had, so he clenched his eyes shut as he walked alongside the train. Every sixth step, he peeked and readjusted his trajectory, hoping not to stumble into any divots in the dirt. When he sensed he was at the engine—when the hiss became unbearable—Charles peeked into the cabin and waved wildly at the train's operator, who waved back.

Charles turned and, with his head down, hurried back toward the storeroom to thank his team. Behind him, the engine exploded with steam and white sound that swallowed him momentarily in a humid haze. The train's cars roused and rumbled beside him as he spotted his men—all eight of them, stepping from the storehouse, wiping sweat from their foreheads and eyes. They turned the corner around the brick building and walked elsewhere into the brewery's grounds, away from Charles.

As the last boxcar lumbered past him, it dragged a breeze that smacked Charles on the back like an old friend, the cars squeaking as they slipped beneath summer's honey sun. Charles sighed, overwrought with the sort of solitude that allowed his soul to expand but that left him feeling lonely, friendless.

Still, this solitude allowed him to soak up the abandoned brewery's silence as he wandered the grounds. His mind tended to float free during the work day, its own defense mechanism; in an effort to ground it, he tried to notice the details he could not during the busy day: Flocks of pigeons flapping clumsily from the dust to the roof of the long malt house; weeds sulking in the breezeless shade beside the crumbling concrete foundation, its whitewash peeling, revealing pink brick muscle beneath. He passed the wooden stairs to the brew house's entrance, the words "Weiseule Brewing Company" looping in long, white letters on the bricks above. Then he turned onto the main alleyway, a boulevard usually sweating with scowling workers in overalls; clogged by barrel-stacked wagons pulled by bitter horses; reeking of manure, of burning barrels, of warm and sticky ale sloshing within wooden casks. Its emptiness seemed peaceful, significant even, though he was eager to trade it for the weekend.

Charles had already turned onto Wakes, beyond the sleeping brewery's gates, when he began thinking about the house. His landlord, to whom he had paid a week's wage and a three-month rent advance, had been scheduled to deliver the lumber for the floor joists earlier that afternoon. As he kicked down the middle of the street, dust curling beneath each footstep, he imagined the golden boards stacked beside the house's finished foundation, flattening the grass. The basement was enormous, as if God had bitten into the earth using only his front teeth; Charles had finished sealing it with stone and concrete and was ready to erect a house over it. Though he was proud of his progress, he sighed at the thought that it took him three months to actually start building a structure.

Stately houses hid behind the shrubs and immature trees—the white one with the row of eight shimmering windows across its facade, four on either side of a bronze door; the mauve mansion with snake scale siding and a third-floor observatory, like a twentieth-century turret; the squat one painted like a peach, with the triangular second story it wore like a hat; and that petite house on the corner, the cream-colored one with the wrap-around porch that inspired his house. This stretch of Wakes Road was one of Wisnago's oldest neighborhoods and one of his favorites to walk through. It represented where he would be in a matter of years.

He sighed. *I needed to be working on the house today*, he told himself, hung his head in sullen disappointment.

Charles crossed and turned onto Seventh Street, where the neighborhood ended and downtown seemed to begin. He could see The Law Offices of J.J. Hampton on the far corner of the block and his family's apartment above it. He avoided eye contact with the wide windows stretching across their living quarters, worried that he might see Elizabeth's sparkling scowl. Instead, he focused on the activity around him—a gang of giggling men with smirking mustaches ducking into a pub, a pair of women with paper-wrapped cuts of meat tucked under their arms inspecting each storefront display, a pack of squealing children chasing each other from the sidewalk into the sunburned street, a pissing horse and a stray spaniel who sniffed the frothy rapids before cautiously backing away.

The entrance beside Hampton's office was discreet. As Charles ascended the narrow passage, the steps complained, each with a different croaking squeal, pleading him to step lightly and swiftly. The door at the top of the stairs creaked when Charles pushed it open. "Elizabeth?" he called quietly. "Becky?"

Despite the amber rectangles of sun slanting across the apartment, illuminating an oak table and the tops of four chairs tucked beneath it, the space was decorated with shadows and dark corners. Three plates waited on the table—two scraped off, one with a congealed glob and two hard biscuits; a mound of butter melted on a saucer at the center of the table.

"Elizabeth?" Charles called a little louder than before, squinting toward the iron bed in the far corner only to find it unmade. His eyes followed the exposed brick wall to the opposite corner where a wood stove waited patiently until October. "Becky? Where are you two?" In another corner, a shelf held foggy jars and bottles, a kerosine lamp, and a coffee grinder with a broken handle. An empty washpan hung in the darkness like some sort of pathetic decoration; a worktable stretched beneath it, but no wife sliced vegetables at it and no daughter danced around her legs. Charles felt the residual heat still radiating from the squatting cookstove, its pipe snaking into the ceiling.

He inched around the table, grabbing a stony biscuit and noticing the door to the back staircase open a crack. Charles felt the air lighten and cool as he descended, noted the quieter cries from these back steps, and found Elizabeth sitting on the stoop watching Rebecca draw pictures in the stale dirt with her dinner spoon. Certainly, he assumed, Elizabeth heard or felt him descend, but didn't acknowledge him.

"Hello," Charles sang from the doorway.

"Daddy!" Rebecca screeched, leaping from the dust, scrambling like a spider up the stoop, wrapping her arms around his legs.

Charles patted her blonde hair, which seemed tangled, tattered even, and streaked with dust. "Someone's getting a bath tonight," he said. "And, then, mom can brush your hair a bit." Charles lifted her into his arms and lowered himself beside Elizabeth, who stared at her daughter's dirty scribbles.

"Where were you?" Elizabeth asked stone-faced and gravel-voiced, as if the sun had dried her out as well.

"Working," he responded simply, but elaborated after a few silent seconds. "A shipment of hops got stuck in Iowa, and we had to wait for it."

"Not at the house?"

"No," he said. "But I'll be there at dawn tomorrow."

He watched Elizabeth's gaze bounce from the dirt to the bricks across the alley, speckled with coffee grounds and feces and uneaten meat, dumped from the window of their back neighbor; two crows shuffled along the rooftop, waiting for the Stonebreakers to leave their stoop so they could feast in privacy. "Your dinner is inside," she muttered.

Charles lifted his drooping mustache lifting above a curled lip. "Becky," he said, his voice perky and playful, "would you draw me a picture?" As she wiggled from his lap and slid back into the dust, he spoke quietly to Elizabeth. "What's wrong, dear?"

Her lips pressed tightly together as her head landed heavily on his shoulder. Her hair tumbled in long, swaying spirals down Charles's shoulder that reminded him of melting chocolate, with the same dull sheen, the same endless drip. "I want to go home," she said in his ear, a wounded whisper like a dying wish.

Charles slid an arm around her back, pulled her so close that their bodies momentarily merged. Still, the solitude seeped through his body, spread slowly like black ink spilled onto a clean bedspread; somehow, embracing the love of his life, he never felt more alone.

Lester Lancaster
March 29th, 1982

Lester's long hair did not absorb the rain. Instead, each drop slipped down the strands that bent down his back. Some dripped from the curls into his mouth. Each drop tasted weird—waxy, bitter—so Lester found himself continuously spitting.

The filthy white awning above him, which advertised Rocco's Records in maroon letters, failed to protect Lester from a rain that seemed to prick him from every side. He hid his hands in his armpits, tucked his chin to his chest, and spit again. A car crawled down Seventh Street and, despite its reduced speed, sprayed gutter water onto Lester. Desperate for an actual sanctuary, he ducked into a bricked-in entryway next to Rocco's twin glass doors. Lester deemed it dry enough to hide until the manager opened his doors for the morning.

The Friday before, Lester had wandered down sunny Seventh Street with money to burn; he had devoured both a sandwich and an *Amazing Spider-Man* as he basked in the golden morning, grinning at the hustle that bustled through Wisnago's streets. At least that's how he remembered the morning.

And, for the rest of the weekend, he had rotated between sleep, cold Cantonese, and MTV—he watched Pat

Benatar's video for "You Better Run" twenty-nine times by his count—until the cycle started to blur. When he found himself singing beside Mrs. Benatar in a warehouse wearing matching outfits—when she warned him playfully not to stretch out her favorite striped sweater—Lester could not uncurl his smile, though he suspected it might be a dream.

Sprawled across his lawn chair like a drying towel, he was startled into consciousness at five on Monday morning by Sparks's video for "I Predict," the one with a Hitler-mustached man in drag performing a strip-tease. Lester decided it was the right time to get some fresh air; he still had a couple hundred dollars of his unemployment check to spend, and it would be good to get rid of it before his sister and mother discovered it.

In retrospect, he should have looked out a window and checked the weather before leaving in just his stained undershirt and sweats. And he should have called to check the store's hours.

Shivering beneath the brick entryway, spitting through his fogged breath, Lester heard the door ding open and watched a white-haired man flip a sign in the window to "Come on in! We're open!" Lester scurried into Rocco's where he was greeted by warmth and sound—side A of Black Sabbath's *Paranoid,* to be exact, a record that Lester loathed.

"Oh, I didn't see you out there," the man said behind the register. He wore wire-framed spectacles beneath his white crew cut, which made him look younger and more hip than he probably was. White chest hair peeked above his white V-neck tee-shirt. "How long were you waiting?"

Lester refused to respond at first. Instead, he tilted

his face toward the low ceiling, taking deep breaths and absorbing every band of heat that hit him. He looked like a lunatic—an unresponsive man in soaked sweatpants—and he knew it. Finally, he said, "Two hours."

"Two hours?" Behind the register, surprise and guilt twisted the man's face. "Wow, sorry, man. We open at 8:00 on weekdays."

Lester wanted to say that he knew—or, rather, that he knows now—but needed a few more seconds to warm up. He also knew the longer he defrosted, the longer he could stave off conversation. Lester hoped that a sigh would answer the man's question and serve as a signal to leave him alone.

"Well, let me know if there's something I can help you look for, or if you're interested in trying something new," the man said. "I just got Iron Maiden's new record in, and it totally rips. They have this new singer performing on it, and it's light-years better than their older stuff."

"Thanks," Lester murmured. The man sat cross-legged on the counter behind the register and picked up a hardcover novel. This sight only stoked flames of annoyance within Lester.

The store consisted of one main space, which seemed too small to house a record store, and two smaller rooms—one listening room, and a room behind it where they displayed stereo equipment. Florid carpeting hid 100-year-old hardwood, making the space feel ancient. Lester liked the way the floorboards croaked with every step and appreciated the windows frosted with a decade of dust. He even liked the contemporary record store decor—the concert posters that playfully scaled the walls; the signs, eccentric and hand-drawn, differentiating the "classical" section from the "country," the "new wave" from the "heavy stuff;" the framed concert tee-shirts hung behind the counter, some with black squiggles on the cotton.

But Lester hated Black Sabbath, especially the song "Paranoid." He hated the guitar's tone, which reminded him of a rusty knife. He hated that Sabbath discovered a catchy chord progression but, instead of building on this riff, repeated it until they bored their listeners. More than this, though, he hated Ozzy Osbourne's blunt and wobbly mewl and the way he seemed to chase the song, throwing his adolescent philosophy at it as it careened away from him.

He tried to ignore the noise as he slithered through the store, snaking toward the top ten section where, on the wall, the week's best-selling single was displayed above three rows of lesser records in a hierarchy of sorts; beneath each 45, a stack of shrink-wrapped LPs and a column of cassette tapes lured buyers.

As he approached, Lester compared the layout to what he remembered from the previous week. He was pleased to see that Joan Jett had crept to number one, though was sad to see "I Love Rock 'N' Roll" bump the J. Geils Band to number three; he found himself humming that "Angel in the Centerfold" song everywhere he went. He shook his head in frustration, though, when he saw that Journey was still at number two; "Open Arms" was the most melodramatic rock ballad Lester ever heard, and he hoped something would come along and kill this intolerable trend.

Lester knew which record he wanted, though, and found it in the center of the second full row.

He had been holding out on the Go-Go's for almost a year, waiting for some sign that their record was worth buying. At some point, though, he found himself hoping to hear "We Got the Beat" whenever he was around a radio. He loved the way the drums smacked against the bass and how Belinda Carlisle's voice hooked during the verses. The group vocals during the chorus projected a picture in his head of friends at a party, half-plastered, singing together with unblushing abandon. Ultimately, Lester decided that *Beauty and the Beat* was worth purchasing.

As he pulled the LP from the stack, the silver-haired manager passed behind him carrying a large cardboard box. "You know," he said, pausing, resting the package on a bin, "records will always sound better, but you can't really beat the convenience of cassette tapes."

"Oh, okay," Lester said. "Thanks." He tucked the album under his arm and turned towards the register, hoping to cut this conversation short.

"Do you have a cassette player?"

Lester stopped in his tracks, but only because he knew that taking a single step away would make him look like the rudest kind of customer. So, in that three-second window, Lester had to decide whether to act like an asshole or to let this idiot pitch him something that he neither wanted nor needed. "No," he said, turning around reluctantly.

"Really?" the man said with sincere surprise. "That's interesting because I always saw you as the sort of guy that listened to music everywhere he went. You know, on a Walkman."

Lester instantly lowered his defenses. He never

considered owning a cassette deck, but a Walkman was different. He imagined the miserable walk back home—drizzle stippling his skin, breath curling visibly from the rank cavern beneath his mustache—made more tolerable by Belinda Carlisle, or Pat Benatar, or Patti Smyth. A portable cassette player could be a life-altering purchase—life-*improving*—a true investment. "Well, I've never been able to afford one of those," he said, suddenly and suspiciously civil. "For now, records are the most economical option for me."

"Yeah, I understand," the manager said. "I'm the same way. But we just got this Walkman II shipment in yesterday afternoon." He pulled a smaller, more colorful box out of the large one he held. "They're more portable than Sony's other Walkmen, and cheaper," he continued, "so I was thinking of finally splurging on one myself. I think I could probably sell you one for $220 or so, since you'd be my first customer."

"Oh," Lester said, caught off guard by an offer that seemed generous. So what if it was a sales tactic? "Well, thanks, but I don't have…" he started, his argument fading before he could finish. He *did* have the money, and he came to Rocco's Records to spend it.

"I completely understand: It's more money than you were prepared to spend today," the manager said. "Tell you what, though; I'll sell you that Go-Go's record on cassette for five bucks. I mean, what's the point of having a cassette player with no cassettes, right?" He snickered playfully, and Lester spotted his shark teeth.

Five minutes later, Lester found himself walking back through the pins and needles on Seventh Street. He shrugged his shoulders to resist a cold that nosed under his arms like a dog desperate for attention. Since his pockets did little to protect him and his new purchase, he shoved his hands (clutching his Walkman) into his sweatpants up to his forearm. Sure, he looked silly, but there's no such thing as pride in a survival situation.

Despite the cold's discomfort, he received some warmth from the Go-Go's as he stepped through the streets to the beat of "Our Lips Our Sealed." Since it was a song he knew, he whispered the lyrics to himself as he bridged puddles. The headphone pads kissed each ear, and the Walkman whirred in his palm. But it was the beat itself, which bounced tirelessly, that actually propelled Lester, and the sparkling guitars that seemed to cleanse the dripping, drab city surrounding him. Already, he was reaping the benefits of his purchase; the reminder that he was out of money for the month nagged at him, but he suppressed it by turning up the volume.

Just as the song took its strange turn toward the chorus—a section in which suspicious "oohs" suspended over dubious chords and Carlisle, almost oblivious to the song's mood shift, asserted her lyrics through a dumb smile—Lester sensed a noise whining in the background. Initially, the squeal seemed to come from the song—feedback, he assumed— though it seemed out of place, and rang louder and meaner as the song slipped into its bridge.

When it became difficult to hear his music, Lester turned to see a fire engine skidding onto Seventh Street two blocks away from him. Its siren soared higher in pitch and louder in volume with each cycle, and its lights flickered and flailed like the fire it was rushing to extinguish. Lester stopped out of courtesy, like a car might pull over to the side of the road. As the engine roared past, it hit its horn—a distorted, deafening grunt that startled Lester so much that he lost grip of his Walkman. It tumbled down the leg of his sweatpants and landed where they bunched around his ankle.

As the engine sped away on Seventh, beneath grey oaks that curled over the road like smoke, Lester tried to picture himself from the perspective of those firefighters: An overweight man waddling down Seventh Street in a tank-top speckled with sweet and sour sauce, his long hair hanging from his head in sticky clumps, his sweatpants pulled past his arms and elbows. *I would have honked at the lunatic too,* he thought, smirking sadly. His face burned, embarrassed.

It was rare, Lester realized, that he ever blushed. *So why now?* he wondered, pulling the player up by its headphone cord, continuing his long totter home. *Just because some stupid firefighters scared me?* He crossed Seventh just before Lilac, the marble sky swirling above budding tree branches. The ancient houses on that side of the street, painted in vibrant pastels, seemed so garish in the grey spring.

The fire engine disappeared down Seventh. *At least they are going somewhere to do some good*, he decided, realizing he was heading home to his MTV, to a well-worn lawn chair, to the sad cycle in and out of consciousness, to solitude. *At least those firefighters have a reason to be awake.*

Water slithered from Lester's forehead, down his cheek toward his chin, slipped suddenly into his cracked mouth; it tasted like smoked socks. He spit it back into the street.

Preston Assad
February 2nd, 1996

A Morse code of cars dotted both sides of the street, stretching from Humble House as far west as Hibiscus, as far south as Sixth. Frost climbed across each vehicle, shimmered beneath the streetlights in the frozen darkness. *They've been sitting there for hours*, Preston thought, his boots crunching down the unshoveled sidewalks he would usually avoid unless he felt it would get him home ten steps sooner.

As he turned onto Coneflower, he sensed a breath of bass, a beat that he felt before he heard. It could have come from any house party on the block, but he knew it was radiating from Humble House, that the show had started without him. "Fuck," he whispered, a puff of profanity that rose visibly into the night.

Earlier in the week, when Schooner asked him to stay late on Friday—until at least seven, but as long as they needed him—Preston panicked. He had planned and promoted a huge show, one with a bill of bands that had drawn well in the past and were scheduled to load in at six o'clock.

"We're fine," McCauley assured him at the dining room table on Wednesday night, reclining uncomfortably in his creaking chair. "All of these bands have played here before, right? Ben's band has played here dozens of times, so they know the drill. Plus, you have me." Preston trusted McCauley, but the demands of running an entire show seemed too enormous for one person. Plus, Preston worried about his PA; without his vigilance, it would be easy for a microphone to walk away, and that's if the entire basement wasn't cleaned out before he came home.

A block away from home, the bass's breath became a melody smothered by the house, muddy and amorphous, and his ears perked at the recognition of guitar chords. *At least no one stole anything essential*, he reassured himself. *The show started, right?*

He noticed the blacked-out silhouettes on his front porch first—a sight that always startled him, but that he had become accustomed to—then the pinching stench of cigarette smoke. Each stride toward his property presented him with a strange sight or sound—the couple twist-tied on his swaying porch swing, the grunting giggles from three lumpy silhouettes hunched over the railing, the slim figure in a dazed spin at the foot of the steps.

He had to sidestep the twirling girl to ascend the porch, whose long hair and skirt swung past their stopping points when she noticed Preston. "Sorry!" she sputtered, embarrassed. The three laughing lumps, in the light, became members of one of the bands. Preston nodded at them before noticing the couple entwined on the porch swing in short sleeves, shivering beneath each other's spindly limbs, were teenagers. Preston decided to leave them alone.

McCauley stood at the front door in his parka, his

hands crammed into its pockets. His face, obscured by a cloud of breath, peeked from inside his fur-lined hood. "Hey sweetie," he said. "How was work?"

"Shut up," Preston said, a smile cracking across his frozen face. He felt the boards reverberating beneath his boots. "How are things going?"

"Great," McCauley said. "The bands showed up on time, and everyone helped each other load in. One guy from one band, I think his name is Sam or Scott, he was able to figure out the board and dialed it in really well. About a hundred people are down there, too. It was pretty crazy getting everyone through the door at first, but we did it. Things sound good and the basement's full."

Preston tried to hide his sigh, but the cold betrayed him, and he was forced to watch his relief spiral slowly toward his counterpart in a cloud of breath.

"Relax," McCauley said. "Everything worked out."

"Right."

"So go down there and have fun tonight. I've got you covered."

Preston blinked twice. "Like, just to watch the band?" he asked as if attending one of his own shows was impossible. "I can't do that. I've been waiting all day to be down there and—"

"Then go down there. Just enjoy the show. Don't worry about working it. In fact"—here, McCauley cast a profound glance across Eighth Street—"I'm giving you the night off," he finally said, a smirk stretching from one side of his hood to the other.

Preston snickered, shook his head as if his friend

had said something so unfathomable it was funny. His heart beat with excitement; it would be fun to lose himself in the music tonight, but his mission was always to offer others such respite. Besides, doing sound was fun enough. "I appreciate the offer," he said, "but I need to make sure Sam or Scott isn't fucking up my PA."

"Oh, come on," McCauley complained, stopping Preston as he stepped toward the door. "We've already made four-hundred dollars tonight—that's a hundred for each band, and another hundred going back to the house." Whatever playfulness existed in McCauley had disappeared, and his mouth had stretched long and level. "I've got this."

Though he rolled his eyes, Preston's smirk gave him away. "Fine," he murmured as a couple of patrons in leather jackets stomped up the icy steps behind him.

"Good," McCauley said, his smile returning. "Now, if you don't mind, I have work to do."

As he stepped inside the house, Preston heard McCauley collect five dollars from each person behind him. He hung his backpack on the hook beside a framed embroidery he had found buried in the basement when he moved in. "God Bless This Humble House," it said in elaborately stitched words that surrounded a house that looked like his. He closed his eyes and inhaled slowly, drawing in Humble House's reliable scent of dusty plaster and lacquered wood. It, along with the music pushing through the floorboards beneath him, provoked a comforting sort of sensory overload. He steeped in the house's spirit until the front door swung into his arm. "Sorry!" some woman said peeking around the door as she unzipped her hoodie. "I didn't know someone was there."

"No worries," Preston answered.

He removed his coat and stashed it on his bed upstairs. Then, after a quick sweep of the house, Preston stepped carefully down the basement stairs into a dark space that seemed to stretch endlessly in all directions.

The heat hit him first, an almost palpable humidity that hovered just above eye level, then the smell—of body odor and smokey clothes, but mostly of body odor. But these were passing distractions, easily obscured by the music, which poured over the room's crowd from the far end of the basement: An unseen band, strumming and screaming, hidden behind a wall of swaying patrons. It was immediately difficult to think, not because of its volume, but because its melody lured Preston momentarily away from his body; he followed the song where it led and, for a split second, forgot where he was.

As he stepped away from the stairs, his eyes adjusted. To his right, Sam or Scott stood attentively behind the soundboard. Around him, small clumps of people tried to talk, doing their best to be social, to see and be seen. They hid in the better-lit back corners and wore bracelets on their arms, bandannas on their heads, holes in their jeans— perfect costumes for the rock 'n' roll show.

It was that wall of patrons in the front, closest to the so-called "stage," that interested Preston. He weaved between people standing in the back rows—squeezed between sweatier, bouncing bodies and slick, bare arms and flannels heavy with heat—and eventually stuck himself between some scrawny high school kid, his voice squeaking beneath the enormous song, and a dude who nodded his fried blonde shag solemnly to the music.

Here, the heat subsided, sucked through the gap around the cellar door behind the band. Here, a crest of lunging kids did their best not to crash onto the so-called stage. Here, forearms and elbows shot into Preston's shoulders, hips bumped his, legs tangled around one another. Here, he rode the bucking animal that was the basement.

In front of him, his high school friend Ben spat syllables into a microphone. Preston saw sweat stains curve down his black Jawbox shirt beneath his neck and arms. Though his body swayed, his stubbled upper lip stuck to the microphone and his bruised Telecaster hovered in place as his blurry hand fluttered around it. Somewhere during the song, he noticed Preston and smiled.

The kids surrounding Preston bounced to the beat and screamed with Ben like they were auditioning for the band, though their voices were snuffed out by chords and syllables. At some point, Preston realized he couldn't hear the bony kid beside him and wondered if he blew out his voice. The kid kept trying, his mouth shaping every word, gasping for air between phrases. Preston didn't know the words, so he closed his eyes and did his best to ignore the elbows and shoulders.

Here, music poured over him like honey, slow and sticky and sweet.

Opening his eyes, Preston watched Ben's bandmates swirl with nervous, kinetic energy, tugged this way and that by chords that their own hands strummed; when they found their footing, they dug their heels into the cement foundation and drew squirming, squelching sounds out of their instruments; smoldering, burnt sounds; booming, mumbling sounds. And, behind them, an apparition sat in the dark shadows behind a set of trembling drums and swinging cymbals.

Everyone else seemed to expect the song's end except Preston, who was pulled suddenly from his hypnotic state by the sound of a hundred clapping hands echoing between the cobblestone walls. "Thank you," Ben mumbled into the microphone before turning to search for his cup of water. His bandmates turned their backs to the basement and dropped ears towards their amps; as they twisted the tuners at the top of their guitars, Preston noted that their sober control seemed to contrast their mid-song abandon. The apparition behind the drums, reanimated and apparently human, blotted sweat from his face.

"Thanks," Ben repeated between short breaths, returning to the mic. "So, tonight's the first night of our tour—we're driving to California and back in the next month or so—and it couldn't have been kicked off in a better place. So let's hear it for Humble House!"

Most of the kids in the crowd clapped politely, but others, who Preston recognized as regulars, raised their hands toward the ceiling and slapped them together enthusiastically. Behind Ben, his bandmates dropped their drumsticks, released the necks of their guitars, and did the same. Preston smirked in appreciation.

"I've known the dudes that run this house and put on these shows since we were friends in high school," Ben continued. "We've toured the U.S. three times, played everything from big clubs and tiny corners, and we've never played a place more comfortable, more fun, and more respectful to bands and fans." He paused, let a chuckle slip from his unwitting smile. "And in Wisnago of all places! Fuck!" His statement elicited sudden hoots from the crowd. "I've spent my whole life trying to get out of here, and, now, there's nowhere I'd rather be."

The corners of Preston's eyes stung. Squeezed between two teenage strangers in his surrendered basement, stewing in the sweat of others. And, for some reason, he was happier there than anywhere else he had ever been.

"If you're here tonight, or any other night, count your lucky stars," Ben continued, his bandmates turning from their tuners and amps. "Feel fortunate that you have a place to go, and that this is that place. This is a new one called 'Friday Night at Humble House.' Thanks, Preston."

Four quick clicks, and the relative quiet of the basement was flattened by a single chord, a tsunami strummed by Ben and his bandmates that seemed to blow everyone backward. As Preston regained his balance, he sensed the snick of a hi-hat, braced himself, held his breath.

As the song surged forward, distorted guitar chords lunged onto and into one another, crashed into cymbals as a lung-crushing kick drum tussled with the frantic and reckless cracks of its snare. He closed his eyes, and felt the song surge around him like a flash flood; he felt the bodies around him swept up by the swirling currents, felt arms reaching for each other, felt hands clasping his shoulders and shirt in frenzied attempts to anchor themselves. He seemed to spin, a weightless piece of debris reeling among the flotsam and jetsam, bubbling in the gushing melody.

When he heard Ben's muffled growl emerge from beneath the deluge, Preston opened his eyes, expecting to see bodies floating beside the beer cans and seaweed in the dark green shadows of the flooded basement, but he found himself in the same place, wedged between two bouncing teenagers, staring down Ben and his bandmates.

He took a step back and a riptide of people pulled him into a faster swirl, a rush of bodies bobbing and reeling in the dark. When he slipped beneath the surface, he felt the cool, slick concrete floor smack against his palms, dent his elbows and tailbone, and suddenly sensed a hundred hands grabbing his belt and pants, pulling him by his shirt back to the surface, back to the heavy air and noise. Though he found himself floating upright, he struggled to keep his eyes open as images flashed in and out of his view.

A hairy, shirtless, sweaty belly.

A flash of cobblestone.

A drooping Fugazi tee.

McCauley sitting from the safety of the stairs.

A streaking line of lightbulbs.

Ben, wide-mouthed, and the blur of band behind him.

A pink knee peeking through a sleeve of denim.

An untied Converse All-Star.

A wrinkled Rocket from the Crypt shirt.

Maryanne's smirk, seen briefly and lost in the blur.

The song receded, caught its breath as it stepped with a slower, half-time drum beat behind which chords droned and shrieked. The swirl surrounding Preston slowed enough for his feet to find the ground; surrounded by swaying, delirious people—friends, he realized—he watched Ben whisper into the mic: "Be here where you can disappear." He repeated his refrain over and over and, eventually, so did the voices beside and behind Preston—hesitantly, then proudly, then heedlessly. "Be here where you can disappear," they repeated as squelching guitars found their notes and rose, as the bass bubbled and boiled over.

"Be here where you can disappear," the basement boomed.

And then it burst, that same first chord, over which Ben roared, "With me." Behind him, his band swung their instruments and screamed, "Be here where you can disappear," with the whirling crowd. As the chords climbed and crashed, as cymbals swished and the bass drum kicked him in the chest, Preston closed his eyes, felt himself expand and combine with his sweaty, nameless companions.

And, as the words "Be here where you can disappear" echoed around him, he realized that he wasn't singing with them, that he had been screaming alongside Ben, his throat in ribbons, slashed by two dull, thin syllables: "With me."

Barbara Farmer
July 17th, 1941

The floorboards crackled beneath Barbara's feet as she made her way across the sun-streaked apartment. It reminded her of thunder before a summer storm—less ominous and immense, maybe, but no less intimidating

It wasn't the noisy floors that worried her about this place, though, or the exposed bricks, which would likely let in winter's cold and overwork the wood stove in the corner. It wasn't the smothering heat that hung in this second-story unit alongside the cobwebs, or even that this bedroom-less loft would provide no privacy. It was the dread that bothered Barbara, something almost palpable that mingled with the scent of cooking oil and stove wood. It was not the sort of place she wanted to wait out her husband's term of duty.

"Oh, there's a staircase leading to a darling alley," Anita shouted, emerging through a door at the loft's far end. "This place is pretty neat."

"I'm not so sure," Joy said pacing the length of one plastered wall until she hit a long table, presumably for preparing meals, and an ancient cast-iron cookstove. "It seems pretty old-fashioned, especially for the price."

"Well, it is right in your price range and in a perfect location downtown," Mr. Peter Bonilla said, a cigarette dangling from his lips, as he slouched on a window sill at the front of the apartment. The sun brought out the subtle blue tint of his grey linen suit, which provided only a fleeting impression of professionalism. "Those were your only two criteria, am I right? An affordable apartment close to somewhere you could find a job?" Barbara could sense his disdain in the straightness of his pencil mustache.

But Barbara couldn't blame him. They had been prowling through this town since noon, seen seven apartments, and passed on each for justifiable reasons. One apartment, situated above a deli, presented signs that they would be sharing the space with a family of mice; another shared its door with a diner, which presented job prospects but reeked of fried food.

Barbara had fewer reasons to pass on this apartment, but something about this dimly lit loft disturbed her. "Maybe we should move on," she finally said after several silent minutes. "I just don't like this place."

As Mr. Bonilla pushed himself onto his legs, the floor sputtered beneath him. "Well, this was the last apartment that matches your criteria, ladies," he said. "There's nothing left in town to rent."

Joy's brow slanted. "Really? There's not a single dwelling for rent in this entire town?"

"That's not what I said," he replied. "What I said was that there was nothing that matches your limited criteria. There are plenty of dwellings to rent in this town. In fact, the landlord of this place has a house for rent just a few blocks away." He took a sudden drag at his cigarette and exhaled abruptly before he plucked the butt from his lips, pitched it onto the hardwood, and stomped it like a cockroach. "But it's a *house*, not an apartment," he added. "Plus, it's a hundred dollars more than your maximum."

A curious grin climbed across Anita's face. "A house? That sounds lovely!"

"We couldn't afford it," Barbara said. "Could we? A hundred dollars more a month?"

Both aimed eager gazes at Joy, whose smirk gave her away. "I think we probably could make it work between the three of us. I mean, if we put in extra hours, worked odd jobs."

As Anita pulled her cupped hands to her chest, her ebony curls bounced. "Mr. Bonilla," she begged, "would you bring us there please?"

Mr. Bonilla sighed as he lit another cigarette.

A minute later, Barbara led what sounded like a stampede down the steps of the apartment and onto the street, where Mr. Bonilla's black Ford sedan sizzled. Barbara squeezed herself into the visible heat of the rear seat and, as Anita climbed beside her, watched the quiet bustle of the block. Automobiles rolled up and down the street, past a mother and father who pushed a buggy beneath the shady storefront awnings, past wandering troops of teenagers— only a year or two younger than Barbara, she realized, but whose lives seemed drastically different. They stumbled into the store whose window advertised Rocco's Radio and Phonograph in large, red letters.

"Did you see that?" Anita asked.

"What, that record shop?" Joy wondered from the front seat.

"Yeah! Wouldn't that be a gas, to get some records for our place?"

"We'd need to get a phonograph first."

"Of course we would. But, when we got one, we could dance at home every Friday instead of at some stinking dance club. Wouldn't that be fun?"

But Barbara wasn't listening. Instead, she rested her head on the hot window and watched Wisnago roll by: An abandoned gas station, two tracks leading to its attached garage; a reclining brick schoolhouse, stretching a single block from head-to-toe; a shirtless kid with a broomstick on his shoulder posing on a drought-stricken ball-field.

And, then, houses: Victorian castles in pastel colors, guarded by shrubs or wrought-iron fences. Lining the street, Barbara noticed oaks—not the divine ones that shaded an acre each on her dad's farm, but swaying trees that made the neighborhood feel comfortable, colorful, friendly. Barbara drew a deep breath and released it back into the heat.

She wiped the drops of sweat off her forehead as Mr. Bonilla pulled the car into the baked dirt on the side of the street. "Here it is," he said. Barbara looked across the backseat through Anita's window at what she could see of a two-story house on a corner lot: A porch, painted cornflower and embellished with maroon; an enormous, wall-sized window facing the porch and whatever street they were on; a swing hanging motionless in the heat.

"Wow," Anita gasped, her view better than Barbara's. "It's beautiful."

Joy led up the sidewalk single file. At first, Barbara fixated on the landscaping—untended, but redeemable bushes; flower beds conquered by saplings and weeds—but, as they approached the concrete steps to the front porch, she perceived more of the house as a whole. Wooden siding, slathered in a sun-faded yellow, produced a pinstriped effect, and maroon trim traced every window and doorway.

"The owner told me the house was built in 1910," Mr. Bonilla said, suddenly sounding like the salesman he was. He flicked his cigarette as the party climbed the porch. "By a local man for his family. Took him six months, apparently, but it was his masterpiece."

"That's sweet," Anita said as she stomped up the steps.

"I love the porch swing," Joy said, though her expression warped when she approached it, an unfinished slab of wood with a wicker back and armrests. She nudged it with her knee and watched it wiggle. "Maybe we could paint it and make it look like it belongs on this porch."

As Mr. Bonilla tried to unlock the door, Barbara stood at the edge of the steps, closed her eyes, and let the neighborhood's heat seep into her skin. She wanted to feel some hint that she could construct some sort of happy life here that John could return to. Her chattering consciousness tried to convince her that this "looking for a sign" business wasn't at all like her, but she focused instead on what the neighborhood had to tell her intuition.

Behind her, Mr. Bonilla conducted a percussive orchestra of rattling knobs and thrashing keys, the thump of leather sole against oak door, but she didn't notice, nor did she sense Anita and Joy as they stepped past her to his rescue, the hollow porch resonating beneath each step.

A breeze swept through the neighborhood. Barbara sensed it several blocks away, heard it waken oak after oak until it swirled around her, blowing back her peanut butter curls, swishing her skirt. It wasn't the sign she was looking for, but it was punctuated by a series of small sounds: The front door creaking open, Mr. Bonilla's familiar sigh, Anita's hands slapping together.

"Our hero," Joy added with a straight face.

As Barbara followed them into the darkened house, she ruffled her nose at the smell of stained wood. When her eyes finally adjusted, though, they widened: Golden stripes of hardwood stretched the length of the living room and into the kitchen, each ignited by a sun that ducked mischievously through the front window. Spotless white walls rose from this almost incandescent floor. Despite the dust that danced in the air, the room seemed clean, blank.

"Wow," Joy whispered in awe.

"Wow is right," Mr. Bonilla muttered through lips that clenched a new cigarette. "I thought this place would be a dump on the inside, considering its price. Something's gotta be wrong with it."

Anita stepped into the kitchen, her heels clicking against the wooden floors, as Joy paced the perimeter of the living room, kicking baseboards, knocking knuckles against window panes. Mr. Bonilla disappeared immediately, though the tail of smoke that trailed him through the house would help them locate him if needed.

Below her, Barbara noticed a trail of footprints set in the stain—the only flaw she could see—and followed them up a narrow stairway to the second story. A window at the summit of the stairs made her feel like she was ascending into a pastel sky and lit the landing that led to a dimmer hallway of doors. She peeked behind one, found a lavatory with a porcelain john and sink, a cast iron tub with claw and ball feet. She discovered a square room behind the next door, a rectangular room behind the door across the hall—both with white walls and glowing gold floors and dust lingering in the sunlight.

She nudged the door open the last door and gasped softly at what she saw; not only was the room enormous, twice the size of the pitiful square down the hall, but it was also endowed with nine windows, three on each exterior wall, presenting a panoramic view of the neighborhood. Through one set, she watched the top of a young oak sway back and forth; through another, the sunlight streaked in at a razor-sharp angle; through the third, she saw the intersection in front of the house, the Ford sweating in the street, that shirtless boy riding his bicycle down the block.

Overwhelmed by the urge to let the summer in, she shuffled from wall to wall and flung open each window, inviting a breeze into the room. Her skirt swirled, her curls swayed, and the room became instantly alive with the applause of little grey leaves. Barbara closed her eyes and pulled the humid air into her lungs, drawing in the house's spirit—but for only a second until the door slammed shut.

"Yeep!" she squeaked, her body taut with surprise. *That's the sign!* some too excited voice insisted inside her.

Barbara opened her eyes to inspect the room—to verify that, indeed, the door had blown shut behind her, but also that it hadn't damaged the beautiful moulding around the door. Except there wasn't much to damage in the pristine room. Above her, she spotted a small, obscure square in the ceiling. *Maybe a door to the attic?* she mused, but was interrupted by Anita and Joy, who tumbled together into the room. "Are you okay?" Anita asked.

"Me? Yeah," Barbara dismissed. "The door was blown closed by the wind. I'm fine. Just scared the ghost out of me."

"Me too," said Joy.

"We thought you fell," Anita added. "Or passed out from the heat"

Barbara worked a smile onto her face, which felt uncomfortable at first; she realized then that she hadn't really smiled since their train ride three days ago. "Not me. Just letting in the fresh air."

The breeze swirled around Barbara as Anita and Joy stepped into the room and up to each window one at a time. It reminded her of the time she visited an art museum in the city with her family. "Beautiful," Anita concluded, her clicking heels echoing in the empty room.

Joy stopped in front of one and pushed her nose close to the pane as if to scrutinize some brushstroke. "You really get a nice view of the neighborhood," she said.

Standing beneath that attic door, Barbara felt like a part of the room, a piece in the exhibit—an ancient statue of Helen or Venus, confident and eternal—particularly as the other two circled back to her after viewing each frame.

"So," Joy started, unwilling to water down her grin, "what do you think?"

"I love it!" Anita giggled. "It's by far the best place

we've seen. And it feels so…" Her voice trailed off, swept up by the breeze and blown out one of the windows.

But Joy knew what she meant. "I love it too. It's worth the extra hundred bucks a month to have a whole house to ourselves."

Both girls turned to Barbara, who hadn't moved. She seemed not to be listening, so Anita asked her directly: "Well, come on, Barbara! What do you think?"

A blast of summer air rushed through the windows and whirled around her, sending her skirt fluttering, her short sleeves flapping. "This room's mine."

Charles Stonebreaker
June 18th, 1910

A *distant clack* cracked the air apart like a walnut, followed by a roar that rolled slowly across the landscape. The neighborhood dogs raged in response—the terrier tied up next door, the screeching beagle down the street, that one bearded mutt from whichever hole he dug the previous evening, each tapped into its inner beast, arched its back and bellowed into the loitering summer sun.

But it was the roar that worried Charles, the way it spread through the neighborhood, slipped across the prairie until it blended with its own echo, becoming a kind of grey, shapeless rumble. No other noise displayed such godliness, deserved such reverence; he recognized it as a gunshot.

Charles noticed his hammer still hovered near his ear—the sound had stopped him mid-swing—so he let the hammer fall on a nail that pinned a wall stud to the floor, pulled another nail from between his teeth, and pounded it beside the other. Sweat zig-zagged down his temple and cheek, collected in his mustache, crept into his mouth; each drop tasted weird—salty, pungent—so Charles found himself continuously spitting.

The house was little more than a platform, a grid of girders and joists that would comprise the first floor bridging over the basement's cobblestone pit. He hopped from the platform toward a golden pile of lumber, picked up a couple of pieces, and shouldered them back. The timbers bounced with each step as he hopped up the cement steps to the front porch.

He wondered whether that gunshot was worth worrying about. Such sounds weren't uncommon in this part of town, but something about this specific gunshot made his knees rubbery, made him want to drop the lumber on the platform and search the block—what for, he didn't know. All he knew was that the resident canines weren't rattled by other gunshots in quite the same way.

Is this neighborhood safe? he wondered as he laid the timber in parallel lines. *Do I want to build my house in an unsafe neighborhood?*

"Charles, come down from there and say hi."

He turned around to see Elizabeth in a cotton dress floating on the trampled grass beneath the platform. Her hair was wrapped into a bun that bulged from the back of her head, which confused him; she always let her hair down in the summer and only put it up during formal occasions. As he scrambled down the steps and gave Elizabeth a gentle hug, he noticed a man with a short beard behind her stepping over the tracks in the dirt road; a round gut bulged behind a pair of oily denim overalls, beneath which he wore nothing, save a swath of chalky chest hair. He coughed as he waddled across the dirt road onto the property.

Charles released his wife and darted, palm extended, toward the gentleman. "Hello Marty," he said. The man's small, pudgy hand seized and out-squeezed Charles before he could offer a firmer, more masculine grasp.

"Six months you been outta my house, and this all you have to show for it?" Marty roared, his beard sculpted into a sort of smirk.

"Now, father," Elizabeth added from behind her husband, "Charles has been working very hard on this house."

"Working hard, maybe," Marty said, then pointed a sharpened grin at Charles. "Not smart, not if this is as far as he's gotten."

"This is not the farm, father. He doesn't wake up every morning to tend to his own property. This is the city, and Charles has to work his job at the brewery just so we can afford the house."

"His *job* is to provide shelter for his family," Marty growled, his voice gravelly and ragged. But his beard still bowed upward.

"I thought we finished this argument earlier," Elizabeth said. "Do we really need to go through this again?"

"With *him*, yes," Marty said to his daughter over Charles's shoulder. "He needs to know how you feel."

"Oh, he knows how I feel, father. If he doesn't, then he's either deaf, dumb, or an imbecile."

"He might be all three," Marty said smirking. He then caught Charles with the corner of his eye and winked.

Charles backed out of the electric space between Elizabeth and her father, its emotional charge stiffening the hairs on his arms and neck. "Well, I think I'm going to get back to the house," he said.

Elizabeth turned to face her husband, her sapphire

eyes making a rare connection with his. "That's why we're here too," she said. "My father wants to help you with whatever you're doing, and I'm ready to roll up my sleeves and do what I can."

Charles hesitated before responding. "Of course," he said through a half-hearted smile, trying to appear grateful, or at least not injured. He now understood that this had been planned, possibly for weeks, and the likely result of one too many tear-smeared letters to Elizabeth's family farm. He could only imagine the response, a dusty letter with semi-literate scribbles and torn corners: Marty could help, of course. He's built half a dozen homes with his bare hands. How many had Charles built? And why hadn't Elizabeth written sooner? Why would she put her family's well-being in the hands of that useless weasel? Marty, after all, could have had that house built by now.

"If you aren't looking for help, Charles, we'll leave you alone," Marty said. He leaned on his haunches, stuck his stomach out, and looked at Charles across his nose. "I just thought you might want a little help giving your wife and child the home they deserve."

The comment spun Charles's attention in a different direction. "Wait, where's Becky?"

"She was following us as we walked," Elizabeth said, twisting toward their downtown apartment, her voice tinted with concern. Marty didn't move.

"Did you let her fall behind?"

"My father and I were talking, Charles. She's old enough to keep up with us."

Charles pushed past his father-in-law toward the

corner where two dirt roads crossed in a lumpy intersection. Fear scraped at his insides like a panicked animal trying to escape—hadn't he just heard that shotgun go off?

First, he looked toward downtown but saw nothing but swaying saplings fading into the summer's haze. Then, he looked south; at the end of the block, he saw a cotton-colored speck that could have been a dawdling goose or an empty burlap sack tumbling in the breeze. "Becky?" he shouted. In response, the shape settled into something semi-recognizable—his daughter in a billowing summer dress dragging an open parasol behind her.

"She's down the block," Charles reported to his wife but mostly to himself. As he marched toward his daughter, his heartbeat softened with each deep breath.

Rebecca met his father between ruts in the dried mud at the center of the street, her parasol scuffing the dirt behind her. "You frightened us!" Charles said, collapsing into a squat and reaching for her hand. "Where were you?"

"I heard the dogs barking and wanted to see them," Rebecca answered, her dress bruised with dirt and grass stain scrapes.

"Never leave us like that again, Rebecca Belinda Stonebreaker," Charles said at her eye level. His voice brimmed with concern, each syllable topped off with a splash of anger—enough to sound like a stern, disciplining parent and disguise his relief. "You could get lost, or hurt, or worse," he scolded, pulling his daughter in for a hug. Sunny strands of hair tickled his nose and stuck to his lips as he talked. "What would I do if I lost you? I wouldn't be able to live."

"I was just looking for the dogs. I wanted to capture their sounds in my umbrella."

A smirk cracked Charles's serious facade as he released her. "And what were you going to do with the sounds after you caught them?"

"I don't know. Maybe use them to make music."

Charles tried to suppress his smirk. It was difficult for him to be a firm father when his daughter said such things. "Well," Charles said, playing along, "Let's hear the music then."

Rebecca gazed into the empty, upside-down parasol—delicate white and trimmed with lacy eyelets, it complimented her cotton dress, complete with bruises and scrapes. "I'm not sure I captured any," she said. Her eyebrows lowered and shoulders drooped, unsure of how to keep playing this game.

"Let me give it a look," Charles said, dragging the umbrella toward him. He stuck his head in its wide mouth and looked around, noticing only a couple of tiny pebbles bouncing around the bottom, something Rebecca had collected, no doubt. "Hmm, I'm not sure I see any either," he said before howling abruptly into the umbrella's bell. He removed his face and quickly collapsed it. "Well," he said with wide eyes, "I think you captured something."

His daughter stood with wider eyes and cackled uncontrollably. "Let me see!" she screeched and pulled open the empty parasol. "Aw, phooey. You must have let it out."

As Charles pushed himself back onto straight legs, Rebecca's hand climbed into his like a small animal seeking shelter from the rain. There were few things, he decided, more precious to him than the feeling of her small hand finding safety inside his. As her other hand reached for the parasol's ivory handle, Charles noticed that, despite the dust and tears and the hand-picked collection of stones rattling around its underbelly, the parasol seemed expensive. "Where'd you get that thing anyway?" he asked, leading her along the ruts in the road.

"Oh, that was grandad. He brung it from his farm." She squinted into the overcast skies, licked her dusty lips. "But it isn't even raining."

The parasol made a grinding noise as it dragged behind them. "Do you think you should be treating it so poorly?"

"I don't know what to do with it, other than capture things. And it doesn't capture things very good, except stones. There was a cat over there—" she glanced backward where she had been spotted, "but it hopped right out."

"Don't put cats in your umbrella, especially neighborhood cats," Charles said, fighting an imminent smile. "They could be mean. And the umbrella is for keeping the sun off of you when it's sunny, not for capturing things."

Rebecca looked upward at the filtered sun. "It isn't even sunny."

The rhythmic patter of their footsteps, combined with the scrape of the umbrella, accompanied them like a quiet Sousa march on their stroll down the block back toward the house, but the cadence stopped as they stepped onto their property. Rebecca froze, refused to move further than the oak sapling beside the road. Instead, some animal instinct kicked in, though she aimed her gaze at the ground instead of scanning her surroundings.

Charles continued to walk, unaware that Rebecca had stopped behind him, and tugged her a step toward the platform. "Let's go, Becky," he said with less patience than he wanted to. "I have to work on the house."

Rebecca released his hand. Tight-lipped, she swung her head from side to side.

"What's wrong? Don't you want to live in the new house?"

"I don't wanna go over there," she mumbled, tangling her fingers into a knot.

Charles lowered himself onto a knee to talk to her. "Why don't you want to go over there, sweetie? Mommy's over there, and so is grandad. Don't you want to say hi to them?"

"No," she whispered.

"Why not?"

She swallowed hard. The swirling clouds reflected in her eyes, obscuring whatever danced around behind them. "I don't like grandad," she whispered again, her voice tissue-paper thin. "He makes me scared."

Charles dropped his head. This was not the sort of concern that she expressed when a spider tiptoed near their bed or when thunder rattled the windows of their apartment; this was sincere, disabling fear. "Will you tell me why he makes you scared?" Charles asked.

She stared at the splinters of grass poking through the dirt and, for the first time, Charles noticed she was shoeless; one foot, stained a tobacco brown, twisted at the ankle and tried to climb the other. Instead of scolding, he put it aside and tried to focus on her fear. Behind her lips, he suspected that she was gritting her tiny teeth.

"Talk to me," he said. "Why does grandad make you scared?"

But Rebecca didn't budge. Charles heard Elizabeth calling in the distance, but he didn't respond. A tear carved its way through the dust on Rebecca's cheek, and Charles wiped it with the brim of his index finger; its enormity against her small face startled him.

"Sweetie, sometimes he scares me too," he said. "He's not always kind or gentle. But," he continued before he knew what he would say next, "I have to trust that he loves us. That's how you treat the people in your family— with faith that they want what's best for you even if it doesn't always seem that way."

Rebecca's gaze remained pinned to the ground.

"We need to go over there so I can work," he said. "And we need to show grandad the kindness and gentleness that he sometimes doesn't show us." His enormous palms wiped her cheeks as his fingers tucked her hair behind her ears. "But if you get scared, come find me and I'll make sure nothing scary happens."

The tiniest gesture, the silent return of her gaze to his, confirmed Rebecca's willingness. Her hand curled back into his and they walked across the lot toward where Elizabeth and Marty steamed, where some conversation cooled. "What were you two doing over there for so long?" Elizabeth asked.

"I was reminding her not to go off on her own," Charles said.

Marty fell onto one knee in front of Rebecca, his beard grinning like a goblin beneath his squinting eyes. "I see you've taken after your father," he said in a playful voice, gesturing at the parasol. "Here, I've given you something nice, but you ruin it because you don't know what to do with it."

"She's five, father," Elizabeth snarled. "She can understand what you're saying."

"Good, because it's true," Marty retorted, turning his grin on his son-in-law. "Isn't it, Charles?"

Charles noticed Rebecca smirk—insincere and scared, but kind nonetheless. It gave him the courage to do the same.

Becky McLaughlin
October 20th, 2011

Becky had been a high schooler long enough to have a routine.

First, she abandoned her brother in his beater truck before he started hitting his pipe to avoid walking into Ms. Sutton's homeroom reeking of weed.

When he wasn't suspended, Tom offered his sister a ride to school, though avoided actual conversation during their six-minute commute. Instead, he rested his thin wrists on the steering wheel while some stuttering dubstep song distorted his truck's speakers. Tom's truck was always one of the first vehicles cutting across the student lot, always toward the space furthest from the entrance. Shoving the shifter into park, he'd mutter, "Out," and expect his sister to hop out; he never noticed that, every day, Becky exited the vehicle before it fully stopped.

Then, she stepped across the quiet parking lot, her still-bleary vision compromised further by the autumn morning's fog.

Here, though, Becky knew she would experience the only ninety seconds of tranquility she'd receive all day so she tried to notice the leaves plastered to the pavement by dew, twilight's gradient above dawn's dissipating clouds, the smear of a school bus's taillights blowing past her.

Once inside the building, she took the first left until it ended dead at the bottom of stairwell D.

The first leg of lockers always felt like the most treacherous. Becky wandered with her jaw clenched past cliques of senior girls, assuming that they were whispering about her, and held her breath as she passed the JV boys soccer team, assembled in a tall, elegant herd. She felt vulnerable weaving between these and other social circles; though nothing ever happened, the potential existed, so she refused to un-flex her muscles until she reached the shimmering trophy cases, a calm stretch of hallway that seemed to span a mile.

Something always happened when she reached the end of the trophies, though—the same three girls would enter the bathroom, arm-in-arm. Each day, they wore the same blouses and capris and knee-length denim skirts, each dated by their modesty, and the same hairstyles, sweeping up and outward, matching their maniacal smiles. It took weeks for Becky to realize that they emerged each time she passed regardless of when she arrived to school or how populated the hallway was. Their appearance made her hands tingle and her heart trip, especially because one of the three smiled at Becky every time, her grin darkened by a mouthful of grey braces. She learned to ignore them, to focus instead on the neon lights reflecting off the waxed linoleum.

"I think I see dead people," Becky told Frances as she pulled a textbook from her locker, the roar of the stairwell clamoring around them.

But Frances was barely listening. "Uh huh," she

murmured sitting beneath the stairs, her back against the wall and thumbs thumping her phone's buttons.

"For real, I feel like I've been seeing and hearing things that other people aren't. Does that make me crazy?"

"Yes," Frances answered. "But we're all crazy. Hey, did you hear what Lisa did with Corey?"

"I don't care," Becky said, collapsing next to her friend. Frances's tee shirt, sized almost too small, shaped her curves; her skinny jeans complimented her black Converse All-Stars. The same shirt would have hung loose on Becky. Her hand-me-down jeans, which had faded to the color of an overcast sky, fit fine, but seemed to contrast the billowing All Time Low hoodie that hid her frame. And she didn't even want to compare her limp hair, the color and consistency of a baked carrot, to France's curls—lush, almost metallic, epitomizing what the commercials called "body" and "volume." Becky pulled her hood up and hid.

"No, you need to hear this," Frances said, still staring at her phone. A slow smile pushed up her cheeks. "Hold on, I'm trying to find the text."

"Why do you care about Lisa anyway?" Becky said, tugging her social studies textbook onto her knotted legs. She fanned through the pages until she found the folded worksheet flattened between pages 316 and 317. "Did you do your World History homework? I forgot to bring my book home."

"Here it is, here it is," Frances said, bouncing in place. "Okay: 'OMG, Lisa snuck out to the parking lot with Corgie'—I think she meant Corey—'and I saw them go into his car'—"

"Serious, I don't want to know."

"'And she had huge hickey when they got back and'—get this—'his fly was down!' Oh my god. How long have they even been going out, two weeks?"

"Frances!" Becky growled through gritted teeth.

"What?"

"Do you have your World History homework?" Somehow, Becky noticed, her anger always came across as whiny and wounded.

"No, I turned it in yesterday. Wasn't it due?"

Instead of escaping through her nostrils, a sigh slipped from Becky's lungs into her brain. She felt her head inflate—the puzzle of her skull separated, stretching her skin like a latex balloon, and bounced against the wall behind her.

"Here's another," Frances said, her smirk subtly lit by her glowing phone. "'Lisa told me that his zipped was busted'—zipper, probably—'and he couldn't get it up.' Weak excuse. I've heard that one before."

"You have?" Becky murmured from the safety of her hood. She rested her eyelids and tried to lure the air out of her head with long, shallow breaths, unaware of the hissing, nasal noises she made as she exhaled.

Frances snickered. "You don't think she meant he couldn't get *it* up, do you?"

The textbook tumbled from Becky's lap as she lumbered back onto her feet. "I'll be back," she mumbled more to herself than to Frances, who didn't seem to notice. Becky was bored of her friend's obsession with who did what with whom, but she also wanted to use the bathroom before the bell rang—and confirm that her head had, in fact, not inflated, that it was nothing more than one of her monthly migraines.

She walked with her eyes shut partially because the light seemed so oppressive and inescapable. Cast from above, bouncing off the floor below, flashing in every display case and windowed door, it compressed her head so that, when she peeked to recalibrate her course every sixth step, she worried her eyeballs would pop pimple-like from their sockets. But she also kept her eyes shut because she didn't want to see anything that might scare her away.

"Hey," Becky heard someone say, and popped her eyes open to see a girl stationed outside the bathroom, a stack of pink paper arched in her arm. "You look like you might like music," she continued, pushing one of the pieces of paper into Becky's path. "Check out these bands. They're playing tomorrow."

Becky accepted the flyer and let her attention skip across, from the crude line drawing (a caricatured jock dumping his soda onto a sorry-looking nerd) to a row of band names, none of which she had heard before. They were playing at some place called Humble House.

"It's a teen center here in town," the girl added. "You should go."

Becky looked up to see a round face she recognized from her art class—Marley Martin, an upperclassman who she always assumed was too cool to talk to her, her black hair teased in a static free-fall, her faded black hoodie bunched beneath a sleeveless jean jacket.

"Thanks," Becky said, swerving around the girl

into the bathroom. She felt bad balling up the flyer, letting it roll from her palm into a tall trashcan, but she lacked the capacity to even consider it.

Instead, she stood with her nose to the mirror and pried her eyelids open enough to inspect her freckled face, which did not seem inflated. Her gaze hopped from speck to speck, climbing her cheeks until they landed in the rainforest of her eyes. She pulled off her hood, taming the few strands of hair that rose rebelliously, emboldened by static. She regretted earlier comparing her hair to boiled carrots when it really resembled stained cedar—a color repeated in her freckles. Realizing that she picked out a maroon tee-shirt that morning, she shimmied out of her hoodie, took two steps back, and stared at the way her freckles and hair naturally complemented her outfit. Becky noticed her reflection smirk back at her before, overwhelmed by the overhead lights, she had to shut her eyes.

She backed blindly into the stall behind her, unbuttoned her jeans, and sat down on the cold plastic seat. In the stall's shadows, she felt comfortable enough to open her eyes and found a stall door adorned with a gallery of graffiti—crude penises, too squat or too thin to seem life-like, let alone appealing; teachers and administrators called bitches and assholes, including the revelation that "MR. VERDE HAS A HUGE WART ON HIS DICK!!" A territorial gang sign, ribbon-like and bold, like a bow hanging from the door. Sporadic pencil sketches of pot leaves, conceding defeat in the competition for significance on this public canvas.

Near the bottom, in red marker, she read the sentence, "becky mclofflan has a ginger cunt hole."

Later that day, in the quiet of her tenth-period study hall, Becky would analyze the scrawl's cruelty—the fact that the writer had taken something factual, her hair color, and twisted it into an insult; the term "cunt hole's" disgusting redundancy; the fact that, once again, the writer had misspelled her name.

But, in the semi-darkness of that stall, her heart fluttered like an inflamed bird in its cage. The corner of her eyes seared, but she withheld tears; instead, she let them boil inside her sinuses, emitting steam that added pressure to her migraine. Becky took several stuttering breaths before she was able to steady her breathing, unwilling to let these words harm her, a promise she made to herself after the "Ugly Freshmen" ordeal a month earlier.

She scanned the words a second time. The word "cunt" repulsed her so much that one side of her lip arched, and "hole" somehow made the ugly word an uglier image. *Why would someone write that about me?* she wondered. *Why me?* Was her hair color something she should be ashamed of? And her hair down there was no one's business but hers— *Except*, the thought, *now it was everyone's business*. One unsteady whimper escaped. She tried to suck back her tears, but her face felt suddenly hot and wet.

Stabbing at the sentence with a licked thumb, Becky hoped the friction would wear away the ink, but it didn't even smear. She gouged until it burned, until she worried it would wear down her thumbprint, then pulled up her pants and plucked her phone from her pocket.

graffiti again, she texted Frances.

Becky barged through the stall door and stepped

directly to the mirror, no longer seeing her own smirking, satisfied reflection. Instead, she stared at an unfamiliar girl with a pale, puffy face slimy with tears whose eyes just seemed strange. The word *ginger* echoed through her throbbing head as she inspected her lifeless hair and the freckles that stained her face. Her faded maroon shirt hung from her shoulders like she was a coat hanger. She found her hoodie balled up beneath the mirror and pulled it back over her body.

Her phone hummed in her hand. **were? what does it say?????**

dont worry, Becky replied without thinking.

The bell rang and Becky sensed the hallway awaken outside. She wiped her cheeks on her sweatshirt's sleeve and retreated into her hood, deciding to hide in it until some adult told her to come out. Stepping out into the hallway, she found herself stunned by the wash of sounds and lights that turned everything into silhouettes. She spotted the girl handing out the flyers, who cast her a concerned look before she had to aim her gaze away.

As she floated in the current of students, Frances sent her a second text. **where are u?** Becky read through squinting eyes. **i wanna find you before class.**

Becky typed back, thumbing her touchscreen hastily until she slammed into a slab of flesh. "Fuck, McLaughlin," said a voice she vaguely recognized. Becky looked up to see Lisa Masters, her jowl rippling beneath a jack-o-lantern smirk. Wall-like, an intimidating width, Becky knew Lisa as the sole senior in her freshmen English class, the one who wore the same cigarette-soured hoodie every day and, according to Frances's sources, had snuck out to the parking lot with Corey earlier in the week. "Fucking watch where you're going."

"Sorry," Becky murmured. As she snaked around her, she noticed the red splotch rising from Lisa's swollen neck.

"What are you looking at, cunt hole?"

Becky's upper lip buckled again before any realization could sink in. When it did, her heart flapped in her ribcage, but Lisa waddled away muttering, "Fucking freshmen."

Barbara Farmer
December 7th, 1941

Through the window, a formation of Canadian geese cruised together through the silver sky. Beneath them, the bleached prairie stretched to the distant tree line. Two houses jutted into view amid a scattering of grey, leafless trees that reached for the soaring flock. Otherwise, though, the landscape seemed silent and bare. *Dying*, Barbara thought cynically. *That landscape is dying.*

On most Sundays, while she waited for Anita and Joy to return from church, she'd sip her coffee and, in the comfort of her housecoat, lose herself in the scenery. Over the past few months, she had watched the view evolve from an overripe, green garden to a flickering autumn fire, then smolder into the ashen, stoic scene she saw that morning. Sometimes, she saw wisdom in the landscape—about aging and change; about the definition of beauty; about simplicity; about one's size in the universe—but had never sensed its decay, never saw death.

Barbara sighed into her cup of coffee, which she held to her lips with two hands, and closed her eyes. She wanted to explore that prairie someday but would wait until her husband returned.

John would wear a red flannel coat, the kind

that tickled her face whenever she rested her head on his shoulder, and tuck his khakis into his rubber boots. They would walk arm-in-arm through the grey landscape in content silence. Every few seconds, she would sneak a glance at his face—indefinitely older and harder, with signs of war forever etched onto it. In the lines carved into his forehead, his constantly clenched jaw, his barely blinking eyes, Barbara would sense his pain, guilt, and shameful pride—emotions she could never comprehend completely. When John would notice her gaze, though, he'd smile and she'd watch those emotions momentarily fade.

They would stroll past the houses, smell the cedar aflame in their fireplace, and John would wave his open palm at the windows, assuming that someone in the house was watching. They would step over downed branches and through tall grass knee-deep and from rock to rock across the small crick that she had never seen from their window. When those Canadian geese would flap in formation overhead, their honks echoing across the prairie, Barbara and John would watch their effort together. "Say, I learned something while I was overseas," John would say, a suppressed smirk cracking one cheek. "Do you know, when geese fly in that V shape, why one side is always longer than the other?" Barbara would know the answer since this joke was a favorite of his from before the war (and since there weren't Canadian geese in the Philippines), but she would shake her head and indulge him. "It's because there's more geese on that one side," he'd say with a subdued smile. And she'd giggle and wrap her arms around his itchy bicep and swear she'd never let him go again.

Barbara heard the front door creak open on the opposite end of the house, heard shoes kicked into corners. Then Anita giggled, but that was nothing new; the girl jingled everywhere she went. The other telltale sign that her roommates had returned was the cold air that slipped throughout the house; Joy, not yet accustomed to the Midwest's miserable winters, kept doors open while she removed her coat and gloves. Barbara pulled her housecoat more tightly around her. "Girls, close the door!" she shouted, her request answered by a creak and click in the other room.

A pink-nosed Anita peeked into the dining room's doorway. "Sorry, love," she smiled, pulling her scarf from her neck. "I hope you saved some coffee for us."

"I did," Barbara said. "But we might have to warm it up. I didn't want it to burn on the stove." She padded into the kitchen where she found the percolator half-full and resting on the countertop. She returned it to the lit stove just as Joy entered the kitchen. "Is it cold out there today?" Barbara asked.

"Honey, I'm from out west," Joy said. "It's cold out there every day."

"Well, a cup of coffee will warm you up," Barbara said, suddenly struck by the irony of serving coffee to a woman who worked as a waitress at a downtown diner. "I'd wager you say those words more often than your hear them."

"You know, you're right," Joy said. "Though I'm not sure I say it as nicely as you just did. You'd make a good waitress, Barb."

"Maybe if there was more than two restaurants in town, I'd find one," Barbara replied, trying not to sound resentful. Joy and Anita both had waitress experience and had no problem finding employment. But Barbara had never worked a real job before John left and could compete with neither her roommates nor the other women whose husbands were stolen by the war, each of whom scrambled to claim whatever job she was offered. It took Barbara a month to find her job on the other side of town, which took her twenty minutes to walk one way. "The bakery will have to do for now," she concluded.

"Anyone up for a game of Rummy while we warm up?" Anita's voice chirped from the front room. The other two could hear the sounds of searching—drawers scraping open and slamming closed, books slapping tabletops, the rumble of an ottoman wrestled away from a wall. "Where is that rotten deck?" Barbara heard her mumble between labored breaths.   Joy rolled her eyes—not in annoyance or anger, but the gesture wasn't particularly genial either. "Did she really lose those cards again?" she groaned in a whisper. "I swear, she is the most forgetful person."

"Look on the stairs, Anita," Barbara shouted. She had moved the deck there this morning after she found it resting beside the phonograph and knew that Anita would have never searched there, though it was in plain sight.

"Found 'em!" Anita squeaked. "Thanks Barb!"

When the coffee was warm again—she stood near the percolator to monitor its progress—Barbara poured two mugs, stirred sugar and milk into each, and walked them into the dining room. Anita was already seated and shuffling the deck; beneath her gentle hands, fifty-two cards slapped onto the table and fluttered into a perfect pile. As Barbara placed one mug in front of Anita, the radio clicked on in the other room. Anita shook her head—not in annoyance or anger, but some sort of exhaustion. "I don't want to hear the news," she whined, then turned to Barbara. "Why is she so obsessed with every update?"   "I hope you're turning on music, Joy," Barbara shouted. "Maybe we can stay away from the war for a while."

"It's Sammy Kaye, don't worry," Joy said, sliding into her spot at the table. Behind her, the radio faded on and the sound of muffled, mournful horns rose through the house, swaying like boat between the ocean's waves. Somewhere within the murmur, Barbara thought she heard a saxophone tantrum and, when the brass receded, a vibraphone's shimmering tones. Even these slow, doleful love songs made her think of her first date with John, of resting her on his shoulder while they swayed on a draining dance floor.

Barbara blinked, removed herself from the memory, and noticed half of her hand waiting face-down on the table in front of her. She scooped up her cards and began arranging them—a four and five of hearts on one side, two jacks on the other, a stray diamond and spade in between— as if this strategy was her secret to success. She stuck her next card, a four of clubs, near the hearts.

"Barb, why not change out of that housecoat?" Anita asked, flicking cards around the table. "We'll wait for you."

"Oh, I'm fine. Sunday is the only day that I feel clean and comfortable, so I'm taking it."

"I think that's swell," Joy said. "I wish I didn't worry

about my appearance as much as I do. I think life would be much simpler if we all just wore our housecoats around." She placed an ace, one, and two of spades onto the table without commentary and discarded a queen.

Anita snickered at Joy's insight, but her attention remained on her cards. Barbara tossed the random diamond in the discard pile and drew a four of spades. She rearranged her hand—the fours and jacks flanking the strays in between. "Okie-dokie," she said. "I'm good."

The song landed softly on its last note, only to be engulfed by a final flourish of horns. Barbara listened as the band began its subtle but telltale transition—the quiet electric organ climbing the scale until it found its key, the piano chord opening as slow as a lily. "How was church?" she asked, hoping to avoid disappearing another memory set in a sweaty ballroom

"It was nice," Anita said, picking up Barbara's discarded diamond. "The preacher talked about being faithful—to your country, and your parents, and your…well, your husband."

The table fell silent for a few reverent seconds. The wind rattled the trees outside, momentarily drowning out the muffled and meandering piano.

"You should come next week," Joy told Barbara. "It's a nice break from…you know…" Her free hand fluttered in the air, gesturing at the frost spiraling on the windows, the cards and cups of coffee, the other two girls.

"It's a return to normal," Anita clarified, "even though we're at a new church in a new town with a new congregation and pastor, it feels familiar." She took a small sip of coffee, seemed to swallow without tasting it. "It's nice."

Joy had dropped a king of clubs into the discard pile when the song was sucked out of the house. In its place, a man barged onto the radio, his cadence rushed and austere. "We interrupt this program to bring you a special news bulletin," he said. "The Japanese have attacked Pearl Harbor, Hawaii, President Roosevelt has just announced. We take you now to Washington."

During the breath of time between reporters, Joy's hand hovered over the discard pile, her absent eyes staring at nothing. Anita cowered behind her coffee cup, around which she wrapped her two trembling hands; she stared right at Barbara, blinked, whimpered inaudibly.

"The details are not available," a new voice reported. "They will be in a few minutes. The White House is now giving a statement. The attack was apparently also made on all naval and…on naval and military activities on the principal island of Oahu. The President's restatement was read to reporters by Stephen Early, the President's secretary.

"A Japanese attack upon Pearl Harbor naturally would mean war," he continued. "Such an attack would naturally bring a counterattack, and hostilities of this kind would naturally mean that the President would ask Congress for a declaration of war. There is no doubt from the temper of Congress that such a declaration would be granted."

Behind the reporter, Barbara heard the ticking of typewriters, or maybe someone tapping out a telegram. The tapping, like muted gunfire, carried the potential to kill her husband; she wondered what messages they already received and hadn't shared. Her thoughts went to John—*Is he under attack too?* she worried—until Anita's quiet sniffles pulled her back to the table. She tapped her bare foot against Anita's, a reminder that they were sharing this terror, that they were there for one another.

"And just now comes the word…from the President's office that a second air attack has been reported on Army and Navy bases in Manila," the reporter announced. Barbara felt her innards drop, felt her ribcage curl inward. Anita's sobbing climaxed—coffee splashed from the cup that bounced in her convulsing hands—but Barbara couldn't comfort her, couldn't move. Her feet tingled beneath her, heavy and dense. "Thus, we have official announcements from the White House that Japanese airplanes have attacked Pearl Harbor in Hawaii and have now attacked Army and Navy bases in Manilla," the reporter repeated. "We return you now to New York and will give you later information as it comes along from the White House."

The radio continued to rattle in the other room, but Barbara no longer heard it. She closed her eyes, noticing that her lashes were heavy with tears, and crawled around her imagination, searching for some corner where she could sit beside John and watch the Japanese planes approach. She wanted to hear the sirens streaming through the sky; smell the heavy, tropical air laced with exhaust; feel her husband tremble beside her so he wouldn't have to be alone. But she couldn't find that corner. She found tears lining her cheeks, found her heart fluttering, but she couldn't find that corner. She couldn't find John.

"Barbara," she heard Anita murmur, her muddy whine obscuring each syllable. "They're in the Manila, right?"

She wanted to say, "Of course they are, you dummy!" But Anita didn't wait for Barbara's answer. Barbara opened her eyes to see a woman slumped in her chair, bouncing with each sob, unable to hide her face or wipe away her tears. She wrapped her arms around her guts like she was hiding a bullet wound. Fighting off her own emotional collapse, Barbara treated Anita as a drowning victim, keeping her distance so she would not be pulled under as well. Except, somehow, it made her feel worse.

Though no one had noticed her exit, Joy re-entered the dining room biting her lip, but with an otherwise calm, collected expression. She wrapped her arms around Anita's slumped shoulders and squeezed her—a gesture that seemed to stabilize her, kept her from sliding out of her seat—and, with a kiss on her salty cheek, released her. On her way around the table, Joy placed her fingertips on Barbara's shoulder. Slowly, Barbara felt her muscles release their grip on her. Anita, still gasping between bursts of tears, also seemed soothed. Only then did Barbara realize that the radio had been turned off.

"Okay," Joy said, dropping into her seat. "Barbara, is it your turn?"

Barbara wiped her eyes, ran a wrist beneath her nose. "You want to keep playing?"

Joy shrugged. "What else can we do?"

"It doesn't seem right," Barbara said. She shook her head faintly, but enough to loosen a leftover tear, which splashed onto the table.

"Well, we don't know what happened at all, let alone

to our boys," Joy said. "So let's just carry on the best we can until we know. It's all we can do."

Barbara glanced at Anita—still shuddering, still whimpering, but no longer drowning—and noticed a short stack of cards had already returned to her friend's ringed hand. So Barbara plucked a card from the stock pile, stashed it somewhere random within her hand, and deposited something to the discard pile without consideration.

When Anita dropped three queens on the table, Joy exploded in exaggerated applause. A puff of laughter pushed through Anita's tears, through her stinging sinuses and congested nostrils. A smile warped her sad face. Anita cleared her throat. "Gee, am I winning?" she said, her sarcasm hidden by equal parts innocence and sorrow.

"Not for long," Joy sneered across the table in mock competition.

As she watched Joy study her hand, Barbara realized that her coffee cup could use a warm-up, but she didn't dare to leave the table. She sensed the need for safety that kept them at the table playing cards, shrouded them with the delicate veil of normalcy. Joy's pale, stoic appearance and Anita's shimmering, tear-stained cheeks reminded her that this veil could tear with the slightest movement. Beneath the shroud, Barbara decided, peace was possible, and so was balance.

So she stayed at the table, smiled, drew and discarded and allowed her tears to dry.

Lester Lancaster
April 12th, 1982

It wasn't the door itself but the ceiling around the door that scared Lester—plaster that buckled like bunched fabric, the exposed wooden frame made of mismatched timber from the start of the century, nail holes where old trim was never properly replaced.

Not scared, Lester assured himself halfheartedly as he stared at the attic door above his bed. *Creeped out, maybe. But not scared.*

A Phil Collins song fought through the static of his alarm clock radio and wafted through the room so quietly that the patter of rain against the roof almost drowned it out. It was eight o'clock, but still seemed dark outside. Lester looked past the tiny diamonds twinkling on each windowpane. Through the room's three-wall panorama of windows, oak trees swayed beneath concrete clouds, their budding branches dripping onto the withered grass, onto Eighth Street's cracking blacktop, onto the hibernating bungalows below.

Lester sighed. He didn't own an umbrella.

"First off, I'm at work," Angela told him over the phone moments later. "So, no, I can't come pick you up. And—honestly, Lester—I wouldn't even if I could. You're a big boy. You can figure out how to get to the comic book store in the rain."

Her words wounded Lester, but he was careful not to reveal this to his sister. "Wow, thanks for your concern, sis. This is the last time I call you for a favor. And, for your information, I had no plans to go to the comic book store today."

"Lester, I gotta go. I can swing by after work, but that's the best I can do."

"Well, thanks for nothing," he said and dropped the receiver into its cradle beside his bed, hoping it helped guilt Angela a little.

The truth, though, was that Lester had nowhere to go, and doing nothing at home was depressing him; he'd rather sit at McDonald's all day than watch another second of *The Price is Right* in a torpid haze from his lawn chair. He thought catching up with his sister could be a diversion from the boredom, and incorrectly assumed she was waiting for an excuse to escape work.

Lester kicked off the covers and swatted his alarm clock. The room became suddenly silent, save the drumroll of rain. As he stretched out across the bed, he caught a glimpse of his body before he could locate what he hoped was a clean pair of sweatpants from a nearby pile. His body bounced with each step, reminding him of how embarrassed he felt in his body. He'd always been big, but never remembered feeling so bad about it.

He was hunched on the front steps within five minutes, having decided not to shower or shave or brush his hair. *Why bother?* he mumbled inside his brain. *It's not like it'll make me look better.* He ran his fingers along the concrete steps stippled with age, over a stone that rose like a smooth, isolated island in the rough sea. Rain ricocheted off the roof and misted onto Lester as he tried to decide whether to wander town or not. Around him, trees drooped beneath the weight of the rain, hung their heads at despondent angles; he rose from the stairs and stepped beneath the low oaks.

Lester walked one block north until he hit Weiseule Avenue. Eighth Street would have taken him straight into town, but he found comfort walking parallel to the rusting railroad tracks. A lumber yard took up one entire block, but its sheltered racks stood lumber-less and dilapidated. Though the former owner had the courtesy to whitewash these sheds before he walked away, the paint had peeled, revealing hints of the silver wood rotting beneath. One shed leaned uncomfortably close to the nearby train tracks. The remains of wildflowers and prairie grass reached through the gravel that covered the yard.

There was something about that lumber yard and the warehouse that took up the next block that reminded Lester of himself: Cast aside when they stopped working the way everyone wanted them to, left to fend for themselves and most likely collapse on their own.

As the rain fell more forcefully, it bounced off of each building in a mist that resembled a force field; when Lester stuck out his arm, he noticed the same effect. The thought that he was protected by a force field, however weak, made him smile until he realized how soaked he really was. His hair smeared down the smooth curves of his back. The extra-large Pepsi promotional tee-shirt he won in a contest stuck to his chest and stomach, swung with the weight of the water.

But it didn't bother Lester. In fact, something about it felt right: Every step and turn he took throughout his entire life led him there to the abandoned buildings on Weiseule Avenue beneath a punishing rain that peeled paint and nurtured weeds. To Lester, the shower was neither a baptism nor a cleansing, but a comeuppance imposed by an objective universe. *This is my downpour,* he told himself. *I deserve to be drenched.*

And so did the buildings around him, Lester decided, including the ancient brick warehouses at the abandoned Weiseule Brewery. Lester gazed through its front gates and studied a property that, at one point, employed a quarter of Wisnago. Even his dad had worked there. He thought about when he would wander past the plant when he was ten, squeeze his head through the iron fence, and count the trucks lined up at loading docks. He remembered the thin lines rising from the smokestacks, the neon Weiseule sign stretching across the oldest warehouse, the men in blue work shirts bustling between buildings. Even to ten-year-old Lester, the brewery felt like the heart of the town, a muscle whose pulse he felt wherever he walked and kept Wisnago alive.

He decided his first beer would be a Weiseule when he turned eighteen but, in the early-70s—months before that birthday—the brand was sold to the largest brewer in North America, and the plant was shut down.

Its asphalt cracked, its windows broken, its cement streaked with rust, the brewery also deserved to be drenched.

Lester had squeezed his head between the fence's bars without realizing it when he heard a car's horn wheeze behind him. He turned to see his sister's Impala, its lights illuminating the rain that flickered as it fell in front of it. Angela leaned out the driver's side window and said something incomprehensible. Lester didn't need to know what she said; without a second of consideration, he scurried to the passenger side and climbed in.

"Yeesh, you're dripping everywhere!" Angela said, her complaint offset by a smile.

"It's nice to see you too," Lester snapped.

"What are you doing out here in the rain? Aren't you soaked?"

"I had stuff to do, and my sister refused to help me get around town."

"Well, I took an early lunch." She adjusted her hair in the rearview mirror, batting out raindrops and maintaining whatever volume remained. "I went by the house, but no one was there, so I decided to see if I could find you walking around the neighborhood."

"Lo and behold."

Lester wiped his wet forehead with a wet hand. He was disappointed that his sister wasn't taking the bait. Though some part of him was thankful for the shelter and companionship—that his sister cared at all—another wanted her to feel guilty for denying him earlier, or at least apologetic. Instead, she shifted into drive and eased the car through the flooded streets with a satisfied smile. "So, where to?" she asked. "Whatcha wanna do?"

"You tell me," he snarled. "I was just fine wandering

around sister-less."

"I can drop you off at home. You can take a shower and get some dry clothes."

"No," Lester responded. "Literally anywhere but that house."

"You're the boss."

The car became quiet, save the downpour popping against its roof and windshield, the shush of street water spraying against its abdomen. Lester didn't notice. He had removed the lighter, unlit, and found himself spiraling around its cool coil. He wondered how much it would hurt to touch it lit, and then wondered how he must look to his sister, a man who committed himself to the downpour now contemplating the car's lighter. He returned it to the dashboard and poked it in to warm it up.

"You never call me at work—or ever, really," Angela suddenly said. "It seemed a little odd, so I decided to put work aside to see if everything was okay with you, or if you wanted to talk. And then I find you wandering around in the rain." The car approached a stop sign at Lily, and Lester looked at his sister; the still-lit streetlights beamed through the rainy windshield and cast squirming patterns down her face. "Everything okay?"

"Yep."

But, as he dripped in his sister's damp passenger seat, he felt like hiding. It was embarrassing that he was soaked, that his see-through t-shirt revealed every bulge and curve. The reminder, though, that his best option for that day's adventure was meandering the abandoned brewery during a pounding downpour made him want to disappear. He rested his soggy head against the window and noticed that Angela had turned north onto Lily, that they were approaching the brewery again.

"When I was little, back before it was bought out, I used to walk past the brewery too," Angela said. "I hoped to spot dad driving some machine around one of the loading docks." She turned back onto Weiseule. The brewery slouched against the asphalt sky. "When I did spot him, though, he usually just waved me on, sent me home."

Lester squeezed his eyes together. "Please don't talk about dad."

"What?" She eased the car onto the shoulder across from the rusting gate.

"I said please don't talk about dad," Lester repeated with sharpened articulation. "And please don't park here."

Memories flickered in Lester's mind, emotional impressions—his face squished between the fence's sun-baked bars; the thin pinstripes on his dad's blue work shirt and burnt work gloves that fit his hands too tight; the inconvenienced grimace on his dad's dusty, shaven face; the words, "Just go home," and the long, lonely sidewalk that unraveled ahead of Lester.

"Why don't you want to talk about dad?" Angela asked again.

Lester wanted to say, "Because he hated us." He wanted to scream it, to roll in his seat, to lunge at his sister with his answer like it was a knife he had just removed from himself. Instead, he leaned with more weight against the window and surrendered. Tears unrolled down his cheeks, mingled with the rainwater and sweat.

"Lester, talk to me," Angela insisted.

He felt her hand massage his sopping shirt and shoulder as he held in his sobs, released them through long, string-like sighs. Her hand massaged harder in consolation, in love.

"Dad worked so much because he wanted our family to be comfortable, and you know that," Angela said. "And, when he left us—" Her sentence skidded to a stop, and she swallowed whatever words remained in her mouth. "All we can do is learn from his mistakes, right? To not be like him."

Lester had made this commitment years ago, even remembered the night that he promised this. Again, the memory came in fleeting impressions—the coffee-stained jacket to *The Who Sell Out* resting the kitchen table, the sounds of his dad's workboots stomping through the backdoor at eight o'clock, the splish-crack of a cold can, the silence as he retreated to bed. Lester resented his obsession with working, with staying busy even on weekends, but he never understood his unwillingness to acknowledge his children when he wasn't at work. *Was this why he decided to abandon us,* Lester always wondered, *why he felt useless when Weiseule was bought?*

Useless, Lester repeated in his head and slid the knife back to the raw spot he had just removed it from.

"Lester, this is old news," Angela said, starting to sniffle herself. "He's been gone for, what, ten years?" She patted her hand against his shirt, stroked his arm. "What's wrong?"

Useless. The syllables bobbed in his head. His muscles became tense and frail, his limbs like the cracked, colorless boards that leaned in the lumber yard unable to maintain their own weight. His hair and shirt and sweatpants, weighted with water, held him captive in his seat and against the window.

"Lester, talk to me please."

Useless. His consciousness fizzed with the word. And he wondered if this was how his dad felt when he killed himself.

Charles Stonebreaker
July 4th, 1910

A *drop of sweat* forced its way across Charles's scalp before finally plopping onto the receipt he was reading. Weiseule had accepted a shipment of one hundred barley bales—he had counted them himself—but the receipt read one thousand. His company would be overcharged tenfold for their order, and on his watch.

Charles knew this was an honest mistake, the distributor's error, and that a timely telephone call to the company would remedy the dilemma. But it was a holiday, and his distributor would be out of the office today and maybe tomorrow, as would the operator in town he needed to connect his call. In two days, it would be too late to correct this mistake. He bit his bottom lip, wishing he had inspected the receipt more carefully before signing it.

Light wafted through the wide window near the ceiling, indicating that it might be afternoon. A casual glance at the clock confirmed this: 1:15 p.m. "Shit," he whispered, another bulb of sweat slipping from his forehead. He told his wife and her father that he'd only be at the office until noon, enough time to pocket some extra money, and that he'd be home by lunch so they could get to work. Centering the receipt on his desk, he decided to resolve the dilemma on Wednesday.

As he stomped down the stairs of the brew house, he saw men, dusky with dust and sun, stacking barrels onto the half dozen horse-drawn wagons that lined the boulevard, presumably orders for Independence Day celebrations throughout the county. The wooden kegs were heavy—Charles wasn't surprised to see one cracked like an egg on the ground, its contents soaking into the dust—so the alley echoed with the groans and grunts and sore sighs of the laborers, whose shirts stuck to their bellies and backs. Their odor mingled with those of the fat horses and their manure, blended with the spilled beer to create a combination both savory and startlingly sweet.

"Hey Stonebreaker," a percussive voice cracked through the bustle behind him. "Heading home so soon?"

Charles turned to see Josh Mingus smiling, his teeth like white pearls in an oyster's mouth. Mingus was maybe twenty, and his sandstone hair was the same color as his sandstone skin. He had been hired as a delivery man earlier that summer and, unlike Weiseule's other workers, was willing to talk to Charles.

"Took half-a-day," Charles said. "I got a house to build for my family. My wife's waiting for me there with my father-in-law."

"Ouch!" Mingus grinned. "Hey, what direction you going?"

"West from here a quarter mile, then a block or so south." He pointed to where the alley emptied into the summer-hardened yard and exhausted trains often sighed in the sun. "Not far—a good fifteen-minute walk."

"Hop on, then, brother. I'm heading toward Stuartville, and it'll be nice to have the company, if only for a few blocks."

Charles balked at his offer, but only for etiquette's sake. Overhead, graphite clouds uncurled toward the sun, staining the sky behind it a bleak silver, and he knew that, if it started raining before he made it home, he would be in much hotter water with Elizabeth than if he had merely returned late. So, when Mingus insisted a second time, Charles climbed beside him onto the wagon's bench.

Charles didn't know much about piloting a wagon with two horses, so he studied each of Mingus's movements— the dramatic way he flicked the reins to get the horses going and the tiny tugs, minuscule and instinctive gestures, that steered the horses across the yard. As they rolled through the dust, wheels popping over pebbles, Charles could sense the wagon's weight, particularly as it turned out of the brewery onto a trail that ran parallel to the train tracks; he felt beer roll inside their barrels, felt the wagon lean over its left wheels, felt the un-sanded bottom of the bench as he clutched his seat.

"So, how long you been working at the brewery?" Mingus asked.

"My wife and daughter and me, we moved out here in the early spring, but I came out a week before them to find an apartment and a job, first week of March. Lucky for me, Weiseule decided they needed someone to manage their shipments, and I had helped with inventory at my dad's store when I was a kid."

"Perfect fit."

"Well, maybe," Charles mumbled. He looked at the neighborhood on his left, the clean yards contained by iron fences, the corniced roofs that peeked above the pubescent trees. Downtown loomed in the distance; littered with celebrating citizens, it vibrated beneath the steel-colored sky. "Sometimes I'm not sure."

"Hey, this brewery's a tough place to work," Mingus said, then spat over the bench's edge. "You're either the muscle hired to sweat, or you're the money that hides in the brew house. If you do something other than one of those, you're made to feel like a snoot or a nitwit. Me and the other drivers talk about it all the time."

A raindrop smacked the barrel behind Charles, big enough to be heard above the thud of hooves and the wagon's rattle. He watched the horses bounce ahead of him, their tails swaying thoughtlessly. Ahead of them, two dirt tracks sliced through the overgrown grass and seemed to divide the sky: An oppressive whirl of mercury on one side crawling across the other's flawless, boundless ice. A rumble crept through the town, rattled the wagon's bench and barrels and wheels, caused the horses to exchange anxious stares.

"Now, was that thunder or a firework?" Mingus asked.

"Hard to tell, especially these days. Back where we used to live, I swear they just lit off dynamite."

"Ha! Now that's funny," Mingus said. He smiled but didn't laugh. "Hey, you still going to work on your house if there's rain?"

"Probably."

A sudden rush of wind roared towards them from town, like God sweeping his hand along the landscape. Charles sensed it several blocks away, heard it wake oak after oak until it swirled around them. Another raindrop, ice cold, careened into his wrist.

"That wife of yours must really have you under her thumb to have you working on a holiday in a thunderstorm," Mingus said. His smile made Charles wonder if his friend also knew how cumbersome a woman's thumb could be.

"I can't argue with you there," Charles responded. "But, you know, I don't mind working on the house. Maybe this sounds silly, but it gives me a sense of purpose." Rain smacked more aggressively against the barrels and the horses' backs. "I'm learning lots too, you know? I've never built a house before, but it's one of those things I'm willing to do for my family and myself, rain or shine, whenever I can."

"Hey, we all have our reason to wake up in the morning, right?"

"And this house is mine. It's the reason I work at that damn brewery too."

As they rolled past Lilac, the storm blasted through town, pushing through the innocent trees and blowing open stable doors, a spectral wall of wind plowing past their trail, into the broadside of their load, nearly knocking the casks from their stack. And the rain, no longer lumps dropping sporadically from the sky, became a full shower that sprayed from all directions. "Woo-wee!" Mingus wailed, flinching against the barrage. "Now *this* is a storm!"

Charles smiled too, couldn't contain the giggles that

galloped in the back of his throat. He released them into the swarming rain. It felt good after his hot, tense half-a-day. Squeezing his eyes, he felt the rain wash away his sweat and the sweet smell of the brewhouse; wash away his clerical error and his inability to correct it; wash away his late return, his half-fulfilled promise, his nagging inadequacy. Thunder rumbled then crackled overhead. Charles sensed its echo stretch in all directions at once.

"Hey, I know a little something about building," Mingus shouted over the din of endless drops. "Let me know when you need help."

Charles's smile stretched into something more, became stony with sincere appreciation. "That's kind, Mingus. I haven't gotten much help, or any sincere offers, so I might take you up on it."

"Sure, brother. We're in this together."

The wagon rolled another block through the storm until it approached the newly-named Geranium Avenue. Charles squinted through the haze of rain and his bleared vision to read the sign pinned to the streetlamp; the neighborhood looked so unfamiliar. "This might be my street," he said. "I'll hop off here." Mingus jerked the reins, tugged them to his shoulders as Charles slapped his sopping back. "Thanks, friend. I owe you one," he said, climbing down the bench. "Be safe in this storm."

"Absolutely," Mingus shouted. He shook his head, releasing loose droplets as he whipped the reins. And the wagon wobbled away.

As Charles trotted down the road, his boots sticking in the muddy wagon tracks, he tried to keep his eyes open through the deluge, to notice exactly what it was that made his block look so unrecognizable in the rain. Maybe it was that the white siding on the street's only other house seemed to glow in the gloom. Or maybe it was the procession of young oaks on the far end of the block, which looked like a parade of leafy people thrashing along Eighth Street. Though beaten by the storm, the grass seemed brighter and spiny weeds seemed to suddenly belong. Even the road itself, resurrected from stiff dirt into loose and sloppy sludge, seemed suddenly dynamic, colorful.

Halfway down the block, the rain slowed and his blurry house became more visible. Charles looked for Elizabeth pacing on the porch, the only area of the house sheltered by a real roof, and thought about what he'd say to her, how he'd apologize: He'd wrap his soaked arms around her and, though she'd momentarily resist, she'd recognize something sweet about his soggy gesture and bury herself in his embrace, even if it ruined the summer dress that draped her summer body. And he'd say, "I love you, Lizzy."

When he didn't see her, he assumed she was in the basement, or maybe working with Marty on the far side of the house, and reconsidered his gesture accordingly. But, by the time Charles was hopping up the steps, he was worried that no one was there—not his wife, not her father, not Rebecca plucking disoriented worms from the road. Beneath his feet, he noticed the words "Went Home" written in white chalk on the porch's unpainted boards.

He ran a hand across his forehead. The storm's ruckus faded, but remained; rain rattled against the porch's roof and the wind pushed through the trees in a whispered roar that reminded Charles of his years on Marty's farm, that decade when the wind seemed to be his only company. Here, that solitude returned. *Maybe*, he worried, *it never went away*.

But then his thoughts shifted to Mingus, to his offer of help. "Sure, brother," he remembered Mingus saying. "We're in this together."

Charles walked into the unfinished house, balanced himself on the slippery floor joists, left muddy bootprints on each streak of wood. All of the walls and windows on the first floor were framed, and he could picture what would become his family's home—the corner in which the fireplace would crackle, the room in which the dinner table would crouch, the window through which they would watch storms advance toward town. For now, though, it was a geometric maze of wet timber and beams, bright orange with rain. Though he and his father-in-law had made what felt like progress in only a few weeks, too much of it was made while Charles was at the brewery.

If Mingus was really willing to help, he realized, maybe that day would arrive sooner—the one when he could stand before his finished house, squeezing his wife's ringed hand, and say "Welcome home;" the one when his wife, admiring their new home through fulfilled tears, would whisper, "Thank you," as her lips floated toward his.

Carefully, Charles climbed between the first floor's ribs into the basement below, splashing into a puddle of rainwater. He had bartered wood laths for a barrel of Weiseule beer and stacked the scrap wood along the wall where he had built steps out of the basement with leftover cement. He found his hammer and a burlap bag full of rusting nails and carried these tools up the cellar steps with a load of laths bending on his shoulder.

As the rain fell in indifferent drops, he reentered the house from the front porch, stretched from joist to joist to the furthest corner of the house, what would become the kitchen. With his supplies secured at his feet, he lined a lath along the intersecting studs and pinned it to the timber, using nails that he kept bitten between his teeth.

He picked up and pinned a second lath, thunder seemingly answering his hammer's clamoring. He picked up and pinned a third, fourth, and fifth. His mouth bitter with rusty iron, his overalls soaked through with rainwater, he picked up and pinned a sixth and seventh.

Charles imagined cutting carrots and potatoes and strips of celery that they had picked from their backyard garden, stirring them into a pot of rolling stew, lifting his daughter to take a whiff of dinner as he finished tacking the stack of lathes between three studs, slipped between the joists, and returned with another stack.

Halfway to the kitchen, he paused and stood in the center of the unwalled space, legs bridged between two slick studs, wood see-sawing on his shoulder. Only then did it occur to him that he was content, completely stressless despite the day's circumstances. He wondered where this peace crawled from, but didn't care enough to dwell in his curiosity. Instead, he closed his eyes and soaked in the emotion. It was a strange sentiment, one he hadn't really sensed since before his marriage and move to his father-in-law's farm, before his Wisnago promise.

"Huh," he grunted, recognizing the long-lost sensation. Rain dripped from his smirk.

And then he tip-toed from bone to bone back into the kitchen where he tacked another stack of laths to the wall.

Preston Assad
February 23rd, 1996

Stretching before Preston, the sky glowed a dusty pink, turning each rooftop into a sharp-cornered shoulder bracing the sunset. Tree branches bounced in the breeze, loosening the last raindrops from a storm hurried out of town by a band of warm air. Sitting on the cement steps of his porch, he tried to admire the unseasonably warm weather and his rose-colored neighborhood.

Except, behind him, a song stumbled out of his basement, slipping on the steps, its feet moving too quickly to maintain traction. Guitars giggled and squealed, like they were being tickled, and the bottom end mumbled incoherently. It sounded like a six-year-old's unsupervised birthday party and, in a way, it was. Preston agreed to host a local metal band comprised entirely of teenagers that insisted it plays thrash, not metal, and that he correct the description beneath their incomprehensible logo on the flyers that Preston had printed and slid beneath windshield wipers at the local high school during his lunch break at the beginning of the week.

Then the song fell apart—guitars tangling around one another, tripped up by dragging blastbeats, tumbling into the nebulous bass that jabbered two measures ahead—and the boys started barking at each other through the microphones.

This, along with one of the band member's dads thumbing through a spy novel on the porch swing behind him, made it difficult for Preston to appreciate the sunset, the just-drying sidewalk, the hints of an early spring.

"Hey," he heard Maryanne say as she approached, a silhouette against a sky that now resembled the rich, ruby guts of a grapefruit. Her winter coat was unzipped, revealing a battle-worn Smoking Popes shirt beneath. "I'm early. Hope that's okay."

"No problem," Preston said, scooting on the cement steps to make room for her. "The earlier, the better. I'm afraid that shirt will get you beaten up tonight, though—unless they mistake them for some black metal band. And they might be that naive."

Maryanne grinned at his recognition of the Smoking Popes, but her eyebrows tugged together in kind confusion. "Really?"

"No no," Preston said. "Just kidding."

"I thought I heard music. Did the bands start already?" She lifted herself onto tiptoes to peek through the front door into the house before finding her seat beside Preston.

"No, they're just sound-checking. Or, they *were* sound-checking. Now they're just jamming, or practicing, or something. Doors don't open for another half hour or so."

"Gotcha."

"I'm not sure that tonight's the best night to be helping out," he told her. "The bands probably aren't going to draw a lot, and—" he turned around to confirm that dad had disappeared into his book. "Well," he whispered, "I don't think the music is going to be great."

"I don't care who's playing. It's just fun to be part of the whole house show thing, you know? Plus, I think it's sort of sweet that you're letting these kids play."

"Shows like this always worry me, though. None of these kids really know the culture of the house. We'll be lucky to have a couple of regulars show up and help keep the peace." Behind them, he felt a song wobble back to life, felt it teeter before staggering forward like a toddler learning how to run. "It also feels weird inviting the town's teenagers into my house for a glorified band practice. That's why we're having such an early show, so it's out before curfew, and why I'm happy their parents are mulling about. One thing I need you to do is keep your eye out for alcohol or any sort of smoking. We could get in big trouble if we let it happen."

"Gotcha."

Preston eyeballed two blobs treading beneath the bruising sky—the sunset had darkened to match Maryanne's mulberry hair, he noted—as they approached Humble House. One tall, scrawny specimen wore all black; something about the logo on his shirt, constructed from inverted crucifixes and batwings, seemed out of its element in southwestern Wisconsin. Chunky calves fell from the other's camouflage shorts. Both boys had longer hair, though the thin one's fell in waxy waves to his elbows, much longer than his friend's, which curved like black claws beneath his chin.

"Hi guys," Preston said as their combat boots clomped up the sidewalk. "We still have, like, a half hour or so until I'm able to let anyone in, just so you know."

"Oh," the scrawny one mumbled. "We're with the

band. They told us to show up early to help them set up."

A dozen little red flags sprang up in Preston's head, which manifested on his face as a cynical smirk. As much as it annoyed him when anyone tried to take advantage of his cozy little subculture, let alone adolescent metal heads, there was something satisfying about these teachable moments.

"Okay," Preston played along. "Which band are you *roadies* for?" He glanced laterally at Maryanne, who watched with the alert eyes of an unsuspecting spectator.

"Sagittal Sulcus," the scrawny one said. "They said we could get in for free."

The last little flag flung to attention, this one yellow with a skull and crossbones. "It's cool that these guys are getting you in for free," he said, suddenly fishing in his pocket. "They your friends, or something?"

"Yeah, I guess so," the scrawny one answered.

"We go to school with them," the squat one followed.

Preston removed a small rubber stamp from his pants. "I gotta stamp you guys before I let you in," he said, gesturing for their hands. "But don't you think they're going to be pissed off?"

"What do you mean?" The squat one offered his left hand.

"No, right hand," Preston said, pounding the stamp into an ink pad at the edge of the porch, rolling it onto his fleshy paw. "Well, Sagittal Sulcus arrived with the other two bands and we all loaded in together at four o'clock. They've been set up for an hour." He snatched the scrawny one's hand and stamped it. "I hope you guys aren't *good* friends because they'll be pissed at you for dropping the ball."

Both boys inspected the stamps; the word "LOSER" bent across the back of their hands it in bold, black ink, seeping into the tiny cracks of their skin. "What the fuck, dude?" the scrawny one whined. His lean posture reared back like a snake ready to strike fang-first.

"Or, I hope you're not just *saying* that you're supposed to get in for free," Preston continued. He rose to his feet and, on the second step, towered over the two of them.

"Buddy, we were told to show up at five and help out the band," the squat one insisted, uselessly rubbing the black back of his hand. "I'm not sure what to tell you. Is there a guest list or something you can check?"

Preston sighed and lowered himself back onto the step. "Guys, I'm trying to support your friends—give them a reliable place to play, you know? Some money to record a demo," he said in slow, neutral syllables. "I don't have time for anyone unwilling to help us build something here. So go home, ask mom for five bucks, and wash the stamp off of your hands. By the time you come back, the doors will be open."

They turned around together with wordless acquiescence, stepping back into the street where they became blobs once again. The sky stretched above them, seeping into the trees and street, staining whatever was left of the day.

Maryanne budged, having observed the interaction with a statuesque stillness. "Wow, that was impressive," she said, "and maybe a little mean."

"You should hear Maculey," he said. "Sends a strong message, though. I've said the same thing to adults."

Preston tried to sound as composed as possible despite the acid splashing around inside him. His hands shook. Though he felt a sense of satisfaction defending his cause, he hated confrontation. "During every load-in, I ask the bands who they want me to let in. All three bands tonight said to let in whatever parents show up, and two of the dudes from one band asked if their girlfriends could get in. They didn't say anything about friends or *roadies* or whatever."

"I didn't know those kids," dad chimed in behind them, peeking over his paperback, "and my son plays drums in Sagittal Sulcus. For what it's worth."

"I figured," Preston said. "Thanks for having our back, man."

Dad gave him the thumbs up and dove headfirst back into the book.

"Were those lurkers, then?" Maryanne asked.

"No, lurkers are more curious and cautious. They don't know what to expect, so they drive up and down the block, or sit in their cars for a little too long and observe us, making sure that this is the right house. But they're always willing to pay." He ran his fingers along the concrete steps stippled with age, over a stone that rose like a smooth, isolated island in the rough sea. It calmed him down, that familiar, reliable stone he had felt a million times. He squinted into the dusk in the direction of the retreating teens. "No, those kids were trying to scam us for sure. There's always one or two. You just need to know the difference."

"That's okay," Preston said. "You will. And you can

always ask me." He faced her for the first time since she sat down, felt the crackle of her scrutiny. It made him nervous. "Anyways, I want you in the basement with me keeping an eye on these kids," he continued. A small smile pushed her cheeks, which bulged like peaches. It was a thankful smile, eager and willing. Her eyes widened, round in the sudden night, a spiral of concentric circles whose sheen kept Preston from completely falling in.

The porch lights ignited. Sound barged suddenly into the evening in a louder, rawer, less-refined form as Maculey cracked open the front door. "Oh, you're here," he said, his head poking out of the house. "Hi Maryanne."

"Hi Maculey," she said. Her attention remained aimed at Preston even as her eyes peeked toward the door. "It's weird seeing you without that coat," she added.

Limp, pale arms, peppered with copper speckles, dangled from his black, sleeveless shirt. "It's hot down there," he said, though stalks of hair still peeked beneath his black beanie, along with discreet dots of perspiration. As he sat down on the edge of the porch, a cash box landed beside him with a ca-chingle. "Things are good down there," Maculey told him. "The board is as dialed in as it's going to get, though they keep turning up their amps. I say we switch. Doors open in ten minutes?"

"Maybe twenty." Preston turned back to Maryanne. "Ready?"

"Let's do it."

They climbed into Humble House and plunged into the basement against a current of the noise that careened up the steps. Preston felt Maryanne's palm on his shoulder as she steadied herself, clutching him as she stepped on one particularly elastic step.

Maculey was right: The basement was warm, though not the sticky sauna it was bound to become. And, with all of its lights on, the space didn't stretch in all directions, as it would in a matter of minutes. For now, it was a regular basement—an occasional spider claiming a corner, the concrete floor dark with humidity, a mildew musk dulled by the soft scent of dryer lint—except for the four adolescents whipping their spine-length hair over their Ibanez guitars and the tomato-faced boy biting his bottom lip as he bludgeoned his squealing brass snare drum. Maryanne squinted against the sonic gale; face-to-face, it felt less like puerile horseplay and more like a premeditated mugging.

Preston waved his hands at the band, whose members, one by one, came down from their breakdown-induced daze. "Guys! Guys!" he barked until he became audible. "Woah-kay. Hi guys. I need you to stop playing until your set. We're opening the doors soon, and I don't want you to spoil the audience's appetite, you know?"

They smiled and snickered, stomped on the pedals beneath their tangled cables, flicked the red-lit switches on their amps. The members of the other bands clustered in different corners; their drumsticks clicked against the cobblestone and unplugged guitars scraped in percussive rhythms without amps. Their conversations ramped into laughter or coiled into careful, philosophical conversation. One boy braided another's beard. Preston took his position on a stool behind the soundboard and, for a second, watched these clusters interact; he had to admit that they seemed happy about being in his basement. *Maybe this show will be more fun than I thought*, he mused.

Amid the fizzing excitement, Maryanne stood in the space's center, facing the "stage," her winter coat folded over her arms. Preston couldn't see her expression but suspected it to be somewhere between bored and bewildered. Quickly, he flipped through a booklet of CDs and plucked a bright yellow disc from its sleeve.

Within seconds of slipping it into the mouth of a CD player mounted on the rack beneath the board, a build-up crescendoed from the speakers pointed right at Maryanne—a snare drum, more of a slap than a tight crack, surfacing slowly from the murmur of gummy guitars. Before the build-up could climax, could break into its simple bop, Maryanne turned around, her lips bent into a surprised smile, her cheeks rounder and riper than before. She approached Preston as the song swirled around her, the singer crooning, "Midnight moon, I hold you for this perfect night / Love is born to linger in your magic light." But when she opened her mouth, nothing came out except an unintended giggle, so she pulled her winter coat away from her chest and pointed to the Smoking Popes logo. Preston nodded, modesty sculpting his lips, the words, "With that girl beside me and you above / You must also be in love," wafting in the stifled air.

Above him, Preston heard frantic stomping across the floor, then behind him on the stairs. "Preston," Maculey yelled. "Get up here now."

Before he even made it through the front door, Preston saw the squad cars, lit menacingly by the streetlights, parked out front—two of them, one on each corner, as if backup had been requested. An officer stood on the porch and another behind him on the sidewalk, like a shadow cast by the lights. Preston recognized both of them; they worked in the same building every day after all. "Hey Roy," he said, the screen door slapping closed behind him. "Everything okay?"

"We got a noise complaint, Preston," the officer said, looking back at his partner.

"No way," Preston said, smiling incredulously. "There's no way."

"We did, about ten minutes ago. You're either going to have to turn it down or stop altogether. And, if we get another, we have to shut you down. Sorry, man."

Preston felt his arms tremble, felt his brain stutter, his vision blur. That familiar acid bubbled up inside him. "There's no way," he repeated. "We've done this every weekend for a year and a half and have never gotten a complaint. I've spoken to every one of our neighbors personally and told them to call us before they ever call you guys."

"I know, I know," he said, his clean-shaven chin rubbing against the bulletproof vest that climbed beneath his stainless uniform. "And, honestly, we're patrolling every night you have one of these things and barely hear it a block away. But we have to respond."

"The show hasn't even started yet," Maculey added, nodding to two kids wandering up the sidewalk. "How could there even be a noise complaint? From the soundcheck?"

As the hesitant teens tip-toed toward the porch, Preston thought about the two "roadies" he turned away and wondered if they would have called the cops out of spite.

"Come on, Roy," he pleaded. "We've always done things the right way."

"Hey Roy," Maryanne said suddenly, prying herself between Preston's pleas. She pulled two folded pieces of paper from her back pocket. "I pulled a temporary amplified sound permit yesterday, so we should be good until ten o'clock. And, just in case, I also pulled a special event permit, so this gathering has been approved by the Mayor's Office, assuming that no illegal activity takes place." She handed the permits to the officer. "And I've volunteered on behalf of the Mayor's Office to supervise this, since there may be a handful of minors."

The officer inspected the permit, ran his fingertips along the notarized seal on the document. "Okay, guys," he finally said. "You're good. We'll visit the individual who issued the complaint and inform them of this permit."

The officers walked back to their squad car backlit by a moon that peeked over the rooftops. Preston and Maculey watched in stunned silence as they signaled to the second car and disappeared down the street, then turned simultaneously to a smirking Maryanne, who shrugged. "I guess it helps to work in the Mayor's Office," she said, "and to have a little foresight." As Maculey turned to the teenagers, inviting them onto the porch with a wave, Preston noticed the way the moon outlined in white Maryanne's tiny nose, her eyebrows, each strand of hair that escaped her ponytail. He turned to the moon, allowed his eyes to adjust enough to view its cracks and pores, then turned back to Maryanne, her sharp, delighted smile trying to pop her balloon cheeks.

Becky McLaughlin
November 4th, 2011

Most days, she could tune out the creaking—like a rocking chair croaking beneath the weight of an old man—but, today, Becky struggled to contain her frustration.

"Mom, what is that noise?" she shouted to Misty, who had sealed herself in the master bedroom next to Becky's to do God knows what.

"Shut the fuck up, Becky!" Misty shouted, her voice ramming into the plaster walls. "I'm trying to sleep!"

The creaking continued, as it did every evening for fifteen minutes until its tempo slowed, until it decrescendoed and disappeared, until she wondered if she had heard anything at all.

"You can't hear that?"

"Fucking shut up! *Jesus!*"

Becky shook her head in short, ragged strokes. *You don't sound tired*, she muttered in her mind, *and since when do you go to bed at six?* Her face tilted toward her phone and iPod, alternating between Frances's sporadic texts and Facebook. What was left of her Halloween candy nestled in a peeled-open pillowcase that sat on the bed beside her; she chewed thoughtlessly on a Snickers, deposited the wrappers between her bed and the wall along with the lesser candies—Mounds,

Three Musketeers, lone Hershey Kisses, their silver foil peeled, revealing milk chocolate gray with age.

Sharp knuckles knocked on her door and, worried about what might be on the other side, her freckles stiffened and her spine snapped taut. She relaxed only a little when she heard her brother's voice on the other side. "Becky, have you seen my issue of *SPIN*?"

"Which one?"

"The one with Das Racist on the cover?"

She had. The three dressed-up hipsters—two with dumb haircuts, another wearing a dumb hat—peeked from beneath an issue of *Us Weekly* in the stack splayed beside her. "No," she said simply. Through the door, she heard him sigh and stomp toward the master bedroom, heard Misty roar, "Fucking *go away!*"

As her house and its occupants crackled around her, Becky clipped a picture of an iridescent insect out of an issue of *National Geographic*. Maybe it was the concentration required, or the search itself—maybe tracing the delicate contours of grandeur brought her somehow closer to it—but she found the process of sliding scissors through paper peaceful. Immersed in the pursuit, she was able to momentarily tune out—and hide from—the screaming and muttering, the stomping and slamming and tense silence, the creaking.

Her scissors snicked and the flat insect fell into her lap just as her phone tickled her ankle. **my mom got me a job interview at ihop monday,** Frances's text read. It was rare to receive a meaningful text from anyone, especially from Frances—something other than "heyy" or "haha" or gossip. Still, something about this news annoyed her.

She scowled across the room at the dented pieces of paper on her dresser, applications for two fast food restaurants within walking distance. When she had returned her applications the previous week, she was rejected by both, told that she was too young—once by a manager, his mustache wet with grease, and once by a bratty blonde cashier smaller than she.

thats awesome, she texted back, adding, **r u even old enough to work there?**

The phone bounced beside her on the bed as she swapped it with the *Us Weekly*. She fanned open the tabloid, scanning the copper bikini bodies, the faces obscured by bug-eyed sunglasses, searching for an image to remove from the magazine but unsure exactly what she was looking for— something beautiful, maybe, or something ugly, but she'd know it when she saw it. She pulled a packet of Sugar Babies from the pillowcase, tore it open, and popped a caramel bean into her mouth.

my mom said if her manager asks shell say im 18 :p, Frances's response read, and Becky felt something bristle inside her. Perhaps suspecting her cruel tone, Frances followed up with, **what r u up to.**

Becky considered ignoring Frances, sending her the message that she was being a mean bitch, but decided to be the better person. **working on my collage for art**, she typed, her thumbs massaging the device's teeny buttons, before returning to *Us Weekly*. When she found a L'Oréal ad with a pair of strawberry lips, stiff and slimy, she traced it with the scissors, preserving its shape with painstaking attention.

Misty pushed through the bedroom door. "Becky, where's Tom?" she asked.

Startled, Becky's scissors slipped, slicing across the corner of the mouth's firm smirk. "Mom!" she whined. "Knock! You screwed me up."

"Where's Tom?" Misty repeated in the same insistent tone. Her eyes, outlined in what looked like charcoal, bounced around the room, scanning nervously.

"I don't know."

Misty backed out of the doorway, disinterested or distracted, as if she had not heard her daughter's answer at all. The door clicked closed, and Becky listened as her mother's feet slid down the hall at a sleepwalker's faraway pace.

Becky burrowed herself further within her refuge of thin blankets, but lifted her left ear in the air, trailing the creaking with her eyes as if it were visible like a cobweb or crack in the swirling plaster, trying to locate the source. *Somewhere in the attic*, she suspected, *but not over my bedroom. Maybe mom's?*

Her search was interrupted by her humming phone, which she fished from the swill of sheets. **sounds boring ;)**, Frances's text read.

Becky's tongue bucked behind her puckered lips as if she had pulled a Warhead from her pillowcase. She wasn't bored. Becky wandered the town with Frances when she was bored, commented back and forth on Facebook with Frances when she was bored. She was the opposite of bored: Busy, absorbed, maybe making something meaningful. It occurred to her that each image she scissored, each insect and candied slab of skin, would soon contribute to an actual collage, some artistic statement. Here, in addition to finding the solitude she longed for, Becky was preparing to say something—what, she wasn't sure yet, but the realization made her hands tremble with anticipation.

And anyway, was Frances trying to say that boring Becky couldn't have fun without her? She watched the display dim only to be roused by another message. **come to my house. it isnt boring here.** Becky read it through a strangled glare, held down the power button until the device shut its eyes, and frisbeed it across the room; it dimpled the drywall and landed facedown next to a crumpled piece of paper—a flyer for that night's show at Humble House, striped with more bands she hadn't heard of.

The door swung open beside her bed and Becky heard, "You fucking bitch." She turned to see Tom in the doorway, his eyes and voice unusually sharp. "Mom said you had my *SPIN* sitting right on your bed." His gaze climbed across her crumpled covers and landed right on the issue. "Give it to me."

Becky felt her extremities activate, felt them tremble and twitch. When her brother was like this, she knew he could cause harm, that he was seeking an excuse to do so. Surrender would mean admitting to the crime and conceding to bruises, and she had learned that resistance if she could summon the courage, might prompt a lesser sentence— refusing to chauffeur her to school, for example, or ignoring her in general. "Lay off, Tom," she said. "I need it to do my homework."

His arm stretched into the room, reaching for the

magazine, but Becky snatched it from beneath his fingertips. "Give it to me," he repeated, baring tan teeth. As he stepped into the room, a whirl of sour air swirled around him—the stench of tobacco and cannabis mingling with his unwashed mop of muddy hair.

"Get out of my room," Becky said, sensing something rising inside her, something that burnt the edges of each syllable. Her grip on the magazine tightened.

"Give me my magazine."

"I'm not in the mood, Tom."

He hunched over her bed, and his stare narrowed beneath his forehead's slick facade. "Give it to me," he said and suddenly pounced onto her. One claw clutching her shoulder, the other on her face, he knocked her sideways, stuffing her into the bed. "Give me the fucking magazine," he said, his serenity more startling than his attack.

Becky's legs bicycled, kicked off covers and scattered remaining magazines, but she couldn't buck her brother, who rammed her into the mattress face first and squeezed her shoulder until she was sure something of hers would crumble in his hand. The *SPIN* folded between her body and the bed. "Give it to me," he muttered, his tone static, his arm snaking beneath her, biting at the magazine.

Becky felt her whole body contract, her molten iron muscles stiffen as she drowned in her bedsheets. Some pinpoint in her consciousness expanded behind her clenched eyes, though she only noticed it as it whitewashed her vision and spread beyond her body. It seemed to feed on her present frustrations—the lonesome creaking, her mother's absent intensity, Frances's oblivious digs—and transform these feelings into physical strength. Beyond the pinpoint, another expanded, a darker one that swelled more slowly, that rose through her, that pushed out her throat as a roar, that seemed to blacken whatever it pressed past.

Screaming, Becky bumped Tom off balance enough to squirm out from beneath him and off the bed with the magazine. She climbed onto quaking legs and screamed, screamed at her stunned brother blinking on the bed, screamed as if some parasite was clawing its way through her ribs and skin, screamed and tore the pages of *SPIN* to pathetic and useless strips, tore whole and half pages of ill-lit faces and bewildering illustrations, tore across neat columns of text, tore through ad after ad after ad, thoughtlessly tore for destruction's sake and let the shreds tumble to the floor.

She took a breath long enough to hear Tom mutter, "You're a crazy bitch," as he retreated from the room.

A whir swirled in her ears, and it was all that Becky could sense for a few seconds. In her mind, she pictured herself standing backlit against the window, bobbing as she soothed her frenzied respiratory system; her shirt, rolled up to her belly by the slide off her bed, and her hair drifting in a haze around her head; tears lining her pink face, tracing the spaces between her freckles; a gutted magazine dangling in her hand, its entrails scattered around her, frosted in white where they were torn from their body.

Slowly, her other senses returned. Her vision, no longer whitewashed, noticed the bed's mess and the missing pillowcase—Tom must have nabbed her Halloween candy on the way out. She no longer heard the creaking, but it was impossible not to notice the punchy music that suddenly shook the house. Becky pictured her brother, pouting in his room as he plucked Skittles from her pillowcase, playing his iPod as loud as he could to reclaim his power over the household, though it wasn't the mechanical electronic music he normally blasted.

She peeked into the hallway, through his room's darkened doorway, but found it abandoned. As her head floated over the hallway's floorboards, it became clear that the music was blaring beneath her.

Gathering the magazines on her bed, collecting each severed shred from the floor, Becky considered her next destination. She'd probably head to Frances's. She didn't want to, but she sure as hell wouldn't stay in a house where its inhabitants purposely violated her privacy, intended to harm her, and played music at inconsiderate volume levels. She snuck out of her room and down the twisting stairs, hoping to escape unnoticed by both her brother and mother, but they were nowhere to be found on the first floor. The living room, hazy in the setting sun, adorned with dirty laundry and dishes, reminded Becky of those deserted houses in zombie movies.

The bigger mystery was the music, which throbbed beneath Becky's feet. It was too loud, she decided, to be coming from any speakers in the house. Itchy with curiosity, she stepped toward the basement door where the music became more comprehensible—a singer's ravaged voice competing against roaring guitars for dominion, drowning out drums that rattled Becky's ribs. She sort of liked the song, she realized, and doubted that Tom would listen to something so alive. *Maybe it's mom*, she wondered, which seemed impossible, since Misty hated all music released after 2001 and hated the basement more.

The basement freaked Becky out too, a place where she was destined to die in a maze of cobwebs. For five years, since her family signed the lease, Becky had been in the basement only two times—once when they moved in, and once when her mother promised to withhold all meals until she flipped the laundry from washer to dryer. But her curiosity prevailed, and she twisted the crystal doorknob.

As soon as the door opened, Becky was battered—with jangling, jagged guitars and tantruming drums, louder now without the barrier between them; with the distinctive scent of body odor sweetened with a hint of spilt beer; with heat, like a huff of hot breath. *Something isn't right*, she decided, and instinctively flicked the light switch. The music disappeared immediately as the lights illuminated the dull concrete at the bottom of the steps, which sent a shiver down her speckled neck and shoulders, down the back of her arms to the skin coiling at her elbows.

She almost retreated, had turned her body back toward the kitchen, but her instinct told her to continue. So she took a step, the stair bending beneath her featherweight, and another, and another. And with each step into the basement, the stink seemed to diffuse, fade into mere must, and the air actually cooled. Standing at the bottom of the stairs, the basement that stretched before her was bigger and better lit than she remembered. There were things hanging on the wall, obscuring the somber cobblestone—fabric stretched across frames. The washer and dryer, which hunched beneath the stairs, hid behind some sort of hand-built bar—except, though the length and height seemed right, its surface was tilted and too wide to serve drinks on. Besides these items and some cobwebs climbing in each corner, the basement was bare, even clean.

As she stepped toward the bar, Becky noted the space's silence, that even her footsteps refused to echo. Despite this peace, though, she felt strong, safe, and confident, felt a heat radiating from within her. *So this is what it feels like to conquer fear*, she almost said aloud. But there was something affirmative in the basement's energy, something that stoked these feelings, though she did not dare to acknowledge this intuition with a thought.

She dragged a stool out from beside the dryer, dusted it off, and positioned it behind the bar before climbing onto it. After spreading the magazines onto its surface, Becky patted her pockets, searched through the stack of magazines and shreds of paper, realizing she had left her scissors upstairs. As she eyed the remains of her brother's issue of *SPIN*, her mind returned to that moment in her room—to shredding that magazine, the terrible necessity of release, the exquisite catharsis that reared from her fear—but only long enough to remind her that she was the creator of such feelings, not the mere recipient.

So Becky tore the pages of *Us Weekly* to pathetic and useful strips, tore whole and half pages of discolored faces and bewildering illustrations, tore across crowded columns of text, tore through ad after ad after ad, thoughtlessly tore for expression's sake in the basement's silent solitude.

Lester Lancaster
April 23rd, 1982

"So, Mr. Lancaster, catch me up," Mrs. Beverly Thatcher said from her side of an unadorned desk, pastel lips pressed together in anticipation, prepared to laugh until she cried. Her squirrel hands drew a pair of sagging eyeglasses away from her face.

But Lester didn't know what to say. He didn't want to reveal that he had spent his last two weeks in that lawn chair in his living room scrutinizing music videos; he had struggled most with the Cars's "Shake It Up," not only with the director's lazy, literal use of automobiles and shakeable objects, but also the disparate image of seductive women shimmying against rock 'n' roll's nerdiest band. Subsequently, he wasn't sure he could allow himself to appreciate this otherwise perfect pop song.

He didn't want to tell her that he hadn't left his house, or that he had shunned sunlight, covering windows with dish towels and doormats and whatever else he could find on the floor of his house. He didn't want to say that he had lost ten pounds, that he had showered only once, or that these last two weeks had been his lowest.

So, instead, he stalled. "What do you mean?"

The expectant smile faded from her face. When

Lester noticed the Tweetie and Sylvester coffee mug on her desk, he remembered their last meeting, that his "putty-tat" impression sent her sliding from her chair. He couldn't help but wonder if its placement was intentional, somehow strategic, and if maybe he should have worn his Looney Tunes tie again, even with the stain, instead of his sweat pants and cleanest tank top.

A different kind of smile stiffened her face, a starchy white one. "I mean, tell me how your life's been going," she answered. "How's the job search treating you? Any interviews?"

"Not many," Lester lied, consciously swerving around her first question. "I've sent out a bunch of applications, and have only been called in for one interview."

"That's great!" she said. "The first month is usually the hardest. A lot of my cases spend weeks preparing and contacting references, so even one callback is a good start." She scribbled onto a legal pad in plump handwriting that was hard to read upside down. "Okay, so where did you interview?"

"Rocco Records," he blurted, because he planned to surrender some of his earnings there after this formality.

"On Seventh!" she almost shouted, and a laugh sprung from her lungs like it had been coiled there since they sat down. "I love that store! It's been there forever." Her starchy smile softened, and her glasses returned to her nose, magnifying a set of melted chocolate eyes. "I'm a bit of a record collector myself. Anytime a Monkees record comes into his store, Franklin sets it aside for me. Franklin's the guy who owns the place. He's Rocco's son—*the* Rocco."

It occurred to Lester that Beverly was looking for reasons to like him, which he had usually credited to his charisma and charm. But this optimism probably qualified her for a job in the unemployment office, he realized. So he put his flip-flops flat on the floor and did what he could to nurture her affection. "Yeah, Franklin's a great guy," he said, a smirk cracking across his face.

"So, how'd it go?"

Lester tried to blink away his anxiety and retreated to his mind where a vision of his "interview" materialized from dust. It formed a steel desk squatting on flattened carpeting and file boxes, stacked to the ceiling, obscuring wood-paneled office walls. Assuming Franklin was that recovering hippie who tried talking him into an Iron Maiden record last month, Lester imagined the meeting—his assured handshake and cordial demeanor as he accepted an invitation to sit, the way his wit turned an interrogation into a lively and stimulating exchange, impressing Franking with his rock 'n' roll wisdom. Lester allowed the moment to play out in his imagination until an outcome came to him—one that made him seem confident, competent, powerful.

"It went great," Lester said, the interview still swirling in his head. "He offered me the job, but had to decline."

Beverly's scribbling screeched to a halt on the page. "What?" she asked, casting the sort of razor gaze that slices painlessly and spills unstoppable amounts of blood.

"I, uh, declined. He only had a part-time job on weekend mornings, which conflicted with—"

"Mr. Lancaster, you're receiving unemployment

insurance. If you're offered a job, I don't care if it's drying cars at a car wash, you accept it. We don't run a charity here."

Something about that statement stuck into Lester like a popcorn kernel between his teeth. "I'm not sure that I agree," he said, starting before fully formulating his thoughts. "That I should accept a job drying cars, that is. I agree you don't run a charity."

Beverly put down her pen and stretched her torso to attention, which Lester interpreted as an invitation to continue.

"I mean, don't you feel that people should be doing what they're meant to do? Clearly, it seems like you're meant to be working in an office like this. Positions like yours were made for patient, hopeful people like you. I feel like I should be holding out for that job, not wasting my time working somewhere that drains the life from me, you know?"

Beverly's starchy smirk returned. "Mr. Lancaster, trust me when I say that nobody believes that more than me. But, as someone accepting taxpayer dollars, you're not in a position to be quixotic—or, frankly, to disagree with me."

Lester cast his eyes down toward her desk. He didn't disagree with her at all, and he wasn't disappointed with her response. Instead, he tried to decide whether he agreed with his argument—that people should pursue what they're meant to do—or if it was simply a card he played considering his desperate hand.

"My advice to you would be to call Franklin back and see if the offer is still on the table," she said as her pen carved pudgy letters into the yellow leaves. Lester looked up to see a different woman, one whose muscles flexed in frustration beneath her blazer's shrugging shoulders, whose smash-lipped smile revealed someone who loved her job so much that she couldn't hide her hatred for it. "I'll follow up with him early next week and put in a good word for you if there's still an opening."

Twenty minutes later, Lester's unemployment check had transformed into a wad of twenty dollar bills in his sweatpants pocket. As he sat on the park bench facing the Civic Center, his tongue streaked across his teeth, feeling for the kernel that had wedged between his molars, knowing there was none. It was a weird feeling, having $450 folded against his thigh and no immediate idea what to do with it.

Beneath the chilly morning that would soon warm into an ideal spring day, downtown rippled in a way that's possible only on a Friday. Traffic moved miraculously as if the stoplights refused to redden; cars and pickup trucks, destination-less, did laps around the square, pulled restlessly into and out of parking spots, stopped mid-block beside one another to converse. Few pedestrians polluted the sidewalks; the ones that did, though, took leisurely steps in pairs, patting backs, laughing. To Lester, the scene seemed surreal, like a cartoon where everything human and inhuman grinned aggressively, bouncing to a beat he couldn't hear.

Meanwhile, the Civic Center leaned into the landscape like the emperor at a bacchanal—imposing, proud, but loose and content in his confidence. As it leered knowingly at Lester, it seemed to say, "You're not as scary as you thought you were, are you?" Lester deflated against the bench's dusty aluminum. He knew it was only a matter of time until he was found out.

For a second, he considered strolling to the sandwich shop around the corner, maybe snagging April's *Amazing Spider-Man* or catching up with *The Mighty Avengers*—it had been six months since he had the luxury of following his favorite superheroine Scarlet Witch—but felt stranded on that bench.

A voice eased out of the morning's noise. "You look lovely, but how do you *feel?*" it asked. "Wonderful. That's wonderful to hear." It sounded like an old stone building— firm, its corners crumbling with age.

Lester twisted on the bench to see that homeless man again meandering across the park's trampled grass. He seemed to lock onto Lester's bench, murmuring more gibberish with each slippered step. "You're the reason, yep, the reason I get up, why I take my medication at all," he chittered, a chipmunk fretting over some invisible acorn. Lester felt his muscles wince as he visualized his impending conversation—how this man would plant himself on the bench, his stench grasping at Lester with obscure talons, and ask nonsensical questions while Lester simply grimaced and averted his eyes; how, as the man doled out gems of hobo wisdom one by one, Lester would study the black cracks on his hands that gave his skin the appearance of woodgrain until some beat cop recognized him as a public nuisance and escorted him kindly out of the public park.

But the man strolled past him onto the sidewalk that stretched along Fourth Street, then the crosswalk. As he passed, Lester studied the man's face, which seemed much younger than it had in his mind, and well-washed. In fact, it occurred to Lester that this man couldn't have been much older than sixty, and that it was his pace, each step preceded by his abused cane, that aged him twenty years. He also noticed his outfit was the same as it was a month ago—the same khaki pajama bottoms, hinting at the long bones that made up his legs; the same corduroy slippers scraping the concrete; the same rubber-banded newspaper tucked beneath the same satin jacket with the same silver snaps (though Lester noticed the words "VFW Post 1525" peeling from its back) and that it was clean—too clean to presume homelessness, perhaps.

The man made it twenty feet to the crosswalk before Lester realized his hand had been squeezing the lump of cash in his sweatpants, guarding it against this murmuring stranger and his cane.

As the man scuttled across Fourth Street, Lester considered how much he had in common with this crazy man. He, too, had nothing to do but wander and had been wearing the same clothes. "The only difference is that he seems to take showers," he said to himself, then realized that this was another eccentricity they shared—talking aloud to no one.

A small, crustacean-shaped hatchback honked its horn twice—once politely, and then again as an agitated squeal—to indicate the man's window to cross had closed. He slid his slippers along the asphalt as quickly as he could, but the hatchback sat and screeched until he had crossed completely, then beetled down the block to the next red light.

Lester couldn't see the man's face, but noticed his quivering cane as he tried to compose himself from the safety of the sidewalk. "Sympathy isn't the right word," Lester mumbled from the bench. "More like empathy. Future empathy. Because that'll be me one day." He wondered what he would do if he was in such a situation—or, rather, what he *will* do *when*. Maybe he'll stop mid-step, blocking the impatient vehicle's path, or exchange choice words with the driver. "Or, I'll beat the hell out of the car with my cane," he decided, a smirk twisting his lips.

The man turned East, tottered toward the Civic Center, and Lester heard his mumble resume, watched his cane calm and stabilize. Creeping closer to the building, he lowered himself slowly onto the steps and secured his cane between his legs. When he stroked the cement beneath him like it was some exhausted dog, Lester made up his mind. "I will *not* become that kooky old man," he declared forcefully enough to attract the attention of a sweating pedestrian power-walking past him.

Lester pushed himself off the bench with a strained, obligated groan and aimed himself north, then cut through the park, kicking across newly sprouted grass. As he ducked under the calloused branches of an ancient oak, he sensed his body on autopilot ferrying him to a destination for desperate purposes. "I've got no other choice," he told himself and began to believe it.

He froggered across Sixth and took Lily toward Seventh Street. In the cooler cement canyon of the financial block where Wisnago's banks sized one another up, Lester convinced himself that he faced a crossroads. He could remain on the same path—which was becoming more complicated and painful with each step—or he could take a drastic turn that would drain some of the difficulty from his life. That's when he thought momentarily of his father, of his crossroads and the course he chose, and swung his head side to side suddenly as if to shake the thought from his mind.

As he turned onto Eighth Street, Lester moved from brisk shadows to the street. Automobile traffic was lighter, but pedestrian traffic clouded the sidewalks like a morning fog. He stepped quickly, intentionally, rolling his feet along the pavement between strolling shoppers and coffee sippers. His hair, hanging like seaweed on a dock, swayed with each step, and a strange grin twisted onto his lips.

When he pushed through the glass vestibule at Rocco's record store, Lester was welcomed by both the splintered chords of the Who's "I Can See For Miles" and a familiar face half-hidden by a stack of used LPs in tattered jackets. "Oh, hey!" he said. "How you digging that new Walkman?"

Lester snarled at the thought of small talk. Here, he was ready to reclaim his life, and some white-haired hipster wanted to talk cassette players. "You Franklin?"

The employee nodded, then peeked anxiously at the front door.

"I'm looking for a job. You got any?"

Preston Assad
March 1st, 1996

"So, Mr. Assad, catch me up," the Honorable Walter Schooner said from his side of a desk cluttered with family portraits. "Unfortunately, I have an important lunch in fifteen, so I may need the short version." He aimed his gaze at Preston, though his attention seemed elsewhere.

But Preston didn't know what to say. He didn't want to come off as rude, especially toward his boss, the mayor, whom he's supposed to please between elections. He also didn't feel the need to defend himself even though Preston had missed his deadline and this last-minute meeting had been called to address why. He sat rigid in his overstuffed chair, anxious to say what he needed to without jeopardizing his job.

So, instead, Preston remained vague. "Slow," he said. "Very slow."

Schooner snickered, laugh lines suddenly sketching across his face. "That's an understatement," he said, his voice tinted more with charisma than derision. "Wasn't your deadline today?"

"Yeah, but you gave me two weeks to make a whole website for the city. You do know how long it takes to build a website, right?"

"Of course, I do," Schooner said, easing back into this chair. "Hey, I was in the computer business before I was elected, and I plan on returning to it."

Schooner sold computers for Gateway 2000, which is why, when he entered office, the Civic Center was stocked with humming PCs (and a storage room stuffed floor to drop-down ceiling with Holstein-patterned boxes). Preston knew that sales experience didn't translate to technical knowledge. *It may account for many of his assumptions, however,* Preston thought, *and his arrogance.*

"You know, then, that our software limitations make it difficult to design anything for a website," Preston said. "That's the first hurdle."

"No hurdle at all," Schooner said. "Gateways share software capabilities with all Windows machines, including state-of-the-art and professional design applications." He spoke so fluidly, with such melodic inflection, that Preston was convinced that Schooner had dusted off an old pitch just for him.

"You might be right, but the city won't buy me Photoshop, and that's what I need."

"Yeah, well, that's an expensive piece of software," Schooner said. "But all we need is something simple, you know? Simple and classy."

They seemed tuned in to separate conversations, so he tried a different frequency. "Okay, then you know that I went to MIAD for graphic design, right?" he said through a dented smirk. "I can design a website, but I don't know much about HTML or writing code. That's the second hurdle."

Schooner leaned forward onto his desk like it was a

bar, like they were buddies. "But you know *something* about HTML and writing code, right?" His spectacles slipped to the edge of his nose, and he peered over them at Preston.

"Only what I have taught myself for this project."

Schooner's smirk spread into a pleased smile. "Mr. Assad," Schooner said, peering down at Preston from his desk. "We wouldn't have asked you to take this on if we didn't think you were the right man for the job. I asked several individuals to tell me who has the skills to make a website and the ingenuity to solve the inevitable problems involved, and your name came up each time. You were the only choice. I can afford you a few more weeks, two or maybe more, but I have to answer to city council members if it takes any longer."

With two taps at the door, Maryanne peeked into Schooner's office. "You're lunch appointment is here, Mr. Schooner."

Schooner rose and shot his titanic hand across the desk; Preston grasped it but didn't shake. "Don't let me down," is all Schooner said as he stepped to the door and showed Preston out of his office.

Maryanne closed the door quietly behind him. "How'd that go?" she asked, inquisitive dimples dotting each cheek.

Preston sighed. "Let's go get lunch."

They pulled their coats closed as they walked downtown between the boutiques that lined Wakes Road, dodging puddles and stepping between the people that complicated the lunch rush. It took Preston the entire walk to summarize his five-minute meeting. Maryanne listened and nodded.

His tirade continued as they ducked into Sal's Sandwich Shop, where his anxieties ricocheted from the oak paneling and onto tile tinted grey by decades of dirty mop water. He paused only to order the number four with no onions or tomatoes.

A window of silence finally opened once they sat down; though Maryanne had taken a bite of her sandwich, she felt obligated to say something. "You're not wrong."

"What do you mean?" Preston replied, plucking onions from his sub.

"I mean, this is super annoying." She swallowed her bite in two humble lumps. "No wonder you hate your job."

Preston's attention popped away from his unwanted condiments and toward Maryanne. "I don't hate my job," he said. "I hate some of the people I work with, but my graphic design work is fun."

"You sure *seem* like you love it," she mumbled, then took a second bite of her sandwich to conceal her smirk.

"Well, I don't *love* it either. It's a job, you know? It pays my bills and allows me to pursue the other things I love."

Maybe it was because she was backlit, the windows behind her casting a veil of darkness over her face, but Preston noticed for the first time the depths of her eyes. Everything about Maryanne was normally bright—her unbuttoned scarlet coat and cobalt scarf, the Easter yellow Chucks he'd seen her don on Friday nights, the edges of her plum-colored hair glowing violet from a sun filtered by finger-smudged windows. Her dark eyes were the curious exception.

"So, what *do* you love?" she said. Her fingers plucked an onion from his plate and popped it into her mouth.

Preston paused, allowing the subtext of her question to trickle through him, before offering his simple answer: "Music."

Maryanne rolled her eyes. "I knew that."

"Well, then you shouldn't have asked," he replied. It was his turn to smile, though his seemed flirtatious, quiet in a wild way. "In my head, though, it isn't that simple. Like, everyone enjoys music, but music is one of the few things I truly believe in. And it's not enough to just listen to music, you know? I have to feel like I'm connected to it, contributing to it, giving as I take. I'm sure you understand where I'm coming from."

But Maryanne's expression conveyed nothing more than patience as she drew a strawful of Sprite into her mouth.

"It's like this," Preston continued. "I want to pour my time and money not only into music, but also the people who play it, even if they aren't awesome at it yet. But, it's like, *want* isn't a strong enough word; I *need* to, and don't feel happy unless I do." He sensed his wild grin mutating into something more defensive, more furious. "Sometimes, it's weird because I feel this intense desperation to maintain my connection to music. I get so excited about new bands and CDs because they work me up and calm me down. Because they're meaningful to me. It's the reason I work at that damn office too."

"So, why not follow this passion further? Why not

turn it into your job?"

"What do you mean?" he said, though he knew what she meant.

"I mean, wouldn't you be happier if you did this for a living? You wouldn't have to deal with people like Schooner and Fred and…who's that one woman who spills coffee all over the place in the break room—Angela? Instead, you could serve the people that deserve it, and you could do what feels meaningful."

Preston had heard this recommendation made many times—primarily from his parents, who were always pushing him to do and say and be more. "It isn't a bad idea, but it's impossible," he had always answered. But, as he snuck peeks at the smile sagging between Maryanne's soft cheeks, he decided she deserved more of his mind. "I wish I could do it," he said instead. "I just don't know how to make my hundred-something-year-old Wisconsin basement a successful venue, you know? I don't have the skills, the manpower, or the space to make it a real business. It's just a thing I do because I love to do it, not because I want to make money."

"But what if making money allowed you to construct a more comfortable space, book more bands, accommodate more music lovers like you? And, then, make more money. And so on."

"I'd still be in Wisnago and would be, at best, catering to the county's bored teens. Which, don't get me wrong, is fine. I like the local kids. I just wouldn't invest my life savings in them."

Maryanne stared at some point beyond Preston

and pondered. "What about Madison?" she asked. "Or Milwaukee? Even Kenosha. Could you move to somewhere bigger?"

A dot of mayo marked the corner of her mouth, but Preston decided it was too endearing to tell her. "See, that's the thing," he said. "After college, I moved away from the city because I wanted to come home. I like Wisnago. It's quiet. Every inch of it feels familiar. I don't want to go back to Milwaukee, even though my parents are begging me to—more opportunities, they say."

He retreated into the cavern of his memory, found himself meandering the murkiest clubs, watching bands that hacked at their guitars, ill-lit by a line of neon signs, ignored by the sweating regulars hunched over the bar. There were a dozen such clubs in the city, backrooms where one nursed a lukewarm High Life, cross-armed but nodding to the beat, shoulder-to-shoulder with the strangers that had settled in the neighborhood, each there for a different reason but united by the collective desire to be seen disappearing. But these images smeared into another, more coherent memory from his senior year at MIAD at a show that winter in a warehouse lit with Christmas lights, desk lamps perched on each amp. There was no heat, and breath tumbled out of every mouth in slow motion, but he didn't remember feeling cold. The kids that ran the show were still in high school, held cigarettes between slender fingers, smiled a lot. They shook Preston's hand and passed him a zine to read between sets. The bands were tattoo-less and blurry, changing chords too quickly and too often in the clamorous space, but the people in the crowd moved together in some kind of chaotic synchronicity. The warehouse only lasted for three shows before it was shut down. For the first time, though, Preston saw music as a place to escape to rather than a means of escaping.

"Yeah, there's a million venues in the city already," he said, returning to the present. "I'd be in a big pond that literally eats small fish. At least in Wisnago, I can provide a service that isn't already here—and that others seem to be seeking out."

Maryanne replied with a soft smile, and Preston understood it; there's only so much one can say to someone who has his mind made up.

They rose from the table together in silent consensus that lunch had concluded, topped their drinks off at the fountain, and left the humming store in silence, biting the tips of their straws, bumping their shoulders together as they returned to city sidewalks thawing beneath an apathetic sun and determined noontime footsteps.

But, before turning back to the Civic Center, Preston's gaze strayed north, pried between storefronts, past the pastel mansions that lined Wakes beyond Seventh Street. "You ever check out that abandoned brewery just north of here?" he asked.

"Is that what that is?" she said. "I drive by it on my way home every day, but never knew what it was. Just looked like some old, run-down factory."

"Yeah, it used to be a local brewery—Weiseule, it was called. It shut down when I was pretty little, though." Rock salt crunched beneath his smooth soles. "We used to sneak into it when we were in middle school."

"Rebels," was all she said, wagging the word like a finger.

Preston snickered half-heartedly as if he had told himself an unfunny joke. "You're going to think I'm crazy, especially after the hopeless conversation we just had, but I've always thought it'd be cool to turn *that* building into a music venue. I mean, it's a cultural landmark, and it's just sitting there, you know?" They stopped at a crosswalk, where he stole a drag of his diet soda. "But I feel this way about every abandoned building—every empty storefront and boarded-up movie theatre and whatever."

Maryanne offered that same soft smile in reply; her eyes, however, sparked and crackled, desperate to be read as they strolled together past the tiny boutiques and corner stores stout with lunch rush customers, then beneath the grasping oaks in the park on the square. As they crossed Fifth and approached the Civic Center's steps, she finally burst into laughter.

"What?" Preston asked, his syllable tinted with worry.

"You're crazy," she said, her smile teased, untamed. "During our entire lunch, you complained that you're stuck doing what you *don't* love so you can chase what you *do* love, but that there weren't enough resources to focus attention exclusively on what you *do* love." She veered into him, bounced her hip off his. "But then, out of nowhere, you say, 'You know, Maryanne, wouldn't it be awesome to turn that abandoned building into a venue?'" She uttered the last sentence in the deep, voice of some doofusy cartoon character.

"I do not talk like that," he said, a guilty smile tightening his face.

A few minutes later, in the wilting light of the office, Preston pulled his Walkman from his desk drawer, hung some headphones on his head, and started pecking code into his computer. In the hiss before the first song started, he closed his eyes and reflected on the preceding minutes in an attempt to render his memories permanent:

The way their bodies became bumper cars as they climbed the steps—round shoulders ricocheting into one another, elbows glancing off ticklish ribs and hips, laughs bouncing beneath the cold awning.

Her sudden recommendation as they climbed the swirling marble steps: "Let's go to the brewery after work, just to check it out." At the top of the stairs, they stood breathless together, and he finally noticed the fireworks flickering in her eyes.

The startling realization that they had been holding hands. *For how long?* he had wondered. He hadn't noticed until she untangled her fingers from his and they separated to their respective desks.

His return to seclusion, where he was greeted by a modest rectangle made of purple, transparent plastic. Two white, toothsome spools in the center. Her words were written in lazy bubble letters: "Shitty Meeting Mixtape".

Only after revisiting this fourth and final memory did he realize how long the song had been playing.

Charles Stonebreaker
July 29th, 1910

"So, Charles, catch me up," Marty demanded, burying his grin beneath an overgrown beard. He tangled his thumbs in his overalls and aimed the tip of his mushroom nose at Charles like the sight of his Remington. "How far behind are we?"

But Charles didn't know what to say. *Truthfully*, he wanted to answer, *me and Mingus made lots of progress, much more in one week than you did in five*, but he didn't want to come across too smug.

He suspected that, if Marty hadn't been bedridden all week, their progress would have been impossible. A case of sunstroke sent him to the Stonebreaker's only bed, where he spent a week tossing and turning and healing despite the apartment's oppressive heat. For that, Charles also didn't want to seem unappreciative; Marty had sacrificed time and strength and health, baked like a biscuit in summer's oven, all for his house and family.

The timing couldn't have been better, though. The day after Mary fell ill, Charles reported to Weiseule only to be told that the brewery would be shut down for one week, maybe more, while they made equipment repairs.

He intended to work on the house uninterrupted that entire time, sunrise to sunset. And, when Mingus had learned of his friend's plan, he offered his shoulders and knees and a shed full of tools for as long as it took to finish the home. Charles and Mingus worked well together. They pushed one another without pressure, taught each another what they didn't know, and laughed often. Their teamwork amounted to visible progress that impressed even them, but Charles didn't know how to report this to Marty, smirking beneath them in the sunny dust.

So, instead, he let Mingus speak.

"Well, we put the windows in on the first floor," he started, standing beside Charles in the shade of the front porch. "Then, we finished the steps going upstairs and framed those rooms. Uh, took a day to brick up the chimney. Gonna frame the roof before we gotta go back to the brewery, if we can. Oh, I got a plumber friend who's gonna put in a water closet and run pipes in and out of the house, but that'll happen next week. What else we do, brother?"

Charles answered with a watermelon smile, momentarily allowing this list of accomplishments to speak for itself. As he rested on the front steps, his body cascading down the concrete like a waterfall, he recounted to Marty the reality of their progress in his head: *We reframed the windows that you built crooked, finished pounding in your nails, replaced the rotten wood you used to make the stairs, and straightened the siding you hung.* But the silence lingered too heavy in the hot air, so he answered his friend simply as if he was too tired to spare a syllable. "No, that's it." "We got a good jump on today and started walling in the rooms upstairs," Mingus added. "That one room's gonna be a beaut." He pointed right above his head, and Charles watched Marty's eyes climb the porch's sanded columns to the skeleton of the enormous master bedroom he had designed for Elizabeth.

Marty's eyes returned to the men relaxing beneath the porch's blue shadows, tightening on the one with the mustache. Charles wondered what thoughts rolled around his mind, whether they clacked into each other aimlessly or circled in careful, single-file lines. He noticed that Marty's grin hadn't eroded, and couldn't decide whether or not the man recognized their victory.

"Well, what are you boobs waiting for?" Marty barked, his body darting toward them. "Let's get upstairs and wall in those rooms."

"We've been working six hours nonstop," Charles said. "We need to take a break for another few minutes." When Marty stopped mid-step, he added, "I mean, if you don't mind."

"Only if you don't want to get that roof started before Sunday," Marty said, stomping onto the porch and past them into the house. His feet thumped up the steps inside like a bass drum in a marching band, as if the house was an instrument he barely knew how to play. They waited to hear him scuff the floor beams above their heads before they felt safe enough to shoot each other uncertain looks.

"I have this feeling—" Mingus started.

But Charles smashed one forefinger to his lips and aimed the other at the father-in-law whose already labored breaths bounced down the stairs. "Let's go get some laths from beneath the house," he said. "He won't be able to hammer a nail until we haul up another load anyway."

Mingus reached out an arm reddened by the sun, pulling Charles onto his feet. They treaded dust on their way toward the cellar, the unblemished sky above faded by a sun that seemed whiter than usual. For a fleeting moment, Charles imagined the strip of land beside the house lush with glowing grass, and his little Rebecca running laps back and forth, chased, perhaps, by a hyper mutt, or maybe an unsteady little sibling, until he heard the clunk of a hammer on iron and returned to the dusty lot. *What could Marty be hammering up there?* he wondered.

"Today's the day, brother," Mingus murmured in the cellar.

Charles stacked a row of laths onto his shoulder. "For what?"

He watched Mingus's eyes widen in the shadows. "Haven't we talked about it all week? He needs to know how ratty he treats you and that he gets on your nerves." Mingus leaned his back against the cobblestone wall. "Hey, I've seen you work all week, and I know you're not the bum he makes you out to be. And up there on the porch? The way he interrogated you about your own house? That was strange."

Charles let out a sigh that spread across the basement. "It *was* pretty strange, wasn't it?"

"It was like he didn't believe us, the way he gawked," Mingus continued. "But the proof's right above us. There're windows now, and a second floor, and a chimney! The damn steps don't creak anymore!"

"I told you how he was."

"Yeah, I know," Mingus grumbled. "I guess I expected someone else—the sort of person who asks for a licking, like some loudmouth at a pub or a ballgame. You can ignore those bimbos. This guy, though, he treats you like you're the one asking for a licking."

"Yeah," Charles answered. He was desperate to push past this conversation and pretend a confrontation with Marty wasn't inevitable. "So, are we going to get back up there?" he asked.

"Not until you agree to say something," Mingus said. "Imagine that, after quitting time, you and I work on this house together the rest of the summer. We'd get it done in no time." His fleeting smile flickered in the shadows. "Now, imagine it's quitting time, and we get to the house to find Marty, who's been working while we were gone. Imagine how much we'd have to redo—and having to explain that to him. Imagine his response. How long would this house take to finish?"

"You're not suggesting that I tell Marty to head back to his farm, are you? That we don't want his help anymore?"

"I'm saying something's gotta change, brother."

Charles cast his eyes toward a foundation marbled with mud. He knew Mingus was right. Charles thought of Elizabeth, though, and her response when her father would barge into their apartment and hastily pack his bags. In his head, he saw the anger that would sharpen her eyes, then watch them fill with fear, worried about her family's safety and future.

But then he thought of that "Thank you," her whispered gratitude as he'd present their beautiful, finished home—one that he had built sooner than expected. She'd squeeze his hand. Their long shadows would lead them up the steps toward the front door, which he'd open for her. He'd have to give her two tours, since the first would be obscured by her rapturous tears. *Maybe I could finally be the man in her life*, he thought.

"Alright," he finally said and stepped back out into the sun.

"'Atta boy," Mingus said, following up the cellar steps.

With his buddy behind him, Charles stamped through the dried dirt and back into the house, stepped from beam to beam without thought, the stack of laths bowing on his shoulder. As he climbed the stairs up to the second story, he drew in the sort of slow, deep breath that made him aware of his ribs. *I'm going up there to work on my house,* he reassured himself, *and I'll speak with Marty when the time is right.* He lifted the laths from his body, held them vertically turned the tight corner, and hopped up a final set of steps as though it were a dance he had done a hundred times. The sun seemed suddenly warmer, meaner, as he strode the beams toward the master bedroom.

"What took you ladies so long?" Marty said as they entered the room, his fingers and thumb wrapped around the handle of Charles's hammer.

"Just finishing our break," Charles said, unloading his laths into a corner. Sweat stung his eyes. "Heard some hammering. What are you working on?"

"I found a few laths. Thought I'd start putting them up if no one else was going to." Marty talked around the nails bitten between his teeth, and Charles noticed that they were the long, thick ones he had used to frame the room.

"Here," Charles said, picking up a burlap sack. "We've been using the smaller nails to tack up the laths. That way, they don't split the wood."

"Nails are nails," he muttered, spitting the iron pins into his palm.

Charles bit the inside of his bottom lip as he spotted the spare hammer, the one whose loose head wobbled with each swing, on the window sill beside an enclosed wall. Up close, it was clear to him which rows were Marty's; fractures shot through each thin slice of wood, and, on two or three, entire chunks had chipped off. Charles wondered if it needed to be redone or if the plaster would keep the wall from falling into their bedroom.

"Hey, Marty," Mingus said, his voice spiced with nerve. "Are those the ones that you were hammering a moment ago?" He pointed to the chest-high rows that Charles inspected.

"Those are them."

"Well, you're walling in a window."

For a moment, Marty stood in stunned silence, squinting across the room at his handiwork.

"He's right," Charles added, his hand patting a stud that spanned the wall at his waist. "Windows are going in here."

"Well, that's obscene. Who needs so many windows in a bedroom?" He reached into his overalls and scratched something. "Seems like a waste of money."

"Oh, I know a window man in Madison," Mingus

said. "I deliver to the bar across the street from his shop once a week, and I made a deal with him: Nine windows for a couple of barrels. He said they were leftovers that were never picked up."

Marty neither nodded at Mingus nor uttered in acknowledgment. Instead, he inspected the room silently, walking his eyes along the walls where windows would be installed. "Still seems obscene," he said. "You want the whole city to see you? Every passerby?" He twisted his head toward Charles, though kept his body square to the window. "Maybe you, but not my daughter."

"Elizabeth told me that she always wanted a bedroom that overlooked the neighborhood," Charles said, an innocent smile cracking across his face. "She said that, if she must live in a town like this, then she'd want to wake up early and watch the sun rise over all the rooftops. This is my try at fulfilling her wish."

Marty eyed Charles incredulously, then retreated toward the corner where he was working. "Well, she always had more looks than brains," he said.

"I'm sorry?" Charles asked. He felt his skin tighten against his skull, felt it squeeze sweat out of his pores.

"She's about as wise as this whole window idea," Marty said. "And I'd know. I only raised the poor thing. Between her and you making decisions about this house, it's a wonder we're on the second floor."

A tremor radiated through Charles, reverberated in the chambers in his chest, and spread to the tips of his fingers. But he couldn't tell if Marty's comments had caused the quake, or if it was physical confirmation that it was time to confront his father-in-law—and far sooner than he had expected. Beneath him, he felt the beams sag, saw the shade of the front room and the basement's black below it.

Marty chuckled as he picked up a lath from the pile. "Sometimes I consider the brains between you two," he murmured between grunts, "and think to myself, 'No wonder that little girl's such a ding-bat. Look at her parents.'"

Charles felt rubbery but tense as if he'd had a too-strong cup of coffee. "You know, Marty, it's impolite to talk that way about a woman, especially to her husband." He spoke without consulting his thoughts or considering his squirming insides. "And I'd appreciate it if you never spoke that way about my daughter again." The hammer shook in his hand, its loose head rattling.

The quills of Marty's beard thickened, swept themselves into an amused grin. "What is this?" he said. His shoulders became rocky beneath his coveralls.

"I just feel like we'll get a lot more done if you knock off the comments," Charles said. "This is my house, my property, and I deserve your respect. *We* deserve your respect."

"You'll get my respect when you deserve it, and I'll let you know when you have," Marty said, his cool, amused tone evaporating with the midday heat. "And, I'll have you know, I'm allowed to say what I want about whomever I want, especially my own family."

"Not when you're in my house."

Marty pushed a dry puff of air from the back of his throat. "You call this a house? This slapdash attempt at a mansion? There are stables in this neighborhood built better. Chicken coops. And you want to attach your name to this?"

"Hey, Marty," Mingus said in a tip-toe. "There's no need to get angry. He's only asking that you knock off the comments. That's a reasonable request."

"Who *is* this clown?" Marty said, sticking his thumb toward Mingus. "Charles, did he put you up to this? That why you're tryin' to look all high and mighty?"

Fear churned inside Charles, tossing his reason around like a carrot coin in a stew. But some awareness boiled to the top above the turbulence: Charles had put Marty on the defensive by simply demanding what he was owed.

"Look, Marty, I'm not trying to seem high and mighty," he said. "We got a house to build, and I'm thinking it'd be easier to get the job done if we got along and treated each other with respect."

"And what if I don't wanna give you my respect?"

Charles swallowed back what bubbled up his throat. "Well, I suppose I'll have to respectfully ask you to step aside so we can finish without you. But why wouldn't you—"

"Hey, we don't want you out of the picture," Mingus interrupted. "We want your help, but we want it because you want to help us and be on our team."

But Marty's intimidated air had already dissipated. "That's what I've been waiting to hear," he said, a lucid sparkle in his eyes. He repeated it as his meaty hand patted his son-in-law's shoulder, then again as he turned and spidered the beams toward the bedroom's door frame. Charles listened to joists creak as he crept across them, heard the pops of his heels hitting the steps, felt the front door open and shut and shake the house.

Peeking over the split laths, Charles watched Marty's stout body barrel away, summer reflecting white off his bare scalp, the hammer still hanging in his hand. Charles wondered if he'd ever see his hammer again. Marty's parting remark bounced around his brain. *"That's what I've been waiting to hear,"* he repeated. *Why was he waiting to hear me dismiss him?* He thought about how he had gone from defensive—like a frightened, cornered raccoon—to relieved in the span of a sentence. The observation weighed on his conscience like a stack of stones, afraid to touch and topple the delicate tower, afraid it might collapse on its own. He bit his sagging mustache and wiped the sweat off his brow with a sweaty arm.

Mingus clawed at a damaged lath with his hammer, ripping them from the studs. "That was weird," he muttered, cracking the thin wood off the wall.

"Yeah," Charles replied.

"I suppose that was easier than I thought it would be," Mingus added. "Hey, it was the right thing to do. You deserve respect."

"Yeah," Charles repeated, but images of Elizabeth flickered in his head—her desperate and frantic tears, begging her father to stay; her desolate collapse onto the kitchen floor, which will likely frighten Rebecca; her rage, which may compel her to storm the house by mid-afternoon if only to scream and cry and kick at Charles. Or, worse, she may hide at home. Each image flashed like lightning in his mind, saturated his soul with sadness.

"It'll be easier this way," Mingus insisted, cracking another of the room's ribs. "Now, we'll have the house done by the end of summer for sure."

"Yeah," Charles mumbled but wondered if he had that much time.

Barbara Farmer
May 10th, 1942

The Rock was silent, except for the wail of some lonely island bird. The breeze swept across the landscape, rattling the skeletal trees; sometimes the ashen sand stippled their trunks. But no leaves rustled, and no grasses sighed. Even the waves, which smashed the nearby beach, seemed dampened by the distance and grey haze hovering over the island.

This silence startled Barbara as she listened for some hint that her husband—or anyone—had found safety. She took small, attentive steps down what once was a road, maneuvering around the stones and boulders and chunks of earth that impeded her path, blown there by a mortar, maybe. Around her, the remnants of a forest stared in accusing silence like still, starving prisoners; she imagined them in their former magnificence, exploding with leaves, glowing green, then imagined them swaying in flames.

The road opened to a space flattened by concrete and surrounded by walls that kept the surrounding hillside out. Cannons squatted four-square in this pit, enormous and aimed in every direction, as if its operators were surrounded or overwhelmed. Around this pit, more bare tree trunks rose into the sky like plumes of smoke. Barbara wandered subconsciously between the cannons; for some reason, it felt safer.

The silence smothered her like a wool blanket. *How can an entire military base be so quiet?* she wondered. *Where is everyone? Where is John?* Barbara backed toward one of the cannons to steady herself but a sound on the hill above her startles her—a rustle, like someone stepping into a patch of leaves. "John?" she said, turning towards it.

Her eyes slipped from the hillside to the concrete barricades that held it back; something scribbled on the wall cut through the mineral and rust and rain, sparking her curiosity. Another rustle interrupted the silence, but Barbara ignored it as the scribble became clear: The letters "JF" scratched into the wall as if by a stone. *John's initials?* she though, her heart wincing in her chest. *Did John write this?*

Suddenly, the rustling wrapped around her, ricocheting between the blackened bones of the forest. Barbara spun and backed herself against the wall. Voices climbed out of the rustling—first one, gargling commands in an unknown language; then another swelling with excitement—but the artillery pit remained empty, the surrounding hillside still. She pressed her hand over her husband's initials, hoping it would afford her courage or clarity, but all she felt was the concrete's stucco, clammy in the tropical humidity. The voices rose in volume, and the rustling became boots on concrete, but nothing crawled from the forest, and no one marched toward her. She squeezed her tear-lined eyelids shut. *This is how they must've got him*, Barbara realized. *They were invisible.*

She jumped at the snap of a gunshot, the bullet

cracking the wall beside her, the concrete quivering beneath her hand. A tangled, wild string of syllables whipped above the boot stomps, the rustling, the clicks of readied firearms, and then she heard a second snap.

Barbara forced open her eyes and became instantly aware of the sweat on her shoulders and neck, the weight of her head, her heart beating against the bedspread. Her gaze drifted to the bedside table, on which an unlit lamp stood at attention beside a clucking alarm clock. Her wedding ring curled at their feet, its band dull in the mid-morning gloom. Usually, it was the first thing Barbara reached for; she would slide it night-cooled onto her finger, and feel instantly comforted, safe, whole. But as she stared at it from bed, Corregidor's silence still haunting her, she couldn't help but wonder.

Am I still married? Does this ring mean anything?

Beneath the bedroom, footsteps stamped on the porch, and the front door creaked open. *Oh no*, she thought, looking at the clock. *Is it ten o'clock already? Are they back from church so soon?* She traced the traffic that traveled into the house—the kicked-off heels hitting the corner where they kept the shoes; the front door closing, sending shivers through the whole house; Anita's melodious laugh dancing up the stairs and stubbing its toes on Barbara's bedroom door.

She sat up in bed and assessed the light filtering through the steely clouds, the still-budding tree branches outside the windows that surrounded her. She tried to tune into the conversation beneath her—distinguished Joy's composed, consistent tone from Anita's, which seemed to frolic through the house like a foal—but could only make out the firmest phrases, like, "We've been worried," and, "Stays in bed," and, "Since the Philippine Islands fell." But then Barbara detected a third woman's voice, one that sashayed through the house quietly, delicately, as if she was listening as she spoke.

Before she could guess who their guest was, she heard stocking feet slipping up the stairs, then sliding down the hallway. "Barbara," Anita's voice sparkled outside her bedroom door. "Are you decent?"

"No," she said, tugging the comforter onto her in case her housemate barged in.

"Well, get ready and come down then. We're making a pot of coffee. Plus, there's someone here who wants to meet you."

"Who is it?" Barbara barked. Then, reconsidering her stiff tone, she sighed and fell back onto the bed. "I don't feel well. Can't I stay in bed this morning?"

"You can't. I'll give you five minutes, then I'm coming in and dragging you out of bed with or without a robe."

Barbara waited until her roommate was halfway downstairs to swing her feet onto the floor. Strands of mousy hair tickled her chin; she wanted to tie it back, but the thought of finding and fiddling with a ribbon irritated her. She paused beneath the doorframe and turned to the ring on the nightstand, suddenly aware of her unweighted hand dangling on the knob. A memory swelled inside her mind— of the stale consignment shop where, her hand knotted in John's, she had spotted the ring in a display case sitting beside a set of brass buttons. Shaking the happy, hopeless thought out of her head, she wandered toward the stairs.

"There she is!" Anita sang, signaling Barbara's entrance into the kitchen.

"How are you doing this morning, sleepyhead?" Joy asked, blowing into the ceramic mug hovering beneath her mouth.

"I've been better." Barbara stretched for the kettle on the stove and carried it to the nearby counter where someone had set out her mug. Only as coffee slid into her cup did she notice that the shadow on the wall behind Joy was a woman, her skin pale against her raven suit coat and skirt. Barbara kinked her lips into her friendliest smile considering her disposition, but concentrated on filling her mug.

"Barbara, this is Lucy LaFontaine," Joy said. "She goes to our church. I hope it's okay that we invited her over for coffee."

"She's a psychic!" Anita chimed.

Lucy climbed out from the corner. "Well, I prefer the word 'medium,' but 'psychic' is fine," she said, holding her tiny hand out to Barbara. "How do you do, Barbara? I've heard a lot about you from your friends."

Barbara accepted her hand but noted how flush her own fingers looked within Lucy's. "It's nice to meet you," she replied, trying to determine why the woman was dressed for a funeral. Her hat—like a small, black satin cake—matched the rest of her mournful outfit; a fog of tulle floated from it around her curled, cast bronze hair. Still, Barbara thought she looked beautiful—elegant, almost regal—and regretted stumbling downstairs barefoot and in her housecoat.

"Last night, after you went to bed," Anita said, "we

decided we wanted to—"

"*You* decided," Joy interrupted. "I allowed it."

"Fine. I decided that we wanted to try a talking board." Her smile stretched into something between embarrassed and sad. "We figured maybe we could find out how the boys are doing."

"*You* figured," Joy corrected her. "For me, it's more for the fun of it."

Anita glared at Joy before turning back to Barbara. "Lucy brought hers for us to use," she said. "Come and look!"

As Anita steered Barbara by the elbow out of the kitchen, Lucy followed, her Mary Janes knocking softly, almost silently, on the floor beneath her. "It was sort of strange bringing the board into church with me," she snickered, "but nothing caught on fire and no one was struck by lightning, so I figured God allowed it."

But Barbara winced at the sight of the board laid out on the dining room table, four chairs circling it ceremoniously. Its warped, blonde wood was marked with black letters and numbers and innocent shapes—moons and circled stars—all of which seemed enigmatic and petrifying. The word "Ouija" twirled near the top in a black scroll, but Barbara was more disturbed by the words "good" and "bye" placed at the bottom.

Lucy snickered suddenly, head slanted, lips split, eyeing a corner where the crown moulding met. "Goodness," she said. "Whoever lived here before you was very unhappy."

"You can see them?" Anita asked, her smile wild with curiosity.

"No," Lucy said, still listening. "I mean, yes—sometimes as shadows or shapes. But, more often, they make their presence known without being seen. This one, he doesn't like me laughing at him." She paused, pressed her lips together, and aimed her forehead at the floor. "He's showing me why he's so sad."

"Why?" Joy wondered, stretching herself across the kitchen doorway.

Lucy's amusement melted away, her gaze glazing with sadness. Barbara saw how small she suddenly seemed—a petite, black speck in a room adorned in gold oak. "None of you have a daughter, do you?" Lucy asked, then swung her head and shoulders like she was shaking something off of her. "You know what? Never mind. Sometimes, I have to remind myself that I can't help them all, right?"

Anita nodded as if she understood.

"Besides, we're here for other reasons, right?" Lucy concluded, casting a kind smile toward Barbara, slipping silently into one of the chairs. Anita and Joy sat on either side of her, but Barbara stood near the doorway to the living room. Sure, she was curious about the board and whether it'd work, but dreaded the thought of what she'd discover. Her ribs squeezed her lungs, but she forced a smile hoping that her concrete cheeks and vaulting brow would convey the excitement this situation called for.

"So, how does this work?" Joy asked.

"We put our fingers on this pointer," Lucy explained, holding up a wooden teardrop with felted feet. "It's called a planchette. But you're not supposed to put weight on it. Just touch it as lightly as you can without losing contact. And then we just ask the spirits questions. They should spell out their answers."

"And we can ask them anything?" Anita asked.

"Well, we've got to be careful," Lucy said. "Don't ask any questions that you don't want to know the answer to. And don't put too much thought into the responses."

"Just don't ask them any questions about me," Barbara said, her arms knotted across her robe. "I'll just watch for now."

"Oh, Barbara," Joy said. "This is just for fun. None of this is—" She stopped herself and peeked at Lucy, whose serenity reassured her. "It's just for laughs."

"Just the same, I'll sit out for a while."

Lucy closed her eyes, dropped her chin to her chest, and started whispering to herself in serious syllables. Barbara comprehended only a couple of sentences— something about the white light, about the highest vibration, about angels and God and good energy—but found herself too startled by Lucy's invocation to pay close attention. *Is this a spell?* Barbara wondered. *Or a prayer to protect us? What might we need protection from?* Her concerns were confirmed by Anita and Joy, who eyed the talking board—and then one another—with hesitation.

Just as suddenly, Lucy lifted her head up and said, "Okay. Ready to try it?"

If Anita's fingers pounced on the planchette like they were a litter of puppies, Joy's hands followed like a cautious mother and father. Lucy pancaked her palms onto the tabletop and let her eyelids droop. When the planchette started to slide, the girls gasped. It jolted twice toward Joy before slipping freely around the board on its felt feet.

"Anita, stop moving it!" Joy yelped, her brow lined, her jaw taut.

"I'm not! I'm not moving it!"

They squealed as it swept from one side of the board to the other, then pulled Anita by the arms as it slid onto the table.

"Anita, you're pushing it off the board! Stop it!"

"I'm not moving it, I swear!"

Barbara's heart bucked behind her clenched chest. She steadied herself by pressing her hand on the wall behind her, letting the plaster cool her palm. Her posture reminded her of her recent dream, though—of clammy cement; of simmering artillery; of an abandoned, burning Corregidor—she pulled away like the wall was on fire.

"So, what do you want to ask?" Lucy said.

"How about, 'Who are we talking to?'" Anita suggested. "Would that be a good question to start with?"

As if answering, the planchette slid back onto the board and landed between letters. It rested there until Lucy repeated the question, her voice slow and patient, after which it whipped to and from letter to letter.

"Becky?" Joy read.

"I don't know any Beckys," Anita said. "Do you, Barbara?"

Barbara jerked her head from side to side, her bones cracking beneath the tension, her eyes wide with fear. It wasn't the talking board; it was the way skeletal trees rattled outside the window, the way the grey haze hovered over Eighth Street.

"I had a great aunt named Becky," Joy said, her fingers stiff on the planchette. "But I didn't know her very well, so I doubt it's her."

"How are our boys?" Anita asked, dumping the words onto the table as if they were bags of flour. But the pointer was already dragging their arms across the board. Anita read it aloud: "I… I am?"

Something snapped within Barbara when Anita read the finished message: I am sorry. "No," she whispered at first, pleaded, then repeated. "No, no, no."

I am sorry, she thought. *He's gone. Your dream. It said so.*

"He's gone," Barbara repeated. "No, no, no." She felt her palm press against the cool plaster behind her, then tumbled into the cold space between the studs, into the smoldering humidity of the Rock.

I am sorry, she thought. *He's gone.*

She heard her roommates mumble, watched them pull their hands from the planchette, reach toward her, but these sights and sounds echoed against the wall on which her husband's initials were scratched.

"I am sorry," she repeated. "It said so."

The wall gave way to Anita's mink-like eyebrows, reared in concern, and Joy's concrete voice crumbling. "Barbara!" she shouted, "Barbara, come back to us! Are you okay?" Lucy hovered behind them.

Barbara blinked as she tried to push herself away from the wall. "I'm okay," she said. "I'm fine. I'm sorry." Tears streaked her cheeks, and she wiped them away with her housecoat's sleeve.

"You really spooked us," Anita answered. "You

started saying, 'No, no, no,' to the talking board and, and—"

"You fainted, hon," Joy said. "You fell against the wall. Does your head hurt?"

Barbara rubbed the back of her head with the cup of her hand. "A little."

"Oh, Lucy," Anita whined. "You don't think it was the ghost that did this, do you?" She didn't notice Joy's crinkled nose and cold, scolding stare, but Barbara did.

Lucy kinked her neck over her shoulder, as if she was watching a bird out the window, though Barbara didn't see any. "No," she answered. "They can't do that." She swallowed a long breath, then listened to the silent, absent sparrows, the strands of her hair drifting in the draft-less dining room. "And this one wouldn't."

Lucy's obscure sentences reminded Barbara of Becky's answer, those four knelling syllables: I am sorry. The haze of Corregidor having momentarily cleared itself out of her mind, she wondered what the message really meant, whether the spirit intended to say John is dead or if Barbara had simply interpreted it that way. *You're silly*, she told herself. *Stop overthinking things.* Barbara yearned to return to her quilt, to the calm of her bed, away from Lucy and Becky and their talking board. "I'm sorry," she said, trying to climb the wall. "I think I'm going to lie down upstairs. I can't—"

"Sit down, hon," Joy insisted. "Take a break."

Anita's hands massaged Barbara's biceps and shoulders, tacked her in the corner between the wall and the wooden floor. "You scared us, babe," she said. "Why not relax until a little color comes back, huh?"

"No, I need to get out of here," Barbara said,

pushing herself from a floor that seemed to give beneath her. When Lucy reached out her hand, Barbara nabbed it and let the tiny medium tug her back onto her feet. The momentum made her mind fizzy, spun her like a toy top; suddenly overwhelmed by the centripetal force of the room, she clung to Lucy, who somehow had the power to keep her on her feet.

When the walls stopped swerving, Barbara realized her hand was inches from Lucy's face, and that the medium was scrutinizing her palm. "Oh, sweetie," she whispered. "Your lifelines, they're intertwined. He'll be back." She looked up at Barbara with brimming blue eyes, which glowed against her wintry skin. "Don't worry, sweetie. He'll be back. You're still married."

Ten minutes later, burrowed beneath the safety of her bedsheets, Barbara inspected her wedding ring—the tiny stone twinkling in the sunless daylight; the waxy band, dulled by a decade's worth of wear by whoever bore it before her—and pondered Lucy's prediction. *Your lifelines*, she said, *they're intertwined.* Below her, the reverent silence from which she departed had flared into laughter and amusement. Anita's shrieks shook the windows in their panes, and each was followed by Joy's jubilant shushes; Barbara even heard Lucy giggle once or twice.

You're still married. She pushed the ring onto her finger. It felt comfortable, familiar. Only with it nestled against her knuckle did she feel like it was safe to fall asleep once again.

She couldn't; the beam creaking above her head kept her awake.

Becky McLaughlin
November 13th, 2011

The basement's inviting silence, dry and grey, swirled around Becky. To her, it felt like floating in the cosmos, in a limitless dim that held all the universe's light within its cobblestone perimeter. She inhaled a lump of air, swallowed it like a vitamin, and crinkled her nose. "I know it's a little musty," she said. "I guess I've gotten used to it."

Frances stacked her weight onto one leg as she stood in the center of the space, vignetted by its darker, distant corners. Ill-lit by rows of dusty bulbs, her new penny hair shimmered and floated on dark shadows like a wig. "This is it?" she asked, inspecting the floorboards above her head. "This is what you wanted to show me?" A confused frown squirmed on her face.

"I guess," Becky said. "I vacuumed up all the bugs and cobwebs and stuff, so it's a lot nicer than it was. And I brought down some speakers so I can listen to music when I'm working." She pointed the tip of her ear toward the wooden workbench, which she determined had most likely been somebody's desk. Whatever it was, she had personalized it. Colorful, ragged ribbons from magazines had been Mod Podged in harlequin zebra stripes along the bench's most visible haunch. On top, a stack of magazines squatted between two tiny speakers, and a pair of scissors waited beside two pitted X-Acto knives, set out like surgical instruments.

"What stuff do you work on down here?" Frances asked. She pulled her phone from her pocket and smudged her thumb across it.

"Homework," Becky lied, then blended it with some truth. "Mostly, I just hide from my mom and Tom. They never come down here."

When Becky focused her attention on her friend, the walls surrounding Frances withdrew into the darkness of her periphery, and the ceiling lifted into infinity, leaving Frances to dab at her device between lines of disembodied lights in a sort of boundless oblivion. She knew this was a prank that the lights and shadows played together, but she appreciated the spooky display and wished Frances would look up so they could enjoy it together.

"I mean, I guess it's cool," Frances finally said, her phone reflected in her distant eyes.

"Yeah, I thought that this could be where we hang out," Becky said, watching her words disappear in the surrounding darkness. "Sometimes. Not, like, all the time."

"Yeah, maybe."

"It'd be cool to get a couch or something," Becky said, aware that she was speaking to herself. "I don't know where I'd get one, though. Or how to get it down here."

Becky had been excited to share this special space with her best friend, begged her to come by if only for five minutes so Frances too could feel its safety and electricity, the vitality that the place seemed to possess. But, as she watched the walls return, as the ceiling dropped back into its place above her head, Becky realized that this basement would have to remain her secret.

"Shoot, I have to go," Frances said, looking up from her device. "My mom's waiting outside. She's my ride to work." Stuffing her phone back into her pocket, she stepped toward the staircase.

"Okay," Becky said following her, but stopped halfway up.

"Sorry," Frances said at the summit. The crystal door knob rattled in her hand, then glinted in the gaudy noontime daylight. "I'll text you when I'm off," she added, the basement door clicking behind her.

Becky stood on the steps, stewing in desolation and allowing the compact space to embrace her, console her. Obviously, the basement didn't impress Frances as she had hoped it would.

She studied a line of grime smeared across the plaster wall; she attributed the marks to the absence of a railing and wondered how many hands had braced themselves as they bent down these stairs. Taking advantage of her unexpected solitude, her fingers tickled the smudges as she hopped from step to step.

She heard his voice before she saw him. "You found it," he said in swift syllables.

Momentum drew her down the steps despite her fear, despite the transparent hairs that lifted off the back of her neck, so Becky couldn't help but see him perched on the stool behind her workspace as she landed on the cement foundation. Her instincts told her to close her eyes, to escape up the stairs, but space swelled all around her, bolstered her as it had the week before. This time, she recognized it, understood what it was doing, tried to trust it.

Frozen at the foot of the steps, she stared at him, then mustered the courage to mutter, "What?"

"You found it," he repeated.

When Becky looked at him, he became difficult to see—his lines faded, stretched too fine, seemed to blur into the background—but his shape sharpened each time she looked away, enough so she could discern his smooth hair, seemingly styled by butter knife; the bold and cumbersome rims of his spectacles; and the sad satisfaction in his smile. When she concentrated, she realized that she saw him better in her mind. She knew what this meant, and the thought made her heels numb. "Who are you?" she asked.

"Just another guy who lived here," he answered. His voice hung from him like something enormous and worthless.

"Why are you in my basement?"

"That question has a complicated answer," he said. "Ask me another."

Becky knew he was kidding, could see it in the dimples that dented his otherwise clean cheeks, but couldn't dam the flood of her curiosity. "What's your name?" she asked. "Are you dead? How'd you die? Why do I see dead people?"

A laugh bubbled up to the brim of his throat but remained sequestered within. "Okay, never mind," he said. "I guess don't really have answers for you."

"Not even your name?"

He shrugged. "That sort of stuff is inconsequential,

it turns out." He twisted on the stool to crack his spine. Becky noticed that the plaid on his unbuttoned shirt matched the jade accents on the otherwise white tee-shirt beneath; on it, the word Hum leaned within two twisting tails of a descending star. His white Converse All-Stars curled over one of the stool's rungs.

"What do you want?" Becky asked, resisting the desire to shrivel into her tattered hoodie.

"Okay, well, that one's complicated too," he said, poking his glasses onto his face, "but I can try to answer it." His fingers tangled, wove a mat that hung between his wrists, then he sighed.

The silence stretched too long, swelled until it pressurized the basement. Becky felt it squeeze her bones. "Are you going to tell me?"

He sighed a second time then stared across the vacant concrete at the cellar door. "Okay. So, first of all, I'm always here, so it's not like I can leave or anything anyway. And it's not like I *want* anything really. I guess I've just been waiting for you to find it. I was hoping you would, and then you did, so I thought I'd say something, since I knew you'd hear me if I did." He heaved his heavy eyes from the door onto her, and Becky felt his gaze push against her. "It took me until college to find it, and you're just, fourteen, fifteen? That's so awesome."

"Find what?" she asked.

As his smirk steeled, Becky noticed that he became easier to see. "Well, this place, for one." He swept his open palm through the air, his wrist flashing into view before disappearing back into the shadows beside his body. "But that's not really what I mean. This basement is just a basement, you know?"

"Is it?" Becky asked.

But the man only snickered; as his glasses hopped down his nose, he let his smirk ripen into a full, firm fruit. His gaze snapped back to the cellar door, where he held it for a few heartbeats before he drew it back toward Becky's wooden workspace. "I like what you did with this, by the way," he said, his fingers tracing the ragged strips of color. "It looks cool."

"Thanks," Becky said. Her thin arms wound around her body ivy-like.

"You know, I built this thing," he said. "Bought the wood and everything. Painted it. We were stupid and built it outside, so my friend and I had to figure out a way to get it inside because it wouldn't fit through the door. I'm glad it's getting some good use now."

He continued, but Becky barely listened. Questions bounced around her brain—about him, about her, about death and this basement that was apparently just a basement. They cracked at her palate and tried to enter her mouth; when they broke through, she concentrated on flicking them back with the tip her tongue until she noticed him pause in her periphery. "What?" she said, her mouth full.

"I said you should cover the whole thing. You know, with strips of paper?" He nodded toward Becky's workspace. "There's something really cool going on here, the way you transformed this thing, altered its essence without really changing its function. Sort of speaks the malleability of objects—of people too, and of meaning, you know?"

Becky's lips puckered and her freckles slid into the creases that cracked across her face.

"You should see your face," he grinned. "Sorry. I went to art school. My brain just thinks like that, I guess. Seriously, though. From an aesthetic standpoint, it just looks cool. You should keep doing it."

Her eyes climbed the workspace, hopped from shred to shred—one pink, speckled texture seemed almost reptilian; the next, white and frothy, reminded her of a waterfall; the third, like tousled lemon feathers, made her shoulders squirm. She couldn't remember where she ripped them from, or why she chose them, or even what they were pictures of, but she loved how each patch of color made her feel something different, and she loved abandoning herself to these swatches, to the process of tearing them from something found, to the innocent violence of it all. They reminded her of the day she accidentally discovered this means of release, the same day she discovered this space— by following a song that throbbed beneath her bedroom, behind the basement, to the bottom of the stairs.

"Wait," she said, her spine taut and alert. "You lured me down here. You were playing music."

"'*Lured?*'" he responded, grinning again. "Like I'm *luring* children into my gingerbread house to cook them in my oven or something?"

"But you did. You wanted me down here."

Above her, Becky sensed a body tramping across the kitchen toward the basement door, then the crystal door knob rattling. "Becky, that you?" Misty croaked from the top of the stairs. "The fuck you doing down there?"

Without thinking, Becky popped her head into the stairwell; it occurred to her immediately that she could have hid and her mother would have never known. "I'm looking for an earring in the dryer," she said. "It's been missing for a week."

"Who were you talking to?" From the foot of the stairs, Misty was a silhouette, the afternoon sun curling around her.

"Myself," she answered.

"Okay, well, I'm heading to work."

"Didn't you just get back from work? How long have you been home?"

Misty's sigh rolled slowly down the steps, tumbled into Becky like a paunchy bag of garbage. "I don't have time to recap my entire day for you. Just bring up the fucking laundry when you're done."

When the door closed behind her, Becky realized that she felt more anxious talking to her mother than the dead man sitting on her stool. When she returned her attention to the workstation, though, he was nowhere to be found. "Hello?" she asked the musty basement quietly so her mother wouldn't hear.

"I didn't play the music," his voice floated somewhere above her.

Becky's soul flinched inside her skin. She turned to find him sitting two-thirds of the way up the stairs, wrists resting on his knees. "Jesus," she said, catching her breath, her hand slapping her stony chest. "What'd you say?"

"That music," he said, "it wasn't me. It was the house. It has a way of…well, it's sort of hard to explain."

"That and everything else," Becky murmured. "So are you going to follow me around now? Are you my spirit guide or something? Is that how this works?"

"No, I'll leave you alone," he said, "assuming you keep at this whole collage thing."

Becky found him harder to see on the stairs, his face fading so far into the shadows that she couldn't make out his glasses, but it occurred to her how unafraid she was at that moment. "So that means no more surprising me when I'm down here, okay?"

"Hey, this space is yours now," he said. "I wouldn't dare."

"And no more reappearing behind me."

"Sure."

"And no more knocking on my bedroom door yelling for me to let you in."

In the darkness of the stairs, Becky struggled to interpret his expression, which blurred between confusion and contemplation. "Oh," he said after a moment. "That wasn't me. That was the other guy."

Becky's knees slipped in their sockets and the hairs on her neck reared row by row, creeping down her shoulders and the backs of her arms. "The other guy?"

"Yeah. He's not a happy camper."

Preston Assad
March 24th, 1996

Outside, perched on a branch that bent beneath her, a bird unspooled her song. The melody—reminding Preston of his mother's piercing, forgivable laugh—reverberated through the otherwise silent neighborhood.

His living room, however, wasn't silent. Five sleeping strangers, strewn across the floor beneath flabby blankets and sleeping bags, wheezed in different tempos and time signatures. Maryanne stretched beside him on the couch, her chin on his shoulder. Preston listened to the rhythm of her slow, content breath as it stroked the length of his neck, meditating for a moment on the weight of her palm on his belly where it ran along the ledge of his ribs.

Preston's mind slipped into a memory of the previous night—the basement stuffed with spectators, kids of all ages, reeling and rolling together in a turbulent, boisterous stew; and the band, glittering beneath bare tungsten bulbs, became incandescent smears that rendered each surrounding spirit a living silhouette; and the kids on the stairs, their legs stretching down the steps, their essence scribbled on the soles of their nodding sneakers; and the air thick with melody and a cleansing, kinetic steam. The show was a success by every measure, maybe because it was a Saturday night, or maybe because spring was finally softening Wisnago's bones, or maybe because the band was bigger, with a recent release on a major label and a song on the radio.

When the house finally drained, when the band unwrapped their bedrolls and claimed their corners, they had insisted that Preston sleep in the living room with them, that he take the couch—as a thank you, they laughed, for hosting them. Preston had not expected Maryanne to stay, let alone land beside him on the sofa, but she had nuzzled her way under his arm before he could even exhibit his approval. All night, he had felt her hair tickle his face and her tee-shirt's peach fuzz beneath his fingertips. Occasionally, her knees would slip around either side of his thigh and squeeze.

He had tumbled into unconsciousness too quickly to consider where he was and with whom. But when he woke up, he smelled the orchard blooming in Maryanne's hair and didn't think about his staggered spine or the static teeming through his hand.

When one of the band members woke—the singer, who had coiled himself onto the wide lap of a chair— he peeked over the lumps of his sleeping bag at Preston, then sat himself up and stared at the still-monochromatic neighborhood for a minute. To Preston, whose glasses were out of reach, the singer resembled a foggy ghost rising from his grave. "Got coffee?" he murmured. With his free arm, Preston pointed toward the kitchen and watched the singer step lifelessly out of the room, his thin legs swinging loose in jeans that seemed too roomy.

Within minutes, the house was heavy again with

sound, however light. The rhythm of respiration was overwhelmed by a slow but chaotic crescendo—the clack of cabinets opening and closing, the shush of the sink, the silent boom of his stocking feet—then the anguished gurgle of the coffeemaker, its death rattle, succumbing suddenly to a peace that Preston often longed for during the work week and rarely appreciated during the weekend.

But, as Preston listened to the house, something felt funny. He buried his anxiety into the cushions beneath him until he heard a metallic clatter—like the clash of cookie sheets—and slipped out from under Maryanne, making eye contact with the singer in the kitchen, whose spooked expression only stoked his concern. Preston didn't pause, didn't grab his glasses; he scampered toward the basement door worried that something had fallen, was broken, or worse.

He maneuvered down the stairs instinctively, but his brain woke up halfway to the bottom. *Hold on*, he thought. *What if that noise was an intruder? What if you're racing into danger?* Still, his bare toes dripped down each step, splashed onto the basement's cool cement foundation.

From the foot of the stairs, Preston could only perceive the streaks of silver light squeezing around the open cellar door. As he crept toward the center of the space, the air becoming cooler, he determined what made the noise—a cymbal safe flipped like a turtle onto its shell, still tottering, having seemingly slipped from a monolithic bass cabinet. Preston remembered resting the safe against a pyramid of drums hours before as the band packed up, though he noticed they were nowhere in sight. "Oh fuck," he muttered.

He had enough time to take stock of what else was missing—a bass amp and two guitar heads, a silver-faced guitar cabinet, and rows of guitar cases, which he hoped the band had packed into their trailer the previous night; but also his own PA speakers and subs, microphones plucked from headless stands, XLR cables slack around their ankles—before a silhouette stepped down into the cellar. A hood drooped over his head. Bony shoulders failed to fill his sweatshirt's sleeves.

"Can I help you?" Preston said, his arms trembling above his elbows.

The silhouette paused, then breached the cellar doorway. He seemed taller than Preston, but not tall. Beneath his hood, Preston could barely make out his stippled chin and oozing lips. "Just picking up my gear," he said, bending toward the cymbal safe, his scrawny talon stretching out of his sweatshirt sleeve.

"That's not yours. Don't touch it."

"Fuck off, asshole," the voice squawked, his sharp nose peeking from his hood. "Let me take my gear and I'll leave you alone."

"You're not taking anything," Preston said, dizzy and tense. He strode toward the silhouette, who straightened himself and reached into the front pocket of his sweatshirt. The gesture was slow and deliberate, menacing.

"I said fuck off, okay?" the silhouette said. "You don't want to fuck with me." He sneered at Preston, his eyes black specks surrounded by white, and seemed to tighten his grip on whatever he hid in his hoodie while he stretched for the cymbals. "I'm just going to take this and I'm gone."

"Preston, is everything okay?" someone shouted down the stairs.

Preston replied, "No," without pulling his stare from the silhouette. "I need your help."

Behind him, bodies careened down the stairs. Preston turned to find the band puddled at the bottom, and Maculey all legs in his boxers, and Maryanne peeking from where the ceiling met the wall. "What the hell?" the pot-bellied bass player asked, shirtless.

"What's going on?" the singer said, his eyes lean, his teeth visible and keen.

Relieved, Preston felt his fear drain down the back of his throat. He turned back to the silhouette with a clearer mind, prepared to back this bastard out the door, but was startled to find his face retreating into his hood; his irises scraping the bottoms of his eyelids; his lower lip peeling down his chin. Tense wire arms rattled in his hoodie. His black-speckled jeans flared around his coiled knees. And then he pulled the pistol from his front pocket.

Maculey flattened himself onto the stairs and breathed an obscenity, but no one else moved. The revolver wavered at the end of the silhouette's arm, which bent from the weapon's weight, and Preston heard every breath, every blink. As his hands rode the air that drifted upward and away from this moment, he heard one of the band members behind him say, "Take whatever you want, man."

"Yeah, just stay cool. Nobody needs to get hurt."

"Sit down," the silhouette said, his voice a vicious calm. "All of you, sit. You too," he added pointing to Maryanne, who dropped from the ceiling to the steps.

As Preston deflated onto the cold floor, he heard the sound of folding legs and palms popping against the foundation, but he refused to take his eyes off the face in front of him. *Memorize it,* some voice shoved through the commotion in his mind. *Cops will be here soon, and they will want to know every detail about this guy.* Past the pistol's nervous tic, though, Preston saw only a lump of a face, obscured by an anxious shadow. He noted the grey sweatshirt again, streaked with dust or sweat, and the flecks of tar that hopped from his sneakers onto jeans that jutted up his leg like a rock face. But he knew that, without his glasses, he wouldn't be able to describe anything more than a silhouette.

So Preston stared, studied the intruder's body unfolded into something wide and thin; his bouncing breath, and how it smacked heavier and heavier; that his magenta face dimmed, turned the color of a cherry shake, then vanilla. Preston wondered if words could be enough to send him back up the cellar steps. "Dude, just put the gun down," he said, his voice a touch too rigid.

But the world cut white for an instant, a blink that whitewashed Preston's perception, and he felt his body blow backward. Behind his closed eyes, he recorded what it could: The shock of the cool basement floor beneath his hands, the acidic ghost twisting into his nose, whatever nipped at his abdomen—*A bee sting,* his brain misinterpreted—but it was the whine that shredded him apart, the highest note on the brightest organ, rending the paper inside his ears. As the noise expanded into silence, he felt the concrete foundation cradle him.

For several seconds, there was no thinking. Preston

felt his brain cramp into something stubborn and smooth beneath his skull—an avocado's slick pit or a glossy chestnut—and felt the universe knock its knuckles against it. All he could do was clench his jaw and joints until his mind loosened enough for sounds to pry in, that's when he heard the voices falling like birds out of the sky, smacking the ground all around him.

"Was someone shot?"

"Should we go after him?"

"Is everyone okay? Did he hit someone?"

"It was a warning shot. He's gone."

By then, the basement had swept Preston underwater and these voices fluttered and wowed with him at the bottom of a pool, skidded off tiny ceramic tiles. His skin prickled in the cool water, and he held his breath as he brushed his belly with his fingertips, then the dip in his back, hoping to sweep the stinger from his skin. He heard Maryanne's voice push through the water. "Preston?"

"What's wrong?"

"Oh God. Preston, what happened?"

In his mind, Maryanne steered her face through the indigo depths, her hair unfurling around her face like ink in the water, her smile straight. She pressed her nose against his.

Then Maculey's voice slid through the water like a spear. "Oh no!" he screamed, and Preston could almost hear him. "No, no, no. Okay, hold on, dude. Okay."

"I'm calling 911."

"Was someone hit?"

"Wake up, Preston. Open your eyes. Come on,

Preston."

Sentences suspended around him. Some sank bubblelessly to the bottom and some floated untethered through the foggy blue. Others pressed like palms against his fevered forehead or landed across his legs, or pinned him through the abdomen to the bottom. They flattened him and made movement a complicated and unappealing prospect. He preferred to recline in the slow, solitary peace of this pool.

"Wake up, Preston. Come on, pal."

"Oh God. Oh God."

"Come on. Open your eyes, Preston."

When he pulled his eyelids apart, Preston saw that he wasn't underwater, that faces hovered above him, that a bare lightbulb burned against the joists and slats crisscrossing behind them. He released a balloon of air, but then his breath came and went too quickly. "What happened," he said without asking.

Maculey's face floated closest. "We're going to get you help," he said, his voice muffled, his cheeks divided by translucent lines.

"Preston, he shot you," Maryanne said, "but you're going to be fine." He felt something curl into his hand, something warm and alive, and looked to find Maryanne's fingers tacky, inky, knotting with his.

"This is bad."

"Stop it! Preston, you're going to be okay!"

"Hi, yeah, our friend was shot."

The bulb above him stretched taffy-like across his vision as Preston turned his head and flattened his cheek against the cool foundation. He sighed and sent his anxiety into the cement slab until something hot splashed against his temple, a tear seeped beneath his chin and cheek, sopped into his hair. His feet twitched, tickled with cold, and his heart thrashed and writhed. "My stomach hurts," he said, feeling each syllable drool from his lips.

"Help is coming," Maryanne said, ducking into his staggering gaze. Her smile steel, soft and firm, accepting. "Hey, you're very brave. You're our hero."

"525 Eighth Street, on the corner of Eighth and—what's this other road out here?"

"Ask them how long it will take."

"He's bleeding too much! Fuck, how do we stop it?"

"We need you, Preston," Maryanne continued. "Don't you know that? Don't you know we all need you?" Her hair willowed around her face, around his head. Beneath this shelter, Preston felt safe, ready. Even as heat escaped onto the cement and surrounded him. Even as the sting bloomed into a bright, white hole in his belly. Even as he heard his own breath blister deep within his lungs. "Preston, hang on," she said. "Please, Preston. We need you here."

His final vision, before he could no longer keep his eyes open, was Maryanne, close enough to be in focus, her round, trembling cheeks greased with tears; her tunnel eyes; her smile bent and dangling from her face. Tiny tears dribbled down the tip of her diamond nose. His final sensation was her hand panicking in his.

And then the voices became hammers on nails, the peel of heels on hardwood, the television throbbing in the other room, the cackle of a distant fire. Tucked in beneath the blanket of his eyelids, Preston doubted Maryanne, that they needed him, but the thought melted out of him along with his limited command of HTML, the twist of his favorite food on his tongue, every song he had ever hummed, every memory. Preston was unaware as it ran out warm around him. He simply felt himself seep onto the concrete and instantly expand.

And suddenly he knew this cement, and these stones. And he saw the stack of slats in the corner, the full-bellied casks, the sun smoking between the bronze beams. And he heard the laughter dancing above him, heard the roars turn to whimpers to silence. And he felt the rope.

Lester Lancaster
April 29th, 1982

He should have known when he walked in—to a bleating Billy Squier, begging to be stroked; to guitars farting on the downbeats and those one-two drums, the snare hitting like a slurp of soup—that it wouldn't be his best day at Rocco Records.

But then, two hours into his second day at his new job, Lester found himself bored and miserable, thumbing through a milk crate packed with used LPs on the counter, daring Franklin to put on another masturbatory arena rock record, to spin Styx or the Scorpions or something he could use to justify quitting right then and there.

Franklin was perched on the counter beside the crate, arching cobra-like over his novel, when he asked, "Hey Lester, you like to read?"

And, suddenly—somehow—his day got worse.

Lester examined his options: He could ignore Franklin, avoiding idle chatter and advancing his quest to remain silent (though this may put his job in jeopardy); or relent, thereby exhibiting a bit of geniality and humanity, but only by abandoning himself to brutal chitchat; and, if the latter, he could answer honestly, though that might invite further inquiry (the very thought of which made Lester snarl); or he could offer curt dishonesty—"Yes."—which might effectively cut the conversation off (or not, which would be so much worse); or he could give a vague response like, "Sometimes," or "Maybe," or—

"Lester, did you hear me?"

"Yeah, I was just thinking," Lester responded. Forced into option two, he decided to answer honestly. "I don't like to read. It is, to me, the most inefficient waste of time."

Franklin's eyes bloated into full circles behind his wiry frames. "Are you for real?" he asked.

"I am," Lester answered, his fingers still creeping across the split album spines in the crate.

Franklin laughed. "I'm gonna need more explanation than that, man."

Lester sighed as though he was being tugged toward the gallows. "Well, reading is a waste of time," he began. "It isn't productive; it's entertainment. Which is fine—we all need entertainment sometimes—but there are more efficient kinds of entertainment."

"Such as?"

"Oh, come on," Lester sneered. "Don't play dumb. You know television is a much more efficient mode of consuming information and entertainment. It's completely passive. I don't have to do or think about anything when I watch TV." The LPs had flopped over in their crate, flipped open to an old copy of Patsy Cline's *Sentimentally Yours*. Lester stared at it.

"I don't know, man," Franklin said, his smile cordial, easy. "TV is very noisy to me. Lots of commercials and interruptions, all out of your control, you know? And movies just feel too fast for me. Books are just my speed." And then he let his attention tip-toe through the store. "Maybe that's why I like listening to records too. It's in your control. You pick the album, you pull it from its sleeve and place it on the platter, you drop the needle—it's all you."

"Even albums are inefficient compared to MTV," Lester said.

Franklin made a noise like something boiling over on the stovetop. "Oh no!" he groaned, his voice balancing between ridicule and contempt. "You're not trying to tell me that MTV is better than listening to music the old-fashioned way, are you?"

Lester felt the pinch of Franklin's gaze, tried to hide in Patsy Clines's distant stare. "I absolutely am," he said. "Think about it this way: Simply in terms of what each offers, music videos are far more efficient. In the same amount of time, I get music, of course, but also visual information to go with it, sometimes even a story."

"Lester, if you have seen even one music video, you know how mindless they are. They're almost afterthoughts, just the band smiling, pretending to play their instruments. It's terrible." Franklin closed the book, then rotated on the counter to face Lester. "Plus, you don't get to pick what song you're watching. Every few minutes, you roll the dice and hope that it's an artist you like." The smile lines had fallen from his face and Lester noticed how his cheeks now hung slack, beat his teeth between syllables. "If you want to hear a Van Halen song, you probably have to wait a half hour or more and suffer through the dumbest videos. That's a waste of time when you could put on *Van Halen II* and a pair of headphones."

Who the hell wants to listen to Van Halen? Lester wondered, then let a laugh somersault through his mind. But he understood that Franklin's point had sharper teeth than his—particularly that "sometimes even a story" comment, which he knew was baloney—and that this discussion had mutated into something far more moronic than, "Hey Lester, you like to read?" Despite this and the aching suspicion that he may have pissed off his boss, Lester decided that wouldn't let Franklin win this one. "But isn't that the point of something like MTV—to discover new music that maybe you wouldn't have discovered otherwise?" he said, tearing his gaze from Ms. Cline to confront Franklin. "I mean, let's not play that game where we criticize something because it doesn't do what it never claimed it could."

"I'm not trying to do that, man," he said. "All I'm trying to say is that MTV—"

"That MTV doesn't provide the *control* that you desire," Lester interrupted. "Hey, man, I hear you." The muscles around his mouth molded each word more than necessary, and his eyebrows bobbed and ducked in a seductive taunt. Electricity itched under his skin; he could almost hear it hum. "But if you're listening to the same Van Halen records, you'll never know that there's something *new* and *better* out there—and, of course, VJs are the curators of what's *new* and *better*."

Just then, the bell above the door rang (the more Lester heard it, the more it resembled a smoker's phlegmy cough than a ding-a-ling) and a middle-aged woman walked in, which was too bad, Lester thought, because he was suddenly winning this chinwag. The woman wore glasses that sagged beneath her nose and an oversized turtleneck sweater the color of congealed grease.

"Hi Lorraine," Franklin said, suddenly content again, his smile the color of laundry water.

"Hi Franklin," she said in a stony voice, her eyes fluttering around the room.

"Shopping for Duane today?"

"Every Thursday."

"Duane's her son," Franklin told Lester. "Lorraine, this is Lester. He'll be working in the store on and off."

She shot Lester a smile that looked more like a wince, so he retreated back to Patsy Cline's perfectly arched eyebrows, her symmetrical bangs, her mouth midway to a smile.

"I'm looking for a particular record today, and I'm sort of in a hurry," she said, her tiny hands tangled and dangling at her hips.

"Well, I'm sure that Lester could help you find whatever you're looking for," Franklin said. "You don't mind, do you? It'll help you learn the layout of the store better."

Lester sat still for a second, trying to determine if Franklin was messing with him, discreetly scanning for hints—a wink, a knowing smirk, that concave face one makes when trying to stifle a laugh—but sensed nothing, which only further stoked his annoyance.

"Sure," he finally said.

He waddled out from behind the counter and followed the woman to where the Billboard singles and their LPs tiled the wall. Lorraine was tiny; Lester loomed like Sasquatch beside her. "He told me the specific album he wanted, and that one of the songs was very popular, so it might be over here."

"What album was it?"

"Oh boy," she said, stopping suddenly and biting the tip of a thumb. "'Escape' is all I remember, but I don't know if that is the band, or the album, or the song."

Lester let his eyelids drop and sighed through flapping lips. "By Journey?"

"Yes!" she said, her little raptor claw pointing at him. "That's the one he wants. It's got that slow song," she added, "with that lovely piano part."

"'Open Arms?'"

"Yes!" She smiled, and her face morphed into something skeletal and frightening. "You know what you're talking about. I see why Franklin hired you."

Lester ran his fingers the full length of his hair and pushed another sigh slowly through his nose. The day before, he had knocked those awful LPs into an unlabeled box and kicked them behind a dusty display of reprinted concert posters so no one would waste money on them. Since retrieving one would seem suspicious, his only option was to lie.

"I'm sorry, Lorraine, but I just sold our last copy of *Escape* yesterday."

Her face rubber-banded back to its natural, more neutral appearance. "Oh, that's too bad," she said. "Duane's going to be disappointed."

"Yeah, it's a pretty popular album, as you said," Lester said. "Does he like Pat Benatar? Her album *Precious*

Time is wonderful, and I hear she has a new album coming out soon."

"No, Duane's pretty picky," she answered. She scanned the wall of Billboard albums like they were Mayan hieroglyphics, each image meaning something, but she wasn't sure what. "Would it be in another section? Maybe not along this wall?"

"No, we actually pull all the records from the bins when an artist makes it onto the Billboard chart and put them all on the wall." Lester was pretty sure that was a lie, but he made a mental note to hunt down and hide whatever fugitive copies he could find.

Lorraine nibbled on her bottom lip. "Well, thanks for your help," she said. "Will you let me know if any more come in in the next day or two?"

"Absolutely," Lester said, his smile tugging his mustache from either end. He watched her return to the front of the store thinking, *That couldn't have gone better*. Not only had he protected that nice lady's son from some of the most insidious songwriting of his time, but he had also made a recommendation. *Like a real record store employee*, he thought. Standing beneath the Billboard wall, Lester allowed himself to be swaddled by a sudden warm sensation—satisfaction, he mused, or self-esteem, or maybe just the mid-morning sun breaking through the storefront window.

But Lorraine didn't exit the store. She had returned to Franklin and kindled another conversation. Lester couldn't hear them, but they exchanged only a sentence or two before Franklin climbed off the countertop, his mouth twisted in confusion, and retreated into the back room behind the register. Lorraine followed with the hesitant curiosity of a stray dog. Lester thought almost nothing of it, though. Instead, he worried about that warm sensation, which seemed to intensify—enough, at least, for him to feel it radiating under his arms.

He understood when Lorraine had returned to the counter with the Journey LP in her hands, when Franklin returned to the register and prodded its buttons. Lester's face blossomed into a crimson carnation.

That warmth, he realized, was guilt. It had been all along.

While he waited for that transaction to conclude, Lester concentrated on his blood thumping through his body an inch at a time, on the draft that pushed past him like a pedestrian on a crowded street, on the Rush song that had been somersaulting quietly throughout the store, anything other than his tarnished conscience. But he found himself wondering what Franklin would say when Lorraine left. *Maybe he'll yell at me*, he thought. *Or maybe he'll fire me.* He bit his top lip, felt his mustache twitch between his lips.

Maybe he'll ban me from the store.

Lorraine thanked Franklin as he handed her a receipt. On her way out, she turned to Lester, the LP jacket's laminated corners already piercing the plastic wrap. "Franklin found one for me in the back," she said. "Thanks for your help, though."

Lester smiled simply—he didn't want to risk additional disgrace by saying something else stupid—and buried himself in the bargain bin, hiding himself between LPs from the 1940s with colorful Bluebird labels, their sleeves like rice paper. As soon as the store hacked Lorraine back onto the sidewalk, he heard Franklin bark from behind the register. "Lester, what the hell?"

"What?" he asked, but his feigned confusion sounded too defensive.

"We almost lost a sale, man, and from one of our regular customers."

"What do you mean?"

When Lester looked up, he found his boss's jaw hinged open. A maze of frustration formed on his forehead. Lester recognized this look as the one his sister battered him with when he tried to lie. "Lester," he finally said. "What are we doing here?"

Something soft and slimy squeezed its way up Lester's throat, something that he couldn't swallow back down, so he spat it out. "I was doing her a favor, Franklin," he said. "That record is so bad, and you know it."

Franklin sawed his head back and forth, his mouth bent into a crooked smirk. "She comes in every week, Lester. She throws her money at me every week. I don't want to drive away customers who—"

"You don't need customers like that," Lester interrupted. He felt that heat flutter through him again, felt it force sweat from his belly and back, and took it as an indication that he should shut up—that he had, in fact, lost.

Franklin pulled off his spectacles and kneaded the bridge of his nose. Lester noticed the crinkles in the corners of his eyes and wondered how old he really was. "Okay, man," Franklin said, re-spectacled and pressing his hands onto the countertop. "How about we try again tomorrow?"

It took the length of Franklin's sigh for Lester to realize he was being asked to leave. "Oh," he said. "Okay." Lester felt like a shoplifter, like a rowdy teenager, a disruption that required removal and deserved management's suspicious stare. But when Lester looked up, Franklin still stared over his spectacles at the countertop, his hands squashed spiders, which only made him feel worse.

A new song had started, still Rush, presumably the same album, though this song more sinister than the last. Lester didn't recognize its rhythm, the way the guitars jerked; the way the snare drum snapped against their short, sharp chords. Whichever song it was, he decided that its menace suited the moment.

"Okay," Lester repeated when he reached the door, debating whether or not to say sorry to Franklin. He didn't, and regretted it as soon as he stepped out of the store.

On the sidewalk, silence greeted Lester, and he realized he'd rather listen to Billy Squier than the passing station wagon or the breeze filtering through the newly emblazoned trees, though he'd never admit it.

Lester didn't know where to go, so he tottered toward the comic book store next door. As he walked, he thought about Franklin and his age. When he mocked the man's appearance and musical taste, then, when he challenged him about books and television, he was debating someone almost as old as his parents. Franklin had informed opinions. Franklin held his own. *Does that make him kind of cool?* Lester wondered. He avoided answering the question, though, fearing what he might discover about himself. But he knew the answer.

Barbara Farmer
September 18th, 1942

The asphalt beneath her feet reminded Barbara of an old, sorry photograph—all silver and gritty, glistening beneath the buried sun—so she tried not to look down. And she tried not to look at the estates that lined Wakes Street, painted like the Easter eggs she used to dip into dye and vinegar on her father's farm. Instead, she looked at the leaves, their edges singed, spreading wide like open palms. The wind rattled through them, shaking dots of rain onto the street beneath.

Barbara twisted a smile onto her lips; these leaves made her happy, and so did her reason for walking into town. She felt the knot of cash tucked into the nook of her bra and thought about the treat she was going to retrieve for the girls: A record from the picture they had seen in Chicago the previous weekend.

She remembered how the city's buildings had loomed over them like scolding parents, cold and critical, and how the wind had wound down the river only to whip their cheeks until they shined like orchard cherries. But the girls had giggled like they were getting away with something, sneaking unnoticed beneath the city's stern gaze. Each time a train passed, the clatter-roar that rumbled between the Loop's buildings had startled and excited Barbara. *This city ain't Las Vegas*, she remembered thinking, *and it definitely ain't Madison.* It was some other animal altogether, some wild species fashioned from stone and steel, steeped in light and grime.

The signs had been something else entirely. On the far side of the street, an enormous "Chicago" sign rose along a boxy, concrete building; its red, striking against the steel blue sky, provided the city's sole color. Barbara walked arm-in-arm between Joy and Anita beneath another, less elegant sign that advertised the State-Lake. They didn't skip down the street, but Barbara remembered her glee as they approached the theatre, "Orchestra Wives" written in red on a marquee surrounded by winking lights.

Inside, the theatre's architecture had swirled and swelled, the walls dripping like ice cream left in the sun. Barbara found it breathtaking, even though she was surrounded by sweating strangers. Though she had to shut herself down during the newsreel, the picture was satisfying—funny—and helped her forget about the burden she carried. The girls stepped out of that theatre unfettered, free to stride back to the train station at their own pace—to window-shop, to stop for drinks, to sip in the starless city's syrupy night—all the while singing that song about Kalamazoo.

The song circled her head as she treaded toward Rocco's, determined to find the record and bring it back for the girls. The heels of her oxfords clicked against the wet concrete to the beat as she hopped onto the Seventh Street sidewalk, its shops quaint—cute at best—compared to those surrounding the State-Lake theatre.

Rocco's Radio and Phonograph was easy to miss; its maroon letters on the storefront window were the only indication that there was a store inside. Stepping through a glass door foyer, Barbara was struck by the smell of polished wood and some frolicking jazz number. A man behind the counter greeted her, but she was too distracted, staring at a row of radios. She crept over to one, petted it like a golden retriever—it was about the same size. Others rose to the height of wood-burning stoves, stretched the length of ice chests. Barbara remembered this awe from when she was in the store last winter purchasing their Philco.

Record jackets adorned the far wall, popping with bright, clownish colors. She felt herself wandering toward them, bouncing to the beat of whatever was ricocheting through the store. She weaved between a cluster of bobbysoxers who swayed together like a thicket of sweetgrass, giggling at some boy stocking singles in the far corner. Barbara silently acknowledged that she had been one of them only a couple of years ago, but their saddle shoes still bothered her, their cuffs bouncing above their slouching socks as if the perfect fold was their only concern.

She turned her back on these girls as she approached the wall of records, knowing exactly what she was looking for. As her gaze hopped from cover to cover, Barbara imagined bringing the record home to Joy and Anita, sliding it from its sleeve and dropping it onto the phonograph amid their girlish squeaks, then scooting across the living room together, slinking and twisting, knees knocking and rocking like bells, until they fell onto the sofa in hysterics, until sweat pimpled their heads, until—

"Can I help you find something, ma'am?" a voice interrupted her reverie. Barbara turned to find that stock boy standing behind her, his arms wrapped around a cardboard box. To her surprise, he wasn't really a boy. A swish of hair unstuck itself from his slicked back style, reminding her of a carefully brushed stroke of paint.

"Oh," Barbara said, returning her feet to the floor. "I, uh, am looking for a record from that picture *Orchestra Wives*. The title has something to do with Kalamazoo."

The stock boy's lips pressed into a graphite line as his eyes bounced around the room, landing only momentarily on Barbara before rebounding back onto the records. "Got it," he said, shooting across the store with Barbara dawdling several steps behind. As he flipped through the row of records in printed paper sleeves, she noticed how his arms filled his sweater and how that defiant strand of hair dangled over his forehead. She wondered if he was annoyed by that plume, if he was even aware of it, when he suddenly plucked one of the records and held it out to her like a tray of hors d'oeuvres. "Be sure to listen to the second side," he said. "It's a lovely slow number from the film, but has vocals. It's great to dance to."

Barbara smiled, thankful to have the record in her hands, mostly because it gave her something to focus her attention on other than the rocky contours of his cheeks. "Gee," she mumbled. "Thank you."

"Say, I haven't seen you around here before, have I?" he asked, and stuck out his hand. "My name's Rocco."

"As in, *the* Rocco? Like, you run this place?"

"Oh, no," he said, a smile cracking across one cheek. "This is my dad's store. He runs it. He just decided to name it after me. But I work here pretty much all the time."

"I see," Barbara said, taking his hand, which felt like a firm piece of fruit. "My name is Barbara."

"Barbara, do you live in town?" he asked.

"I do," she answered hastily. She reached across his gaze to tuck that lock of coffee-colored hair behind his ear. "There. That's been bugging me since I first laid eyes on you."

Rocco's smile spread across his face slowly. "Let me ring you up," he said.

Ring! Barbara remembered, following Rocco toward the front of the store like a curious puppy to where his father, she guessed, had greeted her as she entered. With the tip of her thumb, she nudged her wedding band up and over her knuckle, only semi-conscious of her actions and its purpose, whatever it was. As Rocco poked buttons on a hulking cash register, Barbara transferred the ring to her middle finger, spinning the stone to the inside of her hand. She made sure to reach for the receipt with her left hand, and to flash a stupid smile when Rocco said, "Well, come back to say hi when you can."

The entire walk home tortured Barbara, who, for five blocks, felt the preceding series of events press against the inside of her skin. She bit her lip until it swelled against her teeth. The instant she shouldered through the front door, she said, "You will never guess what happened to me," hoping that someone was, in fact, on the other side.

Anita reclined on the couch, sipping on a glass of something. "Did you break a heel on your walk again?" she asked into the mug.

"Oh," Barbara said, sliding out of her overcoat. "No, nothing like that. See, I was at that Rocco's place, where we bought the radio, and—"

"Did you buy us a new record, Barbara?" Anita interrupted, nearly leaping off of her cushion, her black curls bouncing in excitement.

"Actually, I did. I figured that we could unwind a little tonight. But that's not—"

"Oh, Barbara," Anita's voice twinkled behind her teeth. "You always have been the sweet one in the house. What record is it?"

"Now hold on just a minute," Barbara said. "There was a boy—a man—at the store, and he was really laying it on thick. Boy, was he a flirt."

Anita's exaggerated gasp annoyed her, but it was what she wanted to hear. "Didn't he see your ring, or what?"

"I guess not," Barbara replied, feeling the band

tighten around her middle finger.

"Was he good-looking? Who was this guy?"

"What guy?" Joy said, walking into the room with her own mug hung on her forefinger.

"Some boy made a pass at Barbara," Anita sang as if she were pigtailed and teasing her friend on a playground. She pulled bare feet onto the sofa, folding her legs in that elegant way that sometimes made Barbara jealous.

"Well, it was Rocco, actually," Barbara added but didn't mention that he was a stock boy or that his father ran the shop. Barbara wasn't used to being the attractive one and didn't want to undermine her moment.

"Gee," Anita giggled.

"Did you flirt back?" Joy asked, then laughed, her blonde hair glowing in the dusk that streaked through the living room's big window.

Just then, Anita pounced from her corner of the sofa and seized the small record from Barbara's grasp. "Oh! It's that song from the picture!" she shouted as she pulled the record from its sleeve.

"Put it on," Joy said, collapsing onto the spot that Anita had just abandoned. Barbara kicked off her heels and fell into a chair. In an instant, the drums clanged like Wild West pistols, and cymbals clashed like glass broken in a saloon brawl before settling into a gentle bounce colored by loudmouthed horns, by the tip-toeing piano, by woodwinds like molasses dripping slowly down the song. Anita reached for Joy's hand and tugged her to her feet; she made a face as if she had stepped into a bucket of ice water and hastily handed her cup to Barbara, who couldn't help but chuckle at the spectacle. As the horns swelled behind them, Joy and Anita swayed cheek to cheek with the silliest smirks on their faces. Already, it had become the evening Barbara was hoping for.

But she couldn't help but think about Rocco. Stealing a long sip of Joy's lukewarm coffee, she traced his rocky jaw and stiff lips in her mind, remembered the way his frame filled his sweater and bumped the knot of his tie against his Adam's apple. Barbara shook these thoughts from her mind. Still, it had been more than a year since she felt a man's attention. *Couldn't I enjoy this,* she thought, *even just a little?*

Suddenly, someone shoved a glass of wine in front of her face, yanking her like a fish from the river of her thoughts. Anita had snuck past her into the kitchen and unplugged a bottle. "Let's have some fun tonight," she said, handing another wine glass out to Joy, who swayed by herself in the center of the room, succumbing to the throbbing beat. The singer's voice sounded effortless, masculine but sweet. In the picture, the handsome Tex Beneke sang the song with a certain innocence—"I like her looks while I carried her books in Kalamazoo," and "I'll make my bid for that freckle-faced kid I'm hurrying to." The song made Barbara smile, made her think of Rocco again.

Barbara barely heard the knock at the door amid the stomping and snickering and sipping; in fact, at first, she mistook it as an off-beat kick drum. But it returned harder and distinct, stiff knuckles on an oak door. Since Joy and Anita were too busy bouncing to the record, Barbara opened the door where she found three men standing on her porch, their white sailor hands wrung in their hands. When she saw the uniforms, her knees nearly unbolted, and she felt her muscles loosen beneath her belt. She tried to keep herself together, but bullet-sized tears pushed out of her eyes. "Hello," she squeaked, barely audible beneath Glenn Miller's Orchestra. "May I help you?"

"Good evening, ma'am," one of them said. "Is this the residence of Mrs. Ronald Yarborough?"

"I'm Mrs. Yarborugh," Joy said, appearing behind Barbara. Her lighthearted smile wilted as soon as she saw the sailors in their spotless whites.

The three men looked young—too young, like actors—though the sunset rendered them into silhouettes. The one who had spoken shot a guilty glance to the others. "Mrs. Yarborough," he said, "I have been asked to inform you that your husband, Seaman Ronald Yarborough, died on June 4 aboard the USS Yorktown as a result of wounds received in action. Your husband died serving his country."

Barbara took a step back to feel her friend's body, which stood rigid against this gale, and scooped Joy's hand into hers. Tears fell like pebbles onto the hardwood beneath her. Barbara noticed that Anita had found Joy's other hand, but Joy stood on her own, leaned into the news, fought her face as it tried to contort and twist into chaos.

"Please accept my most heartfelt sympathy in your

loss," he added as the world swirled around him, his face a blur beneath the smoldering summer's shadows. "If I can be of any assistance to you, I hope you will let me know."

But Barbara had already stopped listening, lost herself in the reeling landscape, the way the trees shuttered and seared in the sun behind those sorry silhouettes, the way the neighboring houses exploded in the late summer light, their bricks blood red, their walkways pale. She felt Joy's hand stiffen in her grasp, felt her arms flex tense, but didn't see her friend. Instead, she saw her own black coupe crawling up Geranium Avenue, her own trio of soldiers marching onto the porch, green-suited, sleek-shoed.

Joy stood statuesque between them, frozen in fear or fortitude, her neck stretching out of her dress as if she were waking from a nap. Tears roiled beneath her taut cheeks and her knees locked behind her skirt. *She doesn't need my misery*, Barbara thought. *She needs me to support her. She needs my friendship. She needs me.*

"I'm so sorry," was all that Barbara could say. She wheezed in Joy's ear as she hooked an arm around her neck. "I'm sorry," she repeated as sorrow seeped from her in a steady stream. As she pressed her cheek against Joy's, she saw the ring curled around her middle finger, dull, still spun to hide its diamond. Instantly, Rocco flickered in her mind, sending her plummeting into pity; into that deep, bottomless hole; unlit, lonesome, alone.

"I'm sorry," she repeated, this time not to Joy. "I'm so, so sorry."

On the other side of Joy, Anita floated in her despair and wrapped an arm around Joy to anchor herself, which left Joy standing between two sobbing teens on steady legs, swallowing her terror between every other breath. Her first attempt at movement was to lift her arms, one to soothe the girl wrapped around her waist whose sobs seemed childlike and frail, the other the calm the girl bent around her neck, repeating, "I'm sorry. I'm so sorry," between her tears as if she had killed Joy's husband.

Becky McLaughlin
November 14th, 2011

In study hall, Becky's pencil traced and retraced the curves of his glasses, maneuvering smoothly like a skier down a slalom. She started the sketch during Algebra when she should have been listening to Ms. Boston's lecture, squeezed it in between equations in her notebook—his nose, his cheeks, the swish of his lips that matched the muscular rims of his Ray-Bans.

Becky found herself drawing him wherever she could—particularly his glasses, the most prominent part of his appearance. She decided that, despite her fear and confusion, she owed him some consideration. After all, his advice had left an impression in her that she could almost feel beneath her fingers: "It just looks cool," his voice still echoed in her head. "You should keep doing it."

A reusable grocery bag slumped against the aluminum leg of her desk. In it, a purple folder peeked from between a dozen magazines, burying the rest of her supplies at the bottom—a sixteen-ounce jar of Mod Podge, some stiff paintbrushes, a bunch of Sharpie markers, and a plastic box that protected her X-Acto knife and blades. She thought she might have been able to create in her art class but, instead, her teacher forced them to fill out a worksheet on Gauguin's tropical sunscapes. Becky felt like a crazy bag lady lugging her unused supplies around all day, but she did it for him.

When the bell buzzed, Becky felt like she was ascending from a deep slumber, packing her notebook into her backpack like a sleepwalker as the students in her study hall bunched out of the room. She jammed her pencil behind her ear and shouldered her bag of supplies, the last to leave.

Aside from the odd freshman nose-deep in manga and the pod of swimmers migrating to the locker room, Becky found the school already deserted. A right turn routed her down an even emptier hall, past rows of closed, peanut-colored lockers. These were her favorite seconds of the day—her peace felt objective, true—but also her least favorite; especially when Frances wasn't there to escort her through the halls, Becky noticed she was more prone to seeing spirits.

What Becky assumed to be an apparition approached suddenly, stepping into the empty hallway from nothing, her slim neck stretching from a lavender polo, its collar stiff and wide, and her jeans like an overcast sky. The girl's knowing eyes mismatched her immature face. But Becky walked past without closing her eyes or losing her breath.

The hallway smelled like sulfur and aluminum— elements that chemistry students cooked in small crocks so they could examine the black bits left behind. Becky wondered if they stuck freshmen in the stinking chemistry hallway intentionally, a sort of institutionalized hazing. Still, she was relieved that, besides these phantasmic smells of these elements, she was alone. Her right shoulder ached, stiff beneath the gravity of both bags, so she let them slip onto the floor in front of her locker.

As she pinched the combination between her fingers, Becky felt her phone bristle in her pocket. She pulled out her device and pulled open her locker simultaneously, reading the message from Frances as she tugged her coat off its hook. **wanna hang?** it said. Becky could almost hear her friend's derision and pity as she read the words in her head.

Frances hadn't said a word to Becky since she left the basement on Friday, nor was she waiting in their usual spot that morning either. Becky wasn't sure what she did, but she wasn't prepared to pal around with someone who had ignored her all weekend, then all day. **maybe**, she pecked back with one thumb. **still at school. going to bathroom then leaving**. Beneath these words, Becky planted the implication that the bathroom was the more important priority and hoped that her message would piss Frances off a little.

Her locker clattered shut behind her as she dragged her coat and both bags into the bathroom at the end of the hall. Speckled grey and slate, the tiles that climbed across the floor and up the walls hid the dirt dragged in by sneakers, making the tiny space feel both spotless and permanently dirty. Becky rounded the corner to find two basketball players prepping for practice. One girl's platinum blonde hair, tied into a ponytail, blinded Becky as she entered; her skin looked dark, like cardboard, compared to it. The other's smile seemed clownish, but still lovely beneath her pencil point nose. Sporadic freckles flecked across her face, dark against her complexion like bright, luminous pine. Compared to Becky's, which looked like a pox, this player's freckles seemed perfect.

Becky pictured herself plowing into their space, her winter coat dangling limp in her arms, her shoulder burdened by bags that dragged along the walls, her hair like a wildfire. The players smiled at Becky in that pitied, wretched way that upperclassmen greet freshmen, and she tried to ignore it, scuttling instead into the handicapped stall so she had room to stow her bags.

"I'm not sure what to tell him," one of the girls said as Becky flung her belongings into the furthest corner of the stall, her papery voice reverberating between the tiles. "Like, I want to start, but I'm not sure I will if I ever get the chance to prove myself, you know?" As Becky lowered herself onto the flimsy toilet, she resisted the urge to roll her eyes. When she looked up, she read the words, bold and bloated, scrawled on the stall door in front of her: "BECKY MACLOFFLIN IS A FUGLY SLUT."

She felt the insult shudder through her, felt tiny hairline cracks form at her foundation, and worried that she'd crumble where she sat. Her face clenched and, beneath eyelids too cumbersome to lift, stared at the words, glaring between other thoughtless quips. *Why would someone write that?* she wondered, wondering why disbelief was always the first emotion she felt. Whimpers bubbled in the back of her throat, then burst, allowing the sounds to slip with her tears onto the tile.

"Are you okay?" one of the basketball players asked.

Becky had noticed somewhere in her subconsciousness that they had stopped speaking. Now, she suspected, they had their cheeks pressed to the stall.

"I'm fine," Becky said, then inhaled suddenly, her breath stuttering.

"Are you sure?" the other said. "Is there anything we can help with?"

"Just leave me alone," Becky barked.

Though she shut her eyes, she felt the words burn her cheeks, felt her freckles sizzle and pop like butter on a skillet. But she was stuck, forced to finish on the toilet and face the insult. Her eyes scaled the stall door, swung from one vulgarity to another, each clinging to the door like something flung, but they kept falling back to her name, incorrectly spelled, and its shameful addendum.

Still perched on the toilet, Becky reached over and rifled through her bag, her right hand slicing through her junk like a spade through layers of soil and sand. She searched for a Sharpie, something she could use to scratch out the scrawled words. Her fingertips slipped across a pair of scissors, her knuckles butted a bottle of Mod Podge. She squeaked with relief when she found what felt like a marker tucked between pages of a magazine; when she removed it, though, and noticed its stiff bristles, Becky finally fell onto the floor. Sobs rose from some central spot despite the nervous whispers from the two girls as they retreated from the bathroom.

It was there, forehead pressed against her bare knees, hot tears dribbling down her thighs, that his glasses returned to her mind. She traced them in her imagination while she waited for other details about his face to return. Still slicing through her bag, her hand slid across a magazine cover, cutting her thumb, but she disregarded the sting and sudden ruby rush as the words returned to her mind: "You should keep doing it."

Pushing her shoes onto the tiles, Becky straightened herself, pulled her pants back up her hips, then dragged her bag onto the toilet seat. She scooped her supplies out with two hands as if she were emptying a pumpkin, dumping the guts onto the ground. Her mind retreated into some safe room, someplace tucked away where it could stay out of her body's way while it tore indiscriminately from the magazines' spines, stole textures and colors, a swath of forest here, a sunset there, a gaslit skyscraper at dusk and muddy moss of an area rug, their edges frothy, having been ripped with little concern, torn with little thought beyond the animal act itself.

Colorful puddles of paper collected in a semicircle around Becky. With the meat of her palm, she broke the bristles of a wide, stiff brush then plunged it into the jar of Mod Podge and started coating the bottom corner of the door. The substance smeared on thick in cloudy strokes and almost instantly filled the stall with a chemical smell that stabbed at her sinuses. Becky's consciousness enjoyed only sporadic and disjointed peeks of her activity, where she watched herself reaching for the paper scraps, found the yellows smooth in her hand, stuck them to the stall—sunny cornfields, golden frosting on a cake, crumbles of bronze foundation, each climbing across the door like ivy.

She tore more, the sound vicious and satisfying. And with each page, each corner ripped, she felt something lift from her—something that had perched on her shoulders and slowed her down.

Her spine cracked as she twisted toward the bag

behind her. She plucked that purple folder from its hiding place, fanned it open, and ran her fingers through the clippings found within—of carefully traced faces and objects uprooted from their contexts, of juice boxes and mountains of coffee beans, of blowdryers and tubes of toothpaste. She removed a woman's face, her eyelids draped across her gaze like a blanket on a sleepy child, and placed it on the toilet's tank.

Becky's arms swung around the stall with a finesse and rhythm that surprised her each time her consciousness emerged, curious to inspect her body's progress. The motion reminded her of an orchestra conductor, the way her arms swept slow, low, then fast as she slapped more swatches onto the door, their emerald textures becoming bluer, blacker—a velvety dusk; the cool, steely shadows of a child's bedroom; the waterfall of some runway dress. The textures crawled halfway across the stall door, and Becky felt sweat collect cool at her temples, sting her hairline as she slathered on more Mod Podge, covering what remained of the top corner.

From two feet—the toilet's distance—the collage seemed to glisten in the off-set sun, its yellow band like an unnatural reflection, a trick of the eye. The starry nights and riverbeds that comprised the furthest corner of the door observed Becky as she tore out more swatches, ravaged pages whose tints and textures she did not need, split spines already exhausted. A line of sweat ended in her eye, but she blinked it away, biting her tongue, tasting the sealer's tang as it wafted through the air. She brushed globs of the stuff onto the completed collage, thinned it into cloudy strokes that plastered the paper to the door, and made it one piece. She noticed one corner had dried clear and dull as she sealed the other, spreading the Mod Podge in quick strokes—less graceful, more forceful.

Only when she had glazed the final corner did Becky feel herself return to her body, filling her arms again as though they were sleeves. She blinked, eyelids stamping down dusty tears, and wiped them with the hump of her wrist. When she sat back onto the toilet seat, she saw for the first time what she had done: An enormous collage, teeming with texture, shining in some invented light.

Becky reached behind her for one last image, something she had left for herself subconsciously on the toilet, and held it in front of her, examining the face's perfect make-up. Becky liked the image because the model looked so tired, so fed up; she realized that the face was manufactured, Photoshopped most likely, and at the very least caught by a talented photographer as she shifted from happy to sad. But the image reminded Becky of how she felt, content with her dissatisfaction and exhaustion. She stuck it to the wall in the left corner so that it peeked from the bottom.

As she took her X-Acto to the edges of the door— slicing the crispy pages, trimming the excess that fanned off of the fiberglass—she kept staring at the face, especially those eyelids, the gentle gradient from green to gold that mirrored the door behind her. It was too beautiful, too perfect, too much like the girl that Becky could never be. She fixed it.

The stall door slammed behind her as she exited, sounding like a broken bell, and Becky felt herself fill her body, felt her biceps tremble with adrenaline, felt a smile stiffen on her lips. She pulled her phone out of her pocket, amazed that she had been in that stall for an hour, and flicked through the texts that Frances had sent: **were r u?** and **r u mad????** and **y arent u answering me???** Behind her, the door bounced back open, revealing a glowing streak on a glinting door, a face with black Sharpie eyelids in one corner, and her name—Becky McLaughlin—spelled correctly in the other.

Charles Stonebreaker
August 14th, 1910

To Charles, the scene unfolding inside his house seemed eerily mechanical. The rhythm of hammers and trowels, the predictable course and choreography, the speed and precision—he knew he was watching humans work, but it all seemed so automatic.

There was Mingus, pounding hardwood floors row by row, and his cousin Andrew from Beloit, who knew about plastering walls and offered three week's worth of help. He was a young man, maybe eighteen, but had worked on walls since he was ten, Mingus had assured him, and knew what he was doing. In one week, Andrew had already slathered the first coat on almost all the house's surfaces, but he also had help from a friend, some sixteen-year-old named Guy who worked shirtless in a pair of speckled coveralls and spat tobacco into the basement beneath them as their trowels scraped the walls of what would become the kitchen.

Holding a handkerchief to his brow, Charles watched his daughter Rebecca romp through the house where the floor had been laid, shrieking so she could hear her voice ricochet between the drying walls. Mingus ignored her, treated her like a mare might treat a horsefly, but Charles chuckled at her, wondering what was going on in her head.

When her hand streaked through one of the still-wet walls, she gasped and looked at her father. "Don't worry, hon," Charles said. "It's just the first coat, so it'll be plastered over again."

Rebecca's grimace softened, then thickened again as she pulled her fingers to her nose to inspect what she had scraped off the wall. "Yuck!" she squalled. "There's little hairs in here!"

"It's horsehair," Charles said. "Well, probably cow hair, but they call it horsehair."

"Why is there cow hair?"

"I don't know," Charles said dragging his handkerchief beneath his neck. "Andrew, why do you put cow hair into the plaster?"

"I dunno," Andrew shouted over the scritch of his trowel and the thud of his cousin's hammer and the roaring world outside. "I think it's to keep the walls from crumbling."

Rebecca shuffled toward her father, sticking her hand out to him so he could see the tiny brown hairs snaking through the plaster. "How do they get it?"

"Um, well, I suppose they cut it off the cows," Charles said, kneeling down to her eye level, holding her slathered hand within his.

"Whose cows?"

Charles bit his mustache with his bottom lip. "Whatever cows they can find, I guess," he said and pulled his hammer from his belt loop, hoping that the anticipation of action would end this string of questions. "Maybe they shear them like sheep to keep them cool and collect their hair."

Rebecca gazed at her fingertips as if they contained some secret; her other hand plucked one of the hairs from the paste. "Do they hurt the cow?"

"I don't think so. Does it hurt sheep when they are sheared?"

Charles could tell that she was carefully considering this question by the way her forehead folded onto itself and her stare shot wayward out the window; only last year she had helped shear some of her grandfather's sheep back on his farm and it didn't seem to hurt them. "But there's something that I still don't understand," she said, wiping her fingers on the front of her dusty dress. "Why do they call it horsehair if it's cow hair?"

"Rebecca, hey, I could use your help," Mingus said. He bit long, flat nails between his teeth. As Rebecca toed toward him, he spat the nails into his open palm and pointed. "I just put in these five rows," he said. "Could you step on them and make sure they are sturdy and don't break?"

"What happens if they break?" she asked, her face tipped upward in curiosity, her hands tangled behind her back.

"You'll just fall into the basement," he said and winked at Charles.

Rebecca's eyes sparked, and tiptoes lifted her excited body into the air. "Okay!" she said, hopping onto the new rows near Mingus, her dirt blonde hair streaking around her head. She stamped onto the rows, landed knee-first on them, slapped them with her tiny palms.

Though dusty, Charles knew that the honey-colored floor would become the centerpiece of this palace, making his otherwise modest house glisten gold. The previous week, he was able to purchase enough flooring for his whole house from a building site that had gone bankrupt and was selling its unused assets cheap, and he was eager to install it and finally have a floor in his house. With the plastered white walls and the amber floor expanding beneath him, there were corners of this house that looked complete. He knew that they still had a while to go, but it became easier and easier to envision what would become their majestic home.

"Seems pretty sturdy," Rebecca concluded, laying along the edge of the floor, her hair dripping over the ledge into the basement. While she tested the floor, Andrew and Guy had hopped across a corner to plaster the last of the kitchen walls, and Mingus had already laid another line of hardwood, ready to nail down the next row.

Charles glanced out the open window at Elizabeth, who sat in the shade alongside the house. One of her enormous hats sat in the dust beside her—months ago, she had abandoned any hope to remain what she called "presentable" in what she called "their situation"—and her hair unfurled in relentless waves that flickered in the wind like a flame. Her eyes remained on the cross-stitching clutched in her left hand. Her right hand pushed a needle through a square of frayed fabric, pulled it out, repeated the process, never minding the wind that tugged her hair like a schoolyard playmate.

"What are you working on?" Charles asked, leaning through the window.

Elizabeth flashed her husband a fractured, playful smile, her pupils pin-sized in the sun. "I decided to make something for the house," she said. She held up the biscuit-colored linen with the words "God Bless This" stitched in blocky, elegant letters, serifs fluttering from each corner like tiny banners. Above it, the beginning of a border stretched the width of the words, containing what looked like oak leaves between navy blue bars. "It's going to say, 'God Bless This Humble House,' but I just started this morning. I'm thinking of putting a little house at the bottom, something that looks like our house, when it's finished." She stretched the fabric taut between two hands and tilted her head up to her husband. "What do you think?"

For a second, Charles couldn't think. Instead, his jaw swung loose beneath his face. The embroidery itself was lovely but, for the first time, he sensed excitement within his wife, satisfaction, solidarity—sentiments he hadn't seen in her since he suggested the move to Wisnago.

"So, a little house then?"

"Yes, absolutely," Charles answered but swung his chin from side to side.

Elizabeth snickered. "What?"

"Nothing," he said. "It's just that you amaze me."

Charles leaned out the window to stick a kiss onto Elizabeth's forehead, surprised to see her stretch toward him, to meet him halfway. His lips tasted the sweet, wind-dried sweat on her otherwise soft forehead. As she pulled away, her keen eyes met his for a moment, and her smile spread slow and warm. Around her, the summer seemed to swell, saturated with the kinds of colors that painters might use on a masterpiece, and Charles no longer heard the husky scrapes or house-rattling hammer or the wind pushing across the prairie.

"Can I come inside and inspect your progress?" she asked.

"Of course," he said, clamoring across the house and through the front door, which he pulled shut behind him. "No peeking!" he shouted from the front porch as he watched her wander through the dusty yard, her muslin dress rippling beneath the sun. As she stepped up the cement stairs, it occurred to Charles that this was it—this was the moment he had waited for.

Months ago, he realized there would never be a big reveal, not now that Elizabeth visited the house on a near-daily basis. If she saw incremental progress, there would be no surprise when he lifted his hands from her eyes, and definitely no appreciative kiss, not if she had brushed the paint on herself or monitored the movers as they had hauled in furniture. But Charles thought the floors and walls would be the first opportunity for her to envision this construction as a home, and this instant might be his best chance.

"What are you doing?" she said. Her hesitant laugh bounced between the porch's unpainted floor and ceiling before spinning off into the yard.

"I'm going to cover your eyes while you walk in," Charles said, his hands drifting toward her face. "I want what you see to be a surprise."

"Oh, no thank you." She swatted away his hands as if they were flailing bats.

"No, I insist. This will be—"

"Please, don't Charles. I'm already sweaty enough. I don't need your dirty hands adding to my discomfort." She pried her palms between his hands and her brow, then closed them on his fingers and pulled them back down. "I'll keep my eyes closed. I promise."

Charles nibbled at his mustache. "Alright," he murmured.

"Oh stop," Elizabeth said through a toothy smirk. "This will be fun."

Charles watched her eyelids clamp together, noted how her hands hovered as if inflated by helium. He maneuvered beneath them as he stepped behind her and dropped his hands on her shoulders, then steered her into the house where the application of plaster replaced the wind's roar and pounding hammers quaked the entire house.

The best view was a finished corner in what Charles envisioned to be a foyer—a space where coats could be hung, where hats could be popped from heads and boots peeled from weary feet. Constructed, the space was larger than he had expected and, with a lounge and side table, had the potential to become a full and beautiful sitting room. Charles positioned Elizabeth far enough away from the walls to take in the whole room. "Okay," he said. "Open your eyes."

He tried to experience the finished corner for the first time along with Elizabeth—the tall windows that welcomed in sunlight; the crisp white walls, smooth but for the three dents made by their daughter's curious fingers; the amber floor glowing beneath their feet. "It's only the first coat of plaster," Charles started, "so it'll be smoother before we paint. And, of course, we haven't pinned up any finishing touches, like moulding or trim, but—"

His comment was interrupted by his wife's stunned silence, her statue stillness. Marionette hands still hung in front of her. Finally, she said, "Oh my," and turned to look into her husband's eyes; Charles saw tears, like diamonds, adorn her eyelids as she shouldered into his arms. "Oh, Charles, it's beautiful. Perfect." Her head drifted onto his shoulder, then shot upright with a gasp that shook his arms off of her. "Rebecca!" she shouted and pushed past Charles into the next room.

Charles bristled, turned with tense shoulders, but was relieved to find Rebecca where he left her, smudged feet swinging into the cool basement.

She sat taut, startled by her mother, with square-cut eyes and a wide frown unfolding beneath her dirty cheeks. Mingus stopped his hammer mid-swing to observe Elizabeth stomping into the room; Andrew and Guy clung like spiders to the un-plastered laths, silent and invisible as they stretched between studs.

"Rebecca, get away from that ledge right now," Elizabeth shouted, her voice swelling in the silence left by the workers. Rebecca scrambled from the edge of the floor and climbed up her mother's skirt. "What were you doing? What is wrong with you?" She brandished a rigid finger at the bridge of her daughter's nose. "You are to *never* play in this house whether men are working or not. *Not* anymore." She turned her attention back toward Charles, her breathless smile having bent into a scowl. "Did you know she was lying along the ledge of the floor?" she asked.

"Oh, don't worry, Elizabeth," Mingus said, wiping his silvery forehead with his wrist. "We was watching her.

She was safe."

Elizabeth's head snapped suddenly toward Mingus, her eyes flickering hot. "Are you joking?" She swept Rebecca behind her as she stepped toward where the floor fell into the basement. "I need to know if you were making a joke when you said that, or if you are as incompetent as my husband, so please answer honestly."

Mingus hooked his free hand onto the back of his neck. "Joking, ma'am," he said, his gaze dangling down his nose. The house crackled and sputtered in a new silence, rammed by a relentless summer wind.

When Elizabeth spun to confront her husband, Mingus lowered himself into the basement below where Andrew and Guy had already sought asylum. Charles felt abandoned by his buddies, defenseless as his wife started toward him. He cracked his knuckles one by one as a dreadful tar boiled in his gut.

"What is wrong with you?" Elizabeth barked quietly, close enough for Charles to see that the diamonds in her eyes had dropped in streaks down cheeks that burned hot and raw. Her head jutted from her drooped shoulders like a vulture's.

"Lizzy, we were keeping an eye on her."

A puff of amusement pushed through her swollen sinuses, an incredulous laugh that made Charles sneer. "So, in case she fell into the basement, you'd have seen it, right?"

"Mingus was right there! I was two feet away!"

"I can't do this," Elizabeth said, turning away from her husband, her voice glowing red, then repeated. "I can't do this, Charles. I just can't."

"Can't do what?"

"*This!*" she shouted. "I can't do it! I *can't.*" Her burning voice blistered into ash, crumbled mid-sentence; each grey syllable tumbled onto the amber floor beneath them. "I just can't anymore, not if you…" But the words lodged themselves somewhere within, too big to squeeze through.

"Not if I what?"

Her lips warped, and her eyes retreated behind their lids like they were dropping curtains, and her body bobbed, bouncing the breath out of her in ragged gasps. Tears dribbled clumsily from the corners of her eyes, ran in wide bands across her cheekbones, in droplets onto her dress, collected beneath her neck. Her rigid hands waved like fans in the heat.

Charles took a step toward his wife with open palms. "No!" Elizabeth screeched and leaped backward. "Please no. Please," she pleaded and scooped Rebecca up into her trembling arms. As she shuffled to the front door, Charles saw his daughter's pupils filling their round frames, peeking over her mother's shoulder before they disappeared together into the wild wind.

Charles heard Rebecca's bright voice as they skidded down the front steps. "Don't worry, mama," she said. "I'm safe." But even this was wiped away by a breeze that seemed to steal the world away from him.

Standing in the foyer, Charles lowered his unseeing eyes, took a deep breath, and wrapped himself in the house's silence. He sensed its steady respiration, the roil of its blood, its deep-seated heartbeat; it calmed him to know that this structure was coming to life, cleared his crowded mind.

When he opened his eyes, he saw Mingus pulling himself onto a joist, his broomstick arms shaking as they straightened. "Sorry about that, brother," he said. But Charles remained silent. Instead, he stepped quietly to the window, stared at the swirling, smearing world beyond the building's walls, wondered at the stillness of this space when everything around him was such a mess. "Hey, for what it's worth," Mingus said, sidling up to his friend. "I thought she was alright. I wasn't going to let anything happen to her."

"I know," Charles finally said. "It's not you."

"If you want," Andrew mumbled from the basement, "we can keep working while you go talk to her. We don't want you in no doghouse."

"Yeah," Mingus added, his slick arm wrapping around Charle's shoulders. "We can't have you in the doghouse. You gotta go say sorry."

Charles's gaze slipped from the sweeping trees down to the dust, where he spotted Elizabeth's cross-stitch linen still clamped in a wooden hoop, the words "God Bless This" threaded on a loose flap that fluttered in the wind. In it, he saw Elizabeth's true heart—half-started, dust-speckled, but sincere and loyal nonetheless.

He leaned out the window and reached into the unruly wind to pluck the project from the dirt before pulling himself back inside. "No, let's keep working," he said, clutching the hoop in his hand. "She'll be better when we finish this house." The sigh that shot from his nostrils matched the weather's intensity. "We just gotta finish the house."

Charles didn't see Andrew glance at Guy, a look as straight and taut as a wash line. He didn't see Mingus tuck the corners of his mouth between his teeth, massage his own shoulder as if he had been beaten up. He didn't see the delicate stitches. All he saw was his wife's blessing.

Lester Lancaster
May 14th, 1982

The hiss sizzled in his ears, the tape unspooling, and he decided that he deserved that sibilance more than the birds that bubbled behind him in the park or the shush of traffic.

But then a ribbon of feedback rose from the hush and snapped the song open, releasing the rest of the instruments—drums too simple to strut so confidently, stamping mechanically onto the grunting bass; synth lingering like smoke around a shotgun; guitars looping and slipping all across the song. And that's when the pixie's voice pushed its way in, too certain, too sassy: "I am one of the noticeable ones, notice me," she whined during the chorus and Lester rolled his eyes. Everything about this band and their cassette seemed to beg for his attention—but they had it; he felt his toe tap against the foamy sole of his flip-flop.

Lester looked down at the piece of paper pinned beneath his thumb, considered crushing it in his palm, popping it discreetly into the nearby trash can. He didn't, though. Instead, his eyes traced the "Eighty-Four Dollars" scrawled in the sort of hand that conveys both care and confidence, power and finesse. It was beautiful. At the bottom, Franklin's signature bounced, the "F" rising over the rest of his name like the church on the other side of town, its tall steeple leering at the lower, lesser buildings.

Lester looked up to see someone he had seen before: That homeless man, inching along Fourth Street in dull grey velcro shoes. He dragged a large black garbage bag behind him, clutched it in the same hand as his cane. Each step seemed like a desperate stretch toward salvation, so Lester looked away—at the apple blossoms blooming in the park behind him, with their sweet, powdery smell; at the sunlight twinkling on the dewy grass and streetlights, skidding off the Civic Center's marble and glass; at the white sun pulling itself over the knot of clouds gathering at the horizon line. It was a perfect day, really, but Lester tilted back toward his paycheck. He traced the word "Eighty-Four," slid along the corkscrew "E" like it was a waterslide.

As soon as he entered the record store earlier that morning, saw Franklin perched behind the register, Lester's skin curdled. Walking across the store felt like wading up some stream. Behind his glasses, Franklin seemed unwilling to look at Lester's face. Still, he asked how Lester was in a cardboard tone, how his week had been before plucking his paycheck from a shelf beneath the register.

Lester accepted the piece of paper, but stood at the counter even after Rocco had said goodbye, "See you soon enough," with a prickly chuckle. He stood there even after Rocco retreated into the office, door closed, blinds crimped. He waited for something, some signal or exchange or expression, some major chord to indicate the end of this adventure.

That's when he saw the cassette sitting on the

countertop, the cover featuring a woman's face who stared at him with dreary interest. He recognized the band name, Missing Persons, because he had seen a music video that week, a premiere on MTV. The words "Promotional Copy" were stamped in gold foil across the album's title *Spring Session M.* Lester didn't think twice about pocketing it and slipping out of the store.

He stared at the plastic case. The woman printed on the J-card mesmerized Lester, her gaze piercing a slash of purple paint, her hair a blonde and pink flame that filled the frame. But it was her lips that captivated Lester the most—cherry red, upturned just enough so you only hoped she was smiling at you.

Across the street, the homeless man folded himself toward the sidewalk, reaching for an aluminum can crumpled beneath his feet. Lester guessed that he was collecting cans for change to feed the habit boring a hole into his heart. His sapling legs seemed about to snap behind his khaki pajama pants, and his cane wavered like a metronome. Lester prepared to watch this homeless man fall chin-first onto the pavement, bit his lip in anticipation, but the man snatched the flattened can from the ground. As he swung it toward his garbage bag, the aluminum puck caught its lip and slid down onto the ground. Lester's head shot backward, releasing a silent cloud of incredulous laughter toward the steel blue sky. *This is too painful,* he decided. *I can't keep watching.*

Instead, he thought about the previous week and his last moment working at Rocco's.

It wasn't that big of a deal. Some kid approached him, no doubt already on summer vacation from college.

Lester remembered how unnatural his hair and eyebrows looked against his tan skin, flashing in the light like something metallic, and how his Hawaiian shirt's upturned collar sliced against his cheeks. When he spoke, Lester lost himself in his almost perfectly placed white teeth, almost comedic in their brightness, almost cartoonish. Lester had to ask him to repeat himself.

"Do you have that Olivia Newton-John record," he asked, "the one with 'Physical?'"

Lester's face became stony, tasted bitter words in his mouth, but remembered his lesson from the previous day: He couldn't tell this kid that they didn't have it. So he told him not to get it. "It's a waste of your money," he said. "Plus the song is already sort of passé, isn't it?" It wasn't that big of a deal, but the kid insisted, so Lester walked him over to their Billboard wall to show him that—see?—it wasn't charting anymore, that it was already lost to time, and maybe he could recommend *Beauty and the Beat* by the Go-Gos, whose brilliance he now intimately understood.

That's when the kid noticed the album on another nearby wall in the store's "Pop" section, Olivia's short hair slicked over her white headband, her expression provocative and ambiguous. Lester tried to beat him to it, but couldn't, so he had to pull the album from the kid's hands, assuring the kid that even his boss hated this record. "*That guy over there* wouldn't even sell it to you," Lester insisted. "Hell, he wouldn't even mind if I snapped the record in half." So he did. Lester bent the jacket until he heard the muted pop between his fingers. It was't a big deal, but Franklin saw the whole thing, and he did mind.

At some point, the music in Lester's ears faded to something that sparkled like air rising from a champaign flute, bubbled past that pixie's leaden whisper. A weird synth line descended slowly like a daddy long leg, and Lester knew this was the song he had seen on MTV—that hazy, dystopian video in which everyone's trashed hair became blue silhouettes in the moonlight. The video was stupid, but he still shrugged his shoulders in time to the pixie's wisdom, her voice vaguely confident, strutting with the drums as she sang about life being strange, about not knowing your destination.

When a sour tone stepped between her voice and the song's bare beat—synthetic and aggressive and round, like an aluminum baseball bat—Lester rumpled his brow until he realized the sound was not part of the recording. Half a block away, a car honked its horn at some lumps on the ground. It was the homeless man, his garbage bag convulsing on the pavement beside him, his right arm extended as if some samaritan were trying to tug him to safety. But there was no such samaritan, and it took Lester only a second more to realize he needed help.

Lester's instinct told him to wait for someone else to help this man—that he was too far away, that he couldn't just leave his belongings on the bench, that this really wasn't his problem. But the honking drilled into his conscience, and Lester found himself trampling toward the scene almost subconsciously. About halfway there, he mentally prepared himself for the stench that was about to spike him, took deep breaths in time with his steps. But there was something in that man's expression that made him forget his concern. The angle of his head reminded Lester of a baby bird.

The honking grew more palpable with each step until Lester arrived at the man's side. There, the sound resonated in his ribs and sternum, but he maintained his composure as he hoisted the man to his feet, depositing his knuckly hand back onto his cane. The man looked ragged back on two feet, hair steaming off his head, his expression stirred like pancake batter. Lester plucked his mesh hat from the pavement, noting its constellation of lapel pins, and the lifeless garbage bag.

The horn continued to blare, drilling deeper and deeper into his brain. As the sedan crept forward, he saw the small woman sneering in the driver's seat, her lips a perfect V, but Lester planted himself in her path, knotting his arms across his chest and pressing his mouth into a straight, nearly invisible line. Even when the car's bumper butted up against his knees. Lester stood there motionless, enduring the tearing horn and hot engine, until the man had stepped successfully onto the curb. "What the hell is wrong with you?!" he screamed over the sound, smacking the hood of the car. "You're a terrible human! You probably listen to Olivia Newton-John!" He knew the insect inside the car couldn't hear him, but he felt better releasing his fury.

Lester glared as the car departed, then turned toward the homeless man, who bobbled toward the bench where Lester had abandoned his Walkman. "Let me help," he said, snaking an arm beneath the man's shoulder, the incident still reverberating through his trembling body. "We can sit on this bench and take a break."

"My goodness," the man said, lowering himself

onto the bench. "I know these legs haven't been working right lately, but I've never just flat-out fallen before."

Lester wasn't sure he believed him, but noticed how tightly his left hand grasped his cane, his knuckles like ivory bubbles about to pop. "Well, it looks like you survived at least," Lester tried to joke. "Did you break anything? A hip? A wrist?"

A smile settled on the man's face, and it occurred to Lester that this man wasn't really old at all. "I'm generally pretty bruised and busted, but my body somehow hangs in there." He stuck out a thin hand. "My name is John."

"Lester." John's hand felt frail in Lester's palm, like something he could crush if he wanted to.

"Well, Lester, I owe you a heap of thanks." He released Lester's hand and ran it through his smoky hair, slicked it back like the motion was instinctual; the sparse stands streaked across his pale scalp like pinstripes. "Boy, am I embarrassed," he said, a clumsy chuckle tumbling from his lips.

"Don't be embarrassed," Lester said. "I do more embarrassing things than that every day. Trust me, this is nothing."

The comment coaxed another chuckle out of John and, as it skidded away, Lester realized that he was stuck sitting next to this delicate homeless man with nothing to say. *At least he doesn't smell*, he thought, noticing his ankles stretching out of his velcro shoes and rising into the cuffs of his khaki pajama pants. The image startled him; they were soapy white, hairless, wrist thick.

"See that building over there?"

Lester looked at where John was pointing, but all he saw was the Civic Center looming over the sidewalk. "That building? With the columns?"   "That's the one." John said, easing into the bench. "You know, I built it?"
Here we go, Lester thought, a smirk to tightening his cheeks. "Is that right?"

"Well, I designed it," John added, stabbing his cane into the concrete. "But I was on site when they built it, helped pour some of the concrete, did odd jobs like that. That building's got my name all over it."

"I'm sure it does," Lester said, losing himself in a sky so blue that it seemed fake. "So is that what you do for a living? You're an architect?"   "Oh, no, not anymore," John said. "I've been retired. Not long, but long enough." He let out a small sigh as if by accident. "It's rotten, being retired. I lost my wife five years ago, just before I stopped working. My goodness, it's boring. No one to talk to, to share your life with." He stopped himself, but the momentum of what was left unsaid rolled over him. "That building's all I got," he said after a while, "the closest thing I have to a child."

Lester's eyes slid down the sky, down the Civic Center's overcast facade, and onto the asphalt in front of him. His shoulders slumped. Something about what John said had deflated him—and not the revelation that his man was not homeless. It was his lonely confession. Lester knew something about the subject.

"What about you, Lester?"

"Um," Lester replied. "What do you mean?"

"Your job," John smirked. "What do you do?"

Lester swallowed. His saliva tasted like plastic and slipped through his esophagus too easily. "Well, not much," he answered. "I just recently lost my job." *That's enough,* Lester decided, his gaze stuck on a black gob of gum spat out onto the sidewalk.

"Sorry to hear that," John said. "So you know what it's like—the boredom, the bad television, the suffocating silence that can fill a room."

Lester shrugged.

"I mean, you can only walk through the park so many times a day, right?

Lester nodded; he know exactly what John meant.

John's hand slapped Lester's left leg. "So let me buy you pancakes," John howled, a ragged smile tearing across his face. "It's the least I can do for the man who saved my life."

"No thanks," Lester said before he could consider the offer. The thought of spending an hour or more watching some deteriorating man take messy bites of week-old apple pie and spill his coffee on his shirt, all for the sake of small talk, made him want collapse like a cardboard box, even if something within him really, really wanted to accept the offer. He didn't know what, but he could feel it just behind his heart, easy to ignore but incessant nonetheless.

If he insists, Lester told himself, *then maybe.*

"Oh, come on," John said, his eyes beady behind a pair of spectacles that drooped past his nostrils. "We can keep each other company. You know, a couple of playboys untethered by employment. Plus, it's a free breakfast for you—win-win, right?"

A laugh sprung from Lester's lungs. He felt his ponytail tickle his shoulders as he shook his head. "Playboys?"

"See, I knew I'd win you over," John said. "So what do you want to eat? Know any good spots around here that I don't?"

Lester felt his facade crack further, felt the living thing beneath it show itself. If no one else, he could be real with this flimsy man whom he had lifted from the literal gutter and was now offering him free food. "What if I told you that I got a sandwich guy that'll make you a cold cut submarine any hour of the day?" he said.

"I'd say it's a done deal, then," John said. "Just one favor—could you walk me past the Civic Center on the way? I gotta say hello."

Lester didn't want to say no, though it was a strange request. He hauled the the man onto his legs and helped him steady himself before handing him his hat. John slung it onto his head; it advertised the 803rd Engineers, which Lester assumed had something to do with World War II, noting the gold laurels on the bill. On John's head, he noticed the patch for the first time—a cartoony man beneath an olive beret (*No*, Lester corrected himself, *a helmet*) with six spider legs stringing a web, its gaping mouth and narrowed gaze conveying a playful sort of focus. It reminded him of Spider-Man, but a lovable Disney loaf instead of his friendly neighborhood web-slinger. He also noticed that the back of John's polyester jacket said something about the 803rd with golden letters spelling out the words "World War II Veteran" and "United States Air Force."

As they stepped together across Fourth Street, his

hand spotting John's shoulder, Lester couldn't decide if he was annoyed or relieved. Having breakfast with some strange man who couldn't stand on his own feet sounded like his Hell—especially if he had to listen to this man mumble through his food.

But there was something about John, Lester decided—his humor and humility, his shameless vulnerability, but something else—a kindred spirt that Lester recognized within himself. The things he said and way he spoke felt so familiar. He recognized that pain, even if he hadn't lost a wife or wasn't a war veteran.

"There you are," John said, the syllables slipping from his rigid smile as he stepped onto the curb in front of the Civic Center. "You look good this morning. Strong." With each step closer to concrete facade, John's conversation seemed more candid, more sincere. He placed his palm on the gritty exterior. "Hey, I tried to clean you up up a little this morning but…well, you saw the rest."

Lester stood on the curb and tried not to shine too much attention on John. *He's not homeless*, he thought, *but he still seems crazy*. A person passed by, a businesswoman buttoned from neck to ankle, and shot a glance at John that cut across the sunlight at his newfound friend. For a split second, anger consumed Lester, but a clenched fist was all that manifested.

"This is Lester," John said, tilting toward the man standing on the curb, and Lester's fist twisted loose. "He helped me out earlier. I convinced him to have breakfast with me. Finally, someone I can bore with my stories again, right?"

Lester smirked in silence as he stepped toward the building, its cement pillars no less intimidating than before. On the side of the building, he saw a plaque blackened by years of snow and wind and automobile exhaust: "The Morton Weiseule Civic Center, Circa 1956," he read. "Architect: John Barber."

Dang, Lester thought.

"Okay, that'll do for now," John said, breaking his monologue with the Civic Center. "Now where's that sandwich place?"

Lester turned from the plaque. "Um, well, let's cut through the park. It's faster."

"Swell," John said. "See you later, sweetie."

"Bye," Lester said to the building and quickly caught up with John, who was already darting across Fourth Street.

Becky McLaughlin
November 16th, 2011

"So, Ms. McLaughlin, catch me up," Mrs. Elaine Warsaw said from her side of a desk suspiciously clear of clutter. Her flat palms pressed onto its laminate surface like they were keeping it calm. "How has your freshman year been going so far?" Her lips settled into a smile as hard as cold concrete.

But Becky didn't know what to say. She had never been in a principal's office before and was surprised by how impersonal it felt—no pictures in frames, no mug full of colorful pencils, no dish glowing with individually wrapped peanut butter cups. She still liked the room, with its high ceilings and wide windows and the neat row of filing cabinets—all grey but at different heights—that seemed to quiet the walls painted the color of watermelon saltwater taffy.

She also didn't know what she did wrong. She suspected she was there because of the collage that covered the bathroom stall on the second floor, the one with her signature at the bottom. In fact, she was sure that was why she was there. But why would she get in trouble for covering such disgusting and degrading vandalism? Would she be suspended for standing up for herself and simultaneously beautifying the school? The counterarguments raged inside her mind, ready and unruly; she pictured them hiding beneath black hoods and behind bandanas, hurling molotov cocktails. Her brother had warned her that Warsaw was a wicked bitch.

So to simplify the whole situation, or maybe to distract herself from her anger, Becky told the truth. "Bad," she said, "but better now."

"Oh, I'm sorry to hear that," Warsaw said, her expression relenting slightly. "Why has it been so bad?"

"It's better now," Becky repeated, worried that the principal had missed the most important part of her answer. "But, I don't know, it's just been weird with my family and friends. Bullies too, I guess."

"Would you care to tell me a little more?"

But Becky wasn't sure she wanted to share these details with her principal. She could barely tell Frances about her mom's apathetic intimidation, about her brother's undiagnosed psychopathy; even Becky's best friend had been avoiding her all week, playing a strange game of tug-of-war in which neither side pulled.

The bullying was different. Though the wounds remained, it seemed suddenly surmountable. Becky answered the principal's question by shaking her head.

Warsaw's smile reminded Becky of a carefully sculpted statue. "Well, that's okay," she said. "But you should know that you can always talk to me about what's on your mind, especially if you're dealing with stuff." The way she said "stuff" made Becky's mouth squirm to one side of her mouth. "But things really are better now. I mean it. I have been making my own artwork, and it has helped a lot."

"Of course," Warsaw said. "I'm sure you already figured out that's why I called you into my office, right?"

Becky nodded, melted into the slick fabric of her chair. In her mind's eye, she saw herself, this sliver wrapped in a faded hoodie, all freckles and zits, her hair sticking out the side of her head. She tied her arms around her torso and drew her heels onto the ledge of her seat.

"We became aware of your artwork yesterday morning," Warsaw said. "And I do want to stress right away that I view it as artwork, not vandalism." She stretched over her desk, her elbows supporting broad shoulders that seemed ill-suited for a pantsuit. "Becky, it's really lovely."

Becky blinked. "Wait, what?"

"Your artwork in the bathroom," Warsaw repeated. "It's lovely. What inspired you to make a collage on the inside of a bathroom stall?"

"I don't—" Becky started, then hesitated, looking into Warsaw's widened eyes. Her collages allowed her to stand straighter, but she still wasn't sure they were special, let alone "lovely;" the circumstances of her creation certainly weren't, and she wasn't sure she wanted to reveal that. "I guess I just thought the stall looked boring," she answered.

Warsaw's smile slumped onto her chin. "You know that I used to be an art teacher, right?" she said, but continued before Becky could answer. "Well, we've also been having graffiti issues in the bathrooms—if you think the girls is bad, you should see the boys. I'm not sure how intentional you were, but your collage takes something ugly and turns it into something beautiful."

Becky kept blinking. Her heartbeat clanged bright and bell-like in her ribcage.

"All the teachers have been talking about it too," Warsaw added. "I know this seems bizarre, because you sort of did this without permission, and it sort of seems like vandalism. But, in a way, it's sort of a solution to our vandalism too. I talked to Ms. Browning—you're supposed to be in her class right now, right? She told me that you had turned in a couple of other impressive collages too." Here, Warsaw leaned back again; the buttons on her blazer blinked beneath the room's fluorescent lighting. "So, we talked this morning about offering you more opportunities to create. How would you feel if we commissioned a few more collages?"

Becky bit her bottom lip with the tips of her teeth. Her shoulders scrunched toward each other. "I don't understand," she said. "You want me to do more collages? Like, where? In other bathrooms?"

"Sure, whichever ones you want. You could even sneak into the boys bathrooms after school. And we'll let you use the library's old magazines if you need them." Warsaw gazed out the window at the neighborhood, grayscale and stained. "Of course, we'll pay you too. Maybe $10 per door?"

"You'd *pay* me?" she shouted too loud.

"Absolutely. It wouldn't be right if we didn't compensate an artist whose art provided us with some sort of value, would it? $10 isn't much, but it's all we could scrape up for now."

As her head bounced back between her shoulders,

Becky crawled back into her charcoal mind. *People would probably just make fun of me,* she thought. *They'd probably vandalize my art.* She imagined sitting on some stubborn toilet seat and finding more cruel comments—this time, though, scrawled onto artwork that reflected her soul.

"Can I think about it?" she asked, her smile insincere and desperate.

As she stepped down the mostly abandoned hallway to her art class, eyes open, Becky weighed the pros and cons. Her head fizzed with adrenaline, the kind that made her dizzy, giddy, glad—emotions to which she wasn't accustomed, but set her mind in motion. She started thinking about how she could pull it off—which colors could go where given a certain flooring, a certain stall.

Something in the back of her head stung. *What if this is some kind of trick,* she thought, *or if there's some kind of catch?* Tom would tell her not to do it, not to trust Warsaw under any circumstances.

Her footsteps became brighter as she entered the bathroom. Becky shouldered past the mirrors and headed straight for her stall. *Maybe,* she hoped, *seeing my collage will help me decide.* The door clanked behind her as she fell onto the seat, settled herself for a second, opened her senses to her collage. Her gaze swept across it, moved from one side to the other as if carried by some current. She felt like she was staring at a stream, brisk and deep, a streak of sunlight slicing through it; ancient stones collected on its bed beneath slimy shadows cast by branches that reached across its banks. A smile tightened on her lips; she really felt the life in this collage.

Becky had to lean toward her signature to decipher the blot beneath it, an addendum of some sort: "Becky McLaughlin is a bitch."

She felt something shift inside her, adding weight to her already cumbersome spirit, but these sensations dimmed almost instantly. Her hands reached into her bag and pulled out an issue of *Cosmopolitan* that she found beside the toilet at her house, then scampered through the pages, searching for the right color as if by feel—something green, something alive. She found in blades of grass that swayed toward a mountainous landscape in an antihistamine ad and squeaked as she tore it from the magazine. In an instant, she had Mod Podged the piece over the graffiti, leaving her original signature untouched.

As she walked back to class, Becky realized how alive her artwork really was—glowing and gleaming in the offset light, sure, but growing as well, even evolving. More exciting, though, was the realization that she had complete control over it. Her body bounced down the stairs, floating almost automatically toward her class, but she had descended too deep in her head to notice. *Who cares if someone vandalizes my art*, she told herself. *I can cover it up. I can protect it. I have that control.*

The art room's subwoofers were thumping as Becky entered. The classroom's harsh lighting added to its cluttered, chaotic ambiance. A couple of her classmates dabbed acrylic onto canvas, nodding to the Adele song that vibrated the air around them, and a few more mumbled to each other, some with pencils bitten between their teeth or swirled in their hair, but the rest coiled into themselves, headphones dripping from their ears.

"Becky," a voice squeezed between each beat like a needle through a colorful quilt. "Did you just come back from Mrs. Warsaw's office?"

Becky nodded. Ms. Browning didn't look like an art teacher, with her knee-length skirts and pastel dress shirts. Becky sometimes wondered if she sold Mary Kay after work or moonlit as an accountant. She didn't talk like other art teachers who addressed their students with syrupy voices as if they were kindergarteners. Browning talked like a sorority girl, upbeat and bobble-headed. Becky responded well to it; this teacher's encouragement kept her excited, eager to take risks, motivated to come to school.

Browning weaved between tables of hypnotized students in her sea foam green shirt, her smile long and wide, her ponytail bobbing behind her. "So, did she tell you about our idea?"

Becky stopped just inside the door, allowing Browning to come to her, and offered another nod in response.

"So what do you think?" Her tiny teeth somehow filled her enormous mouth.

"I'll do it."

Browning pinned a smile between her pressed lips. "All right," she said, then repeated it. "All right all right." From her electric and intense eye contact, Becky could tell that, behind her bank teller attire, she wanted to clap her palms together toddler-like, or pump her fist, or maybe rush her with a hug, but was stifling her excitement. "Well, why don't you take time today to think about it a little and run some ideas by me before class ends?"

When she landed in her assigned seat, Becky immediately unpacked her bag—a stack of mangled magazines, innards dangling from between lacerated pages; her purple folder, its corners perky, its contents pressed and preserved; her set of X-Acto knives.

One kid at her table, a senior, squeezed Elmer's glue onto a piece of construction paper; as the blob flattened slowly on the fibrous surface, she sprinkled a finger full of glitter onto it and released a satisfied sigh. Another kid at her table was an impressive illustrator; his line drawings were somehow both realistic and cartoonish, frightening and playful. He was a freshman like Becky, and she had known him since Kindergarten but never talked to him. He uncovered his sketchbook, then peeked over his glasses at the bold, deliberate lines on his paper.

There was one more kid assigned to their table whom everyone called Randall—that wasn't his real name, but Becky didn't know what his real name was—but he spent most days flirting with a short girl whose colorless pixie cut reminded Becky of a mother cardinal, so his seat often went unoccupied. As she pulled her bottle of Mod Podge out of her bag, though, Becky was startled to find Marley Martin sitting in the seat and staring at her mound of magazines.

"Hi," she said, her eyelids dark smudges that contrasted her pale skin and suspicious grin.

Becky tried to look busy, flipping open her folder to inspect the images she had cut carefully from her magazines. "Uh, hi," she said. She still felt guilty for tossing one of the girl's flyers in the garbage a month ago.

"I'm Marley," the girl said. "I saw your collage in the bathroom, and I just wanted to tell you that it's really cool.

"Thanks," Becky said, shooting her a shy smile before rifling through her cutouts for a place to hide. Becky had always thought Marley was cool. Her raven hair fell around her slender face, straight but always teased so that it seemed like static electricity was lifting it from her neck. She was a junior and had cool taste in music, or so it seemed to Becky. Some days, she wore a black leather jacket that seemed a little too tight, unzipped and unbuckled, with weathered grey elbows. Beneath it, she wore shirts with what Becky assumed were bands, always with aggressive and mysterious names like Mastodon and Torche and Every Time I Die, all of them boy's sizes, black and faded. She looked punk, but never rebellious; weird, but always kind of cool; fashionable, but never intentionally. She wasn't a stick bug, like Becky, but wasn't a bumblebee either, and would never have been mistaken for a model; her beauty was mundane and profound.

"Why'd you do it?" she asked, resting her chipmunk cheeks on her palms. Becky noticed her nails, vinyl black and chipped.

"I was just covering up graffiti," Becky said. "About me."   Marley's expression swelled with surprise, and Becky noticed her eye color—a streaky, oily amber that contrasted the rest of her aesthetic. "Woah," Marley said. "That's… pretty cool."

"Why?"

"It's just—I don't know. I thought you were trying to stick it to the school or something, but it's way cooler that you're trying to stick it to the assholes instead."

Becky shrugged, then flipped through her folder, pausing at the cutout of a white plate, untainted but for a smear of red; she was saving it for something special.

"What kind of music do you like?" Marley asked, her smile snarl-like.

"Punk, I guess."

"Cool, me too. What bands?" Becky tilted her head toward her hoodie. "All Time Low," she said. "I like some songs by Sleeping With Sirens and Pierce the Veil too."

Marley's smile straightened. "Hmm," she hummed. "We can work on that. Do you go to shows or anything? Concerts?"

"Warped Tour last summer."

These questions made Becky's stomach tighten. *Is she trying to make fun of me*, Becky wondered, *or be my friend?* As she stared at the folder, a small piece of paper fluttered into her frame of view—a flyer. She picked it up, scanned a list of bands that she'd never heard of, but she was curious about the softer name toward the top, Slumberland, and the dreamy photograph that filled the flyer's background.

"You should come to this," Marley said over her shoulder as she stepped back toward her table. "I think you'd like the bands, plus it's in town and easy to get to. I'll be there too, so you'll at least know me, and I'll introduce you to everyone else."

Becky rose from her folder and, for the first time, felt like she could sit in her seat—really sit, out in the open, unguarded, without slouching. "Okay," she said, her stomach easing, her eyes alight.

Barbara Farmer
August 15th, 1945

It was a strange sight to see, the strands of toilet paper draped over telephone wires, swaying in the breezeless night. Music bubbled out of every surrounding downtown building, a static simmer beneath occasional cheers and screams and wild laughs that seemed so wrong on a Wednesday night. All these sounds boiled over and onto each other, creating the kind of distant din that reminded Barbara of Chicago all those years ago. *Has it really been three years?* she wondered, peeking through the restaurant's front window.

Anita leaned on her, the bronze bracelets on her wrists jingling like a percussion instrument she'd seen someone exotic play in a picture. She had sunk a few celebratory drinks before they departed, but Barbara suspected she had also snuck some drinks in her bedroom while she got ready. They had held hands as they strolled downtown; it was Barbara's strategy for keeping Anita from toppling in her high heels. She remembered minding Anita's feet as they stepped over the confetti that speckled downtown—she couldn't believe that they threw actual confetti in their tiny town—and complimented the celebratory sky above.

Suddenly, the door of the restaurant opened, flinging

shadows across the sidewalk. "Japs!" a woman shrieked, pointing a steak knife at the stunned pair. "You ain't any of them Jap spies, now, are you? The war's over an' you lost! Go back to the Orient!"

A small, pockmarked face peeked over the woman's slumped shoulders. Barbara recognized it as Edna's, but it barely reassured her, as the woman with the knife still stood between them. "Mom, that's Anita!" Edna said, tugging the woman's sagging cardigan. "And put that darn knife away. What is wrong with you?"

Barbara's face fell like a white bedsheet over a clothesline. She squeezed Anita's hand, but Anita just laughed her squeaky door laugh. "Oh, ma!" she said. "You're a gas!"

"She's had a few already," Edna said as she tugged her rambling mother back through the restaurant's darkened foyer.

"Haven't we all?" Anita added with a chuckle. "Come on, Barbara. Let's have some fun."

But Barbara wasn't in the mood for fun. As they wound their way between rows of booths toward the counter, Barbara could think of no one but John. *How is he celebrating?* she wondered, trying to picture a relaxed smile on his face, the cigarette in his hand. Other thoughts invaded her mind—*Maybe he doesn't know the war's over,* and, *Maybe he isn't alive to celebrate*—but Barbara treated them like bees, knowing they would buzz away if she ignored them long enough.

As she dropped herself onto a stool, Barbara noticed that the Sunnyside Cafe was only a quarter or so full. Edna, who ran the restaurant while she waited for her husband to return, decided to close it for VJ Day, opening it only to friends and family so they could celebrate together in private. This was the restaurant where Anita had held down her job since they moved to Wisnago, and Joy too before she moved back home. The restaurant never felt comfortable to Barbara, though.

It was a strange sight to see, the half-lit diner dripping with shadows and smoldering like an untended fire. Normally the restaurant played tight, tidy jazz and swing, the sort even parents would let their children listen to. Tonight, though, the song throbbed and swayed somewhere between too tender and out of breath.

Some patrons clogged the aisles between the booths in pairs or leaned against the Formica tabletops, but most crammed themselves into booths; they melted into each other, dribbled under the tables. A circle of wine painted the bottom of each glass littering the counter's surface.

"So, is there anything I can get you two?" Edna asked on the other side of the counter. She was older than the girls, but not much; her marmalade curls and pink lips had a way of making her seem younger or older as needed, but the scars from her acne made her seem perpetually adolescent. "Whatever you want is on the house tonight."

"Wine!" Anita announced as if she were speaking for the entire restaurant.

"I'd love a glass of water," Barbara said, then turned back to the diner, the swaying couples, gabbing, laughing, somehow filling the half-full room. The low lights and music's sweaty sway, insistent and inescapable, were all almost too much for Barbara. Her lungs shriveled within her ribs, and she reached for Anita's hand to steady herself only to find her friend already draped across the counter like a coat.

"What's wrong, hon?" she asked Barbara, her cheek flattened on the countertop.

"I don't know," Barbara said. "The diner just seems so strange like this, so dim and noisy, don't you think?"

Anita lifted her head like it was a boulder, looked to one side and the other before landing back onto the surface. "Looks like a party to me," she mumbled.

Barbara sighed, flattened her forearms onto the counter, and let her weight hang loose from her shoulders. *Anita's right,* she told herself. *This is a party. Give yourself permission to have some some fun, to celebrate John's inevitable return home.* But Barbara's body seemed stuck to the bar, weighed down by discomfort or fear, by the music or ambiance, or something else.

"I know how you feel," a voice pushed through the calm chaos. Barbara hadn't noticed Edna's mother-in-law on a nearby stool. The way her body stuck onto the seat reminded Barbara of a wad of chewing gum, lilting toward the counter, off-balance but never toppling onto it. "This whole celebration doesn't seem real until my little Terry is home safe and in my arms."

"Your son's still over there?" Barbara asked out of politeness, but then she noticed the steak knife balanced on the counter beside the woman's mug of wine and felt suddenly uneasy.

"He is. Not sure if he'll be coming home, though. He did that invasion at Normandy, I hear, but haven't seen nothing from him since May."

"My husband is still over there too, in the Philippines," Barbara said, but Edna's mother-in-law didn't respond. *Maybe she didn't hear you,* she mused, but she was too shy to try again. Still, she wondered how this woman knew what was bothering Barbara.

That is *it, right?* Barbara asked herself. *You're missing John tonight?*

"I don't know," she answered aloud, pushing her hands into the side pockets of her jumper and fishing out two envelopes folded and faded from years of fret. Her fingers slipped a piece of paper from one of them—a form letter John had filled out at his prison camp, Philippine Military Prison Camp number one—and flattened its creases onto the counter. She always looked at this one first because it was the first she received. John circled the options that said his health was "excellent" and that he was "well," though it contradicted the news she had heard about the Bataan Death March, the horrifying name the newspapers were calling what John went through. She wasn't sure the card even came from John, especially the message below it—to see that "everything" is taken care of, and that she give his best regards to "his friends"—but it was all she had of him after three years apart.

Where the first card plunged Barbara into John's dark reality, the second card, which arrived a year later, offered a spark of hope. He circled the same descriptors on it about his health—"excellent," and that he was doing "well"—but it was his message that dropped her to her knees the first time she read it. He wrote to please see that "sweet lovely lady" is taken care of; that, in the line beneath, (Re: Family) "be good;" and, in one final line, that he give his regards to "barbara." Though the first note hinted at what he had been through, the second reminded her that he was alive, had survived.

Barbara nipped at the inside of her cheek, let her hair bounce around her face as it hovered over the letters. These messages made her anxious about the man she had married—what he had been through and who he'd be when he returned.

Beneath the music, whose beat had become that of an enormous flag's billowing slowly in the breeze, Barbara heard a squeal and a thud. She spun around to find Anita folded on the floor beneath her stool. "Oh dear," Barbara murmured, resisting the urge to roll her eyes. "Hon, are you okay?"

Anita's laughter answered Barbara. It started airy and hushed, but spiraled wider and louder until Barbara felt her face radiate a heat that warmed the restaurant's already humid air. She tugged Anita's forearm. "We need to get you home. You're a little too tipsy tonight."

It took a few attempts for Barbara to pull tangled Anita out from under the counter. Each time she was halfway on her feet, her laughter would bounce her off balance and her slender body would sink back beneath the bar. Finally, Barbara straightened her out enough so she fell into the counter; arms spread, her back bent against the bar and black coffee hair unpinned, she looked both desperate and strangely seductive—until she spoke. "Hey, where's my drink?" she wondered aloud, provoking derisive laughter from the nearby booths.

Anita didn't fight Barbara about leaving. She just kept laughing—violently, painfully—and bumping into the booths, clinging to her friend's shoulder. As they left the restaurant into the sticky August night, Anita moved like an old, noisy jalopy down a dirt road; Barbara prayed that she wouldn't break down halfway home. "Anita, what's wrong with you?" she asked. "I've never seen you like this."

"I'm just in the mood to celebrate," she said, stray strands of hair slicing across her face. "You're not?"
"Not like this."

"Oh, come on," Anita complained, her voice colorful and violent. "We never drink."

Barbara let an exasperated sigh out into the night. "Then why are you?"

"Why aren't *you?*"

It was a throwaway question, meaningless, something a defensive drunk says when someone tells them they've had too much, but it resonated within Barbara. *Why aren't you celebrating?* she asked herself. *Your husband's coming home. Shouldn't you be happy?*

Cool humidity swirled around them, the sort that transformed the night into one of those Impressionistic paintings Barbara remembered reading about in high school. The haze seemed to swallow the celebration downtown as they entered the neighborhood on Wakes, the one lined with the colorful manors; in the dark, lit by hissing gaslights, Barbara thought they looked like gingerbread houses, their edges frosted white.

"What's going to happen to us when they come

home, Barb?" Anita took tiny steps in the empty street, and her hands clamped around Barbara's arms like bonds on a prisoner.

"What do you mean?" "I mean we've been roommates for four years. I've never really lived with anyone else, other than my parents."

Barbara's brow bent and lips bucked but, in the back of her head, she understood exactly what Anita was worried about.

"What if I don't want to leave Wisnago?"

"Then don't leave Wisnago," Barbara said, her friend's fingers tightening around her bicep. The sensation no longer felt confining, though; it felt comforting.

"What if I don't want to leave the house?"

The corners of Barbara's eyes seized and her sinuses tingled. She draped her hand over Anita as if it were a blanket.

As they turned onto Eight Street, Anita whispered, "What if he's not the same?" her voice suddenly steadier, sturdier, more sober. "What if he doesn't love me anymore?"

"Of course he will, hon," Barbara said, suddenly realizing why she had been drinking so voraciously—to blot out her fear. Anita's concerns became clear to Barbara as if illuminated by the streetlight they scuffed beneath, and they felt familiar: *What if the person you've lived for is someone you've learned to live without?*

Barbara glanced at the syrupy shadows sliding across her friend's face. Her tiny, tottering steps expressed what Barbara loved so much about this woman—her childish confidence, her innocent simplicity, the truth and weight of her emotions. She had been Barbara's best friend—her only friend, really, since Joy left—and, sometime soon, would be replaced by her husband, some stranger. "This next month will be real different," she admitted, "won't it?"

"Aren't you scared?" Anita asked.

Barbara wanted to answer yes, but something stopped her despite the questions stirring her mind. Would John be different when he returned? Would he still love her? And how had she changed? Was she still the woman that he had fallen in love with? Would she disappoint him, fall short of his expectations? And what role would she play in his life?

Instead, she lifted her hand from Anita's and pulled her friend's head to rest on her shoulder.

At Lilac, Barbara heard the faraway crackle of fireworks downtown, followed by the flame of its cheering audience. "At least someone's having fun," Anita murmured against her shoulder. It was enough to lure Barbara away from her anxiety, but when the silence returned, Barbara's mind reeled. The weight of Anita's head kept her calm, reminded her that at least one person needed her, if only for the moment.

By the time their shoes scuffed up the front porch steps, Barbara could tell she was losing Anita. "Come on, girly," she said, dragging her body into the shadows that drooped beneath the awning. "We've got to get you in bed."

"But I'm not tired!" Anita whined. In the moon's murky light, her red dress seemed incandescent, like one of those red lanterns Barbara heard were hung for railroad men. But the way Anita walked across the porch seemed more primitive than elegant. Having removed her heels blocks ago, Anita's bare feet slapped the painted floorboards.

She was worse when they entered the house. Having successfully stepped through the inky living room, Barbara let her best friend climb up the stairs on all fours, spotting her so she wouldn't slip. "This is pretty ridiculous, isn't it?" Anita asked, the stairs creaking beneath her palms and knees and the pads of her feet. But Barbara didn't say anything; a smile dented her cheeks, but only because Anita couldn't see it.

The smile lingered as she stretched down the hall to Anita's room, arriving before her housemate with just enough time to pull back her comforter. The neighborhood—illuminated by a murky, inebriated moon—lit the room just enough for Barbara to make out the most hazardous landmarks. Anita's silhouette slid into the room like a silent shadow, but landed on the bed like a beef shoulder on a butcher block.

"Barbie," Anita groaned, "sleep in my bed tonight."

"It's time for you to get some rest, hon," she said softly, as if speaking to a toddler. "You'll sleep so much better without me."

But Barbara noticed her cheeks shimmer in the starlight, noticed her eyelids twinkle, then heard the tell-tale sniffle. "Please?" Anita whimpered.

Barbara pushed a sigh out between her teeth. "Okay," she said. "For you, anything." As she kicked her leg into Anita's bed, she felt her foot tip something solid, heard the unmistakable clunk of glass on hardwood. "What did I just knock over?" she asked, pulling her wet sock into the bed.

But Anita didn't answer. Instead, her body shook in the bed; her tears ran silent, save her desperate gasps for air. Barbara scooted closer to her friend and wrapped arms around her. The stubborn smell of red wine filled the room. As Barbara realized what she had knocked over, her instincts told her to get up and clean it before it stained the floorboards—or, worse, steeped between them.

"If you take care of John as well as you take care of me," Anita whispered between hiccuped breaths, "then he will love you as much as I do."

Barbara felt Anita take a long breath, felt her tense legs relent. *The wine can wait*, she decided. She allowed the concern to evaporate, but struggled to calm her mind. Anita's wisdom echoed—*He will love you as much as I do*—but Barbara wasn't so sure.

She was aware of the absurdity of her situation, of how surreal it all seemed—sharing a bed with her drunken housemate, sobbing silently on VJ Day because her husband was heading home, reeking of spilled wine and counting the fireworks that shattered summer's silence—but only slightly, only enough to mistake it all for a dream.

Charles Stonebreaker
September 30th, 1910

All he could do was drag his brush in slow, deliberate lines across the floor, leaving even rows of lustrous stain. It was the process that focused him, but also the final product—a floor that glowed gold in the late summer sun the same way that rivers did. At the end of each row of hardwood, he'd lure himself out of his pocket of pity and build up the emotional momentum to stain the next row of hardwood that deep amber, sweet like hot maple syrup. It was all he could do.

He didn't know how to tell them. He could hear them outside casting long shadows in the garden, Rebecca's giggles mingling with the melodies the birds saved for autumn. Occasionally, he heard Elizabeth scold her daughter for being a child—"Get out of the dirt! I don't want to have to give you another bath again this evening," and, "Put that worm down, Rebecca. That's disturbing," and, "Get that hat back on! You have your father's skin, and I don't want you to get burned." He loved the innocent way his daughter defied her mother. But, today, it only made his task more difficult.

How could he tell them? The Stonebreakers were weeks away from moving into their house permanently, but that future now seemed uncertain. He swung his head like he was shaking some demon off his shoulders.

Focus, he thought, and aimed his gaze once again at the rows of hardwood stretching the length of the room beneath him. He dipped his brush back into the can, let its bristles soak up the color, then pulled the rest of the five-foot line toward the front door, scrambling over his knees and legs as if they were obstacles.

"Rebecca, come back," he heard his wife caw from the garden. "We don't know our neighbors yet. I don't want to give them the impression that we have one of those children that'll run wild in their yard and pull out all their flowers. Just stay in our yard. It's big enough."

Maybe I could find a job as a carpenter, Charles thought, his hand wavering along with the consistency of his stroke. *Or maybe I could work at that lumberyard. Maybe they need someone to help them with their orders.* He swung his head again; sweat shook free from his hair and dropped onto the stained floor, leaving marks that looked like bullet holes. He scooted back a few feet and started the row again, evened out the golden tone, concentrating on the angle of his brush, on his heavy hand. At the end of his row, he leaned against the wall and sighed. *Maybe there's a farm I could work on nearby*, he thought, *at least until winter.*

He sensed the backdoor sweep open silently, felt it suck a lump of bitter air out of the house. "Oh, you *are* here," Elizabeth said, appearing in the doorframe. The sunlight bleached the room and illuminated her cotton dress; Charles spied the silhouette of her legs behind her skirt. "Why didn't you come out and tell us?"

"I said hello when I got here," he lied. "You just didn't hear me."

"I'm sure I was shouting at Rebecca anyways," she said, closing the door behind her. "Oh my goodness, look at this house! The floors are so beautiful!"

Charles's breath quickened. He swallowed obsessively until his mouth grew stiff and dry, until each inhale felt a few beats behind. "Careful not to step on any of the wet parts," he gasped. "You'll leave permanent footprints."

"I just wanted to hide in the shade for a second, but I can head back outside if you're still working." Charles was relieved to hear Elizabeth say this but, when he looked up, she still filled the doorframe. "You don't look so good. Are you okay?"

Charles nodded, wiping the sweat beading beneath his mustache with his wrist. It was all he could do. "Just want to finish the floors today," he said, "even if it takes me until midnight."

"So do you still think we could get that guy to come out and install the wood stoves next week?" she asked, rounding the corner into the kitchen with cautious feet. "That's all we have left to do, right?

"And the cooking stove, and the gas. And we need water set up with the municipality."

He heard her twist open the tap, which squeaked like a quiet mouse; he pictured her disappointed face when no water tumbled out, the furrows cutting across her brow, running parallel with her straight, tight frown. "And then we're good to move in, right?"

Charles held a sigh in his mouth, then swallowed it like a spoonful of castor oil. "That's right. Legally, we can move in."

"So do you still think it'll be before November?"

He aimed his eyes downward but saw Elizabeth's hopeful grin peeking from the kitchen in the floor's reflection, distorted by variations in the varnish. Even in his attempts to avoid looking at his wife, he still couldn't escape her, so he closed his eyes. "Lizzy, we have to talk about something."

In his mind, he saw her shapely face fade to drab and flat. He opened his eyes to see her featureless expression staring back at him. "What?" she asked, her voice like an open palm slapping something flat.

Something flashed past the window to his right, flickered in his peripheral vision. He assumed it was a bird until he heard chaotic steps scuffing across the front porch and saw Rebecca suddenly spying through the window to his left, a mischievous smirk wrapping across her face.

"They let me go," he finally said. "I was fired."

Charles was relieved to see Elizabeth's brow uplifted, her eyes stretched open, her hand floating in front of her open lips. "Oh my god!" she said, stepping toward him but stopping at the silvery line where he had stained. "What happened?"

"I—" he uttered, but stopped himself, distracted by his daughter peeking in the window, her hair glowing around her head, dirt bruising her cheeks and chin. "I made a mistake. Too many mistakes."

Charles watched his wife's expression change in the floor's reflection: Her brow broke in half and, behind fingers that sagged lifelessly, her lips smashed into a stiff line. "But that was only that one time, right?"

"No, there were…there were more," Charles said, tilting his head back against the plaster. "They said I cost them hundreds of thousands of dollars."

"How—" Elizabeth began, but ran out of breath. She seemed stuck in the kitchen, unable to step onto the stained floor, unable to speak. When words finally emerged, they left her lips dull and heavy, like the rocks he used to build the basement: "What does this mean for, you know, the house?"

"I don't know," Charles answered. It was all that he could do. He knew that, without work, he couldn't purchase the necessities needed to make their house livable over the winter.

"How could you do this?" Elizabeth spat. Her arms trembled rigid at her side. "How could you do this to us after we've waited so long, after how hard we've worked on this house?"

"We aren't giving up on the house, Lizzy," Charles said. An eddy of emotions rose like murky floodwater inside him, clouded with fear and grief and misery, and it burned as he tried to push it back down his throat. "I have a plan to finish the house."

He looked up from her reflection at the real Elizabeth, watched her arms knot themselves beneath her breasts. Her head dangled out and over her body as if it were threatening to leap off. "I'm listening," is all she said.

He heard Rebecca's shoes stamp toward the front door, but could regard her no more than the cricket creaking in the corner.

"I was thinking I'd get another job in town, at the lumberyard down the block from Weiseule, or a butcher—someplace that has goods that need to be shipped."

"And what if you can't get a job shipping goods," Elizabeth asked, "considering that you just got fired for being incompetent?"

Charles felt the flood waters push up again, puddle at the back of his throat. Each breath dove into his lungs with more difficulty than the last, bubbled back up with more panic. He opened his mouth, hoping the muck would spill out onto the floor if necessary, but only air escaped. "I was also thinking that I could join a crew that builds houses. I've learned a lot in the past few months that I might be able to use."

Elizabeth swung her head, released the sort of breath that could easily be mistaken for both pitying laughter or a sad sigh. "You can't work in the winter," she said to her chest.

"Well, I'll find something," Charles said, sensing his tone steel. "And, by spring, we'll be living pretty in this house."

Elizabeth's head shot upward. "By spring? You mean we'll have to spend six more months of living in that dump, trying to keep that little goblin occupied?" She scanned the house owl-eyed looking for Rebecca, retreating back into her ire when she didn't find her.

The word "goblin" sent spines up Charles's arms, but he tried to ignore them. "What do you expect from me, Lizzy? I'm only trying to be realistic. It's going to take me a little time to find a job, then a little more to get paid. By the time I have enough money, it'll be too cold to install a stove and set up water." He heard his voice echoing through the empty house, felt it pierce the plaster and slats. "I'm doing the best I can."

Charles only sensed the front door swinging open behind him as he watched his wife's eyes widen in disbelief. "Your best?" she roared. "Charles, your best is destroying our family. This is your fault. You've gotten yourself fired because of your idiocy and failed to finish this house that you assured us would be done before the summer ended. And now I have to spend a freezing winter in that rathole, sharing a bed with the whole family, unable to draw hot water from our taps for a bath or even dishes!" Each of Elizabeth's breaths bounced out and away from her. "There's no way I'm spending another winter there," she began, displaying the delirious, panicked expression of a cornered raccoon. "There's no—" but then swerved suddenly out of the kitchen, out the back door. She didn't run; Charles only saw her cotton dress drift past the garden and through the neighbor's backyard.

Muddy emotion surged into Charles's brain, the pressure making his head feel so full and ripe and dizzy that he was no longer aware of his emotions. Growls quaked in the back of his mouth, but he heard neither the actual noises nor the words he murmured between them: "I hate this," and, "This is ridiculous," and "I'm done," syllables he let dribble from his lips, unaware of what they meant.

He felt the flood push into his fingertips, felt it tingle beneath his nails. "I hate this," he mumbled, staring at at the sweetgrass swaying in the neighbor's yard outside the window. "This is so damn ridiculous. I do so much for you, for this family, and I ask for is a little faith." His brain folded onto itself; thoughts sprouted in wispy strands, transparent and flaccid. It made sense, then, when he clenched his fist tight enough to pop his knuckles and searched for a place in the wall where he knew there wasn't a stud, a spot through which he could throw his hand. "I'm done," he said again. "I hate this so much. I'm sorry my devotion to my family has caused us so much goddamn turmoil!" He was aware of how forcefully his lips shaped these words, but not that he was screaming, or how violently these half-formed thoughts ricocheted throughout the room.

His fist tightened once again as he roared. "Thanks for believing in me! Thanks for valuing my goddamn existence!" In front of him, beside a window that faced Eighth Street, his mind took aim at a square of wall between two studs. The muscles around his cheeks cramped, and those inside his lips curled and tightened and twitched. "And you're welcome for building you a fucking house!"

As his fist stabbed the wall, Charles watched as an observer, a bystander watching some insane man punch plaster, so the sensation of split flesh, of cold burning bone surprised him initially. The lathes scratched his arm as he pulled it out of the wall, but those scrapes seemed insubstantial compared to his hand, which he pulled to his chest and cradled as if it were a sleeping child. He released an enormous howl into the house. It all happened so fast, but it was all he could do. With his roar still echoing, he looked at his hand; blood steered through the cracks in his skin and his knuckles began to swell into inky bulges.

"Daddy?" A small, hesitant voice poked through the endless echo of his rage. He turned around to see Rebecca standing behind the open front door. Tears sparked in her eyes. Her posture reminded him of a can that had fallen off a shelf.

"Honey," Charles said. "What are you doing here? I didn't know you were there."

As he stepped closer, he noticed fear stiffen her face, her eyes becoming waxy and lips curling out, twisted by looming tears. Charles let his shoulders drop from his neck and sighed; it temporarily halted her tears, but whimpers still wormed out between labored breaths.

"Becky, daddy's okay," Charles said. "I'm sorry you saw that. I'm sorry about everything."

But when he took a second step toward her, Rebecca bolted across the sticky floor and up the stairs. Charles could hear her steps and tiny sobs as they scampered down the hall into the smallest bedroom. He cradled his mallet of a hand and let out another sigh, realizing he had somehow made the worst situation so much worse.

He ascended the stairs slowly, as if testing each step, his head throbbing in time with his hand, his soles tacky with stain. He paused on the landing to listen, stopped to stare out the window at a neighborhood bruising in the autumn dusk. His knees and ankles trembled, tired from an afternoon of work, the gravity of the past ninety seconds.

"Becky?" he said, hushing his voice as quietly as he could, but heard no response. He walked slowly to the smallest bedroom, which would become Rebecca's; it was the only room with its door closed. "Becky?" he asked again, twisting the crystal doorknob. It didn't budge.

"Becky?" he asked again, resting his head on the door in defeat. Tears percolated in his sinuses and seeped out of his stinging eyes. He felt them streak warm down the front of his face, smack the unfinished hardwood beneath him. That's when it hit him: He had lost the people for whom he was working, for whom he had built this house.

"Becky, I know you're there. Please open the door," he pleaded, did his best to invoke whatever parental authority he still possessed, but it withered within him, lifeless beneath his throbbing, trembling body. "Becky, please."

Behind the door, all he heard was a stifled whimper, a thread of breath.

And that's when Charles felt his life dislodge and slide off of him, shatter on the ground like a shoulder of ice. He had lost his job and, with it, any hope of finishing his house. He had lost his wife, who had run out on him in a moment of panic. But the thought of losing his only ally, his daughter, choked him with sadness. He gasped between his tears. "I'm so sorry," he murmured, babbling like a child.

His head slid down the door until he had dripped onto the ground, a puddle of disappointment. His wild, violent sobs shook his whole body. The floor crackled beneath him, slick with tears and the blood that trickled from beneath his knuckles, overwhelmed by the weight of his sadness, his failure, his swollen hand.

And, behind the door, his sadness was echoed in whispers, in hushed sighs, in almost tangible thoughts that wondered why.

Lester Lancaster
May 25th, 1982

As they drifted closer to the house, a tense silence fell over John. He had been cracking jokes the entire walk until they crossed Lilac Street. Lester filled that silence out of obligation. "I'm excited for you to see my house," he said at some point.

The comment seemed to draw John from some faraway place. "Me too," he said a second late.

The oaks overhead reached across the silver sky, their branches weaving into a seamless canopy. Dozens of short, slow steps later, Lester tried again. "I hope I don't screw up lunch too bad," he said. "I guess I'd have to be pretty terrible to botch soup and sandwiches, though."

John offered a knowing smile, but nothing more. He seemed absorbed by the squat houses and sagging chain link fences as if he were planning a painting of the neighborhood. It worried Lester. *Maybe you insulted him*, he thought, *or hurt his feelings*. He decided to keep quiet just in case.

When the house was in view, they sped up. Surrounded by brighter, tidier abodes, Lester's house seemed ramshackle. The paint peeled from every exterior surface; a pallid yellow peeked behind the whitewashed siding, and the porch's steel blue split here and there, revealing bare grey wood beneath. Saplings sprouted in the gardens, and leafy weeds crawled across the yard. Lester wasn't proud of how unkept it felt, but he was excited to show John his beautiful home—except John, it seemed, was leading Lester right to it.

It felt strange, then, for Lester to say, "Here we are," since John had already stopped at the foot of the porch.

The aging man's eyes bloomed bold and colorful. He scanned the front porch, his gaze tiptoeing from the front door, along the maroon railing to the front porch swing, its chains rusting and seat mildewed, swaying in the sweetened lilac breeze. "Incredible," he murmured.

"Well, it's a nice house," Lester said, "but I'm not sure it's incredible."

John pivoted on his cane toward Lester. "Lester, what if I told you that I once lived in this house?"

"Really?"

"What are the odds?" John said, a bewildered smile spreading across his face as he started his hike up the cement steps. Lester snuck up beside him, threading an arm beneath his shoulder to help hoist him onto the porch. He hoped that John wouldn't notice the banner of mold over the front door, and was pleased to see him distracted by the mailbox and its prehistoric screech. "I always loved that sound," he told Lester with a toddler's grin. "Meant there was something good waiting for you. Used to wake me up from my naps."

When Lester shouldered open the door, the odor assaulted him—of sweat and hot sauce, savory and spicy, like a slap to the cheeks. He was horrified when John inhaled ravenously. "Good god, that smell," he said. "It's like it hasn't changed twenty years!" He stiffened his back and sniffed again. "That old wood smell—I suppose it never goes away, does it?"   "I guess not," Lester said, relieved.

At least the house is clean, Lester thought. He had scrubbed the first floor from one end to the other, leaving his aluminum chair, still aimed at his TV, to occupy the otherwise empty living room. Really, *bare* was a better word for it, but at least it was free of paper plates and styrofoam clamshells.

"Wow, Lester," John said. "You live pretty lean."

"I suppose," Lester shrugged, but felt his heart swell with pride.

"Well, show me around!" John shouted. "Give me the guided tour!" His bark echoed through the empty house, his grin like a flashlight illuminating whatever it was aimed at.

Lester led his guest first into the dining room, a cramped space where a normal dinner table would barely fit. Lester's card table seemed the perfect size, though somehow lonely with only one chair tucked beneath it. "We had a lot of dinners in this room," John said. Lester heard him sigh, but it was neither sad nor satisfied; instead, it seemed like a ghost that simply appeared before it vanished.

They walked through the doorway that connected the dining room to the kitchen, adorned with dark blue shadows that hung from the ceiling like garland. "This room hasn't changed a bit," John said. Lester looked at its white cabinets, which stretched to the ten-foot ceiling, and the refrigerator's rounded corners—molar-like, matching the laminate countertops—and imagined generations of women laying out strips of sandwich obediently onto platters, of grumbling men elbow deep in dirty dishes.

When John insisted on climbing the stairs himself, Lester felt his stomach instantly hollow. "I had the same problem with these stairs in the '40s, too," John said with checkered breath, his cane and footsteps beating a waltz beneath them. "Or, well, Barbara did. She wanted to help me up the stairs, but I was too stubborn for her."

Lester was more worried about what John would find at the top of the stairs than his pilgrimage up them.

They poked their heads into each room in order—the bathroom, the wide bedroom at the back of the hall, the square bedroom lit by the noonday sun, all empty, dampened by dust—and John nodded as he silently inspected each. But Lester knew his bedroom was next.

When the door creaked open, Lester flinched, bracing himself for the worst. John's silence offered an opportunity for Lester to scrutinize his room from an outsider's perspective—that spicy smell again, but more palpable, like something stinging the tongue; the sheets swirled like a mashed potato sculpture; boxes of comics, ill-kempt, lined against a wall, the closest thing to furniture; nicknacks line up on the floor or piled like scat in the corners; and clothes everywhere, dripping from the bed and ceiling fan and sole lamp.

John just stood in the doorway like he was afraid to enter, to disrupt what was certainly a volatile ecosystem. Lester couldn't see his face and could only imagine his friend's tortured expression. When John finally did speak, it was through a twisted smile: "I guess this was the one room you didn't get around to cleaning," he said.

"How could you tell?" Lester said, using humor to hide his embarrassment.

John leaned on his cane as his neck stretched into the room, his gaze hopping from window to window to window. "I always thought this room was so magnificent," he said, "as if the person who designed it was trying to impress someone." John turned to face Lester, revealing his slanted smirk, but Lester could tell he simply didn't want to stare at the catastrophe any further. "My wife told me that, the first time she entered this room, she had the overwhelming urge to throw open every window. I used to feel that same urge but never went through with it. Crazy, huh?"

"Crazy," Lester repeated, following him back downstairs, closing the bedroom door behind him.

John asked about the bedroom as they dipped their grilled cheese sandwiches into tomato soup, sitting on either side of the card table in the dining room. "How'd that room grow to be such a mess?" he asked, wiping his chin with his sleeve.

"I don't know," Lester said. He shoved the crust of his sandwich into his mouth before he could utter another word, fully aware of how weak his answer sounded.

"I only ask because a wise man once told me that you can learn a lot about a man by the condition of his sleeping quarters—though that wise man was my father, and he was trying to convince ten-year-old me to make my bed, but never mind those minor details."

Lester blew a half-hearted laugh through his nose out of politeness as he wiped crumbs from his best t-shirt, someone else's souvenir from Fort Lauderdale. "Well, your dad was probably right," he said, his lips tied in a smirk. "It turns out that bedroom accurately captures the state of Lester Lancaster at this moment."

"Interesting," John said. "How so?"

Lester felt like a fly hitting a spider web. He picked up his paper bowl and poured soup into his mouth, hoping it would buy him enough time to BS an answer. But no answers appeared, and John remained patient, dotting his dimples with a napkin, then folding his hands on the table. Lester gulped down the soup and displayed a strained orange smile that immediately melted from his face. "I guess," Lester began, then stopped. "I don't know, man. I'm a mess."

"That's a start."

Lester stole a stuffy breath, and it was enough to keep the walls from collapsing on him. A word swell surged inside him that burned like bile and bubbled up his throat. "Well," he said, staring into his soup, "I'm unemployed— you know that—but every time I get a job, I lose it, and I can't quite tell if I do it on purpose or not, so I guess makes me unemployable as well. I mean, I don't want to work. Who does? But I'm not sure that I want to do anything. Except, it's like, I don't want to do nothing either, you know?"

Lester noticed John nodding out of the corner of his eye, and he knew that John was listening. Thoughts sloshed back and forth, making his mind frothy.

"That's why I haven't been paying my mom, even though she can't afford to support me. And I suppose that's also why I've been spending my unemployment insurance money on comics and Chinese food. All I do is watch MTV and eat wontons and sleep. I honestly haven't cared about anything in a really long time, which is a weird feeling. Every morning, I wake up and decide whether it's worth it to get out of bed. Lately, it doesn't seem to matter either way, you know?"

John said, "I do."

The simple syllables were enough to smooth Lester's anxiety. He released a real sigh, one broad enough to balance him.

Lester's memory suddenly slipped to a moment from two months earlier and, for an instant, a rainbow of emotions splayed in his mind. "You know, the strangest thing just popped into my head," he told John. "A couple of months ago, this fire engine hauled past me on the street and, as it passed, its driver laid on the horn. It surprised me so much, I almost crapped myself."

John nearly spat out his soup but kept it in by cracking a tight-lipped smile. Lester let himself smile at the memory too, but decided not to tell John about how his sweatpants had been pulled up to his elbows.

"The thing is, though, that when the engine passed by, I wasn't even pissed off that it startled me. I was embarrassed. I remember thinking, 'At least they have somewhere to go.' But me? I went home and sat in this lawn chair for forty-eight hours and listened to the same cassette tape over and over." Lester paused to let that thought settle. In two months, he had never confronted or even recalled that morning. Instead, he had let it slide down the drain wherever repressed memories are sent to fester. "It's a little ridiculous to admit, I know, but it was the first time I felt shame in a really long time. And it was the first time I ever looked at someone and said, 'They have it better than me.'"

"Those guys," John said over a spoonful of soup.

"The firefighters," Lester said.

"The ones rushing into the burning building."

"Ridiculous, huh?"

John pulled his smirk up to his nose like a blanket. "No, actually. It's not ridiculous."

Lester spotted the cap on the table beside John's soup bowl, the one with the spider that said 803rd Engineers, and felt his expression drip from his face. For some reason, John's military past made Lester feel guilty. He wanted to ask about the Bataan Death March—how it happened, and how he survived it, and if he knew at the time that it was a death march—but he knew better. Still, as he choked down his tiny bite, he felt a question burp out of him: "So you know what it's like to want to, you know, do something more—to be more than just you." He immediately wilted at his end of the table, appalled that he would let a question like that slip past his filter.

"Of course I do," John said, pointing the corner of his grilled cheese at his host, his eyebrows heavy on his temple. "We all want to do something more, Lester. But there are two types of people out there: The ones who rush into the burning building, and the ones too afraid to go near it."

"There's a third group too. They lay soundly asleep, unaware the building is burning down around them."

John leaned back in his chair, his chiseled stare chipping at the cracks in the ceiling. Slowly, a low-pitched laugh worked its way from his belly, through his body, and out his mouth where its resonance threatened to bring the entire ceiling down. The sound was rich and round and startled Lester, whose own laugh wriggled in comparison.

When the laughter settled, John slurped another spoonful of soup and swallowed it and said, "So, you wanna be a firefighter, huh?"

The question felt like a smack across the back of his head. "Oh, I mean—no…" But even as these words tumbled from his lips, he felt the notion steel him, wrap around him like Batman's cape or thicken his blood like a bite from a radioactive arachnid.

John shrugged. "Well, all I'm saying is that I know a guy from the VFW and that he could use a good man like you."

A knock at the door interrupted Lester's ability to consider the thought any further. He shoved himself away from the table, nearly flattening his folding chair on the way out of the room. As he strode toward the door, he felt John in the dining room behind him, peeking across the house like a curious child. The knocking continued—Lester knew it too well, and offered his usual response: "Jeez, relax. I'll be right there!" He tugged the front door open too dramatically.

"Uh, hi," Angela said. Her hair hung in buckeye-colored bouquets on either side of her pale face. "I got your message and came right over. Is everything okay?"

Lester glanced behind him at the man now steadying himself in the doorframe between the dining and living rooms. His serene smile settled Lester's anxiety and excitement. "Yeah, um, here," he said, searching his right and left pockets on his sweatpants respectively before furnishing an envelope scarred with creases and folds. "Here's $450 for April and May. Would you give it to mom?"

Angela's face twisted suspiciously. "Is this some kind of joke?" she said, and for the first time ever, Lester heard his own acidic tone in her voice. "Like, am I on *Candid Camera*?"

"Hey, if you don't want it, John and I are going to spend it on comic books and strippers," Lester said, cramming the envelope back into his sweatpants.

"And rum!" John howled from the dining room.

The spring breeze blew onto the porch, blowing her hair around a slack expression. "No, of course I'll take it. I mean, yeah, I'll give it to mom." A sincere smile drooped from her face. "Who's that guy?"

Lester shrugged. "Just some guy I met on the street. He and I have been hanging out for the past couple weeks."

"John Barber," he nodded. His wrist sliced back and forth in a wave that reminded Lester of a waiter holding a tray of drinks— a strange and endearing gesture.

"Be nice to him," Lester said. "You can credit him for this payment, sort of, and next month's too—another $450. By July, I should be all caught up."

Angela stood saucer-eyed in the doorway, her posture rigid in her pantsuit. She took a half-step inside and peeked into the house. "It's nice to meet you Mr. Farmer, but what have you done with my brother?" Her brow crinkled as she leaned further into the living room. "Good lord, Lester, did you clean?"

"If he's not going to invite you to lunch, allow me," John's voice reverberated through the empty room. "Please come in and join us. He made enough soup and grilled cheese for three."

Lester shepherded her into the kitchen, where a rubbery grilled cheese sat sliced on a paper plate. He had to admit, he felt good—weightless and hopeful, if not a little exhausted. His arms vibrated, literally shuddered, and he wondered if he had inherited some actual superpower.

Lester landed in his seat as Angela spooned tomato soup into her mouth. John sat in his spot, fingers knitted, casting a smile at Angela, then Lester. "You could see Lester as a firefighter, right?" he asked.

Angela snorted in response, then flung an incredulous glance at John that softened as it swung toward Lester. "Actually, yeah," she said. "I totally could."

Charles Stonebreaker
October 7th, 1910

A *chilly breeze* crept across Charles's shoulders as he stood in the empty dining room. Outside the windows, the sun painted the neighborhood in bright, fiery colors beneath the royal blue banner of the sky. But, somehow, none of that light broke into the dining room. Instead, Charles stood in dusty shadows, his mustache limp beneath his nose, his shoulders dangling from his neck, reading the note he had found tacked to the front door.

He had read it so many times that its sentences only splashed against him, their meaning dripping from his face and forehead instead of sinking in. So, instead, he stood there numb and heavy, lifeless. A cardinal perched onto the open windowsill, bent his head into the house as if to inspect it for food, and flew away without Charles noticing.

The paper felt thin between his finger and thumb—unreal, but somehow so heavy that it was difficult to lift. He gave it another read just to make sure he didn't misunderstand.

Dear Charles,

I know that this note will not be easy to read, let alone accept, but it has been a long time coming. I will not pretend that it is easy to write either, but it does feel liberating, I must admit, and something else that's difficult to describe— like mending a pair of ripped pants that has embarrassed you for too long.

I will come right out and say it: I am leaving you, Charles. And I am bringing Rebecca with me. We are taking the 11:22 a.m. train back to Milwaukee, then back up north to the farm.

I am writing you a note because it is time for us to leave. If I tried to tell you this in person, I know you would persuade me to stay by promising me the impossible. But we can't live that way anymore. Peasants may be able to live in a cramped apartment, but not me, and not my family.

There is something else I realized while I considered whether to stay or go: I cannot love you anymore. It is not that I do not love you. I absolutely do. But I refuse to love a person who continually fails his family—his wife and his daughter, who is suffering just as much from your incompetence. Maybe being raised on a farm ruined me. Maybe I have unrealistic standards for what a man should provide for his family. But I must conserve my love for the people in my life who can return it, who can build it into something everlasting and strong.

I am sorry that this is how it must end. I hope to hear from you soon so we can discuss the next course of action. I will, however, never step foot in Wisnago again as long as I live.

Sincerely,
Elizabeth

His arm relented, gave in to the letter's weight, and let it drop to the floor beside his feet. Another swell of air seeped into the house, nuzzled Charles's shoulder, pushed the letter to the further corner of the room. He stomped to where it curled against the wall, where trim still needed to be nailed. He wanted to feel the ink beneath his fingers, the loops of her signature, the dips and climbs of her cursive, but couldn't convince himself to pick it up.

It hadn't been an easy week. Every day, Charles spent a few hours threading through town, knocking on doors, talking to employers, explaining what he could bring to each business. The new lumberyard had seemed interested, but not immediately. "We only have another couple of months until we quiet down for the winter," the foreman said. "Come back in March." The quarry at the edge of town said the same.

Elizabeth had clearly become exasperated and, on Tuesday, went off like a Roman candle, launching insult after searing insult. "Don't come home until you get a job," she growled while she wrestled socks onto Rebecca, who would only rip them off and stash them with her shoes in one of the kitchen cabinets.

He had struggled with Rebecca as well. Since that afternoon in the house, she hadn't come to him asking strange questions, hadn't brought him flowers with secrets to tell him, hadn't curled into his lap to hide from imaginary ghosts. She hadn't ignored him either, or feared him for that matter, but she hadn't been herself.

This was the reason that he hid at the house until dinnertime. Sometimes, he had work to do. He put baseboard in the living room, finished staining the stairs and landings. But sometimes he just sat on the porch and let summer's leftover cicadas saw in his ears. Even on these sun-flooded days, even as he watched the amber leaves turn to rubies and wave from their boughs, he felt winter wrap its hands around his wrists and ankles.

He felt it in that dining room too—winter reaching in through the open window and paralyzing him. He tried to escape this sensation, shed it like a husk as he stepped into the bronze light of the living room. But that's when he saw the hole in the wall between the front windows, the broken laths bent beneath the crumbling plaster, un-repaired. To Charles, it looked like a gaping wound. He had avoided it for a week out of fear that it couldn't be healed. Now it pussed, infected and swollen, radiating pain. And that's when he realized—the letter, the chill, the wound—it was all his fault.

He had driven them away. He had done this to himself.

The realization worked him like a flame, started at his head and burned through the rest of his body until his legs could no longer handle the heat and he collapsed on the hardwood. His body heaved, bounced and trembled uncontrollably to the beat of boundless sadness—some song that had no ending.

Half thoughts stabbed his brain, but faded away before he could comprehend them: *If only you hadn't lost your job…* and *Why didn't you put your family before…* and *They don't respect you because you didn't…* They flew at him like swallows in a barn, swooping between stuttering breaths before retreating back into the eaves.

"I'm sorry," he yelped, his cries pained and pathetic. He felt tears pool beneath his cheek, felt his shoulder and hips ache where they burrowed into the hardwood, felt the cold breeze slip into the house and cover him like a blanket.

He lay there until the sounds crawled more slowly from his lungs and the tears thinned. Though his body still shuddered, Charles tried to take control by climbing back onto his knees and drawing in gentle lungfuls of air between his teeth. Complete thoughts rematerialized in his brain as if the dust had finally settled.

They're gone, Charles assured himself with this newfound clarity, *and they don't want you. This house is a monument for what you could never have, a testament to your failure.*

These thoughts spurred Charles's body, which began to move independently from his brain. His knees cracked as it lifted itself onto two legs and toward the basement steps—a doorway that still needed trim, steps that still needed a railing and would never get one. He knew where to find the rope, coiled in the corner; they had used it to hoist a wheelbarrow to the second story.

As his muscles moved, his mind was free to rationalize. *They wanted you*, he realized, *not this goddamn house. They never would have left if you hadn't left them.*

A breeze glanced against his face as he returned to

the top of the basement steps and dried the leftover tears still stuck to his cheeks. The rope wrapped around his right shoulder made walking difficult. He felt himself grunt and wheeze with each step through the kitchen and living room toward the staircase, but his mind no longer listened to his body.

That's ridiculous, Charles's brain seemed to debate itself as his body tugged him up the stairs. *The whole reason they left you was because they wanted the house done. And you couldn't give that to them. Why didn't you ask for more help? Why didn't you plan ahead? Why did you send Marty away when you needed his help most?*

The heat hit him as soon as his body climbed past the landing. He dropped the rope on the unfinished wood floor, which shook the whole house, and his body drifted toward the master bedroom. Just inside the door, Charles stopped and tried to absorb the room's beauty. From here, he could see the whole neighborhood, the hills and prairie bulging beyond it, the clot of buildings to the east that constituted downtown. When he closed his eyes, he tried to imagine the room finished: The canopy bed, the curtains shifting in the breeze, the book and Bible stacked on the bedside table. Becky would curl up between him and Elizabeth when she had a bad dream.

It was this image that coaxed tears from his closed eyes. He tried to stop it by squeezing them shut, by concentrating on the sound of the breeze brushing against the windows, but he wasn't strong enough, and the tears overwhelmed him again, cut across his face in relentless lines. *You've lost this,* he reminded himself. *You've lost everything you've ever wanted, everything you've ever fought for. And you'll never get it back. It's gone, completely and hopelessly gone.*

And what will you do now? his mind inquired.

He smeared the tears with his palm and tried to calm his breathing by leaning his head back and drawing mouthfuls of hot air. When he opened his eyes, he saw the whitewashed plaster and the attic door over his head. He blinked through his tears as he tried to remember the space behind it, the joists stretching across the house, and wondered how much weight one could bear.

As he stepped out of the room, Charles didn't think about what he was about to do and why. Instead, he grabbed the painter's ladder in the far bedroom, hung it on his shoulder, and walked back to the master bedroom. His motions seemed destined, already written down. He positioned the ladder beneath the attic door and slung the rope around his shoulder, felt his knees quiver and black knuckles ache as he climbed. After pushing the door onto the attic floor, he lifted himself and the rope into the shadowy space.

While Charles's body trekked through the attic, palming boards and beams, his thoughts paced back and forth, his words wearing a path in his mind with a kind of cadence: *You lost them*, it said. *And what will you do now?* His hands slid along the grain of each joist. Charles found himself at the furthest end of the attic before he realized what he was looking for—a joist that stretched the length of the house—and only had to look up to see it seated above his head. He followed the spine back toward the attic door. The thick, enormous beam was easy to wrap a rope around; he tied one of those unslippable knots, then two more for good measure.

Charles had never tied a noose before, and the moment he realized this, his trembling hands let go of the rope, stepped away from the attic door, and paced to the corner and back. But his mind kept reminding him: *You lost them. And now what will you do?* With his attention tangled around this question, Charle's body took the rope back in its hand, tied something like a bowline down the rope that would hang an inch beneath the attic door, then kicked the thing into the bedroom beneath him.

All around him, the attic rattled. The house felt alive, powerful, pulsing with energy, but Charles paid it no attention. He pulled the rope toward him, slipped a foot into the knot, and leapt into the attic's door as if it were a puddle. The beam above him coughed like something dying, but the knot tightened around his foot, did not slip, and the rope held his weight.

Charles was only somewhat aware of his tears, which had coursed steadily down his face and met with the tendrils of sweat that crept from his forehead. The cocktail stung his eyes, made it difficult to see and think and challenge that convinced voice repeating, *You lost them. And now what will you do?* Swinging himself back onto the attic's floor joists, he untangled his foot from the knot, and lifted his rope to the front of his face. He had no mind left to think about it. The rope already itched around his neck before a corner of his mind became clear enough to see where he was, what he was doing, that his work boots were scuffing the air over the attic door, that his spine was straight and ready, that his tears had ceased, that his hands trembled too much to be of any use, but that he was still alive, and his family too, and that there might be some way to repair the hole in the wall downstairs.

But that voice, incredulous, scolded him, reminded him: *You lost them.* And then wondered: *What will you do now?*

When he stepped off the landing, he wasn't aware of his last breath or his wife or daughter, or the house that he had built for them. He was only aware of the room's blinding brightness and the tension around his neck, the emptiness of the surrounding space and the way his vision gave way to grey, the sound of the beam barking above him, something he felt in his muscles, his bones.

Charle's body bounced at the bottom of the rope, then swayed for fifteen minutes, the attic creaking in pain and pity, in misery and grief and guilt until the noise calmed to nothing. Dusk bowed through the windows, painted his body a gold so bright and beautiful that the bedroom seemed momentarily filled with a sweet music that made his death seem somehow important.

But he would never hear the music, only silence—a real silence, the sort that stretched beyond the boundaries of his life and bled into the lives of others.

Becky McLaughlin
December 2, 2011

A *wall near the front door* crawled with stickers, advertising things Becky had never heard of—bands, maybe, or radio stations, record labels, websites, music festivals, she wasn't sure. Each sticker expressed alternative music's noisy sneer—or indie's cold shoulder, or heavy metal's dead centipede essence. During shows, Becky never noticed the wall of stickers but, with afternoon's dusk filtering through the finger-dotted windows, she found Humble House's sticker wall overwhelming, hypnotizing; it was hard to find her way out.

Despite this, there was something undeniably comfortable about Humble House, and she felt it in those first moments during that first show she attended.

The space used to be a factory of some sort—a brewery, she remembered someone telling her. From the gates, it looked like little more than a cluster of abandoned brick buildings. The lot leading up to the front door felt eerie and magical in the moonlight; she stepped carefully over patched pavement that rippled in stiff waves, over gravel walkways that started and stopped without warning, over train tracks and ornamental weeds. The specter of some song wafted foglike across the lot, coalescing as she approached the front doors; an unlit sign above it welcomed her to Humble House, as did some sort of hipster cross-stitching hanging behind the guy whose shivering hands collected her money inside the door. "God Bless This Humble House" its words read.

When she thought back to that first night, she remembered the porous floorboards bowing beneath her feet, how enormous the pitch-black ballroom felt at first, how it shrunk as the night went on, as the first band finished their set and wheeled their amps through an exhausted audience that offered to help them. Marley sought her out and introduced her to girls and guys with weird names that matched their weird hair. Becky met almost everyone in the room—kids older and her age, kids younger who slow danced to fast songs, kids who had just left the stage, who asked Becky her name in voices that somehow cut above the clattering chords, who wiped sweat from their brows between breaths. She remembered meeting Maryanne, who ran the place; she was older and reminded Becky of the sort of teacher who wasn't afraid to hug you when you needed it. When the last band played, Maryanne grabbed Becky's wrist and tugged her onto the side of the stage to watch with her, like she was some sort of VIP. Afterward, Becky stayed behind to help clean up.

Since then, Becky hung out at Humble House almost every day after school—to talk to Marley, to finish homework and start artwork, to hide from her brother and mom. Becky thought it was cool that Maryanne kept it open until 7:00 each weeknight, brewed coffee and baked bread in a stickered-up bread maker, played music by bands called the Weakerthans and Jets to Brazil and Denali (bands Becky was learning to love), helped kids balance equations and fill out college applications, let them complain about their parents, their boyfriends and girlfriends. It was a non-profit teen center, Becky later discovered, when it wasn't putting on punk-rock shows.

During one of these weeknights, as Becky sunk herself into an overstuffed couch and tore thin blades from a technicolored *WIRED*, Maryanne asked her what she was doing. "Oh, it's so cool," Marley bounced on the cushion beside her. "She makes these collages that are all colorful and abstract and stuff. She has been putting them in the bathrooms at school to cover up graffiti. You should see them." Becky barely had a chance to blush before Maryanne requested one of her own for Humble House—"Right inside the front door," she smiled, "so everyone can see it."

Becky's face crinkled at this memory as she leaned against her completed collage, her gaze sorting through the swarming stickers on the wall across from it. One read Merge Records, another Code Orange Kids. She spotted several that said Make Do and Mend, and she wasn't sure if it was a band, brand, or command.

She wanted Maryanne to be the first to see her finished wall, then Marley, then the rest of the world. So when Marley barged through the door, her hair in a pair of perfect braids, Becky squeaked in panic and pressed herself onto the wall like one of her Mod Podged strips.

"Is it done?" Marley smiled. She inched out of her leather jacket, revealing a half-tucked-in Botch shirt beneath it. Her boots boomed on the worn hardwood as she hung her coat on a nearby hook.

"I don't want you to see it yet," Becky said, pin-toed, her body plastered against the collage like a slender starfish.

Marley snickered. "No offense," she said, "but do you really think your little twig body can block out that whole wall?" She took a few steps back until her shoulder blades and elbows stuck into the stickered wall. Becky winced as she watched Marley's gaze scale the wall, as it dipped and dropped and meandered with the motion of the strips. "Wow, Becky. It's incredible."

"You're just saying that," Becky said, trying not to lift her eyes above the buckles on Marley's boots.

"Is that a face?" Marley asked, bending her neck to trace the thin lines that climbed across the scraps. "That's cool. Where'd you come up with that idea?"

Becky's shoulders shrugged imperceptibly beneath her baggy hoodie. "Just something I've been drawing a lot lately."

Relief unfolded within her when she saw Maryanne's stout frame round the corner, her hands crammed into the front pockets of a purple hoodie. Bands of dusk streaked through the front door, leaving cherry highlights in her chestnut hair and wiping half of her face clean of shadows. A smile swung on her face as soon as she spotted Becky. "Is it done?" Maryanne asked.

"You're going to love it," Marley said, dimples piercing her round cheeks.

Becky cracked an uncomfortable smile. "Before you look," she said, "I tried some different things, so if you don't like it, I can cover it up." Then she pivoted away from the wall, planted herself next to Marley among the stickers. Her eyes snapped toward a bright spot in the lower third where it was difficult to tell the shreds of paper apart. From there, the piece flowed upward, lifted her gaze along a stream of creams and vanilla greens, beer suds spilling onto rolls of mint chocolate chip and sunlit sidewalks and profiles of surf guitars. The flow spouted at the top, allowing her attention to dribble slowly down back to the bottom amid deeper greens and browns—moss and soil, grilled meat and overgrown beds of lettuce. Cutting across the patches of paper, Becky's attention tangled around a thin black line, almost invisible, then broadened to take in the entire drawing—a face, its crooked smile smirking, its sculpted hair upswept, its thick Ray-Ban frames balanced on a precariously slender nose.

"What, what is—" Maryanne mumbled, interrupting her inspection. Her voice trembled softly, but enough so she had to restart. "Who's face is that, Becky?"

The muscles in Becky's back set like lumps of concrete, strained her shoulders until they tensed, until they could no longer hold up her head. "It's complicated," she answered like she was addressing Principal Warsaw, then remembered it was Maryanne. "It's just a face I've been seeing in my head lately." Becky's gaze clung to the collage, to that bright core in the center that encompassed her like a womb, but she broke from it to peek at Maryanne, whose expression seemed layered with emotion—her brow bent up and mouth bunched beneath her nose, curved into a suppressed crescent; her squirrel cheeks speckled magenta, squashed by her shivering fingers. But when Becky saw the tears, she couldn't contain herself. "You don't like it, do you?" she asked.

"No!" Maryanne burst, releasing the tears and breath that she had been holding back. "I mean yes, I love it, Becky." She shut her eyes, turned them into whetted slivers, then pulled her hands from her cheeks, opened her arms so that Becky could walk into them. "It just reminds me of an old friend," Maryanne whispered, her sniffles sharp in Becky's ear. "A very special friend. And it couldn't be more perfect for this place."

Slowly, Becky felt herself disappear within Maryanne, like a soul retreating into a body. It made her feel full and free, though her friend flattened her arms against the buffer of Becky's hoodie until they matched temperatures. It was the first time Becky felt this sort of affection—unconditional and complete, reserved for her—and didn't know what to do besides abandon herself to it.

Becky felt Maryanne's warmth radiate deep within her hoodie, lingering like a lantern's mantle, even when she released her. "Oh my goodness," Maryanne said, pushing a laugh through her warped lips, wiping the beneath both eyes with a poly-cotton sleeve. "That was emotional. Sorry about that." She blinked half a dozen times as scanned the collage a second time, then looked back at Becky. "Thank you," she said, her eyes bottomless wells. "It's beautiful. I can't wait for everyone to see it tonight. Maculey will—well, I don't know what he'll do."

"Are you staying for the show?" Marley asked. Becky noticed swollen spots beneath her eyes as well.

"I want to, but I have to go home first," Becky said, her hands retreating into the sleeves of her hoodie. "I have to drop off my supplies and change."

"Okay, I'm coming with," Marley said, pushing off of the wall and stepping toward the hook on which her coat dangled. "I've never been to your house before."

Becky made a mush-mouthed face. Before she could vocalize her concern, Maryanne christened their trip together by saying, "Well, I have to help the bands load in. Hurry back, okay?" before disappearing around the corner.

Humble House was only a few blocks from Becky's house, but she contemplated taking a detour downtown to buy herself a few more minutes before she was forced reveal her fucked up family to Marley. As they skipped down the steps, stretched their short legs across the rail yard's rows of rusted train tracks, she imagined how the meeting would unfold in her mind: Misty would screech as soon as she heard the screen door slam, demand that Becky finish folding laundry—a chore she had finished days ago—and ask where Tom had gone and whether he was hiding any pills in their house. Marley would freeze in the door frame, refuse to enter their terrifying house—*No*, Becky reassured herself. *She would laugh, and ask a million questions on their way back to Humble House.*

"So what happened in there?" Marley asked, stepping through the old factory gates.

The question brought Becky back to the neighborhood tinted in pre-winter shades of grey, back to the tangerine sun ducking beneath the roofline, to shadows stretching half a block as they stepped onto Weiseule. "I'm not sure," Becky answered almost automatically.

"Maryanne recognized him," Marley added. "Did you know him?"

A carnation of breath bloomed in front of Becky's mouth as she sighed, then wilted in the cold air. "I don't know," she said. She wasn't sure how much she wanted to say. Marley might think she was a freak. *No*, Becky reassured herself. *She would think it was weird and cool. She'd want to know more about it.* "Okay," she said, blowing another carnation. "You have to promise not to think I'm crazy, okay?"

"But I already do."

"For real."

"Okay!" Marley screeched, "I won't!" She veered a haunch into her friend's bony hip, almost knocking her into a puddle of leaves.

Becky steadied herself, swallowed the cold air, and

then said, "I can see dead people."

"No way!" Marley gasped, grasped Becky's shoulders with claws of disbelief. "You are fucking with me."

"I'm not."

"Like, what to they look like?" Marley asked.

"I don't know," Becky said. "I try not to look at them." She retracted her arms into her hoodie, stuck her hands beneath her bony armpits to defend herself from the cold, letting her sweatshirt's sleeves swing at her sides. "I guess, they look like normal people—just, dressed a lot different sometimes. But when you try to look at them, they get harder to see. It's weird."

"Uh, yeah," Marley said, her wide smile shaping her words.

"One time, one of them started talking to me," Becky said. "It was in my basement, and it was pretty scary at first, but then it wasn't."

"So, your house is haunted?"

"Yeah, every place is haunted. I mostly see them at the school."

"This is so fucked up," Marley said, kicking little rocks with her scuffed boots, snuffing out little leaf flames. "Is Humble House haunted?"

The grey streets seemed too grey to Becky, almost hazy, as she thought about this question. "Actually, I don't think so," she answered. "Which is weird, since it's the sort of old building that should have a lot of spirits."

"Maybe they don't have any reason to show

themselves to you," Marley said. "Is that how it works? Do they give you messages? Send you on missions?"

"The one guy in my house didn't," Becky said. "He said something about how he wanted me to find something, but I still don't totally understand what he meant."

"Maybe it's treasure."

The haze thickened as they approached the old lumber yard. It moved almost visibly, convincing Becky that it was no longer the faded winter air. "Do you smell that?" Marley asked as they turned onto Geranium.

Becky did, like hot plastic or simmering chemicals, like when she threw styrofoam cups into a campfire. "What is that?" The answer revealed itself as they continued down Becky's block. "Oh my god, is that house on fire?" Marley asked, spotting black smoke lumbering across the road like a pack of wolves. She took off toward it.

Her hands still wedged under her arms, Becky trotted behind Marley, but stopped when she saw a house half hidden by whole walls of smoke. "Holy shit," she managed to squeak, stealing hesitant steps—inches—down the street. The fire revealed itself in increments, first the feral smoke, muscular and fast, leaping over the fence, clambering under the shrubs. *It could be the house behind it,* she reassured herself. *The smoke could be coming from somewhere else.* But when she saw the heat warping the front porch—bending the air, the floorboards, the siding's straight lines—Becky knew that it was her house. A few more steps revealed the smoke tumbling from the front window, through the screen in the front door, up through cracks in the attic. "Holy shit," Becky repeated, noticing the light show in her own bedroom behind the wooden blinds.

"Come on!" Marley shouted from the corner. Where a herd of concerned neighbors had gathered.

"Marley," Becky said, her syllables creaking quietly. "That's my house."

"What?" Marley ran back to Becky, who had stopped on a sewer cover in the middle of the street.

"That's my house."

"Oh my god, are you serious?"

The smell had become painful, poisonous. Becky put her hood up and hung her collar on the bridge of her nose. Behind the black beasts stumbling out of their front window, Becky watched the flames claw the wall, cast strange shadows on the picture frames and kitchen cabinets. The fire was so loud, a hissing rumble that she knew would drown out any syllable she would utter, so she stayed silent. She pushed her arms back through her hoodie, no longer feeling cold.

The first thoughts that slid through her mind as the flames jabbed through the windows were not of her mom and brother—those came later. Rather, it was relief that she had her purple bag, her phone, her All Time Low hoodie. And then it turned to the basement, to a stack of magazines she had stashed down there, but also the workbench, fully collaged; for a split second, she debated whether she could drag it through the cellar door.

"Becky!" she heard someone shriek from across Eighth Street. Through the steel grey swirl, Misty shuffled in Becky's robe toward them—a cherry red Wonder Woman thing that had always been too big for Becky and had grown dusty on its hanger. Her mom looked ragged; sacks of skin sagged beneath her eyes, wide and weary, dyed by mascara and stress. Her slick hair swung in thickets around her head, and relief flickered in her eyes, like she had found her valuable wedding ring, or that she had made it to work on time. She immediately sidled Becky, hooked an arm around her, and said, "I'm so glad you're okay."

Becky threaded an arm through her mother's embrace, but the gesture seemed mechanical and automatic, almost emotionless. She rested her head onto a shoulder that might as well have been a bathroom sink. "What happened?" Becky asked her mom.

She felt Misty's muscles contract, squeeze her like a blood pressure pump. "That little prick," was all Misty murmured at first. Instead of continuing, she peered into the fire as it smeared itself up the walls of the living room, watched the smoke trip and tumble out the dormers in the attic, lift into the sky in a perfect black plume.

"Who?" Becky asked. "Was it Tom?"

"I caught him selling weed right on the front porch," she said, crowing over the rumbling fire so that the gathering crowd could hear. "So I told him to get out. I went to my room to take a nap and, next thing I know, I smell smoke."

Becky felt the fire vibrate the air, felt it numb her

cheeks and chin and nose. Her forehead tingled in time with the back of her hands. She looked past her mother toward Marley, whose eyes reflected the fire's wild, unruly spirit. She didn't know how to respond to her mom because she knew it was not the whole story, that there was some other side that her mother was keeping to herself, but also because she was hypnotized by the surrealism of it all, the slow flames consuming the house like a snake swallowing an egg.

A silent squad car slid down Eighth Street, its lights swinging against the stubborn dusk, and stuck its landing near the gathering neighbors. An officer exited and immediately asked the spectators to disperse, to at least back down the block. Sirens rose in the air, its howl subtle beneath the hissing, spitting fire, the rumble of its heat. Without a word, Misty drifted toward the squad car, leaving Becky motionless on the sewer cover, imaging what few possessions the fire had already consumed—her iPod, her Harry Potter Legos, probably her bed spread.

"I'm so sorry," Marley said, but the sympathy bounced off Becky, who searched for but couldn't find her sadness. She might have been sad a month ago, she realized, or if Tom or Misty had been hurt. Becky basked in the horror and heat, let it ripple on her sweating skin, but couldn't find the pain inside her, couldn't feel the sting.

Could she stay with Marley tonight? At Humble House? Hell, Francis would probably take her if she asked. Becky's realization moved her past the flames, past the tragedy still flaring before her. She was trying to find a way to tell Marley that they should head back to Humble House soon, that she didn't want to miss the show, when she was tugged onto the curb to make way for the fire engines—two of them, each snaking down different intersecting streets, their lights stirring up the smoke. To her, they arrived in an eerie silence beneath the roaring inferno, like they were sneaking up on the beast still thrashing in the house. Men in khaki jackets hopped out and swarmed the property, each with a different mission—one with a hose, another working machinery on the truck, a third pacing the length of the house looking for easy entry. Becky couldn't pay attention to all of them and the fire, which had pushed through the windows of her mother's bedroom, shattering them with a sigh beneath the fire's drone. Glass glittered onto the porch's roof like fairy dust.

"What should we do?" she heard Marley say, but Becky's mind was too busy to answer. In her periphery, she noticed the crowd swelling, wrapping around the corner of Eighth Street onto Geranium where they were hiding. These bystanders spoke to each other, but in the sort of reverent hush reserved for church services, holy monuments, miracles. Meanwhile, the fire ripped through to the outside, climbed the siding like creepers. It kicked onto the front porch, stabbed at the ceiling; the swing's chains snapped, and it fell into the flames.

The firefighters floated around the site like gnats, seemingly doing nothing. They hovered around a hose but did not pick it up. A few feet down the road, she even saw a firefighter sitting in the dirt, his legs unrolled in front of him, a paunch dropping out of his unzipped fire coat. His mouth hung open under a silver-streaked mustache. "What's that guy's problem?" Becky wondered aloud.

Marley studied the man as he squinted into the fire. He seemed out of breath. "Maybe he's hurt," she said.

"Okay, you two," a voice said behind them. "We need to clear this area. Why don't you two head home, okay?" They turned to see a short woman in a firefighter's coat and overalls, her hair hidden beneath her scuffed helmet.

"That was her home," Marley said, barely audible above the fire's rumble.

"Oh," the woman said. "I'm sorry to hear that." Becky watched her mouth straighten, her gaze bounce onto the ground. "Well, you need to back up onto the sidewalk at least, okay? We're gonna try to control this fire and need the space."

As they backed onto the sidewalk, Becky asked, "What's wrong with him?" She pointed to the firefighter sitting in the street. "Is he okay?"   "The chief?" she asked, looking over that the man bent over his belly, panting like a hot dog. "Someone told me he used to live here too way back when. When you become a firefighter, you never think that you'll watch your own house burn down."

As the woman clomped toward the next clump of bystanders, the thought of this man residing in her house rolled around Becky's dizzy brain. When she blinked, she saw him in that instant sitting in the darkness of his living room, greasy, tank-topped, ponytailed, amused by his own boredom, but the image lingered only as long as her eyelashes touched. She stared at the man, his head shaved and lustrous in the lingering daylight, his body crumpled, defeated, but daring the inferno to make a move, to take anything else from him.

Beside her, Marley stood enrapt by the flames and their apparent celebration, dancing in honor of their victory. Her eyes reflected their revelry, though her body, her face, remained motionless, too scared to move.

The surrounding crowd seemed terrified as well, worried that even a stray cough might provoke the fire further. Becky spotted her mom, still talking to a police officer, though now her shoulders toweled, surrounded by paramedics, the victim she always yearned to be. She recognized a few neighbors too, people she had never uttered a word to in the three years she had lived there. All of them shared the same solemn expression, observed the chaos with a sober obsession, a mesmeric dread.

But, as she inspected the rest of the crowd, Becky saw too many unfamiliar faces—too many mustaches and bonnets, too many overcoats. Their faces blurred when she tried to study them, washed into watercolor portraits that bled into the background, and the realization rippled up her arms. When she saw the man with the glasses, his hair tousled, his frown robust and real, she knew that half the gathered crowd was not physically there.

She wondered what this meant, that these souls

had returned to watch this house burn, or that the town's strongest firefighter had to sit at the sight of it. She wondered what this house meant to these people, previous occupants, she presumed, or neighbors, guests who had connected with the house. Though entire faces were difficult to discern, the pieces represented the whole—a teary eye blurred by the radiating heat, a bitten lip or an open mouth smeared by the smoke. Still, a silent sadness veiled their presence, smothered Becky, made it hard for her to breathe.

But Becky also wondered what it meant that she wasn't sad. These souls stood entranced by the fire, and all she could do was watch them, entranced by their emotions, by her own wonder, by a connection that dragged them from the dead to watch a building burn.

Above the fire's cackle and roar, above the mild murmur of observers both real and not, Becky heard something else; before she could determine its source, she saw silver streams punch into the house, drenching the first floor and porch, burying it not in water but in a grey steam that erased the house from view. And, for a moment, the gatherers gasped and sighed, stared at the smudge that blotted out the building, banished it to a void that made Becky feel alone surrounded, lost among so many, at least until the house reemerged, black and broken.

But all Becky could think about were these washed-out spirits and their stunned expressions as they watched this house become something else. She felt the muscles tense around her hot heart, felt her own fire simmering behind her eyes; these souls should know nothing is doomed to absolute destruction, that everything becomes something else—and that, even when it's gone, it's still recognizable behind the collage and Modge Podge, in thin black lines that scale whole walls.

Some things need to be lost before they can be found, Becky thought, feeling the mist tickle her face on the chilly December evening when she became momentarily homeless. *Found things are more valuable, the reason we live, the reason we die— to find, to help others find, to use what we find to help others.*

Steam blotted out the house's second story, billowed into the boysenberry sky; somehow, the house's shaky black bones found the strength to keep it aloft during these critical seconds. The refreshing scent of hose water, of sprinklers and spring, replaced the smell of molten poison and plastic, and a peaceful, sibilant hiss replaced the fire's thunder.

Becky felt Marley's arm wrap around her, but Becky didn't need her condolences. She was ready for something else to replace this doomed house, to transform the old and broken into something new and beautiful.

Barbara Farmer
October 17, 1945

It was far too chilly to sit on the porch swing, Barbara knew, but she wasn't sure what else to do with herself. The feeling had stalked her for more than a week now, almost two—this boredom, this listless anticipation that kept her at home, on call, prepared to instantly put on a pot of coffee.

Past the porch, past the little brick houses that sprouted throughout the prairie like tombstones, the sky gleamed a metallic blue, reflected the very sun it yearned to contain. The grass had already gone gold, some of it grey, and the distant smell of smoldering leaves seasoned the air. But, beneath the porch's blue, geometric shadows, Barbara rested, content, ready—shivering, even beneath her sweater, but ready.

She dug her heels into the porch and hovered over a cooling cup of hot coffee, the wrong posture for swinging. But she wasn't there to swing.

It all happened so quickly, all at once. First, there was the telephone call from some Air Force rep, his voice flat despite his message—that John was heading home, first to recover in San Francisco, then to Wisconsin. But, she was assured, it wouldn't be soon. "He was a prisoner of war," the voice recited like he was reading something typed on an index card, "and the U.S. government is committed to ensuring his full health before he reenters the civilian world." Barbara, who had been doing dishes, struggled to speak. All she could do was nod, blink back tears, ferret for a towel to dry her dripping hands; by the time she found one, he had hung up, and she had lost her chance to ask any questions.

Had Anita been there, they would have driven out to San Francisco that night together. They would have scrounged up enough liverwurst and white bread to last the trip, refueled with coffee and pastries at whatever oases they could find on the route, slept in the car if they had to. But Glen had knocked on their door on Labor Day in a leather jacket and hat like a folded napkin, his clean shaven face as chiseled as a movie star's. By the time Anita caught her breath, her bag was packed, and she was gone.

After the Air Force had hung up, Barbara had begun to pack her bag too, prepared to hop on a train or a bus. She was shoving underwear into her suitcase when she was interrupted by a knock on the front door, had scampered down the stairs so fast that she answered with a pair of pantyhose crumpled in her hands. It was a telegram from John. It said he was safe in the States again, sleeping restlessly in a hospital bed with the whitest sheets he'd ever seen. He was fine, but had lost a lot of weight and felt weak. "Stay put," the note ended. "If the war didn't kill me, another week won't either."

Since that evening, Barbara had learned the meaning of patience. She would allow a shift at the bakery to take her attention off of John—there was nothing like rolling dough till your wrists dropped to keep your mind in the moment.

Then, she would return to sit on her swing to watch the sun dribble down the sky, the shadows stretch across and consume the neighborhood, the lights snap on one at a time in each of the surrounding houses.

She wanted to be the first person John saw when he stepped out of the car, to be the first breath he inhaled in Wisnago.

A book hid half beneath the swing's cushion—some green Penguin paperback—and a crinkled copy of *McCalls* beneath that, but Barbara didn't want to read either. Her attention shifted between swishing trees and the song seeping through the living room window, some peppy number on the radio that needed more piano. On occasion, she pulled from a stack of letters, but discovered her attention span wasn't what it used to be; she'd comb haplessly through one letter, too excited to concentrate, or stop halfway though another, tears of happiness or sadness overwhelming her, rendering reading impossible.

A block behind her, Barbara heard the unmistakable sound of an engine panting in the sunset, of rubber tires on gravel crackling down Seventh Street. Her heart vibrated, a buzz that revived and betrayed her every time; she had been waiting on her porch for ten days, and no cars ever stopped. She calmed her breathing, closed her eyes, pulled a slow breath through her body.

When the car—a rusty thing that her neighbor cursed at each morning—rambled by, she felt her heart bend. A breeze rose around her, rippling the pages of her magazine, ruffling the flames that consumed the saplings lining the street.

She stole a sip of coffee to calm her down and drew a crumpled letter from the stack on the seat beside her, a recent one that she had scanned 200 times since receiving it on Tuesday. Its promise always quieted her, always stilled her shaking hands by the end of the second sentence.

Dear Lovely Lady,

With every passing day spent apart, I feel myself growing more and more anxious to see you. I also must remind myself that, with every passing day spent apart, I am growing stronger, healthier—becoming more of myself—so that you will recognize me when I return.

The hospital food is wonderful. I never remember enjoying mashed potatoes much, but I have developed a deep respect for the food in the past few days—a true understanding of its majesty. My doctors and nurses insist that I keep eating, and I certainly am not one to question their professional judgement. I just don't feel like, well, me when I am eating a third bowl of strawberry gelatin, a second serving of turkey and gravy, a whole pot of tomato soup. As much as I enjoy it, it feels wrong, and I worry.

That's my biggest fear: That I will return and you won't recognize me. I had nightmares about it overseas.

Barbara tried to envision John at his prison camp, balled up in his barracks, staring for hours through jagged shadows at a string-hung moon. Complex emotions brewed in her brain, seeped through her body: Sadness at this lonely thought, but also guilt, shame that she had contributed to his pain. She swallowed, loosening the tight lump at the top of her throat, and chose not to look up as another car—royal blue, a richer hue than the kitschy sky—crackled by.

Glen and Anita surprised me yesterday during supper. Boy, it really caught me off guard. He looked great, like those men on enlistment billboards, all dimples and muscles and perfect white teeth. By comparison, I look like a ghost. Anita looked great too, but cried the entire time. She said you were doing great, and it made me miss you even more.

When she thought back to reading this section for the first time, Barbara felt her cheeks pink and prickle. She had been so jealous that they had seen him before her that she had crumpled up the letter and thrown it at the front door. The thought that Anita had been the first woman to speak to him besides his nurses made Barbara seethe. But over the better half of a week, she had come to see their visit differently: John needed to see a familiar face, and Barbara was thankful it was them. Now, she felt more embarrassed than anything, but she still didn't like reading this paragraph, didn't like the shame it summoned.

Some other soldiers on my floor received special permission to go see a picture at a nearby movie house tonight—some comedy with Ginger Rogers. I passed, though. It didn't feel right to see my first movie out here and not at home. It is strange to think about home, though. I'm not yet sure where home will be. Probably in your house in Wisnago, which will be much better than home with mom and pop. It'll take some getting used to, though, because the town will be new. I wonder if it'll feel like home, or something else. I have put so much—

Something beyond the corner of her eye tugged at her attention—something strong enough to steal her from her husband's letter, but too subtle to consciously notice. It was that blue car again, which had almost certainly circled the neighborhood and was now creeping east down Eighth Street. Barbara watched it approach, muscular and elegant, silver trim streaking along each side.

She didn't know what to do when the car stopped outside the house, when she spotted a shadow shifting inside. She didn't know what to do when a solider climbed out, his uniform the sort of peanut brown that she associated with saying goodbye. She didn't know what to do when he walked slowly toward the house, solemnly, with his head down and hands behind his back.

She didn't know what to do when she saw the face— slack, unshaven, unsmiling—wasn't John's.

She calmed her breathing, closed her eyes, pulled a slow breath through her body. *Everything is fine*, she told herself, feeling the world rise around her like a flash flood. *Keep calm,* she told herself, but fear boiled beneath the surface of her skin. She felt simmering tears about to bubble over. *Wait to hear what he has to say,* she told herself, and took every sound she could, every smell, into the black silence of her mind.

"Barbara?" he heard the soldier say in John's voice. The words echoed between her bones like a sound that never left, and it woke her spirit up.

She ran, the front porch beneath her bowing with each stride, leaped down the cement steps, heard her coffee cup hit the floorboards hard. She felt like she was falling and hoped someone would catch her before she hit the ground. The cold sky swiveled around her, the hot leaves, the sun filtering between branches, flickering in her periphery until she was dizzy and disoriented and convinced she was about to crash.

John caught her, but Barbara knew her impact knocked him off balance; instinctively, she wrapped her arms under his shoulders, stuck her heels into the soil, and held him against her, surprised by how breakable he felt in her embrace. She lost herself in him nonetheless—the savory smell of his skin beneath the sweet singe of his cologne, both so familiar, so frightening; the creases of his soft linen uniform and the weight of his hand tangled in the back her blouse, of his head pressed against hers—scared that this wasn't real, that this was one more tenuous daydream about reuniting with her husband.

It required all of her willpower to pull herself from John, so she slipped her palms into his, afraid to fully let go. She stood before her empty house, squeezing her husband's ringed hand, and said, "Welcome home."

The house loomed over Barbara's shoulder, steel blue, trimmed with a deep red that gave the house a tempered color, a quiet vibrance. Her husband, admiring his new home through fulfilled tears, whispered, "Thank you," as his lips floated toward hers.

John's kiss was clean and tight like she always imagined his bunk would be. On tipped toes, Barbara pushed against him, her hands pulling his collar closer so they wouldn't lose each other again. Sound trembled in her lungs as his tongue poked politely between her teeth, as hers poked back. She sensed their rise into the dusk as the neighborhood reeled around them, houses and trees and telephone poles uprooted and tornadoed over their shoulders and under their shoes, the cobweb clouds and sunset and sky.

Somehow, they both landed on their feet. As she pulled away from his kiss, Barbara took her first real look at John's face—full and fleshy, dark and deprived. Skin sagged beneath his eyes, but his cheeks and chin seemed too round, mismatching the frail weight of his body beneath his uniform. "I didn't recognize you when you walked up," she said, placing a soft palm on his shaved cheekbones.

"Oh," he said with a wince. "Is that a good thing or—"

"It's a good thing. I have you back. You're home, and I couldn't think of anything better."

John's shoe shine eyes reflected her portrait, and Barbara saw herself as he did: With longer hair and shorter fingernails, more demure and mature, stronger. "You look the same as in my dreams," he said, "but somehow better."

Barbara fell back into him, back into the pressed

cotton comfort of his embrace, into soft muscles that felt safe and sweet, but noted her own stiff knees and flat feet; she couldn't shake the feeling that, instead of melting in his arms, he was melting in hers.

John tottered behind Barbara her as she pulled him by the hand along the sidewalk toward their house. She didn't think much of his stubborn pace until they hit the cement steps when she felt his hand pull hers down. His breathing stalled, then pushed out in strained puffs. "John?" she asked, her voice bent in concern.

"I'm fine. I just need to take stairs slow."

And they did, one at a time—John concentrating on the mechanics of each muscle in his legs as he lifted them, his hand wavering in Barbara's as he fought for balance, his lips pressed into a tense line that mirrored the ones forming on his forehead. She wanted to ask the questions that crowded in her mind when they reached the top of the stairs, but "Are you okay?" was all she could squeak out.

"Yeah," he said, calming his breathing. "I… Well, I took a bullet in the leg early on, before Corregidor fell. It's sort of a long story." Here, he smiled the sharp-toothed smile that made Barbara dizzy as a teen. "Let's just say I've gotten pretty good at pretending I'm not injured."

"Why didn't you tell me?"

"Same reason I didn't tell you when I was coming home," he said, his attention swaying toward the porch swing, the broken mug beneath it, the hot coffee steaming off the floorboards. "Barbara, I… I was worried you wouldn't be here. There I was, shot in the leg, starved half-to-death—and four years is a long time, you know? If I told you, I wasn't sure if…" His voice trailed as the wind rose around them, roused the trees, which seemed to shush him, soothe him. "Well, I wasn't sure."

Tears hardened in the corners of Barbara's eyes. "Oh, John, I—"

"Now, I know what you're going to say," he interrupted. "I've heard it a million times in my mind, every time I imagined this day. I just need to know one thing: That you still want to be with me, the man I am now."

"Yes," Barbara insisted.

"Even though I'm broken."

"Yes."

"More broken than you know."

"Yes, John," she whispered through the tears that tore down her cheeks. "Always."

It surprised Barbara, the way John swept her up, his arms shaking beneath her weight. Before she could think any further, she felt his lips on hers again, felt one hand on her back shoulder, another splayed on her cheek, his fingers curving around the nape of her neck. She was only somewhat aware of how her body bent, its obtuse angle, and only because she felt her hair's languishing waves swinging even with her tailbone.

And in a sudden swell, the wind swept John's letters from where they had been stashed on the swing. They somersaulted through the air, circled around the porch like bats. Barbara felt the breeze glance against her face, but didn't think twice about the letters (she would never need them again), nor did she think about her husband's lips, how firm they seemed, muscular, and yet how submissive—or how forcefully her lips played on them.

Instead, she thought about Anita, about laying in bed on that low-slung summer night, tangled together in darkness, and those words she whispered when Barbara needed them most: "If you take care of John as well as you take care of me, then he will love you as much as I do." However dark and cloudy the moment seemed at the time, she allowed this gem glisten in her mind, allowed herself to grow fuller, thicker; felt herself become something sturdy, something strong, something against which one might lean.

She shifted her weight and, supporting herself, eased John into her arms.

The wind rushed through the trees in the neighborhood like it was waking a sleeping world and, all around Barbara, the silent autumn reveled in its own shy way. It was only then, as John's nose tickled hers and her hands gripped his shoulders, that she realized how suddenly and silently her fear had been snuffed. Their world would be different, but within their control—and even when it wasn't, she knew could handle it alone if they couldn't handle it together.

In her head, she acknowledged that she would have to help her husband acclimate to civilization, conquer the demons that nested within him, reconstruct a life in a world that had turned without him. She would support him, she decided, not because she had to, or even because she should, but because she could, and because she wanted to.

By the time they pulled their lips apart, these thoughts had set in Barbara's mind, hardened as monoliths of truth against which other thoughts would forever orient themselves. Though some of the inaccuracies of Anita's statement remained—no one, Barbara knew, would love her as much as Anita and Joy did, and John would love her unconditionally—she pitched these cherry pits aside so that she and her husband could step into the open heart of this house, their home, the only building whose beauty and wisdom would ever rival that of their love.

Becky McLaughlin
February 24, 2012

It was far too chilly to sit on the front steps, Becky knew, but she wasn't sure what else to do with herself. She looked out at the slushscape that she once called her front yard, at lumps of snow that lingered in little white islands, at puddles that would stiffen into crispy slates of ice by the time she went to bed. Along Eighth Street, a row of shrugging oaks let their bare branches weave through the vacant sky and drip onto the drying pavement.

She decided not to look behind her.

Sometimes, Becky stopped on her way home from school to sit on the steps or after a show at Humble House, though she hadn't yet figured out why. She only stayed five minutes or so, usually after the sun had already set, and always alone, without Marley or any of her new friends. But it was still afternoon; the sky still glowed ghost grey, and the neighborhood still reverberated with the sound of dripping gutters and a sole stubborn bird.

Beneath her finger, Becky prodded a small pebble pushed into the cement steps. Her hand had dropped onto it before—while on the phone or waiting for a ride or hiding from her family in the public privacy of the front porch—and sometimes automatically. As her fingertips swept against it, she felt it wiggle like a loose tooth.

If she stayed on the steps long enough, stayed still enough, she knew she would feel the house behind her—hear the swing creak in the breeze or feel the front porch shudder beneath someone's footsteps. But she knew it wasn't there, that it had been bulldozed the day after New Years, and that the basement had been filled in. For some reason, they left the front steps, rising like some ill-sanctioned monument to what once disrupted this landscape; Becky never found out why, but she also never asked.

Her fingernails pried at the pebble subconsciously, reserving the forefront of her attention to wondering why she was there, what compelled her to perch on these steps. It was technically trespassing, she knew. *And blatantly pathetic*, she told herself, shivering within her hoodie, which still smelled like smoke. She closed her eyes, concentrated on the light that filtered through the clouds, through her eyelids, and tried to remember the house—the way the stairs croaked beneath her feet, the way her room echoed when she cleaned it, that strange blood stain on the living room ceiling. The basement. Her workbench. The cellar door.

But the house didn't come back. Behind her, she sensed an empty lot—a slush swamp, even and ambivalent.

When she brought her hand up from the step, Becky was startled to see the little stone pressed in the hollow of her palm. A frown firmed on her face. She rolled the stone between her thumb and fingers before flicking it onto the sidewalk in front of her, where it bounced twice before rolling into a puddle.

Maybe I do miss the house, she thought, then released a sigh into an afternoon already too full of air, too full of light and sound. Her gaze traced along the edge of the sidewalk, grazed against stalks of grey grass, skidded through slush, but then bounced back to the pebble. She lifted her eyes toward the phantom sky, balanced on the black branches that sliced it mercilessly, bounded from bough to bough, but then dropped back to the pebble. In the street, a bird shook a shock of street water from its checkerboard feathers; Becky smirked, but then returned back to the pebble.

Stupid rock, she thought, pushing herself off the steps.

Momentum carried Becky away from her lonely monument and all its memories. As she stepped from curb to curb, corner to corner, she felt cold water splash onto her cuffs and seep through her canvas shoes, felt cold air bite her numb nose and frozen freckles, felt cold clouds unfurl in front of her stiff face. But she also felt the cold stone bobble in the fortress of her hands, warmer in the hanging front pocket of her hoodie. She wasn't yet sure what she'd do with it, but she was sure she'd do something, if only carry it with her wherever she went.

Acknowledgements

Before it was published, *Friday Night at Humble House* had been sitting on a shelf for seven or eight years. I started writing the book in 2011, which means that it's older than my children. I poured years into putting all of its pieces together.

When the whole picture formed, I realized that *Humble House* really is the book of my heart. It contains themes and ideas and subjects that make up my core, even if some of it reads a little overwritten to my ears now. Each character is a little bit of me for better or worse. Sharing it with the world made me nervous and vulnerable, but I didn't want to keep it to myself.

I queried this book for two years and, looking back, am surprised by how few replies I received from literary agents. I could count them on one hand. It landed on the proverbial shelf with a heartbreaking thud, and I wondered for a while if I was cut out for this whole writing thing.

After a year or two of moping—of trying to write but not quite finishing anything—I started another book and found a voice that suits better and feels more natural. I've written a few more books in that voice since, each containing a piece of my heart, but none sharing so much of it as *Humble House*. So if you're reading, thanks.

A lot of people supported me while writing this book and offered assistance, but I forgot who. It's been that long. I'm sorry if I missed you in these acknowledgments.

David Schwantes read multiple drafts of this book, offering me a lot of encouragement and good advice. Truly, he was my beta reader, alpha reader, and, sometimes, my only reader. I probably would have never finished this book if he hadn't kept asking for pages.

For a little while, I was part of the Cary Area Writer's Group. Here, I met some friends who offered me a lot of useful feedback and encouragement while drafting this book, especially Mary Jo Wallace, Eileen Lynch, and Debbie Marcussen. I made a lot of progress on *Humble House* during those years, and CAWG significantly boosted my motivation and productivity.

Even when a manuscript is fresh, it's not always easy to keep track of who actually reads my writing. That said, I appreciate the family members who read this book, including my mom, Midge Erbach, and my aunts Jenny Koppe, Marsha Gepner, and Judy Seaver. It makes me happy knowing you were some of my first readers. I owe my dad Chris Erbach and my brother Alan Erbach for supporting every endeavor I've ever pursued. Our creativity flows from the same well.

The story of Barbara and John Farmer is based on the story of Leda and Jack Miller, my in-laws who are no longer with us. Like John, Jack survived the Bataan Death March; like Barbara, Leda found a way to keep going even though she wasn't sure she was still married. Their love story inspired me, and I hope I did it some justice. I appreciate the

Miller and Barber families for accepting a guy like me, who prefers artificial bait to real bait, into their families.

Family really is one of the most important support systems a writer can have. My wife Emily and my children Emmett, Finn, and Maeby cheer me on, give me ideas, let me ramble and vent about my writing, and offer me space to write. I don't know if I would have ever finished or published this book without their unconditional support.

I don't think I could write another book like this again, which is why it was important for me to usher it into the world. If you read it, thank you. It means a lot.

About the Author

Dane Erbach is a writer from Chicago's northwest suburbs, where he lives with his wife and three kids. He teaches English and journalism at a public high school.